KATE

Kate

Brian Cleeve

Coward, McCann & Geoghegan, Inc. New York

First American Edition 1977

SBN: 698-10812-4

Library of Congress Cataloging in Publication Data

Cleeve, Brian Talbot
  Kate.

  I. Title.
PZ3.C583Kat3   [PR6053.L43]   823'.9'14   76-57150

To the memory of
Aunt Kate, who
helped to make this
Kate possible.

KATE

Chapter 1

She crouched against the stone pillar, hugging her arms round her thin body not so much for warmth as to prevent herself from shivering. If she did not move at all, if she scarcely breathed, the cold was not quite so terrible.

If she did not move—

Behind her, behind the thick, squat pillar of the crypt that was their prison, one of the English nuns was praying. "Holy Mary, Mother of God—"

Other voices whispering in the darkness. There were only two candles left, stumps of tallow guttering on stone ledges, doing no more than stir the shadows. The Marat who had brought them their bread that night had said they would not need any more candles. What had he meant by that? *They will let us go. They must mean to let us go. And then?*

She is dead, she thought, and bent forward with the pain of thinking it, remembering. In the wood. Seeming no different from when she was alive. Only that look of astonishment. "My darling—oh, my darling—" And then afraid. "Stay with me! Kate! Kate!" Her eyes seeming to change, to become blind. But nothing else changing. As though she were still alive. And Kate had clung to her until she had grown cold and heavy and it was no longer her mother in her arms, but a dead body, strange and terrible and more and more frightening, more and more bewildering as she sat there looking at the still familiar, still beautiful face.

"—and at the hour of our death, Amen. Holy Mary, Mother of God—"

Half a dozen voices praying now. One of the remaining few children whimpering. Footfalls, old and slow and heavy, as out of the shadows the Vicomte came pacing, his hands behind his back, his head bent. As though he did not know where he was. Old and tall and white-haired—thin white hair—staring down at the stone floor in front of him as he paced this way and that, hour after hour. While his wife and daughter watched him from their own places in the shadows, against the far wall. Watching him as though all their care was for him. None for themselves. Except that the Marats should not see them afraid. They had been arrested because the Vicomte's son had escaped from last August's conscription, and was in New Orleans. The family of an *émigré*.

At least, Kate had thought bitterly, *they have a reason to be here*. She had tried to talk to the daughter, because they were the same age or near enough. Seventeen. "They killed my mother," she had told her. "The Blues came into the town where we were acting. There was shooting, and we ran out of the theatre—and—" She had cried so much in trying to tell the story, to tell it at last to someone who might understand, that she could not go on. Only see it behind her tears again. Over and over. The audience struggling to get out of the small theatre. And the sounds of the fighting coming nearer. Her mother in her black velvet gown and coronet as Bérénice, standing alone in the middle of the stage, half-lost, still in her part. And she herself running from the wings crying to her, "Mother! *Maman!* Quick, the Blues are coming!" Her mother still hesitating. She had had to pull her away, out of the theatre, into the lane at the back, and they had run, stumbling in their gowns, their Greek sandals, hearing the fighting in the main street behind them. Shots upon shots. And one of them—her mother stumbling again, falling onto her knees.

Kate had not known what had happened, had thought it was only a stumble, and had helped her mother up, and they had run on, more slowly, come to the end of the lane, had been among cottage gardens, fields, the safety of the wood. There her mother had sunk down onto her knees again, and Kate had seen the dark, wet stain of blood on her back.

"I wanted to help her—" but what help could she have got? And her mother would not let her go. "I should have gone in spite of her," she whispered. "No, no! Do not leave me, Kate!" Clinging to her. She must have known that she was dying, that nothing was any use. "You must go home, my darling, go home to England. It is no good here any more." As though it were no more than buying a ticket for a coach. Growing paler and paler, her face silvery with sweat, her eyes huge. Her hair a dark mass of chestnut spread out on the dead yellow leaves. "Promise me you will go to England. It will soon be spring, and—it is so beautiful there."

Kate had held her as though holding could keep off death.

"What should I have done?" Kate had whispered to Mademoiselle Blanche that first night they had talked together. And the other girl had looked at her across such a gulf of difference that it was as though she had not understood the words. As though she could not conceive of a woman dying in a wood. "God's Will be done," she had said at last, folding her thin hands together and lowering her eyes.

She was to have entered a convent a year ago, she told Kate another time. But the convent had been closed and the nuns driven out. When her mother, the Vicomtesse, learned that Kate was an actress she contrived to draw Blanche away into another part of the crypt with her, and after that the girl answered Kate only with pale smiles and inclinations of the head.

"What should I have done?" Kate whispered to herself. If she closed her eyes the wood was there—there—and the pile of leaves and branches she had heaped over—over the— "Stay with me! Kate! Kate!" What could she have done? Only heap the dead leaves over the black velvet dress, the white, astonished face, to hide it while she went to search for someone who—who would bury— She had no more than walked out of the wood when she herself was taken prisoner. No one would listen to her about her mother. Who cared for one more dead woman at such a time? And more prisoners and more, until there was a column of them, to be dragged and beaten into forced marches for eight days, to the coast, to this prison that had been the crypt of the Church of St. Anne before the Revolution.

They had been here three weeks. Those that had survived the march. And others had been added. The Vicomte and his wife and daughter. The English nuns. The abbé. The nuns had been brought from Rouen in a cart. In every market square the cart had been halted so that the villagers could throw stones at them. And yet most of the other prisoners in the crypt were villagers.

"It is the time of Anti-Christ," the oldest nun had said. She had understood Kate's story, and had wept for it. Old, soft tears. "But it is a sign of Our Lord's tenderness towards us that He permits us to share His sufferings. All is forgiven to your mother now, my dear. She sits at Our Blessed Lady's knee and watches Our Infant Saviour smile at her. She died for God's cause, and we must not wish that it was not so. Let us say the Rosary for her, child."

The little boy who had been whimpering began to cry aloud. *"Je vais te dire un joli conte,"* the mother was crooning. "Listen to *maman*, my precious." But the child would not be quiet even for the familiar cradle song, and two of the nuns and the abbé went to help the mother quiet him. If the Marats heard him crying, it would make them angry.

"Hush, hush," one of the nuns whispered. She made her Rosary into a toy for the child, the great round wooden beads falling and clashing together, up and down, up and down. The little egg-seller came to them and began to wring his hands at the noise. When it did not stop, he came and knelt beside Kate.

"Mademoiselle! Citizeness, I mean—go and stop him—please, help them to make him stop. It will bring the guards down on us! The Marats!"

"Leave me alone!" Kate whispered. But even the effort of resisting him, of answering, made her aware of how cold she was, as though the cold was deep in her body, like a pain. Like stone. She tried to get to her feet and half fell. The egg-seller pulled her upright. He did not seem to feel the cold, although in the three weeks they had been there his red cheeks had turned leaden grey, like all of them.

"He likes you, Mademoiselle. He will be quiet for you. He is afraid of the sisters and the priest."

She went to where the child was, surrounded by the dark shadows of the nuns and the abbé. "Give him to me for a moment, Madame," Kate said. But the woman looked at her with blank eyes and held the child tighter.

"She will make him stop crying!" the egg-seller hissed at the mother. "Give him to her!"

"No, no!"

"It is because the guard Le Moel favoured you the other day," he whispered. "She does not trust you any longer." The guard had given Kate an extra ladleful of hot soup and had tried to fondle her. "You should have let him," the egg-seller had said afterwards. "Then you might have some influence with him if—"

The child stopped its crying, its mind caught for the moment by the Rosary beads, the glitter of the silver Christ on the wooden Cross. The egg-seller followed Kate back to her pillar. "That guard who has taken a fancy to you—you know—you could—they are good men, the Marats—really—at bottom—good Republicans.

Like I am myself. It is a misunderstanding that I am here—and you too, I am sure. If you would only be a little—a little agreeable to him—"

The door crashed open at the head of the stone steps. Two Marats carrying flaming torches lurched through the doorway and the shadows leapt and staggered in the crypt. The light glared red and burning on the grey walls, the pillars, reached into distant corners where figures were crouching. There was a stirring, a murmuring, then a silence broken by the child's crying, its voice rising to a pitch of fear, cut off into a stifled sobbing as the mother pressed its head against her.

"Stop the brat's row!" the guard shouted, "or I'll stop it for him, and permanent."

"It'll stop soon enough," the other guard said, fumbling drunkenly with some papers in his free hand, "where they're going." Both men laughed, leaned their heads together to peer at the documents, turning them this way and that. "Roll call!" one of them shouted. "Answer your names smart and sharp, damn you! Bercard, Joseph."

"Here, here, Monsieur," the egg-seller cried, waving his hand eagerly. "Present!"

"'Monsieur,' he says," the guard shouted mockingly. "Royalist scum."

"I meant citizen, I meant citizen, your Excellency!"

"Quiet, damn you. Boussy, Jean Pierre."

"Here."

"Chartier, Anne."

"Here."

The roll call staggered on, half the names mispronounced, shouted again and again until they echoed among the pillars, mangled and unintelligible. A third Marat came and a fourth and fifth, all of them drunk, moving unsteadily, kicking at anyone still crouched down against a wall or a pillar, routing into the corners for anyone hiding. "Get your bits together, you're going travelling again." Laughing and cursing and pushing, making the roll call even harder to follow.

"Arro—Arrio—Haricot, Kathérine."

"Here," Kate said, guessing that it must be Harriott they were trying to say. Two of the Marats had found a prisoner still lying

[11]

down against a wall, and were kicking him. But he did not move.

"There's one here that's dead," one of the Marats shouted towards the steps. "Or dying."

"He'll make a body just the same. There's a cart for them that can't walk. Lechantre, Nicholas!"

"Here Mons—Citizen."

All the crypt in anxious movement and whispering. Gathering bundles, those that had any possessions to gather. Huddling together. Kate stood against her pillar as though it had some safety about it, some familiarity. Where would they be taken now? All the nuns forming into a small group, whispering prayers in unison. The abbé forced his way through the press towards the steps.

"I demand to see the Commandant," he said. "You cannot move us in this weather, at midnight. There are old women, children— they will die of exposure. They are dying even in here."

"He demands!" one of the roll-callers cried out in mock astonishment. "Eh, Vourc'h, d'you hear him? What had we better do?" And then, turning on the priest, he shouted, "You'll see the Commandant soon enough, you old cretin. And where you're going you won't worry about the weather."

They are going to kill us! Kate thought, and then, *I am mad. It is impossible.*

"We have had no proper food all day. Only bread."

"Silence! Rieux, Tanguy." There was no answer. The old Vicomte was standing in the midst of the crowd of prisoners, his eyes looking over their heads. He was the tallest there and seemed to have nothing in the world in common with anything round him. Someone touched his arm, and again more firmly, to engage his attention.

"They are calling your name, Monsieur Le Vicomte."

"My name?" the old man said.

"He is here, Monsieur de Rieux is here, Messieurs."

"Let him answer for himself, damn him. Citizeness Rieux. Diane."

"I am here," the Vicomtesse said.

"Rieux, Blanche."

"I too," Mademoiselle Blanche said. The two women, the old one and the young, stood up, and joined the Vicomte near the foot of the steps. People made way for them. Mademoiselle Blanche's hair was long and pale blonde, like a veil. She stood with her eyes downcast as though she were the nun she had hoped to be. More guards had come with lengths of rope and began calling the prisoners up two by two, binding their hands in front of them and linking them in pairs.

The woman with the little boy who had been crying stood near Kate, rocking him in her arms. She stared at Kate as though she did not recognise her. "He will die," she said. "He will die of the cold."

"I will help you carry him."

But the woman only stared at her and repeated the same words.

Three villagers, a woman and two men, were trying to tie up a bundle. A Marat kicked it away into the darkness and laughed. "You won't need that. Just bring your gold. Eh, *ma mère?*" He ran his hands over the woman's dress to feel if there was gold hidden about her. One of the men tried to protect her and the other held him back. But there was no gold to find.

"Get on with you, damn your eyes," the guard shouted at them. He came lurching round the pillar and found Kate standing there. It was Le Moel. He was thickset as a barrel, with tiny eyes in a red, sweating face; sweating wine and brandy and food in spite of the ferocious cold. Black moustaches drooping over a wet red mouth.

"The little citizeness," he said.

"Don't touch me!" But she could not back away from him. He had put his hands on either side of her shoulders against the stone-work.

"Whyn't you be nice to me, eh? I could"—he twisted his head on his thick neck, trying to look over his shoulder—"I could keep you with me," he whispered.

"No!"

"Don't be too hasty. You don't know where they're going." He leered into her face, licked his mouth, his tongue rasping against the ragged fringe of his moustaches. "They're going for a swim. Ssssh!" He tried to look round again. He was very drunk and his neck and body were too thick to let him turn his head enough.

"A—swim—?" She could not understand what he meant, could not allow herself to understand.

"Sssssh!" He moved a hand like a bear's paw and forced it over her mouth. "Not a word! I'll tie you last," he said. He had rope in a pocket and began fumbling with it while she stared at him, still not understanding, not wanting to understand.

"You are going to kill us all? To—to—drown us?" It was not pos-

[13]

sible. He was drunk—trying to frighten her—to— He was pulling her hands in front of her, tying them together, making a drunken business of it while the crowd of prisoners round about them were dragged up the steps two by two.

I must shout out to the others, Kate thought. *They do not know.* But it could not be true—Her hands were bound and he was dragging her, not towards the steps but away from them, making a pretence of looking for anyone who might still be hiding. In the darkness behind another pillar he caught hold of her, his hands feeling her shoulders, her waist, as though he were buying a chicken in the market.

"Be nice to me," he said, his voice mumbling and slurring. "An' Le Moel'll be nice to you. Feed you good. Make you warm. Commandant has his woman, why not me? A countess he has. Like cream. You stay with me, eh?"

"They are going to drown us!" she cried out, but her voice did not answer; it was only whispering.

He pushed his hand over her mouth again, shook her violently. "Sssssh. Secret!"

"It is not true! You cannot be going to—"

He began to drag her towards the steps, hurrying now in the echoes of the crypt, the shadows. The last of the coupled prisoners already vanishing. A Marat was standing by the doorway, forcing them through, lifting his torch high up. Black doorway, red torchlight. The woman with the child, a man tied to her. The woman stumbling, repeating over and over, "He will die of the cold."

I must tell them, Kate thought. Through the church. *But he is lying—*

It was a full moon, silver-white, the night black and white like the day's ghost, ice sharp, brilliant. The prisoners in a huddled column of pairs. A cart. The salt smell of the sea beyond the houses. Grey-black, shuttered. The Commandant standing by the stone cross in the middle of the square—plumed hat, sword, cockade and sash—shouting, "You are going on a journey, my friends. To where you will become good citizens, servants of the Republic. Down the hill, march!"

Shuffle of feet, a voice calling, *Monsieur le Commandant!* Excellency! Where are we going?"

"Silence! Make that man keep silence!"

The sound of a fist striking. Shuffle of feet.

As they went down the hill, the cart rattling iron wheel-rims on the stones of the road, Kate could see the Vicomte seeming to lead the way, head and shoulders taller than the others. Mademoiselle Blanche's hair turned to silver by the moonlight, ghost-white. The black submission of the nuns. *It cannot be true,* she thought, closing her eyes against them, against the night. The cold piercing, and yet not so cold as the crypt. Le Moel dragging her along, like that poor something he had bought at market, behind the others, separate.

The houses shuttered, secret, sleeping. But they could not be sleeping with these feet going by. *They know!* she thought and it was as though she were asleep, dreaming, in a black-and-silver nightmare. She had no will. Could not shout aloud to wake herself.

The road turned and the sea was there, below, ahead. Black glass inside the curved grey arm of the harbour. Touched with silver caps beyond it. And the path of the moon like silver cloth. In the harbour a ship lying, black and derelict. Down the last of the hill. Onto the mole.

Along the harbour wall there were fishing boats, four, five, tied up and waiting. The head of the column had already reached them. The guards were forcing the first couples on board. The Vicomte. The abbé, tied to him. Behind them Mademoiselle Blanche, her mother. Two of the nuns. Kate opened her mouth again to cry out, but the nightmare held her, she could not make a sound for horror. And then someone screamed, the egg-seller, Bercard, screaming, "No, no, no, no! I am innocent! Where are you taking us? No, no, no, no!"

A guard clubbed him, and the echo of his scream hung in the sharp air like broken glass. Half a dozen of the prisoners screaming, a dozen, a great fountain of screams for mercy. Was she herself screaming? "They are going to drown—"

Le Moel dragged her away, drove his palm at her mouth so that her lips were cut against her teeth. The woman with the child turned towards her, holding her child to her breast, her mouth open, a black hole in her silver face. "Give him to me!" Kate screamed, trying to hold out her bound hands. The woman made no answer, no sign. A Marat pushed her violently, pushed the man bound to her, and both of them went over the side of the mole into the waiting boat that was already full of prisoners. The sounds of clubs and fists, of cries for mercy. Floating across the water, already distant. Le Moel holding her, behind a pile of baskets on the far side of the harbour wall.

"You come with me now," he said. He let go of the end of her rope to catch her round the body, bury his face against hers.

She pushed him with all her strength and he staggered back, the heel of his boot catching something, slipping on an icy stone. Waving his arms, falling. A heavy thud. She stood for a second, expecting to hear his shout of rage, someone shouting. And a cry came across the water, the sounds of oars, the lap and suck of water against rocks. But no sound from Le Moel. She went to the edge of the quayside and looked. He lay head downward on the rocks below her. Not very far below. One arm already in the sea, the sea moving it. His eyes were open, looking at the moon.

Is he dead? she thought. All round her only silence. And the lapping of the sea. The oars, the voices farther and farther off. More crying out. She could not force herself to look towards the hulk. Uncertain, hesitating, she began to move, stupidly, on tiptoe, in the remnants of her sandals, in what had been her white gown as Fénice and was now grey rags. Began to run. Expecting at every step, every second, to hear shouting, guards running, her breath harsh with terror, her eyes blind. She did not know where she was running, where to run. Only the shuttered houses. Could hear nothing but her own sandals running, stumbling, her heartbeat, her gasping for breath. She could not run properly with her hands bound. The end of the rope trailed, caught at her feet. And she still ran. The shuttered houses. The black-and-silver streets. Until there were no houses. Fields, a hillside, grey stone walls and pale grass. Her side hurt so much that she could not go on.

She knelt down, the ruts of the roadway hard with frost, black earth. Like iron. Every breath like iron. She bent over trying to breathe. "O, *mon dieu.* O, God have mercy." On her? On them? She dared not look, and had to, had to. Turning her head very slowly. The sea spread out. So beautiful under the moon that it was like the road to paradise. The hulk was moving, two of the fishing boats dragging it out beyond the harbour, into the open sea. She thought—it was impossible—it was her heart beating, the pulse of her own blood—but she thought she could hear the oars creaking. Could hear the voices echoing, echoing in the empty dark, in terror.

[16]

It is not possible, she thought. As though to say it would make that true. She lay in the roadway, crying. When she looked again, the hulk had reached the broken sea, the waves. It lay lower in the water than it had done.

"O God, have mercy," she whispered. Do not watch. Do not watch. She gathered the end of the rope into her hands, got to her knees, stood up. *I cannot go on,* she thought. But something made her go on. "I did not—" She could not understand anything. Not her own thoughts. Only feel the horror. And a voice whispering, "I am alive. I am still alive." And did not know whether the voice was whispering in an agony of relief, or of still greater horror.

The hillside. Grey stones like animals. The coldness of the sky. *I shall die here,* she thought distantly. But not drowned. Not clawing at the timbers as the sea poured in. "O, God, have mercy." The tears running. Like ice. "I am alive," she whispered, and shook her head in agony, in horror, in unbelief.

There was a low shape in front of her, a mound, a kind of roof no higher than herself. A roof made of earth, grass. She leaned against it, the grass brittle, cold. No sound. She made her way round and there was an entrance, so low that she must crawl to go in. A sour, thin smell, of smoke, of cold earth, of long-dead grass and bracken, dry rustling under her knees. A shepherd's hut. His bed. Not used since summer. She lay down, her bound wrists chafed and numbed, her hands useless. She must try to free them—try—the knots hurt her mouth, her bruised lips where Le Moel had struck her. Like gnawing against stone. She was so tired. So—

Chapter 2

The coach horn cried its warning, high and clear and arrogant, as they thundered and rang and jangled through a village street, the houses ghostly in the dawn, humped and crooked shadows against the lowering December sky. English sky. English houses.

I am home, Kate thought, peering through the misted glass at the countryside. The other passengers slept, snoring and swaying with the coach's movements, leaning against one another, the man beside her crowding her into her corner.

I am home. English fields. English trees. Great spreading silhouettes of trees, the sky behind them burning, beginning to burn crimson. Clouds like thin black islands in a crimson sea. *And I am alive.*

She wondered what province they were travelling through. If it might possibly be Hertfordshire. "You were born in a place called Hertfordshire, my darling. And how you cried on being born! Oh, *mon Dieu,* how you cried! As though you were saying 'I do not want an actress for my mother, an actor for my father! No no no!' Oh, my wise little Kate. But we have no choice in such things, my love. And you must make the best of it."

Across the fields in the growing light of the dawn there was the dark grey shape of a wood, and she closed her eyes against it. But that was worse, because behind her eyelids she could see the branches, the piled leaves. She drew the edges of her hood closer round her face, although the other passengers still slept, and there was no one to see her eyes. When they did wake, she would pretend to be asleep. The second day of pretending to be asleep for hours at a time to avoid talking, answering. Betraying that she could understand scarcely one word in four that they said to her, because of her nervousness at having to say anything in return. Betraying by her accent that her natural language was French, and had been for twelve years, since she was a tiny child.

She had not thought of it, among all the other terrors, the far greater ones of escaping, of lying hidden for ten days with the farmer and his wife and children. Had not thought beyond reaching England. Had half thought that she would recognise the countryside, the roads. It had been roads like this, this one, up that hill in front of them, that they must have travelled. With the company, the carts. Her father carrying her. All she remembered of him was that carrying. And singing small songs to her when she was very tired. A dark, smiling face, and a bristle of beard that pricked her cheek as she lay against his shoulder.

"Not much farther, my tiny one. Only a short while, and then, hup-la, supper. And a warm, warm bed." Always the roads. And the theatres. Candlelight, and crowds, and her mother and father standing there before all the people, saying wonderful things. And the clapping, and the shouts of applause. There could not always have been crowds, nor always applause. But those were the times that she remembered. Her mother on the stage, tall, splendid, one arm flung out, and all the brilliance of the candlelight, and she herself sitting on a basket in the wings, adoring.

She could not remember when the theatres and the roads had ceased to be English and become French. She must have been no more than five. There had been debts. Someone had run off with money. So her mother had told her, later. She half-remembered, half-dreamed of remembering, a ship and sailors, and the strange, strange feeling of the ground tilting as she walked, and a sailor catching her up in his arms before she fell over into the sea. He had smelt of tar, and had carried her into the cabin to her mother.

Strange to remember that, and not remember her father dying. It must have been soon after. In Calais. Or Amiens. Or farther south. And still the roads. Still the theatres. The long hills. After a time another man had carried her when she was tired. And after a time more that man had disappeared as well, and she had grown too big to be carried. And unwilling also. She had begun to be jealous of the men who acted with her mother. Without knowing why, or even what jealousy was. Had begun to act herself without knowing that it was acting. All the people there in front of her. The candlelight. The barns. The stable-yards. The real theatres. The roads between. The jealousy. And the love.

The tears ran, and she drew the hood closer still. The man beside her woke and jerked himself upright, stretched, yawned, shook his head violently as though to shake the sleep out of his eyes.

"I beg your pardon, ma'am."

She did not answer him. The others began waking, three other women and another man. "What o'clock is it?" the second man asked of the company in general. The first man pulled out a watch, and told him a quarter before eight. Kate could understand that much, but when they began talking of other things, she could understand scarcely anything at all.

The shock had come within a few minutes of her being landed on the beach in Cornwall. All the way across, with the smugglers, she had never thought of it. Speak English? Why, yes, of course, it was her own tongue, by birth, by— And the Cornish smuggler who had received her onto the beach, as the Breton crew were helping the Cornishmen unload the ankers of brandy and the bales of silk, and the tobacco; he had needed to speak to her in low Breton before she could understand him. It was he who had told her that she still had reason to be afraid.

"I'd not make myself noticed if I was you," he had said. "There's a new Act just passed to keep out what they call aliens and they might put you in Bodmin gaol and send you out of England again."

"Send me—but I am English!"

"Aye, maybe. But can you prove it, my dear? Your tongue is no proof of it, and that's for certain. I believe you, but I'd take no chances if I was in your shoes."

A big, grey man whom they called the King. The King of Prussia, although she had not understood why "of Prussia." But he had been like a king. It was he who had given her the handful of guineas. Not counting them. Merely diving his big hand into a leather bag and pulling out gold to put into her lap. And she had been so ashamed, so astonished and ashamed at such a careless magnificence of generosity that she could scarcely thank him, and stayed looking down at the small heap of gold there. The dreadful suspicion coming to her that such a gesture could not be purely kindness—that there must be some other motive behind it. Stumbling over her thanks as if her tongue were made of wood.

"No need to thank me, m'dear. We gains so many o' they little coins in our trade we scarce bothers to count 'em, 'cept by the handful. I'm ashamed to give ye so petty a bit o' help." And he made as though to add more guineas to the heap.

"No, no! *Mon Dieu*, how can I—you have given me so much already—how can I hope to repay you ever?" Her cheeks burning. Almost afraid that he had read her thoughts. "How can I—?"

"Easy enough, m'dear. When you do come to your rightabouts,

mebbe you'll find a poor soul as needs help and then you'll pass on that little bit o' help to them. God send you'll be soon able to. As for me, that boat out there as brought you'll keep me in guineas a fair length. I hope all of 'em are spent as well as those few are likely to be."

But for all his seeming carelessness, he had questioned her at first shrewdly enough, with more penetration than his grey sailor's eyes might have given warning of. Her mother's death. The crypt. The drownings. The child from the farm who had come on her in the shepherd's summer hut and brought her to his father. The kindness of the farm family that had kept her hidden and fed and clothed her, until there was a smugglers' boat willing to bring her across to Cornwall.

"And they took ye in as easy and comfortable as that? Ye had no fear they'd hand ye back to—what is it ye called 'em? The Marats?"

"But they were Catholics!" she had cried, half bewildered at his question. "Hand me back?"

"And these fellows in Callac—in the town—are they not Catholics?"

"Why—I suppose—I suppose once—but now—now they are Republicans—or pretend to be while the Republicans are winning."

"But were ye not just telling me about these poor souls of nuns? That the villagers pelted stones at 'em as they sat tied in their carts? Have the villages turned Republican too, as well as the towns? And what differ' was your farmer from village folk?"

She could not answer him; as she thought of it could not unravel it herself, except that it had been so clear to her that any single family she could have stumbled on would have given her shelter. If there had been a group of people together it might have been—would almost certainly have been—different. She tried to explain that as the King rubbed his chin and considered her with those disconcertingly shrewd eyes.

"How can I explain it? If there are others there, they are afraid—they do what the others do—but in their hearts they are with the Chouans—the rebels. Even those people who threw stones at the poor sisters—by themselves they might have been quite different." She shook her head in despair of making an Englishman understand what was happening in France. Even in the Vendée, even in the rebel towns, among the Royalists, she had understood little enough herself—until prison had taught her.

The King was nodding slowly as he looked at her. "Aye, ais,

there's nought simple about folk, once you pry into 'em, and start asking whyfor they do this an' that. Aye, I believe your tale." Resting his hand on her shoulder for a moment, beginning to smile again, as though doubts were clearing away from his mind like clouds fading. "I believe ye better than if ye had a clearer-thought-out story and account o' everything. Aye." Smiling down at her whole-heartedly now. "And if ye know as much English as ye say, and the sounds come back to ye, ye'll have nought to worry about. But until ye can speak and answer easy and understand all that's said, keep your mouth close and be better nor careful. 'Tis war now, and they have powerful fears o' spies an' Jacobins. The first magistrate as laid hands on ye down here'd be certain sure as how he'd caught Madame Robespierre herself. Ye'd have a mort o' trouble before ye were free of him. If ye got free. Go up to Lunnon and get lost in the crowds."

He had looked at her clothes. The farmer's wife had given her an old cloak and heavy stockings. "Ye'll need different gear to that, m'dear. Leave it to me a bit."

She had lain up in a cave all that day, sleeping, and eating what the Cornish smugglers gave her, great mugs of broth and mulled wine that she fell asleep over before she could finish them. And that night the King had brought her English clothes: a gown and half-boots and some linen, a shift and petticoats and stocking

"My wife sends 'em to you with all her heart," the King said, "and but that she's abed of a putrid sore throat she 'uld be here herself to make the gift. She's nothing above your size, and if she's a bit thicker about than you, you may take a tuck in here and there, she says. No doubt you'll know how."

The linen was very fine, such as a lady might be glad to wear. It was then he had pulled the gold out of the leather bag and dropped the handful of guineas into her lap.

"I cannot! I cannot take all this! Any of it! Why should you—I am a stranger to you—a—"

In the end shame had taken away her words altogether and she had covered her eyes with her hands. She still felt so weak and ill, even after the days in the farmer's house, that the tears came whether she would or not. And she had not slept. She thought that she would never sleep again. "I am sorry. I am not yet strong again."

"No wonder. And ye must be strong enough to have stood all."

[22]

He had brought her a mirror and a comb, and soap and towels, by his wife's commands. "I cannot bring ye to the house," he had apologised. "Maids talk. They'll not talk of brandy, they're reared up to that trade. But a strange young woman that seems to have no word of English might be a different thing, and too much temptation to go gossiping. If ye can make do here until nightfall, one of the lads'll bring ye a basin and a ewer of hot water."

She had been shocked to see her own face again. The eyes hollowed out and haunted, her cheeks ghost-pale and thin. She had her mother's eyes, brown-hazel, and her mother's chestnut hair, the same dark mass of it; and the darkness of her hair and eyes made her face more a ghost's than ever. Her body too had grown so thin that she could feel all her bones as she put on the clean linen, and that also had been a kind of shock, of pity for her body, as though it belonged to someone else and she was thinking with sorrow of what it had been. She had been pretty once. It seemed very long ago. Young men had looked at her and her mother had laughed at her for blushing and being troubled.

"They have been looking at you for two or three years already, my darling, my little goose. Have you not noticed it? You will break many, many hearts, my love, and must grow used to it. It is very pleasant trouble to grow used to, I promise you."

And before Kate could restrain herself she had cried "No! Never! I will never grow used to it!"

It had been as though she had struck her mother across the mouth. She had seen the beautiful, still beautiful eyes seem to grow sightless with the pain of it, with the pain of that cry of revulsion, of shocked innocence and knowledge. And even in that second, before she knew fully what she had done, what she had said, she would have torn out her tongue to have unsaid it.

She had looked into the Cornish woman's mirror and remembered like a wound aching, years after the flesh has seemed to heal. But the hidden bone continues its aching. Her mother lying under the leaves.

"How could I have done that to her? Hurt her in that way?" And again. And again. As the men became younger, and her mother older, and more desperate to be loved.

"How can you? *Maman! Maman!*" Had cried with shame, threatened to leave her, to leave the company. It had seemed to her at times that it was she who was the older and her mother the child.

And she had felt as though her own heart was becoming a stone inside her. "I will never love anyone," she had told herself. So much pain. So much shame in it. That wakening in her mother's eyes, that dancing in her mother's voice, in her movements, that told that she was in love again, and had been loved. A kind of youthfulness come back, like the ripe bloom on fruit—a glowing of the flesh, of satin skin. Her acting took on a new, slow richness of gesture, her voice a new depth of passion, like the trembling sound of a great drum that has been softly struck. And the young man would move himself like a leopard, or a cock, would stretch with slow content, or strut or preen. And then grow bored. And ashamed. And the agony in her mother's eyes would begin.

"Never! Never!" Kate whispered. Whispered aloud in the coach, as she saw her grey reflection in the glass.

"Beg your pardon, ma'am?" the man beside her said, leaning slightly forward and peering sideways at her with curiosity. "You said summat, ma'am?"

"Nothing," she whispered again, even her lips cold with remembering, stiff with shame. "I slept." Hoping she had understood him properly.

And now she is dead, she thought. *And forgiven. Oh pray God that she is forgiven. And I? I who am alive?*

The coach stopped to allow them to take breakfast, and she was obliged to get down and pretend to understand what people said to her. But it had been early accepted by her travelling companions that she was not talkative and they left her alone at the table and talked among themselves. Of its being only one more night and day to London, and what each of them meant to do there. She had begun to find that she could follow the drift of their talk, so long as she was not required to answer anything. And the man and his wife who had joined them yesterday, replacing travellers who had got down, spoke much more clearly, almost like her mother. They were saying how expensive the London inns were and how, the last visit they had made, they had had to pay above a shilling each for a dinner of quite an ordinary kind.

She had already learned that there were twenty-one shillings in a guinea, and twenty in a pound, and twelve pennies in a shilling, and how much a traveller's meal should cost. But in London? To find lodgings—to— She found herself almost glad that there was still that day, and the night, and the next day before they must arrive. As though even the coach had become a kind of safety, and these companions, to whom she never spoke except to murmur something indistinct and sketch a smile at them, had become friends.

What shall I do there? she thought, staring down at the kidneys growing cold on her plate. At the coffee that she could not have forced herself to drink even if it had been drinkable. *What shall I do there?* Find lodgings. A room. Be alone. Sleep. Now in daylight, in this room, beside people, she could think of it. *It cannot go on,* she thought. One could not go on like that. That kind of dreaming.

Her neighbour asked her something and she nodded, and he put his fork into her plate and ate what was there, smacking his lips and thanking her. "Very tasty," he said. Tasty? She did not answer him and he did not appear to expect an answer but said something about the sky, and snow. A red sky.

If there could be a way of sleeping without dreams. She shut her eyes and thought, *Why do you come to me? Why? Why? What could I have done?* And they were behind her eyelids. Drowned faces. Drowned hands. The child.

The coach horn blew its shrill warning to them to be done and the waiter came bustling for them to pay.

"You didn't ate nowt," the man beside her said. He seemed to be making an offer to pay her sixpence for her and she shook her head and made haste to pay herself.

"A young leddy travelling alone," he said confidentially, "is liable to be put on. You 'ave folks in Lunnon, I hope?"

She nodded again at the "travelling alone," and he seemed both satisfied and disappointed. She climbed back into the coach and pretended to be quickly asleep, or drowsing.

The day went by. Dinner. Supper long after it was already dark. The street lamps of a town. Her companions slept. She slept herself, lulled and swayed, exhausted. Tried to keep awake. "Please, please—why do you trouble me? What could I have done? *But it is I who am torturing myself!*" she thought. "I am giving way—for what? What is my guilt? That I am alive and they—they are dead? How could it have served them if— And if I had cried out then—then, in the crypt when— What could that have served? And it was too late. I tried—I tried to cry out—"

Round and round. She could no longer remember the exact sequence of things. What Le Moel had said. When. Whether she had tried to cry out then or— And going down the hill? Then? If she had cried out to them then?

"Have mercy on me," she whispered. But they came swaying with the coach's darkness, in the shadows, in her mind. Like creatures of the sea, sea-pale. Mademoiselle Blanche, the Vicomtesse, the old Vicomte—floating in the dark—the woman with her child, the nuns, the abbé, the egg-seller with his mouth still screaming in drowned silence, "I am innocent! You—you—you—!" And his hands— What was it about his hands that he seemed to hold up like that? And her mother, her mother lying hidden in the wood. Her own mother of whom she had been ashamed. The eyes grown of a sudden so young. And then so old. So blind. And yet still open.

I am creating them, she thought, *out of my own weakness. O God, protect my mind from myself, protect me from the dead.*

If she looked at the coach glasses, they became dark mirrors. "No! No!" She made herself look through them, reasoned with herself. "If I go on like this, I shall grow truly ill. I shall die. If I am still alive, is it not because it was meant that I should live? For what? Could there be a purpose in such things?" Look through the glasses. Hedges. The dark roofs of farm buildings.

"I am home. I am safe. Now that we have left the coast—even my accent—how many French people there must be in London—and I am beginning to understand. Suppose that someone knew French, remembered it from childhood, from one educated companion— the French of Paris—and was set down in Brittany—how much would they understand at first? Not a word. I am quite safe now. After a week or so no one will guess that I have ever left England."

She forced herself to close her eyes, leaned back her head. Her companions snored, breathed in the restless way of upright sleepers, lurched and woke muttering and slept again. She slept herself and at the same time some part of her mind seemed to stay on watch, to drive away the dead. It was not an easy sleep, but it was something, and towards morning she sank deeper into it, so deep that, if she dreamed, she remembered nothing, and woke to find her companions getting out for breakfast, and her neighbour touching her arm to wake her.

One more day. Neat villages, pretty woods and hills. The road improved. Her companions still more eager and important about their business in the capital, mentioning shops and theatres and famous places they meant to see if there was time. She felt a sudden envy of them, thought—if only she was that stout woman with her black bonnet and rosy face. To visit her married daughter. To be met. She had talked of it so much that Kate had long ago made it out. A widow with four daughters, all married, all content as apples. And this one most content of all, married to a lawyer.

"How must my Susan be feeling at this minute!" the woman was saying. Black woollen gown. Black cotton gloves. Black beads. Such a comfortable, rosy widowhood. A cook and a maid and a serving man left behind in Cornwall for the month of her holiday. "Iss, iss, it will be a holiday for them, too, with none but themselves to consider." Rosy and jolly and content. "I declare I am excited as a girl. 'Tis more than a whole year since we have seen each other."

The man beside Kate was a shopkeeper from Bodmin, going up to a warehouse to look over new goods.

And I? Kate thought, fear swooping like wings. She clenched her hands in her lap. *I have money. I can understand at least some of what is said to me. What is it? Only a new town? A new place? How is it so different to Paris? Or Bordeaux? Or Lyons? I shall—I shall be alone.*

She wanted to put up her hands against her face. *"Pour la dernière fois, adieu—"* They had not reached that line in *Bérénice*—would never reach it again. It was not possible—"I am alone—I am alone."

"Courage, *ma petite, toujours* courage. You cannot follow our calling without it, my love. Always you must be very brave."

That her mother had always been. That lifting of the head from defeat.

"I did not know it enough!" Kate cried in her misery. "If only I could go back and love her enough—tell her how much I loved her bravery." That walking from town to town behind the overloaded carts. Only one cart at times. The poor jade of a horse tottering. And they themselves so tired that another mile was impossible. And at the end of how many miles, another theatre. Not four livres in the audience. Five livres of expenses to find for tomorrow morning. And half a dozen drunken fools trying to ruin everything, even the little that there was. Be brave? And her mother striking a gesture. Making them smile. Her poor, stricken companions. Lifting them up. As though she was their soul.

The coach had stopped again to change horses. Ring of harness, bustle, stamping of hooves as the great animals were put to. Maids on the inn balcony above the yard. The scalding liquid that they served as coffee. The sharpness of the air that seemed even itself to say "London is near, London is near." How many more miles? But there was still dinner-time. Still the whole afternoon, the evening.

"Eight o'clock!" the widow was saying. "To think that I shall see her at eight o'clock this very evening! She will have grown so big I shall scarce recognise her! Iss, iss. She is to be brought to bed in April, you know. I was that big when I was carrying her! Like a barrel of cider!" Her laugh ringing out through the yard, as though the street must know her excitement.

Kate walked up and down, avoiding a small boy trying to sell her pencils, or a comb, and another larger boy with ribbons and threads and scissors. An ostler chased them away. What would she do? What would her mother have done?

Dinner. Dark. She felt her heart beating. And then grow still with fear. "It is only another town. Another town. I am alone. I am alone." The wheels took up the rhythm, the horses' hooves, the ringing of their harness, the creaking of the springs. Even the post horn cried, "Alone, alone, alone!"

"We are upon the stones now!" the shopkeeper beside her told her with an air of consequence, as though she would not have known it but for his telling her. She guessed that he was speaking of the town pavé. The sounds rang differently, iron on stone road. There was a street lamp, houses lit. Her companions began to peer out with a new interest.

"I have only to find a bed. And tomorrow—"

There was traffic, a coach going the other way, with a great sounding of horns like a salute, a galloping and rumbling. Foot passengers, more lamps. She was, in a different part of her mind, astonished at how many lamps, at the brightness of the streets. How great a city it must be! Shop windows, bustle, a rainbow of lengths of cloth in a draper's windows, people shopping—buying bread, meat, books—carrying parcels, talking, hurrying, muffled against the cold. Such lights and crowds and shops and buildings, such traffic, that what had gone before was like a large village, nothing, and she felt her heart beat sick with terror.

"What should I do if my Susan's Edward was not here to meet me? Oh lord ha' mercy what a place it is, what a bustle!"

"The Fleet market," the shopkeeper said, pointing to flaring lights, stalls. "I come here near every year, you know. Iss, that I do, but I would not live here if I was to make twice my money. Oh no, Bodmin for me."

[28]

They were all getting themselves ready for the journey's end, feeling about them in the dark for anything left behind, buttoning coats, adjusting bonnets and hats. Kate tightened her own cloak about her throat and shut her eyes. "I wish for a room with bed—a bedroom?—for a bedroom—and to wash—hot water—soap—" But she need not ask for everything by name. Just say "to wash." "And I must eat—they will expect me to order supper." She tried to think that she was hungry.

The coach swung sharp round, lurched, the horn blew triumphantly. They were stopped, arrived. And the door pulled open, an inn servant there, offering her his hand to help her.

"I'll get yer box down for yer, ma'am. Which is it?"

Box? She stared at him, her mind blank, and he said it again, louder and impatiently, as though he were used to stupefied travellers who could not understand English. Box?

"I have no box," she said.

"Yer portmanteau then."

"No, no portmanteau—*rien*—nothing, nothing. I—"

But he had turned away, shrugging, and was already clambering with a colleague onto the rear step to wrestle with the widow's great trunk and the shopkeeper's portmanteau, and the other travellers' provincial luggage, while the guard and the coachman swung their arms against their huge coats and blew on their fingers. The yard full of people. Other travellers, ostlers, grooms, a waiter in a bright-lit doorway, boys dodging about with their pencil trays and cottons. The horses steaming in the cold, their haunches like brown sweating satin. A man in a beaver hat and surtout, and with an air of busy consequences greeting the widow. Cries of "Edward!" And "How is my Susan? Oh Lord ha' mercy how shook up I am! My legs are giving under me, I declare! How is my dearest girl? Is she very large?"

"Here? Shall I ask for a bed here?" A man jostling Kate, and from the other side a tray of cottons pushed under her nose. A boy's bright, dark face, swarthy and Jewish. "Very cheap, ma'am. The cheapest yer'll fin' anywheres. On'y a penny!"

She made her way towards the bright doorway, uncertainly. The Jewish child followed her. This inn would be very dear—they had spoken of how dear such places were—a shilling for a supper—how much must a bed cost? But— The boy had grown frantic, seeing her escaping him. "Only a penny! A penny for such cottons as them! Look at 'em!"

She looked, not at his cottons but at his face, his eyes. Dark velvet. Black curls. "I do not want cottons," she said carefully. He began to urge again. "But I do want lodgings," she said. "If——"

Could she trust such a boy? But his very Jewishness, his foreignness, seemed in a way to make him nearer to her for that moment, less strange. And although his eyes were very sharp and businesslike, they did not look deceitful or evil.

"Lodgings? Yer want somewheres to lodge? Yer got blunt? Cash? Money? 'Ow much yer want to pay?" He was all business, as though a hundred different kinds of lodging lay at his command, his tray no more than a pastime.

"They must be clean," Kate said. "And respectable."

"Respectable?" The black eyes snapped, considered, judged. Her cloak, her face, her voice, her boots, her lack of luggage, her ignorance of the town. "French, ain't yer?"

"No!"

"The Frenchies all goes to Somerstown. I knows a cheap place there."

"I am not French!" If he had been an adult, she would have been terror-stricken at his immediately guessing, and as it was she was sorry that she had been so foolish. "It does not signify anything—I shall go in here. Thank you—good-bye—" She did not know whether to give him a penny to quiet his suspicions.

"Orl right, orl right," he was saying. "Yer ain't French. I don't care if yer a Rooshan. 'Ow much yer want to pay?"

"It does not signify!"

But he would not be put away. He had caught her cloak with one not very clean, supple hand, and was drawing her with him. "If yer goes in there," he said, "they'll twig yer."

Twig? She tried to put him from her, but he would not let go.

"They'll 'ave yer," he said. "Jus' landed, eh? No passport?"

"Let go of my cloak!"

"Yer don't need to be afraid of me," he whispered. "I wouldn't turn yer in—we ain't that sort. I got a real safe place for yer. Cheap, too. Yer can trust me."

"I do not wish to go to Summertown—" The last place on earth that she wished to go if there were French people there.

"Nao, nao. I won't take yer there. Come on!"

If he began to raise his voice? It would be madness to trust him, but worse madness to argue with him here. Already an ostler was looking at them, the waiter's attention had been attracted. If she asked them to free her from the boy, and the boy should say, "She is French. She has no passport"—Why had she ever spoken to him? To save a few shillings. *I am mad, mad.* And now?

"Is it—near at hand? Near?"

"Only a step." His eyes glittering with business triumph, his hand on her cloak possessive. "My granfer's place. Clean? You should see some places! Ours yer can eat orf the floor." He was tugging her towards the yard gates.

The serving-man who had discovered that she had no luggage watched her go with scorn and indifference. No loss in such a customer. The other passengers were already crowding into the inn, their faces full of ruddy-cheeked expectation of fires and supper and mulled ale and negus. The widow with her Susan's Edward laughing for happiness.

"Jus' round the corner!" the boy said.

And in reality it was not very far or she must have made up her mind to escape from him. But the bustle in the streets—the press of people, the air of business, of buying, of lit shops, of hurrying; of drays creaking by still laden with goods, although it was so late at night; the sense of vastness of the city that must spread mile upon mile in every direction—robbed her of the power of decision. Where should she go? Which way? Which turning? How should she find lodgings by herself? Were there signs to tell which house took lodgers? And if she asked—

While she argued with herself, the boy guided, darting and tugging, his tray of cottons closed up with a cover and hung from his shoulder, banging into passers-by who cursed him for a little villain. He took no notice of them. "Only a step more."

They had turned out of the great street into another, just as crowded and as busy, but narrower, less lit, only a globe here and there on a post or a housefront with its oil light guttering dull yellow inside it. Rubbish in the roadway, mud freezing again with the darkness and the lessening traffic, so that Kate had to be careful of her steps and not let him pull her along too fast. So careful of her steps that she scarcely noticed that they had turned again, into a still narrower street—a lane—like a dark entrance rather than a lane, with blind walls on either side of it almost touching her cloak as she tried to hurry with him.

"Where are we?" Not fear, not fear of a young boy—but alarm—*I am mad to follow him so far.*

The passage opened, became the strangest of narrow streets, the sides rising like cliffs, dark and crooked above, ill-lit below by candles, oil lamps, lanterns on wooden stalls, a brazier burning red and smoky; the smell of food—meat cooking, sausages, potatoes baking, chestnuts roasting on trays of burning charcoal. The people like shadows, shadows hurrying, hanging in darker shadows, in cellar doorways, in windows, in blind entrances to still darker, even narrower lanes. No street lamps. Slush underfoot. Worse smells overcoming the wretched smells of bad food and liquor. Putrid. Decaying. Thick, rancid sweetness from an open drain, choking. As though she had come into a circle of Inferno.

"Nearly there now." Tugging her along. There were faces staring. Pale women. Children. A drunken man lurching across their way. The boy dodged round him, pulling her by her cloak. "Don't mind 'im. 'E ain't wicked."

They turned another corner, and there were children's voices shrieking something at the far end of the next lane. The boy began to run, unslinging his tray. Kate heard the sounds of blows, shrieks of pain and anger, a scattering of feet. Yells of "Jew, Jew, Jew, dirty Yid, Yah, Yaaaaah!" The boy came back to her, wiping his face with his sleeve.

"Oh *mon Dieu!* What has happened?" Should she run? Where?

"It ain't nothing. Bloody kids. I taught 'em something. My name ain't Mendoza for nothing." He had slung his tray again, and caught her once more by the cloak. " 'Ere we are."

"But I cannot—"

"Yer'll be safe as 'ouses 'ere. That's what yer want?"

She understood only the word "safe." Hesitated. It was enough. He began drawing her with him again, and since he knew what he wanted and she did not, he had his way. They came to where the shrieks and fighting had just taken place. To steps, leading down into a cellar, into near blackness. No more than a hint that somewhere below a candle might be burning.

"Gran'pa? It's me, Izzy! I got a lodger! A goy!" He added something in another language that sounded to her like Spanish. "Come on!" he said to her, now not only possession but pride in his face and accents. " 'Ere we are!"

He went down first, holding up his hand to assist her after him like a small swarthy courtier from old Versailles. The hint of candlelight became stronger. They were in a doorway. Inside there was a smell of mustiness, damp, old clothes, that same rancid sweet-

[32]

ness of drains. How could she escape from here, tell him that she had no need of—did not want—?

An old man was shuffling towards her, carrying a candlestick and lighted candle. The light fell on piles and racks of clothes, like corpses, men and women hanging. The old Jew himself seemed to be hanging in the dark, only his face, his grey-white beard turned yellow by the candlelight; the shape of his skull cap, his black kaftan melting and fading among the old clothes he brushed against. He lifted his candle higher and peered at her.

"A young lady?" His accent was heavier than hers.

The boy spoke rapidly in Spanish. She caught the words "French" and "passport" and "afraid" and watched the old man's eyes. Again, like the boy's, there was nothing there of wickedness. Rather of concern. And with no better reason than her judgement of faces and eyes she thought, *perhaps—perhaps I might truly be safe here? For this night.* And she was aware in that moment of being so tired that to attempt to find some other lodging, more respectable, in less frightening surroundings, was next to unthinkable. And God knew she and her mother had lodged in places almost as strange as this. Under hedges, more than once. She leaned against the jamb of the doorway. In the lane above her head feet pattered, a child's voice shrieked, "Go to Chelsea! Go to Chelsea!" Followed by a scream of triumphant laughter and feet running away. The boy made to run up the steps but his grandfather prevented him.

"I'll kill 'em!" the boy said, his fists doubled.

"We have a guest!" the old man said. "Welcome to our house, lady. You need have no fears of us." He spoke to her in a slow, rusty French, more provençal than French.

"Three bob, my grandpa says. Three bob a week. You understand? For the room?"

"I said two shillings, Isaac. We do not make profits out of fear."

"A week?" She was suddenly so tired that she could fall. "I shall not wish to stay—so long." She would fall.

"I meant two," Isaac was saying. "That's what I said, two bob a week. Yer won't get cheaper—nor cleaner."

"The lady is not well," the old man said. "Support her, Isaac." The boy gave her his shoulder. The old man came close and looked into her face, slowly, carefully, as though he were a doctor. "You must sleep," he said. "Without sleep one dies. Come. I will show you the room."

[33]

He led the way, and she followed, leaning on the boy. He was much stronger than he looked and was proud of being leaned on.

At the back of the shop there was a kind of yard, more like the bottom of a deep well than a courtyard, and wooden stairs leading upwards. They creaked dangerously as the three of them climbed, the railing loose, the treads slippery with damp turning to ice, the brickwork against which the stairs were fastened black with soot as the candlelight fell on it. The bricks themselves seemed loose, as though the whole house might be taken to pieces, brick by brick. Three, four, five flights of the sagging, frightening staircase. Although she was too tired to be frightened of it, or anything else. All she wanted at that moment was to lie down. Let it be a straw mattress on a wooden floor and it would be enough. They had passed doors, windows, heard voices, sounds, someone—of all things— playing a flute. Thin music, sweet and birdlike.

"'E plays in a orchestra!" the boy said. "A real one! Only the theatre 'e plays in is shut tonight. 'E's a Jew, too."

The flute stopped and there was the sound of coughing.

One more flight. They seemed to be at the level of the rooftops. The air smelled cleaner. Of soot rather than of drains. Chimney pots leaning black and squat against sharp starlight, the glisten of frost on slates. Echoes from the streets.

The old man unlocked a door, thrust it open with a gesture that combined hospitality and encouragement and humility. The boy had no such complex reservations and, snatching the candlestick from his grandfather so that the flame guttered and almost vanished, he dived through the doorway and said, "Come in afore yer gets frozen. Look, there's a carpet!"

There was. Worn thin, ragged at the edges, but still with faded colours in it that glowed in the candlelight, and, in the way that unimportant details may, gave her an immediate sense that here was security, as much home as she could have hoped to find. As though an old man with such a carpet on his attic floor would be sure not to cut her throat or steal her gold. She smiled at the old man, to show him how pleased she was.

Even more important than the carpet there was a bed. She saw the shape of it. Would have given her two shillings rent simply to lie down on it in that same instant, and fall asleep. But she must be shown the chair, and the basin, and the blue and white delft ewer in which the boy promised to fetch hot water from down the street.

"There's a bake'ouse round the corner. They'll give me some if I buys a loaf. D'yer want supper?"

She did not know whether she did or not. But it was easiest to give him a sixpenny piece out of her store. And she must eat sometime. Tomorrow. If she could just lie down—

The old man set the candlestick on a shelf and drew out a table from a wall. That too was much better than she could have expected, if she had expected anything. Mahogany, with drop leaves. And a drawer. He took a cloth out of the drawer, and a knife and fork and spoon. The boy took down a plate from the shelf where the candle stood burning.

"I'll fetch yer a pie, an' a loaf. An' some ale." He dived away. She heard the stairs shake under his hasty feet.

"Have no fear," the old man said, standing by the doorway. "We ourselves know what fear is. We understand. If you are cold, Isaac will bring you another rug. And he will light the stove."

He closed the door, to make his way down slowly by no more than the starlight. She sat on the bed. There were cotton sheets, and thick blankets, and a bolster, and a feather pillow. And the bed was iron, so that there should be no bugs. She could not have hoped for better in an inn.

I will lie down until he comes back with the food, she thought. And was asleep.

Chapter 3

There was daylight. No more than a greyness through the thin curtains, the attic window—but daylight. And she had slept. She lay very still, so thankful for the light that she did not want to move, did not want to do anything, not even remember. Only lie and look. Grey ceiling, grey walls, grey window. The shape of the stove, the table. There was a large water jug on the table, and small, strange shapes beside it. What could they be? As though she had been very ill and was now mending.

I have been ill, she thought. What were the shapes? A mug? Her supper that the boy— She was still dressed as she had been—had laid down—slept. There was a cover over her. He must have— She had been so ill, so tired that the tears came without her knowing that they were come. To find kindness. And to have slept. In spite of the cover she was very cold and began to shiver. And still did not want to move, holding the last tepidness of warmth around her.

"I am in London. I have shelter. Even some money." The tears came faster. All the ghosts vanished away. As though with the daylight all the ghosts were destroyed, had never existed except in her imagination. It was true. Where else had they been? The nightmares, the shadows? Only in her mind. She could think even of her mother without that fearful tightening round her heart. Only with sadness, not with terror. Could weep for her, say prayers for her; like another wound already—not healing—not that—it would never heal; no more than the other, older wound would heal. But not that terror as though the grave itself was there behind her eyelids if she closed them for an instant. And the others? God, have mercy on them all. Even—even on— She let herself remember that dark shape stretched out on the rocks, head down, arm touching the sea, lifted by the lifting waves as if it were still alive. Perhaps—perhaps he had been. And there was no terror. Only the cold that made her shiver as she remembered, looked.

They understand, she thought. *For a time they did not understand— they thought—* "Oh most merciful Saviour—" Ghosts crying in the dark, "Why were we drowned? Why, why?"

"Forgive me," she whispered. "Please forgive me. All my life I will remember you, I will light candles for you, and surely already you are in Paradise. You cannot want to torture me. Only let me be in peace. Let me be quiet." How good she would be. Always. "I will try always to be—to make up—make up for—for everything." For what had happened. For being still alive. "I will try so hard." Try to—try to make others happy? Yes! Yes! Or was that being proud? "I do not mean it proudly, I promise, I promise. Only that I know that I must make amends." Why had God permitted such things? And chosen her to live? Why? If one could know. If one could only know the why of things, what one should do. If only one could be truly good.

"But I can try! I can try!" She would find a church, a priest—as soon as she had money she would have masses said for all of them. And the tears ran down her face in happiness that she could promise them a gift, that now, now they understood. *My mother will have told them,* she thought. For surely, surely she was with them? Must be with them. All that past forgiven.

She said her prayers, glad to be cold as she said them, and for the last Hail Marys she made herself get up and kneel on the floor. The carpet somehow friendly under her feet, her knees. When she was done, she touched it with her fingertips, stroked its dusty, threadbare surface. *Maman was right,* she thought. *They are kinder here than they are in France. I am so fortunate to have come home.*

On the table the hot water of last night, grown icy. The mug of ale. The pie. Bread. She ate and drank, and washed in the cold water. For the first time since—since—almost afraid to think, "I am happy. I am almost happy." She could not, must not think yet of such a word. But quiet? "For the first time I am quiet. I can think of—what I must do." Be good. Find work. A theatre. There must be many theatres—one of them—she thought of her accent that must be so obvious. But she would learn very quickly. She knew the words themselves. It could not take very long.

She went down the outside stairs into the well of the small courtyard. There was a trace of sunlight that tried to follow her, abandoning her halfway down. She needed to hold on to the half-rotted rail in order not to slip on the ice of the wooden treads.

In the cellar the old Jew greeted her. She had slept? Had breakfast? Had been comfortable? If there was anything more she desired—?

She had not meant to stay more than that night, but he looked, sounded so kind. And the thought of finding another room was frightening. She took out her money-kerchief and a half-guinea. "I did not pay you my rent last night. If—if I can give you this in advance? While I still have it to give," she said smiling.

And he smiled and took the coin in old, soft fingers, like a matter of courtesy, a gift, rather than a matter of business.

He made a gesture towards the racks of clothes. "If you have need of any clothes, my dear—" As though he were making her a gift of treasure in return, into which no base question of payment would enter.

She looked round, shaking her head in polite refusal. Women's bonnets, men's hats, pelisses, coats, jackets of thick grey fustian, boots, slippers, gowns, old blankets, chairs, tables covered with piles of coats and cloaks, breeches and petticoats and shifts, old leather stays, corsets, more boots, a pyramid of iron cooking pots, some copper jugs.

"The best are in another room," he said, lifting his hand towards a half-hidden door.

"I must not spend more money," she said, "until I have found work. Is there—do you know of a theatre near to here where I might look for work as an actress? Your grandson said—that one of your tenants—"

"There is the Parnassus Theatre—where Mr. Solomons plays. You might apply there perhaps."

But he did not know precisely where it was. He spread his hands in apology for himself, his situation, the nature of things. "I do not go about the streets very often," he said, his hands including his gaberdine, his beard, his skull cap, all his history. And in her new— not happiness—but quietness of mind Kate would have liked to say something, to tell him that she was sorry that the world was as it was.

"I think that you must first turn to the right, and then—then you may ask someone. I do not think it is very far. I wish you good fortune."

The gold coin was still in the palm of his right hand and he touched it with the fingers of his left hand like a talisman for her, and bowed.

In the street there was also sunlight. No children screaming insults. No one at all. She turned to her right, away from the direction they had come from the night before. To have slept! She felt already as though she were well again. It would not matter how small the parts they might offer her; she would take anything. And then they would see! She would learn so quickly! She could almost imagine her mother was there beside her, giving her strength. The thought was like a pain that almost made her stop as she walked and hold her hand against her side, against her heart. And yet a kind of sad lovingness, of dearness in the pain, as though her mother were truly beside her, only hidden from her eyes. But made new, and wonderful, and— *"Maman? Maman?"*

There had been a song her mother had always hummed and sung and laughed about when things were worst for them: *Mahlbrouk s'en va t'en guerre. Mironton. Mironton. Mirontaine.*

And at that Kate had to stop, had to clasp her hands together under her cloak, close her eyes against the blank brick walls that pressed on either side of her in the alleyway. *I shall die,* she thought. *I shall die without her.* All the roads. All the days of the walking, riding on the carts. Coming to the crest of a hill and seeing the valley below. And the plans, and the dreams, and creeping into cold beds and warming one another and thinking of tomorrow. Oh, my dear. My dearest. All the theatres. All the plays. "You must be brave, my darling." Not when the house was full and shouting and contemptuous, but when it was almost empty. A barn with a few peasants in it; dulled, wondering faces, and none of the gentry come. "Now is when we must be brave, my love. Now we must conquer them. Give them a remembrance they will talk about all winter."

What had the young men mattered against that?
Mironton. Mirontaine.
Be brave.

The brick walls almost closing above her head, the hint of sunlight high up, and down here shadows. Ice under foot. Black mud.

[39]

Someone had just passed without her noticing. She came to a wider space, with doorways, windows. A line of rags hung up to dry, or to get filthy again before they dried, in the soot. Half-naked children, a few women. An old woman smoking a clay pipe on cellar steps, her hair like grey twists of yarn, her face seamed with black.

"If you could tell me"—the woman looking at her with uncomprehending eyes—"the way to the—"

A child crawled towards her, small, wizened, like a monkey with naked buttocks, but the head too large, grey and lolling, the mouth open, making mewing sounds.

"—the Parnassus Theatre?" Kate whispered. She could not help herself backing away from that crawling, monstrous approach.

The women spoke together, said something to her. She did not know what they said, or whether they understood. The child reached her cloak, clawed slowly at it. If it raised its head—looked at her— She was taken with a sudden panic—said, "Thank you, thank you!" And turned and ran, did not stop until she was between blank walls again. A maze of alleyways, closes, courtyards. The blank, deathly faces seeming to become greyer, the rags more terrible. As though step by step she was descending into poverty's last circle. She asked again, and again could not understand.

A man eyed her cloak that in this misery was like magnificence, seemed to be thinking of following her. A woman came staggering out of a doorway, whimpering. The sounds of shouting from a window high up, the sounds of blows.

She wanted to run, and no direction was better than another. The man was following her, like a shadow against the wall behind her. She began to run, turned a corner, slipped on the icy mud that filled the kennel in the centre of the lane, almost fell and grasped at something, someone. A child in a doorway. Sheltering. A thin, ragged boy.

"Bring me out of here," Kate whispered. "Please—please—" She heard the man's footsteps, and shrank into the doorway beside the child. The man went by. Perhaps he did not see her. Perhaps he had no ill design in following her. She leaned in the doorway where she stood, shut her eyes, breathed very deep. The child stayed where he was. He did not say anything, or seem surprised. When Kate looked at him again, he looked at her as if he were waiting for her to explain why she was sharing his doorway. Although as Kate looked, she was less certain that it was a boy. A boy's rags, but the thin, dirty face had something of the girl.

"I am sorry," Kate said. "I slipped."

The eyes considered her. Huge grey eyes in the grey, thin face. Very slowly a thin filthy hand came out from inside the rags of the shirt, cupped its palm.

"Gimme a penny," a voice whispered. Like a scarecrow's whisper in a field. But with no conviction in it, no real hope of a penny. The eyes huge with the knowledge of hunger.

"You are a girl?" Kate said, her own fears momentarily lost in horror of those eyes, of their knowledge. She felt for her purse, would in that instant have liked to empty it into the child's hand. "A girl? Not a boy?" She touched the shirt, held the torn cloth with her gloved fingers to illustrate what she meant.

The child nodded, her neck like a stalk of grass. As she bent her head, Kate saw blood on the scalp, dried reddish black, like a wound that had just finished oozing, the hair matted with blood. It was not possible to tell the colour of the hair, it was so filthy, so bloodied. There were other marks visible through the tears in the shirt, the breeches. More dried blood.

"Oh, *mon Dieu!* What has been— Show me the way please, out of here!"

She found a shilling, pressed it into the child's hand, and was ashamed; found another and gave that too. The child stared at her, stared down at the two coins. Her mouth began to tremble. She looked at Kate again, seemed unable to believe what her eyes saw.

"What has been done to you?" Kate whispered. She pointed to the marks, to the child's hair.

"She give me a 'iding." The whisper very soft, frightened.

The sense of it was obvious enough. A she? A woman had done this to a child? "Your—your mother?"

The child shook her head. She had a strange look of patience. Such violence must have happened to her many times before she could acquire so much patience.

"Show me the way out of here," Kate whispered. Her mouth was dry. "To—to where there are—"

The child closed her fingers on the shillings and nodded slowly in understanding. They went down the lane, the child's feet naked on the ice. They were blue-grey with cold. A tall, thin child, almost

[41]

as tall as Kate. She had crossed her arms over her torn shirt as though she were protecting herself from the cold, but she showed no other sign of it, did not pick her way round the patches of ice between the stones, the frozen runnels of mud. Another corner and there was the sound of traffic. Coaches, people, shops. The child pointed, as if they had reached a frontier. She did not look at Kate, but down at her shillings.

"You are hungry?" Kate said. "If—do you know a place, a theatre—the Parnassus Theatre? Parnassus?" She repeated the name in different pronunciations, until the child understood her and nodded again. "If you will bring me there I will give you—"

The grey eyes were so filled with patience that Kate thought she would die of shame, of wretchedness at the sight of them. How many days had she let herself be in misery: warmly dressed, lying in a bed, travelling in a coach, pushing away good food from in front of her, dwelling on things she could not alter, bathing in grief? While this child—

"Why does she beat you?"

"I don't get 'er enough." She saw that Kate did not understand and opened her hand, to show the money.

"You—have to beg? For this woman?"

"Yus." Again the whisper so quiet that it was difficult to hear her.

"You must have food," Kate said. She took the child by the arm. Like a stick. Ivory. There was a look of alarm, terror. The hand opened, offered Kate the shillings.

"No no no!" Kate cried. "I will buy you food. You must eat something. There—there is a pastry shop. A cake? A pie? Would you not like a pie?"

She did not know whether the girl understood or not, but the alarm faded, became only bewilderment. Kate drew her across the street. People stared momentarily, at the beggar boy and the young woman seeming to have captured him, to be taking him to justice.

They came to the door of the shop and Kate tried to make the child come in with her, but she hung back, alarmed again. Kate went in and bought pies and cakes, more than any child could eat, however starving—as if she were buying peace of mind—and came out with her parcel. All the time in the shop she had watched the girl from the corner of her eye in case she vanished. Outside in the street she opened the parcel and gave the first of the pies to her. "Eat."

The girl took it uncertainly, looked at her, seemed about to put a corner of the pie to her mouth and then did not, but put it inside her shirt.

"It is for you!"

The child nodded and smiled and, as she smiled, looked for a moment almost as she ought to have looked, almost like a child, almost beautiful.

"I'll bring yer to the 'nassus," she whispered. She held the pie against her ribs as if she were drawing the warmth of it into her before she ate its substance.

Perhaps, Kate thought, *she is ashamed to eat here in this street with people watching her. If I could give her my cloak,* she thought, and was filled with humility and a strange new happiness, as if God had sent the child in her way as—as—an answer! An answer to her prayer to be good—to make—to be allowed to make others happy! How much money did she still have? *I will give her half of it. Was it not given to me? As soon as I know that I have work I will give her all of it. Only keep enough for my food.* She wanted to touch the child's arm, to tell her "I will give to you—give to you."

If they are watching me, she thought, *they will know. I could not help them, but I can help this child. God has sent her to me.*

She put her arm round the girl's shoulders as they walked, and without allowing it to seem deliberate let the edge of her cloak fall round her, held her closer. After a few steps she thought that the child was crying, and did not look down for fear of embarrassing her.

"It's 'ere," the girl whispered. "Down 'ere." She shivered under Kate's cloak as though to be made part warm was worse than nakedness.

They went down a brief turning, and there was a theatre, familiar as a friend's face; the portico, the columns, the steps, the air of ambitious poverty; ambition in the façade and poverty in all else. Playbills fastened to the columns, beside the doors. There was a lane beside the theatre and Kate turned into it, the child hesitating.

"It is the stage door I must find," Kate said. "Do not be afraid of me. We shall find somewhere for you to shelter while I am inside. And then you shall guide me—" She had been going to say "Home." Home? That room? The old Jew? The boy?

"In here." The stage door. Another playbill. Kate's eye took in a detail of it here and there, from instinct. "Mr. Thos. Benedict, as

Jack, in THE FARCICAL ADVENTURES OF JACK AND THE BEANSTALK."
And farther down "MAJOR; THE WORLD-RENOWNED MINIATURE
HORSE, WHO DISCOVERS LOST OBJECTS HID ABOUT THE STAGE—"

That kind of theatre? She felt a momentary sinking of spirit. But
if they had nothing here—what was JACK AND THE BEANSTALK? She
took off her cloak and put it entirely round the child to hide her
rags, and the worst of her dirt and the marks of where she had
been beaten. The eyes widened. There were tear traces in the dirt.

"They will let you wait inside for me, I am sure. And you may eat
your food in shelter." She pushed open the stage door and brought
her in. There was a passage, and a cubbyhole of a doorkeeper's
room, with an old man sitting on a chair and reading a newspaper,
as though he and chair and newspaper had been there forever. A
smell of dust. Echoes.

"I am looking for the manager."

The old man tilted his head so that he might see her above his
wire-framed spectacles. Like an old, grey, dusty crow, in black
breeches and black coat, and heavy steel-buckled shoes; dusty wig.
A refugee from a play of thirty years ago, and forgotten there on
his chair, with his newspaper.

"Misser Gosport?" he croaked.

She nodded, swallowing, thought, *How many times did my mother
do this?* But her mother would have swept in like a queen returning
out of exile. "And if—if this child with me—may wait here?"

The old man nodded, returned to his paper, holding it up to the
grey dust of light from a window.

"Wait here for me. Eat." Kate touched the girl's face with the
palm of her hand, brushing at the cold tears. Put the parcel of food
into her arms. *When I come out again*—she thought, *I shall have work,
I shall have work, I am quite sure of it. God has sent you to me for a sign of
love. Of good fortune.* But she said aloud only, "—you shall show me
the way back."

Familiar kind of corridor. The smell of tallow candles and oil
lamps and scene-painter's paints; of raw wood, and new canvas,
and old brick. The sounds of theatre: violins, voices echoing, echoes lost in the flies, someone shouting, someone hammering. First
green room. Second. Dressing rooms. A woman singing a high
note at half-voice: "Aaaah aaaah aieeee, aaaah aaaah aieeee." A
man leading a tiny horse towards her. Major. Red velvet bridle, a

[44]

tossing, impatient head and mane, as if eager to be finding more lost objects, here or anywhere. "Aaaaaah aaaah—"

"I am looking for Mister Gosport, the manager."

The man jerked his thumb, incurious at foreign accents in that home of them. Two girls tripping by, dressed as nymphs in muslin draperies and ballet slippers.

"Mr. Gosport?"

She found him on the stage, supervising the Beanstalk, a great, gimcrack, twisted ladder of greenery, with gigantic red beans on it like nothing that ever grew. A small, fat, harassed man with his hair on end and his cravat untied, small hands half hidden by lace ruffles. Another man—Mister Benedict?—beside him, dressed as a boy-hero in tight white cambric shirt, not overclean, and sky-blue breeches, the beginnings of an unheroic paunch held in by a red cummerbund, surveying the beanstalk with a doubting eye.

"Mr. Gosport?"

The little, harassed man turned to her, his face seeming to have written on it, instantaneously like a book opening, almost before he had time to look at her: *Actress. Out of work. Wants something. Nothing for you. Go away.*

"Yes?" he said, with a maximum of unencouragement. She began to explain. English. Trifle of accent—soon learn—Racine—Corneille—Molière—Scarron—but mostly tragedy—her mother—Shakespeare—her catalogue of qualifications fading into nonsense in front of that beanstalk, the remembrance of the little horse.

Mr. Gosport's eyes had grown veiled with lack of interest. Like glass. Mr. Benedict began attempting the beanstalk as though already resigned to breaking both his legs.

"Can you dance?"

She shook her head. "Only—just a little—"

"Sing?"

She shook her head again. A large, red-haired woman coming onto the stage, dressed too young in a white muslin gown, her hair too red, her bosom too bursting out above the pink ribbon of the gown's high waist, her hands gesturing. "Gosport! That 'orse! That 'orse—outside my dressing room! *Il est intolérable!*" She saw Kate, stared, threw out both hands. "Margot? Marguerite? *Mais c'est impossible!*" She came close, stared into Kate's face. "Pardon! I thought—I thought for a moment you—"

[45]

And recognition came to Kate. "Madame Pariglia!" Lyons. Five years ago. A singer who was ill, in the hospital, and Kate's mother had befriended her. They had travelled together for a fortnight afterwards. To Bordeaux.

"You are Margot's daughter! The little Caterina!" Cries of delight in Italianate French; of recognition, explanations—

"Go away!" Mr. Gosport cried furiously. "I'm trying to——"

"It ain't safe," Mr. Benedict said, two steps up the beanstalk. "I can feel it giving."

Madame Pariglia took Kate away, still in a cataract of talk, into a small dressing room that smelled like a box of scented powder spilled in a stuffy wardrobe. Clothes on the floor, on the two gilt chairs, on the dressing table. Powder and clothes and boxes of pomade; candles burning; a dresser crouched almost hidden on a stool, sewing beads onto a hooped skirt. A vast pompadour wig on a stand, decorated with a galleon made of silver filigree. The dresser looked up, bit off a thread, attacked the skirt again. "I'll never get this finished. What did he say?"

"About what?"

"The horse! The horse! The smell of it!"

"Oh, the 'orse! I forgot—I have found a friend. Chérie, my love—darling Bunny—go out and fetch us a jug of 'ot punch, eh? And two glasses? Caterina—this is Mrs. Bunn, my dresser. My dear, dear Bunny. And this is an old friend from France, Bunny—Caterina 'A—'Arri—'Arriott—" The Triumphant. "Such a name! I could never pronounce it. The daughter of my saviour. And she is dead? Oh, I cannot believe it! Margot dead! Oh my dear, my poor child! She was so beautiful—your *maman!* A jug of punch, Bunny? *Three* glasses."

"Give me the shilling then. That skirt'll never be finished. I'm half blinded as it is."

"Let me—please," Kate said, offering a shilling of her own.

Mrs. Bunn took it with an ill grace. Thin and bent and fierce, with a pointed nose and chisel teeth that seemed created for biting off threads, and fierce little gimlet eyes for threading needles.

"I am so afraid of her," Madame Pariglia whispered, falling into her hissing, Venetian French again when Mrs. Bunn was safely gone. She leaned forward, her arms fat and round and milky white, her bosom filled with promises, her red hair toned down to splendour by the candlelight. So overwhelmingly a woman that Kate felt a sudden consciousness of how little of a woman she herself must look, how thin and wretched and ill-dressed in the kind Cornishwoman's sensible strong gown and too large petticoats and much too large black boots. Five years ago Madame Pariglia had looked the ghost and Kate herself at twelve years old had been ashamed of growing fat. She smiled at the memory and Madame Pariglia held her hands and said, "How like your mother you have grown! But so thin! So ill! What must they have done to you! And what are you doing here? You are looking for work?" She was shaking her head as she asked the question. "My dear, my dear! Did you see that 'orse? That is what they want! And acrobats!"

"But is there no—there must be a proper theatre—real ones—"

"Two! In the whole of London! Two! And to get a place in one of those! Santa Madonna! And with a French accent!"

"Is my accent so bad? I thought—I was so sure my English would be perfect." She smiled again, sadly. Tried to make the smile gay. "But I must find work. I must! It is—" She stopped, helplessly. Not to find work? It came to her like a shiver that she might not—that there might truly be no work for her. Nothing at all. She stared at Madame Pariglia. "And in the countryside—the small cities?"

"My dear! Perhaps—after two, three months of trying. Perhaps."

Kate sat looking down at her hands. How thin they had grown!

"Until your English is better you should get something else to do. There are so many French here now—and some are still rich. Your English is good enough to teach their children English—"

"No! I shall not go near any French! I—I cannot—"

"Or an English family to teach their children French. But"— Madame shrugged her beautiful white shoulders, made her mouth sad in sympathy—"there are so many poor young French women— and with such names! Madame La Marquise teaching the butcher's daughters."

"But I must find—"

"If you need money—"

"No! I—thank you a thousand times but—"

"There is one other possibility," Madame Pariglia said, not looking at her guest, but searching on her crammed dressing table for a jar of rouge. "Let me touch up your cheeks a little, my dear—you are so pale!"

"No—no, please. What other possibility?"

"You could find—I could find you—a friend."

Kate did not understand at first. And then had no need of rouge.

"Madame!"

Mrs. Bunn came back before either of them could say more. The dressing room was filled with the smell of punch. Madame Pariglia took the quart jug, held it to her nose with a great show of connoisseurship to hide her embarrassment. Mrs. Bunn set down the three glasses with sharp sounds, sweeping away powders and pomades as though she hated them.

"O Bunny, Bunny, I 'ave shocked my young friend," Madame Pariglia cried with affected laughter. "I said that, if she cannot find work, she can always find a gentleman friend."

"And she's honest, is she?" Mrs. Bunn said angrily, banging herself down on her stool again, snatching up her needle and bowl of beads, attacking the skirt as though she hated that too. "La-la. Well? No harm if there was more of that about." She bit her thread, her teeth clicking like scissors, knotted the ends together, stabbed the skirt with the needle. "Why can't she find work? There's work to be done. Give me back my candlestick. You don't need it to drink punch."

"But what work, Bunny, my darling? 'Er accent——"

"You don't need an accent to scrub floors."·

"That is very true, Bunny. But she is not so strong, you see—and she is an actress——"

"Actress! Actress! Every girl with a powder box and a pot of rouge thinks she's an actress. She could sell oranges, couldn't she? Ma Casey's gone. Thrown out yesterday. Drunk. On too much punch probably. Insulted Mr. Gosport once too often. Why can't your friend sell oranges?"

"Because, Bunny chérie—" She looked at Kate. "At least it is in the theatre—"

"Sell oranges?" Kate said.

"Buy them for tuppence," Mrs. Bunn snapped. "Sell them for threepence. Pay Mr. Gosport a guinea a week. You'd make a living. An honest living. If you didn't drink too much punch."

"I have not had a drink all day, Bunny!" Madame Pariglia cried.

"All day? All day? What time do you think it is? Midnight? Of course, Mr. G. may have someone in mind for the job. *I* don't know." Snapping another thread. Rattling her beads. Stabbing. "Since I fetched it, you might as well give me some. There's no fear of *me* drinking too much. All day! And still morning!"

"Here you are, Bunny; here you are, my love. Don't be cross." Madame filled a glass to the brim, and over, and gave it to the small, crouched woman, who took it in both hands like a squirrel taking a nut, sniffing, sipping, almost dipping her sharp thin nose into the steaming surface. Kate drank hers, glad of the warmth of it, the strength of the brandy. Grains of nutmeg floating like black dust on top of it, catching at her throat. Madame Pariglia drank as though she had truly waited all day for this moment, sighed, her eyes shut. Drank again, almost emptying her tumbler. Emptied it. Refilled it with an air of absent-mindedness, her thoughts busy about Kate.

"Of course you would not dream of it—the oranges—"

"Oh no, oh no," Mrs. Bunn said. "Better have a gentleman friend. Two gentlemen friends. Much much better than selling oranges. Three gentlemen friends, why not?"

"Bunny! Bunny!"

"I'm not saying anything, I'm not casting aspersions. Of course, if the cap fits anyone within hearing, they're free to wear it. But I'm not saying a word. If there's another drain in that jug I'll have it, since it was me that fetched it."

"But I do not know how to sell oranges."

"La-la, it must be very difficult, oh lud, yes. You'd need to be put apprentice to it, I shouldn't wonder. Seven years at least. *I* don't mind what anyone does. The Haymarket's only half a mile away, and no one needs apprenticeship for that—or so they tell me."

"BUNNY!"

"Give me patience!" Mrs. Bunn said, savaging a blue glass bead with her needle point. "I just mentioned a possibility, that's all. What's it to me what anyone does to earn their bread and butter? Or their punch? I'm only a dresser. The dirt on the floor. That's all *I* am. *I* don't have gentlemen friends at beck and call."

Within a quarter of an hour, without quite knowing why, or what she had committed herself to, Kate possessed the right to be sole orange-seller within the Parnassus Theatre, and had pledged herself to pay Mr. Gosport one guinea the next Saturday mid-day, and a guinea each Saturday thereafter; to be of good behaviour and sober habits; not to make assignations with young gentlemen in the audience—or old gentlemen for that matter—to sell no rotten or unripe fruit, to give the proper change even to drunken customers in the audience, and to be on duty from half-past seven in the evening until the performance ended, whether at eleven, or later. She might, she was told, hope to sell between fifty and a hundred oranges a night.

"But that means—" she began, trying to calculate how much the profit on fifty oranges a night might be, at a penny an orange, with a guinea to be paid at the end of every week. "It will only leave four shillings a week! How can I——?"

"Oh, but you will sell thousands, my dear! Thousands!" Madame Pariglia cried. "So pretty as you are! Ma Casey! You should have seen her! A monster! A fright! Oh, my dear, you will do wonderfully well. I know it. I know it in my bones."

"Some are grateful," Mrs. Bunn said. "And some are not. I'm sure I don't expect gratitude. Who am I to expect it? No one."

"Oh, but I am grateful." Kate even tried to believe that she was. And walked back past the Green Rooms and the other dressing rooms, and down the stone corridor to the stage door still trying to feel it, to feel pleased that at least she had something, something. And thinking, *If I had said 'No,' and in the next theatre and the next had still found nothing?* Tried to imagine what else she might have found. To sell oranges? Was it so much worse than standing at the door, for example, to take the entrance money? And she had done that often.

The old doorkeeper seemed not to have moved, unless to turn the pages of his newspaper. His head still tilted in its dusty grey wig, his spectacles dustily glinting in the flakes of daylight. A shadow stood up, white-faced in the dark cloak that Kate had put round her. The child. She had almost—had forgotten her. The girl began to take off the cloak, hurriedly. Held out the parcel to her, the parcel of cakes and pies.

"But that was for you! For you to eat!"

The doorkeeper did not condescend to look at them. Kate brought the child outside. "We will share the cloak," she said. "I have—I have found work!" As though to tell it to someone made it better news. "I am to sell oranges here."

She held the girl against her. The way home. To the old Jew's cellar. And when they reached there? Her step hesitated. *I will give her the cloak*, she thought. She could not give her much money, she would need it for oranges. For her own food.

"This woman that you live with. She is not your mother? An aunt? Some kindred to you?"

The girl shook her head. "She bought me fer a quid," she whispered. "Off of another woman."

"She—but that cannot be! Bought you?"

"Yus." The low, throaty whisper, no protest in it, no indignation. Kate stopped, turned towards her so that the cloak fell away from the child, left her as she had been, torn shirt, thin rags of breeches, scars. Dirt. Was she lying, lying for sympathy? But the scars could not be lying, the dried blood. And in the eyes that patience, that knowledge of suffering. Kate felt her face flaming at the ugliness of her suspicion.

"What will she do when you go back? If you bring money, she is pleased?"

The head nodding. And something strange about the child, something untouched by the hunger, by the rags, the cruelty. Something—a kind of withdrawnness. Almost hauteur. As though her patience were saying, "This at least is mine." In her eyes. In the way she bent her head. A thing that some animals have, however terribly they are ill-used.

"You shall have this cloak for your own," Kate said, taking it off, wrapping it round the thin, high shoulders. "I do not need it—I have another—much better, much much better. Quick, let us go to my home, and you shall see how warm the cloak is." She herself welcoming the cold, the wind.

She still held the parcel the child had given back to her, and they walked quickly, the child nervous in the cloak, looking at Kate sideways, fingering the ties that Kate had fastened for her, looking down at the dark blue wool that hid her feet. That threatened to trip her up. It was too long for her. But within a few moments, with an odd gracefulness, she had learned to hold up the hem.

They came to the market laneway, turned to the corner, were at the cellar steps. The boy Isaac was there, belligerently holding a cudgel as well as his tray. He saluted Kate, stared at the girl, seeming to be judging whether she threatened insults or not. Kate gave her the parcel for a final time, found another shilling. The girl began to take off the cloak.

[51]

"No, no, you must keep it, it is for you! It will keep you warm—"

Isaac looked shrewdly at the child, the cloak, Kate. "It won't keep 'er warm long," he said. "Yer chucking it away fer nothing." He fingered the cloth. "Worth a quid that is, anywheres. . . . 'Oo runs yer?" he said to the girl.

"Missis Sullivan," the girl whispered.

"She'll 'ave that orff of yer in two minutes, won't she?"

The girl nodded.

"See? Yer chucking it away. An' 'er missis 'll get so drunk on the blunt she'll knock 'er senseless jus' for the fun of it."

The child finished taking off the woollen cloak and held it out, beginning to smile. It would not have surprised Kate if she had curtseyed, the smile was so sadly beautiful, so unlike the rags. Kate took the heavy cloth in her hands, held it unthinkingly. The child turned away, holding the parcel against her chest, her head slightly bent. When she was half a dozen paces off she turned and smiled again, but not looking at Kate, looking at the ground between them.

"What's she still got there?" Isaac said with suspicion.

"Food. Pies."

"You won't keep yer blunt long. I 'ope you 'as lots of it." He settled the leather strap of his tray on his shoulder, took a better grasp of his cudgel. "I'll be orff," he said. "Unless yer wants me to fetch yer some dinner?"

"She said that the woman—Mrs.——"

"Missis Sullivan?"

"—that she bought her for money—for—a quid. How much is that?"

"A guinea. Yus, that'd be it, for one like 'er."

"What do you mean? One like her?"

"One like 'er what's only good for begging. Too thin for anythink else, for men. She'd be worth five if she was fatter."

"You do not know what you are saying!"

The boy's eyes looked at her, dark with knowledge—more than knowledge, a terrible contempt for ignorance, for all that was implied in what they had both been saying. "What do you think," his eyes said. "What do you think a Christian child is worth to Christians? . . . D'yer want any dinner?"

"No," Kate whispered. She began to run after the child, who had disappeared round the corner of the lane. *If she is gone!* she thought. *If I cannot find her again!* And saw her in the distance. Thin, a shadow. Turning at the sound of Kate's running steps, seeming to poise herself to run, to run away from anything that followed.

"Wait, oh wait," Kate cried out. "Please wait." Brought her back as though something more precious that anything she knew had been escaping her. Would have knelt down to hold her. "I cannot let you go back to her," she whispered. "I cannot. Would you stay with me?"

The child only stared at her, with that unreachable patience, that air of something untouched, untouchable, deep within her. They went down the cellar steps.

Chapter 4

Kate knelt on the floor beside the child, slowly cleaning the open, suppurating wounds. Feeling each one as though it were in her own flesh. The fragile, naked body shivering now and then under her fingers as she gently sponged, and cleaned, smoothed on the apothecary's ointment of mercury and coal tar, wrapped and bandaged the raw welts with long strips of linen. The jugs and basins of hot water steamed, grew cool, the water turning an ugly colour. The child never cried out, did not so much as whimper. Only a catching of the breath, that shivering.

If I had let her go! Kate thought, and it was as though she had let her go, as though the child was not here, was out there in the cold, in the December twilight. Holding out her thin hand at corners: "Give me a penny. Give me something for the love of God, that I may not be beaten again."

The child did not cry, but Kate cried as she sponged and cleaned and soothed and bandaged. The wound in her head was terrible, and twice, when Kate was cleaning it, the child gripped hold of her. But still she did not move otherwise, or try to pull away, or cry out. Until that too was cleansed, and Kate could dry her in the great towel she had bought from the old Jew, and take up the cotton shift, and the petticoat, and the green kersey over-gown that she had also bought from Mr. Mendoza's cellar, and dress her. The stove burning, the curtains drawn, food on the table with its white tablecloth. She tied the black silk Barcelona kerchief round the child's neck and shoulders, loosely, stood back to admire. "Now you are beautiful!" she said. The child seeming to have grown still taller in the long gown. Her hand touching the knot of the kerchief, feeling the silk. Her eyes looking down.

She began to cry then, the tears rolling. She put up her washed hands to hide her face, knelt down on the floor beside the blue and white china ewer, bent down until her head almost touched her knees.

"It is all right," Kate whispered. "It is all right. You shall never go back to her, I promise you. Look! Here is food, our dinner! We are going to eat together, and then you shall sleep in that nice bed while I go out to buy my oranges. You shall sleep and sleep."

Like a possession. Like her own child. As though she could not have done touching, caring for her, surrounding her with tenderness. She lifted her up from the floor, held her, made her sit, made her eat and drink. Made her lie down. But when Kate went towards the door, softly, thinking her already asleep, the girl sat up with a look of such terror that she had to come back to her, hold her hands. "You must lie down and sleep," she said. "Get well."

She could not call her by her name, the name the child said was hers—Tit. What had it been to be corrupted into that? "Titine," Kate said, pronouncing it in French. "Shall I call you Titine? There is nothing to be afraid of here. You must sleep. Listen to the stove burning! It is burning so that you may be warm and safe."

But when she reached the cellar, was thanking the old Jew, old Mr. Mendoza, for giving her credit for the clothes, and for all else that he had done to help her, she felt, rather than heard, a soft, shadowy movement behind her back, looked round and saw the child there.

"Oh *mon Dieu!* Why will you not stay in bed?"

"She has probably never slept in a bed," Mr. Mendoza said. "She is afraid. And afraid to be here without you, in case that woman should come for her." He looked thoughtful himself as he said that.

"She would not dare! Even if she knew where the child is."

Mr. Mendoza shrugged. "She has paid for her," he said. "She depends on her."

"What shall I do? Is there no law——?"

Mr. Mendoza shrugged again. "For her?" He smiled. "Perhaps if she died in being beaten. Perhaps then. You could give the woman money. Buy the child from her. Then you might have no more trouble." He did not look convinced.

"I will do that," Kate cried. "If she comes here, tell her—she shall have her money." She grasped the child's hand as though in that

[55]

moment there was the threat of losing her. "We will go together to buy the oranges, that will be best." She looked down at the child's feet. "But she needs boots, stockings."

And there was such sudden pleasure, such joy in looking through the heaps of boots and slippers for a pair that would fit the girl's narrow feet that it was like a game. Long ago Kate had had a beautiful doll, with golden curls and ringlets and a painted wax face. It had had clothes and boots and shoes that could be put on and taken off and changed. She remembered it now, and the joy of that time seemed to add itself to this moment. Making Titine sit on a table's edge, trying on stockings, morocco half-boots, short laced boots, Kampschatka slippers of black Spanish leather, with turned-up toes. It was those that she had to choose for her; all the boots too large and clumsy.

And in a burst of pleasure Kate bought some for herself and gave Mr. Mendoza her own Cornish boots in exchange. They had already worn blisters on her heels and toes and she had the feeling as she put on the slippers, felt their lightness, their comfort, their clinging to her feet, that now all would be truly well; that finding Titine was truly a sign of new beginnings. *I shall no longer be alone,* she thought. She walked about the cellar between the crammed, heaped tables, the racks of clothes brushing against her shoulders and head, feeling her feet ready to dance they were so light, so comfortable.

Titine sat on the table, lifting up now one foot and now the other to look at her own slippers. She had begun to smile, bending her head to hide her face from Mr. Mendoza, from anyone who might see her smiling, as though such happiness was punishable.

"I will buy you a bonnet!" Kate cried. "And one for myself!" There seemed in that moment no end to the things that fifty oranges a night might buy. "Have you bonnets?"

Mr. Mendoza bowed and went into his inner cellar; came out carrying a great armful of hats and bonnets of every fashion of the past ten years and more. Lunardi balloon hats, Devonshires with their brims turned up and swaggering cockades, chimney-pot hats, cocked riding hats, beavers with rolled brims and feathers, and one on top of the pile so beautiful that it was the only hat that anyone could consider buying—with a tall crown and pale blue riband gathered and tied in a bow round it and a sloping brim. She looked down at her outdoor cloak, the heavy darkness of its sensible strong wool; imagined how she would look in that cloak with that hat.

"I think we must wait," she said, trying not to feel sad, "until it is spring." But she found a dark green velvet pelisse for Titine and put it round her. There was a pale green satin lining and fur edging, and a cape hood of the same materials. Next to the wonderful hat it was the most beautiful thing in the two cellars, and came also from the inner room.

"It is two guineas I am afraid," Mr. Mendoza said. "I cannot give it to you for less. But you may pay me when you wish." Kate could not tell whether he was pleased to sell so much or nervous of giving so much credit. Perhaps he was both. She was glad that Isaac was not there to look at her with his knowing eyes full of hidden scorn for every kind of weakness.

"You must make a list," she said hurriedly. "And I shall pay you so much every week." Out of four shillings? But she would not think of it. She wrapped the pelisse round Titine, adjusted the hood. "Now we will go to buy oranges," she said. "And you are not to be afraid."

They went up the steps. It was dark, the market round the corner full of business, shadows, lanterns and torches lit. But Kate knew already that she would get nothing there to her purpose. "Will you bring me to a great market?"

Titine nodded, and they began hurrying against the cold. Too cold for rain, even for snow. The air gripped at their throats. Ice underfoot. Kate half afraid at every corner, at every instant, that she would hear a woman shouting after her to give back the child. She clutched her purse against her. There were four guineas remaining in it, and seven shillings, and a sixpence. One guinea for the oranges. *She may have all the rest. All of it.* She would sell all the oranges tonight, a hundred at least. She would make them buy two and three together. If she sold a hundred oranges, it would mean—eight shillings and fourpence profit. How much did she owe Mr. Mendoza? She did not dare to think.

A street of shops and traffic. More lanes. More streets. One of them becoming a market, almost insensibly. Shops giving way to stalls, to barrows, to covered spaces echoing with voices, the grinding of wheels on the cobbles. Trestle tables, meat, chickens, eggs, piles of cheeses, oranges, apples; rabbits stretched, furry and sup-

[57]

plicating as they lay dead in piles; loaves, butter; tubs of oysters, lobsters crawling; torchlight flaring yellow, red; smoke blackening the haloes of light for a moment; men crying, "Going cheap, larst fer today—'oo'll gimme a tanner for a nice plump 'en?" And a woman shouting hoarsely, "Two bob the 'undred for lovely oysters, fresh as tomorrer, two shilling the 'undred."

A sack of oranges for eighteen shillings. "Becorse of yer pretty eyes, my dear. Twelve dozen beauts in that there sack, an' not a bad one in the 'ole lot." The man swinging the sack towards her as though it was nothing. "Ain't yer got a barrow, duck? Yer won't never carry it without." A big, red-faced man with a black shiny apron of oilskin over his corduroy trousers, his red flannel shirt and grey moleskin waistcoat. She had not thought of having to carry them, of what a hundred, a hundred and fifty oranges would be like.

"Perhaps we could carry them together?" Looking at Titine. But they could not. "Or find someone—"

"I knows summun as 'll carry them," Titine whispered. "If 'e's 'ere. I'll go an' look for 'im."

She went, almost backing away as though she did not want to lose sight of Kate until the last possible moment, even for this short space of time. And Kate also felt a tightening at her heart as the child disappeared, wanted to call her back. The fruit-seller still crying his oranges, his apples and his medlars, his grapes and pears and chestnuts and walnuts. The day's market business ending, the street barrow traders having long ago bought their loads and gone with them, and the shopkeepers, and the housewives, and the servants from rich houses. Rotten fruit underfoot, the smells of oil and roasting chestnuts, charcoal fumes from braziers, fishwives loading empty baskets onto drays and carts. If she did not come back—if the woman—

Kate saw her coming, hurrying, followed by the strangest creature, no taller than herself, no bigger; a thin, strange, ragged child with black hair and yellow skin and eyes like black slits, like knife wounds in the gaunt, yellow, bony face. An idiot's face. A starved idiot. All the skin yellow. The naked arms. Naked shins below the flapping, too-large breeches. No shirt. A waistcoat that must once have been a gentleman's, traces of colour in the torn and faded satin, the inside of the rolled collar. One button holding it across the narrow, bird chest.

[58]

"'E'll carry 'em," Titine whispered. "'E's my frien'. Would yer give 'im a penny?"

"But he is only a child——"

The boy had already bent down, lifted the sack with a small grunt of effort, and balanced it across his shoulders. He stood waiting, his slit eyes watching Kate for her next orders. He did not seem to feel the weight of the sack.

"He cannot carry that!"

"'Im?" the fruit-seller said from behind her. "'E can carry anything, that kid. 'E's a lascar. 'Ere, 'Ang, run with it; show the lady."

The child began to run, ten yards down the market, and back again.

"Go all day like that," the fruit-seller said. "'E can't talk o' course." As if that explained it.

Kate still did not think that it was possible, or at least right. Yet nothing else suggested itself, and she must have the oranges brought. Brought first to the cellar, and then to the theatre. "Tell him I will give him threepence," she said to Titine, feeling that the boy would not understand her if she made the promise direct. "And the moment he is tired he is to set them down and rest."

The fruit-seller, hearing the words "threepence," and "tired," laughed heartily.

Kate began hurrying away, and then, contrite, stood still until Titine and the boy caught up with her. They must make, she thought, a strange small procession. But no one paid any heed to them, and they came by ways that already were acquiring a semblance of familiarity for her, to the market lane, and the Jews' corner. In sight of the steps down into the cellar. Already feeling in her purse for money, changing the "threepence" to "sixpence" in her mind, and wondering whether she might ask him to come back in an hour or so to bring them to the theatre.

A shadow came rushing out of a doorway, a woman's voice screamed, "Ye villain, ye kidnapping whore! Where's me girl, me baby, me darlin' child, hell's ruin to her?"

A woman like a maniac, her hair like greasy serpents twisting under a broken straw bonnet, a mass of shawls and skirts and waving fists. Grabbing hold of Titine, holding her at arm's length, ripping at the hood of the pelisse, half releasing her in astonishment at the finery, as if doubting her recognition.

"Let go of her!" Kate cried, trying to push the woman away, and the woman turned all her fury on Kate. A stench of drink, her feet staggering under her so that her weight bore down on Kate's shoulders. A hand clawing unsteadily for Kate's eyes. "Stealing me child, me living, me heart's blood! Ye whore, ye thieving bitch, I'll murder ye."

Kate tore herself away and the woman fell on her knees. "I will give you money for her!" Kate shouted. "How could you treat a child so? You are wicked, wicked!"

"Wicked, is it? Holy God, I'll teach ye something—" But the promise of money had penetrated. "How much? Ten poun' she cost me, the ungrateful villain. Leavin' me that loved her like a mother to go off with a young whore the likes of you. How much'll ye give me?"

"Nothing!" Isaac's voice cried. He came racing up the steps, armed with his cudgel. "I knows yer, I knows yer! I knows 'oo yer owes blunt to. I'll 'ave yer took up for debt and gaoled if you ain't gone out of 'ere in 'arf a minute. Ten pound! You ain't never seen 'arf of that yer 'ole life together, yer filthy drab. I know 'oo's looking for yer for 'is 'arf a quid. An' more than 'im." He stood over her brandishing his cudgel, like David with a female Goliath fallen at his knees.

"Who's lookin' for me?" the woman said, but the fury had gone out of her. She rocked herself backward and forward where she knelt, tore at her bonnet, at her hair. "Who's lookin' for poor Mary Sullivan that never did harm to a livin' soul? What'll I do without me 'prentice, me little child? Who'll feed me? Who'll look after me? Ochone, ochone!" she wailed in a high, piercing shriek of grief.

Others had come running at the sounds of fighting, screaming. There was already a crowd growing, a circle of shadowy onlookers, pushing forward, looking at the fallen woman, the boy with his cudgel seeming to have felled her.

"She is drunk!" Kate cried. "We are trying to make her go away."

Isaac made himself small, invisible, lost himself in the adult crowd before it could turn on him. The woman rocked herself on the ground, tore her hair, the front of her dress under the mass of shawls. The crowd laughed; someone pushed her so that she fell on

[60]

hands and knees. Her bonnet fell off and she began to crawl about, looking for it. Kate had pulled Titine away, could scarcely see what was happening. Isaac re-appeared, tugged at Kate's cloak, whispered, "Get down into the cellar quick."

"Who pushed me, damn ye?" The shriek rising. "Let me get at ye, ye whores."

"They'll see to 'er," Isaac whispered, leading the way down. Men laughing. As Kate went down the steps, went below the level of the lane, she could see between the legs and skirts of the crowd for a moment, could see the dark heap of the woman crawling, crawling; someone kicking at her, sending her sprawling to the other side of the ring they had made. A woman crying in mercy, "Don't kick the poor wretch, she's only drunk."

Isaac closed the door of the cellar, pushed a bar across it. "They might think of coming down 'ere next." His grandfather was standing holding a dark lantern and a box, his eyes afraid. "It's all right," the boy said. "I got us barred up. 'Oo's this?" He had turned to see Kate's porter, still carrying the oranges, standing obediently in the shadows.

"You can put them down here," Kate said. "He has brought my oranges from the market. May he stay for a little until—until they have gone? The people—that woman—I would have given her money."

"She'd come back for more."

"What will they do to her?"

"Chase 'er, if she runs. Pelt 'er a bit. Serve 'er right. What's yer name?" Isaac had turned back to the porter, with the authority of the master of the house. More the master than his grandfather. Something strange, almost frightening in so much authority in so young a boy. The porter, older, taller, stood submissively, without answering.

"'Is name is 'Ang," Titine whispered. "'E can't talk."

"Then 'ow d'you know 'is name?"

Titine was bewildered at that. "It's what 'e's called."

Above the cellar steps the shouting and laughter of the crowd, the drunken wailings of the woman rose to a pitch. There was the sound of running, the pounding of boots as the woman ran and the hunt gave chase to her.

"Will she come back?" Kate said, leaning her back against the barred door, and feeling that in another moment she would faint.

Isaac shrugged his shoulders. "Not if they roughs 'er enough."

Like the sea. As though the cellar were an island. And even that island threatened.

Chapter 5

"Lovely ripe oranges," Kate whispered. "Only three pennies each." Her heart beating. Such madness to be afraid! What was it but an audience? Only another kind of part? "Lovely ripe oranges." Titine and the boy 'Ang waiting with the sack of oranges in the passage beside the doorkeeper.

I shall never sell them, she thought. *Who will buy an orange?* But a young man did. Bought two. A young man in a high cravat and a bottle-green coat, with two girls, one on either side of him. A girl beyond them wanted one, and demanded that her boy should buy it. And then another. A fat man in the middle of a row bought half a dozen for his wife and daughters.

"Lovely ripe oranges."

Men asking her where Ma Casey was, was she Ma Casey's daughter. Pinching her as she went by, making jokes that she did not understand, making comments about how she looked. That she understood well enough, although they were in English and not in French. The kinds of comments she had learned to endure long ago. Years ago. Even so she thought she would die. She swallowed, could not so much as whisper. Feeling the crowd surrounding her, no safety of space between her and the audience, no lines to say, no other actor. The faces staring. And she kept thinking of that crowd surrounding the drunken woman. The sound of them as she ran, as they began to run after her. "Lovely ripe oranges."

But she had sold a dozen, a dozen and a half, and the coins began to weigh against her, in the wide pocket under her skirt. A crowded house for the new programme; for *Jack and the Beanstalk*; for Madame Pariglia; for a Signor Giacommetti, who would "swing on the slack rope in all the forms of a monkey," the handbills promised. And the tiny horse. And the acrobats. And the ladder dancers. The orchestra already playing. She could see Mr. Solomons, who had walked to the theatre with them. Blowing softly against the mouthpiece of his flute, preparing to play. Frail and sad-seeming and old. From Poland. He had told her as they walked along that he had lived in London for thirty years, and gave lessons on the flute. "If you would like lessons?" he had said, smiling to show that it was a joke, that he was not really looking for business.

"Lovely ripe oranges." She must have sold twenty, twenty-five. She went back to refill the basket Mr. Mendoza had lent to her. Titine and the boy were crouched facing one another in the passage, playing with the oranges, and Kate felt a momentary pang almost of jealousy to see how quiet and happy they were together, like two thin shadows, a small golden pyramid of fruit between them. Their hands touching. They stood up as she came, ready to be frightened, and the half-beginning of that pang of—not jealousy—how could she be jealous? How monstrous she would have to be to feel anything of the kind. The feeling changed into an almost-pain of tenderness, so that she wanted to touch the child's face, hold her, reassure herself that the child was truly hers, truly there.

"You are not cold? Not tired?"

Titine shook her head. Smiled. And Kate had to touch her, hold her hands. "We shall have supper when we go home," she said. And thought, *What will the boy do?* But she could not—it was unthinkable—he must have somewhere that he went to at night, that he too called "home." And if she sold enough oranges now she could carry home the few that were left herself, without any need of him. Until tomorrow—

She refilled her basket, and they helped her. She wanted to say something kind: That he should have his supper, that—What could she say? Wishing to surround herself with the warmth of kindness like a shield. Against all that was terrible. Like a bird weaving a nest against the wind, the cold.

"He shall have supper too," she said hurriedly. Went quickly away before she should say more, more than she meant to say. *I cannot*, she thought. Already—Titine's voice whispering in her ears, "'E's my frien'. Would yer give 'im a penny?" How had they been friends? Begging? Shivering on the corners of empty streets?

"Lovely ripe oranges." Her voice louder, no longer so afraid. And, as she grew less afraid, noticing the theatre more, the audience. An audience of tradesmen and shopkeepers and their families, of apprentices, of girls who might be anything, muslin dresses and feather tippets and bright, painted faces. All of them better dressed and better fed than any such audience could ever have been in France. An air of jollity about everyone, of self-satisfaction, of the feeling that they had a right to pleasure, to sit there in their best coats and bonnets and be amused. The young men and women in the front rows already growing impatient for a beginning of the entertainment, beginning to shout, "Curtain, curtain," and stamp their feet and clap. The violins and the 'cellos playing for dear life to please them, keep them quiet. Mr. Solomons shaping his old, worn lips to his flute; entering a thin high sweetness into the music like a bird singing in a wood. But lost in all the stamping, the shouting.

Above the stalls there was a row of boxes, curving in a horseshoe round the whole theatre, and the only near-gentry of the audience were there. A pale, young-old man with a quizzing glass; a stout, red-faced man with a young, painted woman not much different to the apprentices' girls, except for the flash of jewellery in her hair, and her expensive fan; two young men with curled hair and curled lips, who had begun to throw down walnuts at chosen targets in the pit. An elderly man alone in his box—wearing a wig, sitting far back so that it was difficult to see him. But as Kate looked up towards him he leaned forward and beckoned her. He did not seem the kind of man who would eat an orange in the theatre, and she stared in surprise for a moment. He beckoned her again.

She went round to where a staircase led up to the boxes on that side, and found his door. "Come in! Come in!" A strange air of excitement about him; an elderly gentleman dressed with a particular kind of care and elegance; a long brown frock coat and buckled breeches and slippers, lace ruffles, his wig clubbed and powdered, his bicorne hat on the gilt chair beside him. Like a young man meaning to impress a lady, and the same kind of excitement in his manner. He held out a small parcel to her, wrapped, not in paper but in red velvet, and tied with a rose satin riband.

"Do you know Madame Pariglia, the singer?" he said.

Kate curtseyed, and bent her head to say yes. Afraid to say even "Yes" to someone so authoritative-looking, in case he should notice her accent and question it.

"If you will take this to her," he said, "I shall be much obliged to you. Does she sing early in the programme?"

[65]

Kate was forced to answer then, to say that she did not know, but if he noticed her accent, he made no remark on it.

"You shall be my messenger to her often," he said. "If you will. And here is my earnest money."

He pressed a coin into her hand beside the small, velvet-covered box. That strange air of excitement about him extended even to his hand. She thought that she could feel it tremble slightly as it touched hers, although he must be sixty years old. And if he was of the cast of mind that gives presents to singers and sits solitary in a box to watch them, it was hard to imagine that it was the first time he had done it. Yet that was the kind of excitement that he appeared to have.

When Kate was outside the box and near a wall-sconce in the passage, she looked at the coin he had given her. Gold. A half-guinea. A half-guinea! She stood for a second staring at it, wondering whether he had made a mistake. But he had had the coin ready for her, with the box. As much money as she had hoped to make in profit in the entire week! She began to run down the corridor, as though to earn the money the better, but in reality because she needed to run, to do something. Allowed herself to realise now how frightened she had been of earning nothing. And Titine—she must tell Titine—to have someone to tell! And the boy—'Ang—how could anyone be called 'Ang?—she would give him supper—give them both the most wonderful, wonderful supper. They would have a feast, they would have wine—she gave a jump down three steps to the lower corridor and spilled her oranges and had to stop to gather them up. Half a guinea! Ten shillings and a sixpence! How many oranges—one hundred—the profit on one hundred and twenty-six—one hundred and twenty-six times crying, "Lovely ripe oranges!"

The candles seemed to burn brighter, the audience to be handsomer, the music more wonderful. She could hear the flute and thought that, if Mr. Solomons would walk home with them, he should share their wine. And she would buy cottons from Isaac to mend her gown where it was torn, and buy needles—and pins—ten shillings and sixpence—half a guinea! If she could only sing aloud!

But the curtain had risen and no one would have heard her if she had sung at the top of her voice. The "garden fairies" dancing in Jack's mother's garden, fairy skirts swaying, legs kicking, heads bending, chorus singing, the apprentices stamping at the flashes of pink tights and plump calves.

Kate hurried down to the door that led to the back of the stage, climbed wooden steps, passed Jack standing in the wings, tightening his cummerbund and flexing his knees, preparatory to dancing on at his cue. Even he seemed touched by magic at that moment, and she said, "*Bonne chance*" as she skipped by him. He did not hear. The giant was trying on his papier-mâché head, and groaning "Fee Fi Fo Fum" inside it, like a monster in a cave. Up more steps, the dressing rooms, Madame Pariglia's.

She knocked and Mrs. Bunn cried out in her snapping voice, "Who is it? Who is it? What do you want *now?*"

"It is Kate. With a message."

The door opened. Mrs. Bunn beckoned her inside. It was almost impossible to move for clothes on the floor, on the wooden stand, on the chairs, on pegs driven into the walls and the door. Madame Pariglia like a great white statue, naked but for her shift and pompadour, having her shoulders creamed and powdered; standing in the billowing heaps of velvet, satin, silk and muslin, cambric and whalebone. An overpowering scent of Chypre, of Jessamine, of Maréchale, a faint background odour of brandy punch. The warmth of an orchid-house. Wax candles burning, reflecting and re-reflecting in half a dozen mirrors, showing that soft whiteness, that richness of flesh from every angle: the great thighs, the haunches like a sweet white mare, the rich white column of her neck. Madame Pariglia was a staggering sight and for a moment Kate could understand the old gentleman's excitement, if this was what his gift was leading to. Whether he was sixty or twenty, this should make his blood run young.

And as thoughts do come, not singly, in good order, but pell-mell together, she thought also of her mother, of seeing her more than once like this, preparing, and knowing that in reality she was preparing not for her performance on the stage but for her lover in the audience or in the company; and the fury of jealousy, the shame of it, the anger. "But chérie, he is so good, he is so kind to us! May I not be a trifle kind to him in return, little mouse? We are only to have supper together, that is all. What do you think that ladies and gentlemen do together at supper-time, what have bad boys been telling you, eh? We laugh and talk, that is all, and drink wine."

All the memories pell-mell. So that for a second, seeing Madame Pariglia there so big and creamy-white and splendid—like a magnificent flower being unwrapped from all its coloured leaves and petals to reveal the heart of it, the honey—Kate felt anger, such an anger as she could not understand herself, and she could have run out and slammed the door between them, hidden the woman's nakedness.

"Well?" Mrs. Bunn was snapping, the powder puff shaking clouds of the Maréchale powder over the rich curves of bosom. "What is it? What do you want?" And Madame Pariglia turning languid eyes towards her, in an ecstacy of being cared for, made even more beautiful. A great creamy mare being groomed.

"Someone has sent you a gift," Kate said, her voice harsh.

She held out the velvet-covered box. The white hand reached towards it, closed round it with pointed finger-nails. They would touch flesh like that. A man's flesh. Kate shut her eyes for a second as the fingers did touch hers, a finger-nail lightly scraping her palm.

"Who is it from?"

"You don't need to go jabbering away in French again!" Mrs. Bunn said angrily. "If you don't want a body to understand what you're saying, I'll go outside. Don't mind me. I'm only a dresser, nothing, just a piece of furniture, like a servant."

"Oh Bunny, Bunny, someone has sent us a present!"

"Us, us. It's likely they have sent it to me, isn't it? Well, who's it from? Why don't you open it?"

Madame Pariglia was already tearing the package open, her nails rasping at the tied ribbon, at the velvet, exposing a flat, small jeweller's box covered in red morocco, embossed with gilding. "Look, look! My initials! An A, and a P! Amalie Pariglia! Com'è carina!" Springing the box open. A dazzle of green fire. An emerald the size of the half-guinea that Kate still clutched in her palm. Surrounded by other stones. Opals. Tourmalines. Chips of diamond. Burning on the velvet lining. A thin gold chain coiled in the white satin of the lid. "Che meraviglia! Oh, Bunny, look, look!"

Even Mrs. Bunn was momentarily silenced.

"Who is it?" cried Madame. "Tell me. No, no, let me guess—was it—'E is young and like an angel, with blue eyes and soft, soft blond hair, was it? And a lisp when he talks so that you want to kiss him at each word?"

"Oh, yes!" cried Mrs. Bunn in a fury. "It's sure to be him. This is repaying the money you lent him last week. I expect he won a thousand guineas with it at Faro and bought you this for a keepsake. Oh, it couldn't be anyone else, could it?"

[68]

"It was an old gentleman," Kate said. The half-guinea was still real. They would have supper. Titine and 'Ang and she. And Mr. Solomons. A wonderful supper.

"An old gentleman? With a clubbed wig?"

"Yes."

"*Che noia!* But it is still a pretty thing, eh?" She dangled it by its chain, so that it flashed in the mirrors, seemed to concentrate all the light of the dozen candles in one rainbow of fire. "What did he say?"

"He asked only—if you sang early in the programme."

"And then he will be round here like an old billy-goat—you did not see the young man I 'ave described? You could not mistake him, he is so beautiful."

"Yes, yes!" cried Mrs. Bunn. "If we're going to have a gentleman friend, let's have one who borrows our money and has a lisp to say thank you with, instead of an old billy-goat who'll pay our rent and give us jewels worth a hundred guineas just as a good-wish present before we sing. Oh, yes, if we're going to make fools of ourselves, let's do it properly."

"Bunny! You are forgetting yourself!"

"Forgetting myself? I'd need to, with this kind of carrying on. When was I last paid my wages, eh? Answer me that. Oh, we have money to pay young gentlemen's debts for them, to give them to go off gambling with—but not to pay me my wages, that has a mother to keep, and a crippled father. Oh, no, there's no money for that. How could I expect it?"

"Bunny, you told me your father was dead!"

"And if he is dead, what of it? Dying of chagrin at how I'm treated. And he *was* crippled, not able to move out of the chair to feed himself."

"I don't believe you even have a mother."

"Don't believe I have a mother!" The powder puff descended furiously, smothered white bosom and throat and shoulders in a snowstorm of powder, an avalanche.

"Bunny, Bunny, I am joking. You shall have your wages tomorrow. I promise, I swear it."

Kate wanted to leave them, but was fascinated by that vision of nakedness, of luxury—of—of what? She did not know, felt a strange shiver in her mind, a curiosity not to know—she knew already—had known since she was ten, nine. Too young to know what knowledge it was that she was gaining—but a curiosity to feel—to feel that languid heaviness that was in Madame Pariglia's eyes as she was powdered, as she thought of her young man, her golden, lisping Adonis.

Kate felt a shock of horror at herself, as if she had caught herself in treachery, in the most shameful of betrayals—had looked within herself and seen that same crawling weakness of corruption as— "Never! Never!" her mind cried. And vowed again to be as empty of such thoughts as though she were a boy—that boy, that painted, dark-haired boy with the angelic face she had seen once in a picture in a church. A boy shepherd with a pipe, bending towards Our Saviour's wooden crib, among the sheep, and the gentle, wondering cattle. Such a pure and perfect boy! If she could only tear away the cloak of her girlhood and be so quiet and pure.

Although she did not know it, she looked in that moment like a young boy dressed as a girl, a boy with chestnut hair caught back from a pale, thin face; shocked in a purity that few boys have, or preserve so long outside of holy paintings; standing poised by the door, her head held very straight, very upright on the thin, beautiful neck; her lips slightly parted; her eyes so shocked, so haughtily curious, so on the brink of depths of discovery that Madame Pariglia stared at her with a kind of lazy yet startled greed; a sensuality that must reach out to any promise, any challenge. Nothing truly conscious in it. As though indeed a young boy had been placed in front of her like a choice morsel set down in front of a cat; and the cat's eyes must narrow in reactions of delight, her claws unsheathe and sheathe themselves, her sleek body arch and stretch and shiver with languid expectations of gluttony satisfied.

Then Madame Pariglia was yawning, dangling her jewel in bored impatience. Mrs. Bunn dusting off the surplus powder; wrapping the whale-boned stays round her mistress's full, soft waist; settling them on the richness of the hips over the thin cambric shift. Pushing her bony knee with venom into the smooth, beautiful back.

"Oh oh oh! BUNNY! You are 'urting me!"

Mrs. Bunn's lips pressed together, her eyes gimlet sharp, her hands fiercely tugging at the laces as though she would have liked to tighten them until her mistress was cut in half. And then with a swift spasm of something like tenderness running round to Madame Pariglia's front, and adjusting the stays under the magnificent bust, tucking and touching and placing and adjusting so that no uncomfortable fold of cloth should injure the cream-beauty of skin.

Kate let herself out and ran down the corridor, her face flaming for no reason that she could understand, except for those memories of her mother. And then stood still, that image of the white statue rising out of the heaps of velvet seeming to have burned itself into her mind, to be glowing there like white-hot metal, frightening in its power of burning. She looked at her left hand where the small gold coin lay like a golden eye. Half a guinea. *I shall buy roast meat,* she thought absently. *And a bottle of wine. And——*

She went slowly down the corridor to find Titine, and tell what they would do. But Titine lay asleep, sitting on the stone floor, her head propped on 'Ang's shoulder. And again, Kate did not know what she felt. She put her finger to her lips so that the boy should not move, should not disturb Titine, and took more oranges and went back into the body of the theatre.

The *Farcical Adventures* gave way to acrobats. To the little horse. To Madame Pariglia singing Mozart. Although the pit was not much taken with opera, and began after the second aria to shout for more popular songs.

Kate watched her, as sometimes she had watched her mother, almost able to think of her mother as a stranger; to see her standing, moving, see her gestures—listen to her voice—and not need to think *tonight she will—with that man—the one who—*To think only, *How beautiful she is!* Feel herself almost faint with tenderness. But a vague, impersonal tenderness like looking at the stars on a summer's night; to feel a drunkenness of beauty, as the words came rolling, rising, whispering, full of music, of that wonderful cold passion that was her mother's secret. She did not act, in the ordinary sense of acting, Kate had sometimes thought. Almost *could not* act. Scarcely moved about without a kind of stiffness. And yet out of her came welling—not only passion, but a cold purity like the purest water from a spring. With a man, with a lover, oh dearest God, there was no stiffness then. And as for purity, that chastity of passion— But on the stage! She had once thought her mother the only true actress in the world, had thought the King and Queen must come to see her if only they could be told how wonderful she was. She had dreamed of writing a letter to the Queen.

"*Ma chère Majesté,* if you would only come to Dijon to the Theatre here—" or Marseilles. Or Bordeaux.

She had learned since then more of what acting was, and could be, had seen fine actresses. And yet still she had thought that her mother possessed a secret that none of them had found. Nor Madame Pariglia. Curving out her white arms, bending in a low, sweeping curtsey like an invitation to the audience to—to—not to share chastity. Certainly not that.

Kate stood withdrawn in a dark corner of the theatre, watching and listening, unconsciously with that same expression of shocked curiosity, of a purity of anger, that she had felt in the dressing room. Seeing Madame Pariglia on the stage, her vast pompadour with its silver galleon for decoration, her panniered skirts of the court days of Versailles that the Revolution had destroyed, her fan covering her broad white bosom, the black ostrich feathers touching, caressing, revealing, sweeping. '*O zittre nicht, mein lieber Sohn.*" And the pit beginning to whistle, to shout "Give us 'Sally, Sally in our Alley'! Give us 'Hearts of Oak.'"

In his box the elderly gentleman was leaning forward, his face alight with an excited admiration. Madame was wearing his jewel and he must have taken that for a confirmation of his love, his acceptance. *That he has bought his mare,* Kate thought in fury. And as though the old gentleman was aware of his indiscretion he drew back into the shadows.

"'Hearts of Oak'! 'Hearts of Oak'!" The apprentices whistling, shouting down Mozart. Madame Pariglia made her sweeping curtsey again, rose like a white swan from the stage, held out her arms. The stamping and whistling eased.

"*Mes amis! Mes chers amis!* You are my masters. 'Hearts of Oak' it shall be. *Attendez vous!*" She held out her hands to the small orchestra as though it spread in seven rows of musicians as far as her eye could reach to left and right of the stage. The violins, the 'cellist, Mr. Solomons, who had let their music die away, tilted their bows and instruments again. The pit's *chers amis* grew quiet; the violins threw jaunty, arrogant notes into the air, like waves dancing; and when her moment came, Madame Pariglia sang their song for them like the opening of a sailor's love affair: "Come, cheer up, my lads, 'tis to glory we steer—" The apprentices stamping again, but this time with triumph, banging their elegant canes on the floor, smacking their knees, readying themselves to roar the chorus, the sailor grasping his love: "Hearts of oak are our ships, Jolly tars are our men. We always are ready, steady boys, steady!" The roar spreading through the stalls, even the boxes with elegant, amused embarrassment adding quiet voices to the burst of passion, "We'll fight and we'll conquer again and again!"

Madame Pariglia possessed her audience as though she held each man there in her arms; even the women sharing in the wave of physical attraction welling across the lights, breaking in an ivory foam of sensuality against their minds. Even Kate felt it, was shaken by it as almost never had she been touched or moved by Racine or Corneille. Something frightening, tearful, choking in it that made her furious against it and yet helpless, as though an unfair advantage had been taken of her emotions.

The song ended, and another began: "Of all the girls that are so smart, there's none like pretty Sally; She is the darling of my heart—"

They would not let her go, until at last a furious Signor Giacommetti, glowering at her from the wings, persuaded Madame Pariglia that she was tired, and she curtseyed half a dozen times, blew kisses, held out her arms, was almost tempted to a third encore, but at last drew away from her loves, to give way to the "Human Monkey who would Dazzle and Astonish his Audiences by his Performance on the Slack Rope." And after a short period of prejudice against him because he was not Madame Pariglia, nor even a woman, he did indeed begin to Dazzle and Astonish, lying on his arched back across the swinging rope, doing somersaults on it, hanging by his toes from it, walking five steps and falling straddled across it, bouncing up again; until the apprentices clapped and whistled almost as heartily for him as for "Hearts of Oak" and "Sally" and Madame Pariglia's white bust and loving arms.

The excitement gave a thirst, and perhaps because Kate was sober, while at this stage of the evening Ma Casey had usually been drunk, she sold out her third basket of oranges, refilled it, and saw that there were only three or four dozen left in the sack. As she came back from the doorkeeper's cubbyhole, and Titine and 'Ang asleep beside his chair and the oranges, she saw the old gentleman walking on eager feet, with a boy's nervousness, towards Madame Pariglia's dressing room, tapping at the door. And heard Mrs. Bunn crying, "Well, who is it? Who's there?"

He turned his head as Kate came by and smiled at her as if they were friends, and he was half-ashamed and half-proud of the situation she found him in. The door opened enough to let him sidle in. Madame Pariglia's voice cried, "Mr. Jardine! Who could imagine—?" Kate hurried away.

Another hour and it was over. The Dancing Burletta. The Human Pyramid. The Fencing Match. The Company. Kate had scarcely a dozen oranges left, and her pocket weighed against her with a wonderful heaviness of silver and copper. And that gold half-guinea tied safe in her handkerchief. She had forgotten about Madame Pariglia and the old gentleman, at least as far as her contradictions of thoughts about them were concerned. She had lost any curiosity about them; felt a warm glow of joy towards the whole world, and especially this audience if only they would all go home, and let her go home as well. She was so tired that she did not know if she was hungry or not, and wanted only to sit down in a quiet place and count her money on the floor. A hundred and twenty, a hundred and thirty oranges? At a penny profit a time? But more than that, she had paid only a penny ha'penny for each of them. She was too tired to work it out in her head. Fifteen shillings? And the half-guinea besides. They would be rich.

The audience went at last, and Kate found Titine, and the boy, and Mr. Solomons, and they walked home by the frosty starlight. There were no shops still open, but they found an eating house that would let them buy pies and meat and bread and cheese and two bottles of wine to take with them. Kate found herself singing "Hearts of Oak" as they walked, and then "Mahlbrouk." Mr. Solomons hummed Mozart, and what perhaps were Polish tunes of his childhood. Titine walked with 'Ang, carrying the wine and the food, and every now and then Kate turned round to make sure that she was safely there.

It is all well, she thought, with a happiness like fear, a kind of trembling of happiness. *It will all be well.*

Only when they had almost finished eating, in the inner room of the cellars—old Mr. Mendoza and Isaac sharing their wine, Titine and 'Ang sitting side by side on a box, holding hands—did Kate allow herself to face the problem of the boy. But what problem could it be? He must have somewhere that he lived. Twice she was on the point of asking Titine, and stopped herself, in case she was told something that she did not want to hear. And what could she do? How many stray children could she—And would not allow herself to think of Titine as a "stray child," as one like hundreds, thousands, who at this moment must be shivering in doorways, anywhere they could find shelter. *He will go home,* she thought. She pushed the last of her wine away from her, could not finish her bread and cheese. *He may take that with him,* she thought. *It will be breakfast for him.*

She pushed the food towards him and stood up. "Tomorrow you shall come to the market with us, if you would like to. I am so tired. And you, Titine—say good night to your friend." Feeling like a murderess. *Yet he has been better fed today than for the past year, from his looks. He has earned money. He shall earn money from me every day,* she promised herself. She could not look at Titine as the two children took leave of one another. Isaac went with the boy through the outer cellar, holding a candle to light him to the steps. Too clearly not for politeness but to make sure that he took nothing with him as he went, beyond his bread and cheese. Even that, Isaac's expression said, was foolish extravagance.

Isaac came back and they all went to bed, Kate and Titine climbing the outer stairs, Mr. Solomons behind them as far as his room below theirs. "Good night. Good night." The sharp stars. The chimneys. The dying smoke. The cold.

Isaac had lit their stove for them, and they sat for a moment in front of it, Kate too tired even to count her money, holding Titine's hand. "Where will he sleep?" Kate whispered.

"Somewheres," Titine said, when she had understood. "'E finds places." She put down her face against the knuckles of Kate's hand that was holding hers, and rested her cheek there.

[75]

Chapter 6

Kate woke to hear Mr. Solomons's music, sad and sweet and full of immense distances, of plains and forests stretching forever towards the sky; drifted awake out of a dream of Madame Pariglia singing, holding out her arms. Kate's own arms were round Titine, the child's body thin as a bird's, scarcely any weight in it, her breath quiet and warm and comforting.

We shall be rich, Kate thought. A remembrance of the hat. The broad blue ribbons, the shape of the high crown, the brim. She had never seen such a wonderful hat. She began to imagine a gown to go with it, remembering the ones she had seen last night, taking a sash from one, and a cross-over neckerchief from another; and bodices and skirts and open gowns and buffons and long tight sleeves—or perhaps three-quarter sleeves? She was asleep again, satins and paduasoys and muslins and sarcenets unrolling their brightness out of the shadows, the music of Mister Solomons' childhood weaving in and out like a silk thread. Madame Pariglia's gown, Mrs. Bunn stabbing.

Kate sat up, alarmed. "We must buy oranges!" Suppose there were none left? Suppose—

Titine had woken with a small cry of fright, more frightened to find herself in bed than back with Mrs. Sullivan on a layer of dirty straw in a cellar, being kicked awake. She did not know where she was, felt round her in the dark, touched Kate's body, cried out again.

"I am here!" Kate said, catching hold of her, drawing her close. "You are safe; it is all right." Smoothing Titine's hair, the wound in her scalp still rough with dried blood under Kate's palm because it had not been possible to bandage it. Nor necessary any longer, old Mr. Mendoza had said. It would heal best uncovered. "We will light the stove. And have breakfast. And then we shall go to the market. And 'Ang shall come——"

He had slept on the cellar steps all night. Isaac had found him there when he had opened the cellar door for business. "'E's got a cheek!" Isaac said.

"But you must have somewhere else—where have you slept until now?" Kate cried, wanting to be angry. 'Ang looked down at the ground between them, clasping his hands together in front of him, his yellow face expressionless, or with no expression that she could read. The black hair chopped raggedly. The slanting eyes almost closed, invisible. The absurd waistcoat, five sizes too large for him, falling away from his bony chest as he bent himself forward. "Titine! Does he understand?"

"'E understands everything," Titine whispered.

And he did not seem like an idiot on closer looking. Only strange. A Lascar, the fruit-seller had said. What was a Lascar?

"'E's Chinee," Isaac said. "Deaf an' dumb Chinee of a ship."

"'E ain't deaf," Titine said, taking the boy's hand protectingly. "'E can 'ear." The boy bent his head and smiled.

"Tell him—" Kate began. She felt Isaac looking at her, his eyes judging all her follies, weighing her weakness. "Tell him he must not sleep outside this cellar," she said quickly. "It is very wrong of him."

They went to the market, and she could think again of money, of how much money she would make. Bargain with the fruit-seller who remembered her, was friendly, amused at her two followers, possessive of her as a customer. Promising to treat her right, to keep the good fruit for her. "Try some apples," he said. "Some of 'em loves apples. An' pears."

She took a dozen apples for a trial and felt herself a business woman, began to look forward to the night. And when the night came, she sold almost as well as she could have hoped. There was no half-guinea from the old gentleman, Mr. Jardine, but a young man in one of the other boxes gave her a shilling to carry a supper invitation to the prettiest of the garden fairies, and another shilling when she brought an acceptance back. She would not allow herself to think what she was doing. "What affair is it of mine?" she cried in a kind of medley of self-contempt, and self-excuse, and scorn for the garden fairy in her dirty pink tights and her eagerness to be taken out to a midnight supper by the elegant young man.

Kate had told 'Ang to go home, to leave them, as soon as he had carried the sack of oranges and small parcel of apples to the theatre, and she left Titine sitting alone to guard the fruit, beside the doorkeeper. "I have no obligations toward 'Ang," she told herself. "None! None!"

When she went back to refill her basket, Titine was gone. She could not believe it for a moment, looked round at the corners of the room, the passage, into the shadows. The old doorkeeper half asleep in his chair, his wig nodding. "Where is she? Where has she gone?" Shaking him awake. He started up, blinking his eyes behind his spectacles, his newspaper falling from his knees onto the stone floor.

There was an empty quart pot beside him, and a smell of porter. "Where did she go?" But he could only open his mouth and stare at Kate's urgency. She left him, ran to the stage door, outside, her heart beating like a hammer, a cold panic that had more and less than reason in it, a terror as though she herself was threatened, something beyond the reach of thinking. The dark, the cold. Which way? *Oh God, which way could she have gone? Why? Why? Let me find her, let me—the woman! The woman has taken her! I shall die!*

Two shadows against the wall. One shadow. The two children close together, sharing Titine's pelisse. Coming slowly, timidly to their feet as Kate saw them, turned on them with the fury of relief, her fear become anger, shouting, "Why did you go outside? What are you doing there?" Could almost have—catching hold of Titine, almost shaking her, then holding her against herself, not able to speak, to think, to see. Feeling the child tremble. Making herself say, "It is all right, it is all right. I was only afraid that—Why did you go outside? Did I not tell you not to stir, not to—?"

The child whispering. Kate bent down her head a little to hear what Titine was saying. " 'E was cold."

Kate would have driven him away, struck him—and then, as though she had already struck him, her hands burned like Cain's, with shame, with—"What shall I do? What can I—how—?" The boy had backed away from her a pace or two, beyond her reach, and she thought, *He knows, he knows what I was thinking*—and could have died of shame, have held her two hands in the fire to cleanse them. Remembered the woman Mary Sullivan, crawling on hands and knees among the kicking feet, blind with drink and misery. As though it was herself.

"Let him come in with you," she said. "With us." Thinking, "But what shall I do with him? What shall I do?" She held out one hand towards him but he did not come near. And when she took a step towards him, he backed away until his shoulders were against the wall. Only a shadow. Until she was touching him. He bent his head, expecting to be struck. "Please," she whispered. His shoulder naked, like old ivory. "Tell him not to be afraid."

She put her arm round him, drew him away from the wall. "You shall have supper again," she said. "And—and we shall find somewhere for you—for you to sleep—Does he understand?"

"Yus," Titine whispered.

They went back into the theatre and later that night Kate arranged with old Mr. Mendoza that, in return for sweeping out the cellar, the boy might sleep in a corner of it.

Isaac looked at her sideways across the supper table, curling his mouth, but after a day or so even he accepted the boy's presence, calling out possessively, "'Ang, you yellow villain, where's me tray? Where 'ave yer put it now?" And when he left in the morning to sell his cottons, ordering 'Ang to guard the steps from any Christian children who might dare to come and shout down them at his grandfather. In fact 'Ang's mere appearance on the steps was a protection. More of a protection than Isaac's cudgel. The Chinese boy had only to come running out of the cellar doorway and start up the steps, and at the sight of his yellow face and slanting eyes, his black porcupine quills of hair, his fists doubled, the sleeves of his new flannel shirt rolled back, the boldest of Christian paladins took to their heels and fled for safety.

Christmas Eve. Christmas. New Year 1794. On New Year's Eve Kate had a whole guinea from old Mr. Jardine in the theatre. He seemed to believe that she had some influence on Madame Pariglia and was always attentive to her, treating her with a courteous gravity; seeming to value her good opinion, to be asking for her understanding of his elderly passion. And Madame Pariglia gave her a silk gown that Kate spent the day after Christmas cutting down to her own size.

She paid the first instalment of her debt to Mr. Mendoza and it began to seem that she had always lived in the attic room under the roof, with its rattling window, and its iron stove, and Titine beside her. To wake, and hear Mr. Solomons's music; to walk home from the theatre in the icy moonlight, or the wet dark, and know that supper was waiting, that they would all sit round the big table in the inner cellar and for half an hour have no cares in the world beyond the food and drink. To feel the past fading, taking its proper place in remembrance, healing.

I am grown happy! she thought, and was afraid, and ashamed of herself for being afraid, and was still half afraid. Like the timid sun in January, snow in the dark sky surrounding it. But January becomes February, and spring. She no longer dreamed of the sea, of the dead; or if she did, the dreams were buried deep under other dreams and she did not remember them when she woke, except as shadows, fading to Mr. Solomons's flute.

Mr. Solomons had come to a patient, wordless friendship with 'Ang, and for lack of any other way of communicating had begun to teach him music. Early in the mornings, when the cellar was swept and the door opened, 'Ang would climb up to Mr. Solomons's room, bringing him a cup of tea from old Mr. Mendoza's pot, and for half an hour would blow sad notes. The strangest of music. He learned very quickly. "A natural," Mr. Solomons said proudly. "A natural-born flautist." He even learned Mr. Solomons's own Polish tunes. But when he played them, they sounded different. As if he had reduced them to their simplest essence, taking one note at a time, and letting it dwell in the air until it faded away and died before he would play another.

"No no no!" Mr. Solomons would cry. "That is all wrong, *nein, nein!*" And yet, strange as it sounded, there was a haunting quality to 'Ang's music that gripped Kate's heart when she heard it. Just those single notes, like stars in the dark. And both he and Titine growing smooth-skinned with food, the shadows going from their faces.

And I myself, Kate thought sometimes. Mr. Mendoza had given them a mirror for their room and when she brushed her hair in front of it, or dressed Titine's hair with ribands, she could not help thinking that she was looking well again, as she had used to.

She liked to put her head beside Titine's and compare their colourings, their hair; an ivory paleness in both of them, but Titine's cheeks beginning to glow with childhood; a bloom on the skin like peach bloom, the same soft beginnings of colouring; and Kate's hair a dark mass, auburn, copper, chestnut; Titine's pale gold, her eyebrows a shade darker, arched in that expression of mute questioning above the huge grey eyes; the strange almost-hauteur of childhood; of a traveller who has come to a place of whose nature he is unsure and who holds himself back from any too-great intimacy.

Kate thought at times that Titine held herself back even from her, that there was an inner self in her that no kindness could reach, although it was not apparent to any sense but instinct. To every other appearance the child was all yieldingness of gratitude. And sometimes it seemed to Kate almost too much happiness to bear to see her becoming a child again, playing with a doll that Isaac made for her out of old cotton reels and rags. Isaac stitched it himself, neat and furious by candlelight at the supper table over Christmas, saying scornful things about girls and dolls. Making a gown and bodice as neat as a tailor could have done, and a bonnet and a cloak of blue velvet pieces. Painting the face on cotton stretched over a small oval of smooth wood, while 'Ang watched him, his eyes growing wider and wider, until Isaac drove him away: "Get out of me light!" Like Mrs. Bunn. As though the handling of pins and needles induced a sharpness of character, an infection of the spirits.

In the theatre Madame Pariglia was herself growing sleeker if that was possible, and even Mrs. Bunn seemed to have some of her sharpness smoothed away under the old gentleman's influence. He owned a bank, and a mad wife, and a grown-up family of proud, indifferent daughters, and at the age of sixty-one, for the first time in his married life was having a love affair.

"*Che noioso,*" Madame Pariglia would yawn about him when Kate brought her a message, or a gift, or flowers from him; or at any time, simply for the pleasure of talking about him and belittling his value. But all Madame's debts were paid, and Mrs. Bunn had a new gown and bonnet and boots, and an air of consequence. When she and her mistress quarrelled now, it was only about the insanity of allowing some new young officer with debts and a lisp to throw any shadow on the affair. There were more jewels, and a gift of three shares in a new Canal Company.

"Shares!" Madame Pariglia cried in disgust. "What should I do with such things?" But she handled the document with a sensuality of pleasure, making it crackle between her fingers, and looked sleepily at Kate with the air of a woman of property considering her estates.

"We must find you a *cher ami,*" she said to Kate, who had learned

[81]

not to answer such suggestions. "You are beginning to look quite pretty, on my honour. You are too thin, of course. You should eat more, my darling, and run about less. Such 'air! If all of you was in keeping with that! But there are some gentlemen who like thin girls." She stroked her own bosom with tender thoughtfulness.

Mrs. Bunn, instead of a pungent defense of virtue, merely stitched at a new chemise gown for her mistress, in white muslin with sprigs of green, and pressed her lips together, as though thinking, *Not everyone has a mistress who has a banker for a lover.*

The Farcical Adventures of Jack and the Beanstalk gave way to *The Merry Pranks of Robin Hood* with a Ballet of Country Maidens pursued by King John. Signor Giacommetti went off to be a Monkey in Edinburgh, and the little horse went to Belfast, their places being taken by a Mermaid who sat combing her hair on the stage in a tank of water and who ate raw fish thrown to her by her keeper. According to the playbill he was a fisherman, who had caught her off the rocks of Wales. There was also a cock which crowed when any volunteer from the audience told a lie, such as that he was not in love with anyone, or that she had never been kissed if the volunteer was a girl. While truthful answers were rewarded with furious scratchings of the boards of the stage.

The man who owned the cock tried once or twice to make Kate come up onto the stage to answer questions, but she would not. And several young men in the pit, and more than one or two in the expensive seats, began to take notice of her and add a more serious note to their attempts to pinch her as she went by, or bent over them to give an orange or an apple to someone farther along the bench. And as with Madame Pariglia's lazy suggestions of good will Kate had learned not to shiver, not to be afraid. Only to be so calmly definite in her rejections that the young men felt she must have an escort somewhere near, and that he might be dangerously jealous, so that they had best leave off tormenting her.

Indeed, she had an escort in Mr. Solomons, who looked forward to their walking home as one of the great pleasures of his day, to be crowned by supper. And there was 'Ang. And there was Titine. It was as though Kate already possessed a family without ever having possessed a young man as a preliminary, and she was glad of it, like a protection against—she was not even sure against what. For God knew she felt no temptation to—to anything that had ever tempted her mother. She shivered again at the thought. And found herself at the same time with a sense of—not loss, but of—of almost expectation. Although of what? Of what? When already she was as happy as anyone might dare to be.

"There is a look in your eye!" Madame Pariglia cried to her one night. "Bunny, Bunny, look at 'er eyes! She 'as a lover, I swear! You secret little thing, tell us 'oo he is. I command it!"

Kate felt herself burn with anger. But that night by candlelight she examined herself very carefully in the mirror as they went to bed, and could see nothing strange.

"What yer lookin' at?" Titine said, sitting up in the bed and holding her knees. "Yer been ages lookin'."

"I am looking at my eyes." And her eyes danced at her from the shadows, against her will at first, and then quite with her will, and she went and threw herself into the cold sheets beside Titine and caught hold of her so tight that the child gasped with breathlessness. Could not one be in love simply with life itself? In love with happiness? What need was there for any such thing as a young man?

"What's the matter? What's up?" Titine was saying, and they lay holding one another, laughter quietening into smiles, murmurs; falling asleep, dreaming, Kate dreaming of a young man. No particular young man. Until he was that dark boy by the Crib, the shepherd boy, and she smiled in her sleep, and held Titine's hand as if it were his. And the young man smiled at her, and bowed, and they were by the Crib and—and—she did not dare to look, felt a cold terror of what she might see in the Child's eyes. Wanted to cry to Him, "It is nothing, nothing—it is not love—only the joy of seeing anyone so beautiful! May I not touch his hand?" And the Child looked at her with love, and she was her own mother kneeling there, her face grown lined and ruined, only her hair still beautiful, and full of autumn leaves.

"He is forgiving you," the old nun whispered. "Did He not forgive the Magdalene?" And such forgiveness was so terrible it was like her heart being torn out of her and burned by white-hot fire, burning away the shame, the long caravan of shames.

"I am not her!" Kate cried, and the Child looked away from her, as if by crying out like that she had hidden herself away from His sight, denied herself.

"Oh, please," she whispered, the tears running in her dream—
"must love hurt so much?"

And the Child was gone, and the cattle and the cave. Only the young shepherd boy was there, with his purity of face.

"Love is a wound," he said. And who would dare to wound such beauty? He seemed to be looking about him for the Child.

"I did not mean to deny—" Kate whispered. "Oh, believe me, believe me, please." But the young man was gone, and she was alone in the dark. Until out of the dark came other dreams, and at last a merciful depth of sleep beyond the reach of dreams. To let her wake to the sounds of 'Ang's lesson on the flute, the single notes, each one floating pure as starlight, like lips touching. Waking very slowly, turning her head on the pillow, still with the mark of tears on it. Although she had forgotten why they might be there even if she had been able to see them. The shadow outline of Titine's cheek, a sense that she too was waking, a strange feeling of there having been a dream a long time ago, and that perhaps Titine might know what it had been. Might even have shared in it.

"What are you thinking of?" Kate whispered.

"Me alphabet. Why does there 'ave to be so many letters?" And the last shadowy remembrance of the dream faded, and they were both very young again.

So young that it was of immense importance that Kate should be the wiser of the two and able to teach Titine everything that she would need to know in order to grow up into proper young womanhood. Among such things, almost first among them indeed, being the alphabet. But, as Kate herself did not know it quite perfectly in English, the teaching went on slowly enough. Sometimes Isaac heard them at it, and corrected them scornfully: "Yer've forgotten J. What yer want 'er to spell for anyways? Girls don't 'ave to spell."

Titine had also begun to help in the theatre. They sold not only oranges and apples now, but hot pies and cakes. Mr. Gosport increased the concession money to a guinea and a half, and still they made more and more profits. Three, four, almost five guineas one week. Kate had paid all her debts to Mr. Mendoza, had bought the longed-for hat for a guinea and a nearly new gown for another two guineas for the spring, when at last it would decide to come, and wore them both even though it remained winter. She had dressed Titine and 'Ang, and given Mr. Solomons a woollen scarf in return for 'Ang's music lessons, and still she had money in her purse. She began to study the *Lady's Magazine* for the newest fashions. Realised, with a sense half of shame and half of triumph, that she was earning much more money than Mr. Solomons, and tried by small stratagems to prevent him from paying his proper share of their supper expenses. "It is only payment for 'Ang's lessons," she said. "It is only just that we should give you at least something in return."

"But that is my pleasure, to teach him!" Mr. Solomons smoothing his old, knuckly fingers down the thick red woollen scarf at his throat. "And you have already given me this beautiful, beautiful comforter." His voice, his smile, the movement of his hand full of a courtesy as antique as his clothes, his wig; and at the same time full of irony, a self-mockery. The irony was almost painful; the gentle acceptance of his ridiculousness as escort to two such young women, of his poverty, his failure as a musician.

Kate found it hard to understand the failure. He played so beautifully, taught so well, and, as they walked to and from the theatre, he would sometimes talk of music with such joy that it came as a shock to remember that in reality he was no more than a thin thread of sound that scarcely anyone listened to, while the garden fairies, now become country maidens, kicked up their sturdy pink legs or the Mermaid ate the raw fish that her keeper threw to her.

It made Kate think uncomfortably of her mother. And even more uncomfortably of herself. But her mother had not been a failure—not that kind of failure? And she herself? Selling oranges—but only for a little while more. And then?

"It is more than talent that is necessary," Mr. Solomons said, when she managed to touch obliquely on the question. He had a way of looking at her as if he could see more than was ordinarily visible about her. As if he could read her thoughts, and worse than that, her future. She wanted to cry out to him, "It will not be like that for me!" And he seemed to know what she was thinking and smiled; sad, ironic, self-mocking, his old, thin, blueish lips delicately curving, his eyes bird-bright under their wrinkled yellow lids, his head slightly inclined. They were at supper and he held up his wine-glass against the candlelight. Towards her. "More even than beauty. But I am sure——"

"It's luck," Isaac said, thoughtfully taking the last large piece of

[85]

sweet cake. "And push. That's what does it. Push. But yer got to 'ave luck too."

"I am sure that if you want it—truly want success—even great success—then it will come to you."

"We all wants that," Isaac said, his mouth full. "It takes more than wanting."

"Indeed it does. But that is the most difficult thing. To want it, truly. For that means that you are willing to pay the price."

"What price?" Kate whispered. It seemed to her that the conversation had taken an almost painful seriousness, although they were only filling those last happy few minutes of the evening, or rather of midnight, before they went to bed. Food, wine, idle talk. 'Ang and Titine sitting together as they always did, a trifle drawn back from the company, in shadow, holding hands. "Do you mean—that one must be willing to work hard?"

"Much, much more than that. The price is everything that you possess. Everything."

Mr. Mendoza listening to his friend, his lodger, twisting his fingers in his soft, grey-white beard. Isaac's eyes darting from Mr. Solomons, to Kate, to his grandfather, as if afraid that something of value might escape him if he did not keep constant watch. "I'll pay," he said.

His grandfather frowned. "You do not know what you are saying."

"Oh, yus I do. I ain't goin' to stay in this cellar. Not me."

"I believe you," Mr. Solomons said. "Success is written in your eyes, Isaac. Great success." He turned towards Kate as though he had heard her saying, "And in mine? Can you see what is written in mine?" He was no longer smiling. "Sometimes it is not a question of paying," he said. "Of paying willingly. Sometimes the payment may be taken by force."

She shivered uncontrollably. "Someone is walking over my grave," she said, trying to smile. "It is time to go to bed. Titine, 'Ang—if you will excuse us?" turning to Mr. Mendoza.

After that she did not allow herself to approach the subject again with Mr. Solomons, and was half afraid that he might commence on it himself as they walked along, or sat at supper. As though she had a feeling of guilt at not being willing to pay the kind of price he was talking of. Although that was ridiculous, for every reason. How

[86]

could she pay it, when she did not really understand what it was? Or how to begin. How can an orange-seller pay a price for success? What price could her mother have paid? More than a whole life of effort, of self-belief and courage? And pain, and still more courage? Had her lovers cancelled out that payment?

I do not understand at all what he meant, she decided, and was half angry with him as though it had been he who had first begun the subject, and not she. And who in Heaven's name was Mr. Solomons, playing his flute for the garden fairies, to talk of the price to be paid for success? What could he know about it? And what was "success"? To be rich? To be famous?

"I am very happy as I am," Kate told herself, more than once. "I have everything I want—almost." One day she would act again. Quite soon, perhaps. When her accent—and if she did not, would that be so terrible? She tried to imagine a life for herself in which there was no more theatre. *I could still be happy,* she thought. And thought too, *I might even be happier!* Remembering a thousand things, that seemed each like a separate pain: the fear, the hunger, the being so tired that her bones ached, and still having to go on stage. And behind all else, all the other agonies, the shame. Of seeing her mother shamed.

"I shall be much happier!"

And felt as though she had escaped from something. Surely the true business of life was to be happy? And to make others a little happy as well—if one could? Surely that was quite enough? Titine. 'Ang. Titine growing up. The child might, Kate had thought once or twice—scarcely even thought—merely touched on it—day-dreamed—Titine might have the makings of an actress if she were trained. It was difficult to say why. The way she carried herself— that kind of self-containment—she was a strange, strange child. How wonderful it would be if—She imagined teaching her—and in the half of a moment that such day-dreams take saw her already a success—at Drury Lane, Covent Garden—heard the applause—felt the tears of happiness—that she had created her, created this magic that a thousand people were applauding.

And the payment? What price might Titine have to pay? Kate would catch hold of her then if she were close, and smooth her hair as though she had just rescued her from great danger, and say to herself, "Never, never!" Unless—unless Titine should wish it—?

While as for 'Ang—she had long ago overcome that shadow of jealousy, and loved him because Titine loved him, and also for himself. Like loving a good and loving dog. She felt ashamed at such a simile, and yet it was exact. The silence. The obedience. He seemed always to know before she asked him what she would want him to do next. And he guarded Titine as though he was truly a kind of watchdog, not allowing her to go anywhere, not even twenty yards down the lane to the little market beyond the corner, unless Kate first gave permission.

Only 'Ang's music kept reminding her that he was more than that. He had found a piece of stick the size and thickness of a flute, and had marked the keys and stops on it. When there was nothing else to do, he would sit in a corner of the cellar, or beside the door-keeper at the theatre, making a ghostly music, his fingers flying and caressing, his lips pursed against the stick.

"Don't do that!" Isaac would shout at him. "Yer gives me the creeps. It's 'orrible, 'orrible! I'll buy yer a bloody whistle if yer wants one, only don't do that!" And 'Ang would stop until Isaac went out. And then take up his length of stick and make his silent music again, his eyes lost. Kate imagined at times that she could even hear it. It made her shiver, and she could almost have echoed Isaac's horror of it, as though they both heard the same thing, without knowing what it was. It held her back from promising to buy him a real flute when she could afford it. What music would he make? The thin shadow, like a ghost, his fingers moving, moving, stilled, raised. What was he hearing as he played?

In the streets there was a day of spring. The sky blue crystal, promise of warmth in the sun glittering on windows, shining on the mud, on the grey stones of the gutters running down the centres of the reeking lanes, on the black rooftops; the black and red and yellow carriages, smart-painted, swift-running; the sleek coach horses with their brasses shining, the great haunches of the dray horses; the sedan chairs with the chairmen trotting, brandy in their eyes; the ladies' bonnets and straw hats and muslins and satins; here and there trees over garden walls showing green leaves. Every living thing in London welcoming spring; the sparrows and the pigeons; the cats drowsy in the new sun.

They almost danced their way to the market, Kate and Titine holding hands, wearing new slippers—rose-coloured, with flat heels and pink ribbons tied in criss-cross round their ankles, these showing, Kate allowed herself to think, to great advantage as they went along, the light wind tucking their muslins against their legs, or puffing them forward. More than one gentleman passing by lifted an eyebrow, or turned his head to look, or raised a lorgnon in polite pleasure at the sight of two such pretty creatures, one almost a woman, and the other no longer quite a child.

"They are looking at you," Kate said handsomely to Titine. "You are so pretty today." And then thought, *They are really looking at 'Ang, because they think him so strange*, and was depressed for three paces until another gentleman looked unmistakably at her, and made her blush.

But Titine *was* pretty. More than pretty. It was difficult to find a word that described how she looked, how she had become in no more than two months of being loved. The hoarseness gone out of her voice, the violet shadows from under her eyes. Her hair beginning to grow longer, to curl in a pale, wheaten gold; her neck very slender; her head beautifully shaped, beautifully held; held by an instinct, by that child's hauteur of surprise at the world; a narrow oval, with delicate, thin bones that made Kate want to fondle them, take them between her hands. Like growing a flower, holding the tight bud of a rose between one's palms, not quite touching the petals for fear of injuring their purity.

Titine seemed even in those two months to have grown taller. Like having a sister. At times. And at others, like having her own child, so that Kate felt very old and full of love and fear. Would watch Titine sleeping, lips parted, eyelids almost transparent, waxen, blue-veined, dark gold lashes grown thick as silk fringe, lying on the fading remains of those violet shadows, hiding them.

God has had such mercy for me, Kate thought in those moments, and got out of the bed to kneel beside it, and pray for her mother, and all the dead, and for herself to be good, and for Titine and 'Ang, and Mr. Solomons, and Mr. Mendoza, and Isaac. And for Madame Pariglia and Mrs. Bunn. And even for old Mr. Jardine, and Mr. Gosport, and Mr. Benedict and the garden fairies, and the fruit-seller, and the people in the street who had looked unhappy that day. Even for Mrs. Sullivan, that God might forgive her. For without her she would never have found Titine. "O God, please let us live gently now. I don't care about a new pelisse, truly not. Not about anything, so that we may go on as we are, and have enough to eat. I don't care about acting again. Not about anything, so long as we may go on in happiness. And I may be always wise and good." Until she grew so cold, and her knees on the boards hurt so much, that she was forced to bring her prayers to a hurried Sign of the Cross and Amen, and jump into the bed again beside Titine.

"Wha'? What's the matter—?" Titine still asleep but murmuring, stirring.

"Nothing, my darling, nothing—go back to sleep." Holding her hand, then letting go of it for fear her own hands were too cold, would wake her.

"Look at 'im!" Titine said now, as they trotted and skipped, and reduced themselves to a more sedate progress towards the market. "Don't 'e look a queer ol' buffer?"

An old man in a wide-brimmed beaver hat so strange that it could scarcely be called old-fashioned, but was a fashion of its own. With under it a hanging curtain, a visor of green silk to protect its wearer's eyes from the pale sun. He wore a long brown camlet coat to his knees, and his legs were so swathed round in grey flannel bandages that they seemed to have no shape at all, the wrappings spilling down over his flat, square-toed, countryman's shoes, half covering the old, thick silver buckles. A woollen scarf swathed and wrapped round his neck, drawn up over his mouth. A thick, monstrous figure, like a fragment of the winter left over into spring. Standing dark and lost at the corner of the street, leaning on a crutch-headed stick as thick as a man's wrist. Even his hands hidden in black woollen gloves.

They were crossing the road towards him, and he lifted his blind, invisible head as if somehow he was aware of them, was watching their progress towards him. And Kate had a sudden, dreadful imagination that behind the green silk veil there was nothing, no eyes, no head. Nothing. And was on the point of grasping Titine's arm to draw her another way when a carriage drew up between them and the strange, muffled, invalid figure, and hid it from them. Inside the carriage two people. Both leaning forward as though looking at the old man. Opening the far door for him. There was no footman on the dicky seat to get down to open it. Nothing there but a black trunk, as sombre as the carriage, like a dark, cold shadow in the sunlight.

[90]

Kate looked away as they passed behind that black heaviness of leather and scarred, ancient varnish. And then, with a kind of shiver of curiosity looked to see what the old man was doing, and why the carriage had stopped. And stood, unable to move, to think, to say anything to Titine. The shepherd from the painting. From— the dream come back to her in an instant, clear, complete, at one and the same time wonderful and desolately frightening. The young shepherd with his beautiful, absorbed pure face, kneeling by the Crib. And in the next instant it was a young man like many young men, and nothing like the painting at all, except—except— and she forgot that there had been any sort of dream and only remembered the painting with a quick feeling of something like indignation at the likeness, as if the young man had tried to deceive her in some way. Tall, thin, pale, with dark hair that fell loosely and rather untidily across his forehead in a way that a poet might affect, but that made him look simply too young and countrified, Kate thought with scorn. And not very fashionably dressed, either. A kind of country-town air about his hat, and his dark brown coat, and his pantaloons, and his not completely London boots. And yet there was something about the way he stood so kindly and patiently by the old man, helping his slow and agonising progress up the lowered steps of the carriage, such courtesy in the bend of his head, the pressure of his hand beneath the grotesque, padded elbow of that dreadful figure, that Kate continued looking at him. Wondering if he was the old man's son—*Oh, no! not that!* she hoped for him—and was ashamed at the hope and suddenly very pleased to think that he must be the old man's son and was so bravely courteous, so good to him there in the street, so indifferent to what passers-by might think.

He is wonderfully good, Kate thought, and wished almost that she might tell him so, find a way of showing her recognition of his goodness by a look, the expression of her face.

"What we standin' here for?" Titine said. "Are yer still lookin' at 'im?"

"No!" Kate said. "No indeed I am not! Why should I stand looking at anyone? I was waiting for you, you are so dreamy and slow!"

"Me?" Titine cried indignantly, but before she could protest any more Kate had caught hold of her and dragged her along, away from the young man, and the carriage, and any further possibility of day-dreaming. But more than once in the next days and weeks Kate thought of that odd tableau, and its strange details. Once or twice she even thought for a moment that some young, tall man walking in front of her in the street, or in the crowd in the theatre, was the same one, and felt an odd quickening of interest as though to see him again might explain the mystery of that old, muffled man, and how such a father could have such a son. But she was deceived each time.

February became March. The cold returned, filled the streets with an icy wind, sleet, hail, snow flurries that turned to an ugly yellow slush at mid-day and froze by evening. Gales cried round the chimney pots, made the roof creak above their attic, rattled the small window as though wanting to drive it in against them. The too-early, pale green leaves on the trees shrivelled and died. *It will never be warm again,* Kate thought. *Perhaps in England it never does grow warm.* And she thought for the first time of France with a longing sadness—of the sun, and the spring flowers, and the blue sky. But people still came to the theatre, wanted hot pies more than ever. She had six guineas put away in a handkerchief. And Titine could spell "Titine" and "Kate" and "'Ang," although sometimes she got them mixed up.

"I shall buy 'Ang a flute," Kate promised herself. "The first fine day." Mr. Mendoza knew someone who dealt in musical instruments he said, although he was vague as to what a flute might cost, second-hand. Mr. Solomons, who had a professional grandeur to maintain, thought that it would cost at least two guineas for something worth-while.

It does not matter, Kate thought. *He shall have it all the same.*

The fine day came. As suddenly as the last, a fortnight before, had disappeared. In mid-morning, the clouds blown away. The sun bright, warm. The air dancing.

"We shall do something very special today!" Kate cried. "It is to be a surprise!" She made them hurry back from the market, and ran by herself up to the attic to fetch her handkerchief with the six guineas knotted inside it.

"Now! You are not even to ask where we are going. 'Ang, put down your stick. Come, come quick, Titine. Not a question, not a word till we get there."

She already had the directions from Mr. Mendoza. The other

side of Holborn. A street like a frontier between gentility and poverty. A narrow river of business, of old-fashioned shops with bottle-glass windows, and secret-seeming premises where clerks scratched at ledgers in deep shadows, no more than shadows themselves through the dusty green panes.

Impossible to tell what they were doing, or why, or what kind of business they conducted. And at the far end of the street, at the very beginnings of poverty, a pawnbroker's, with his three gilded globes remembering Florence and the Medici. A narrow window, a heap of violins, their cases ajar, flutes, bassoons, trumpets, hautboys, heaps of music in leather folders; deep inside the shop the glimmer of a spinet, a harpsichord, a harp, music stands, a drum. As though Mr. Mendoza's friend had longed to be a musician and, driven to pawnbroking, had yet bent his necessity towards his art, and served music by giving impoverished musicians loans on their instruments.

He must also give loans on other things, as they saw when they entered the shop. A shabby-genteel lady with her embarrassment hidden by the sides of her bonnet was fingering a gold watch and chain on the counter, reluctant to let go of it for what she had just been offered.

"Ten shillings and sixpence, Mr. Levi? Oh surely it is worth more than that? My husband paid—he told me that he paid——" She heard Kate and her companions entering, and her voice fell into a whisper. Kate made herself busy examining the spinet, and then the harp.

"What we doing here?" Titine said.

"Ssssh! Wait."

They did not have to wait long. Mr. Levi came round his counter, as unlike Mr. Mendoza as could well be, short and fat as a balloon, and as lightly dancing on small feet in black, varnished, glistening slippers. Fat round cheeks and a fluff of white hair supporting his embroidered black skull cap, a fluff of white beard on his fat round chin and his nose jutting out as rich and shining as if it were carved from the best butter, and on the point of melting. His eyes dark and liquid and luminous, seeming to brim over with his customers' tea s. He was heaving a great sigh for his last customer, now hastening from the shop with her half a guinea, her head bent in shame that anyone might see her leaving; shabby skirt, shabby boots, worn tippet, carefully-kept best bonnet. Kate had a moment's wish that they had not come there, felt as though behind every object in the shop there must be sorrow. But Mr. Levi, sensing a buyer and not a seller, had grown happy on the instant, and was touching the keys of the harpsichord with loving fingers, short and fat, running light as white mice on the keyboard, filling the shadows with the beginnings of an air, gay as a music box, and as sad as a music box playing alone in an empty room.

"What may I do for the young ladies?"

"We wanted to know—how much is a flute? A good one."

"'Ow much? Oy, oy, oy, there's a question! 'Ow good is good? 'Arf a guinea? Two? Three? You play the flute, little ma'am? Is it fer you?"

"For my friend." She pointed to 'Ang, and Mr. Levi, with no signs of astonishment, waddled lightiy, balloonly up to him as though he meant to measure him for the exact size and quality of flute that would go with his appearance, like a tailor with a suit of clothes. And intended then to float round him as he played it.

"For you? Ah. Ah. For you. Hmmmm." Mr. Levi bent himself into the piled treasures of the window, exposing a great rump of black breeches, rather worn and shiny, and came up breathlessly with a flute, black and silver, that he dusted on his sleeve, and flourished slightly in the air before offering it to 'Ang. And in the moment of 'Ang's taking it in his hands Kate determined that if it should cost twenty guineas she would somehow buy it for him. All his expression in his hands. His fingers so thin, yellow ivory, so gentle as they touched, curved over, held. Unbelieving. Like a lover touching his just-seen beloved. Lifting his eyes towards Kate, his mouth slightly open, as though if ever in his life it should be given to him to say a word, it would be then. And bending down his head again, lifting the mouthpiece, shaping his lips. Soft, soft notes. One by one.

"How much is that one?" Kate whispered to Mr. Levi.

"That one? Oy, oy, I'd 'ave to say one guinea—and a 'alf—one and a 'alf quid—not a penny less, I couldn't take. Such a beautiful instrument you don't find many places, young lady. Listen to 'im play it! Virtuosos should be glad to play that flute; Mozart should be glad to play it. One and a 'alf guineas the very least. And 'alf a guinea for the case. Eh?"

She could have bargained; one part of her mind told her that she

should. Two guineas! A third of her savings! She was mad, completely mad! And she saw 'Ang's face, his hands, heard the strange
music still echoing, fading, and untied her handkerchief with trembling fingers for fear that Mr. Levi should discover it was all a mistake, and that a beautiful flute such as this should really cost much
more.

She almost ran out of the shop with Titine and 'Ang, Mr. Levi's
gratitude and courtesies following them into the street. She did not
know what to say, and 'Ang could say nothing, and they hurried
along the pavement as though none of them could wait until they
were out of sight of the three golden balls of the pawnbroker's
shop.

"I have lots of money left!" Kate said at last, trying to sound gay
and careless about it. "Such a lot! What shall we do? Let us have a
holiday until tonight. We—oh, we shall find wonderful things to
do. We have not had a holiday at all, all these weeks of working."

It was not a very long holiday. But long enough to spend the
chief of another guinea. They wandered down the length of Lea-
denhall Market, to where the sideshows had their booths at the bottom, and saw the Irish giantess who was seven feet eight inches tall,
and had a beard. They saw the performing fleas that drew chariots
in a race across the lid of a box, and fought with swords. They
watched the strong man bend iron bars round the neck of a young
lady dressed in spangled tights. They had ice cream, and spruce
beer and lemonade, and grilled sausages, and cakes, and went into
a coffee-house and ordered hot chocolate and toasted cheese.
Three separate gentlemen made the most determined efforts to at-
tract their attention at different times during the day, one of them
very handsome in a new French hat and cream-coloured pantaloons, and all in all it was difficult to imagine a more successful
holiday. They bought ribands to re-decorate their hats, and wine
for supper, and a new piece of music for Mr. Solomons to teach to
'Ang—the only slight shadow on their happiness in returning to
Mr. Mendoza's house that they must go out again in an hour or two
to work in the theatre.

They ran down the cellar steps, Kate calling out "Mr. Mendoza!
Mr. Mendoza! Imagine what we have been doing all this time! I
give you a dozen guesses!"

He was in the doorway, waiting, his face grave. "There is someone here for you," he said. "To see you."

His face so grave, that all Kate's excitement died on her lips. "To see me?" she breathed. A dozen fears, each more frightening than the last. "Oh, what is it—what is wrong?"

He did not answer her, but drew her into the cellar that was so dark after the street, the sunlight, that she could see nothing at all. Until out of the shadows she began to distinguish the shape of a man sitting: a wide-brimmed hat, a bent and aged bulkiness, leaning both hands and chin on the handle of a stick. Even there in the half-dark of the cellar she could make out the green silk visor hanging like a curtain beneath the brim of the hat.

A shallow wheezing of breath, a rasping noise as the old man gathered his strength to speak. "Come in, Mademoiselle. Come close to me."

And there was no young man beside him, bending down by him in courtesy.

Chapter 7

Kate could not speak, could not move. She felt Titine beside her, heard her whisper something without knowing what it was. As though she had known, expected, waited for this—since— She tried to answer. The darkness of the shadow. The sense of being watched from the shadow, that horror of thinking that behind the veil, the green silk shade, there was nothing. Like an image of Death. Out of her nightmares. And it seemed to her in that instant that this figure had haunted all her dreams since Callac, that she had known it would at last take shape. She felt a terror beyond reason. Like a sickness that took her strength. If she had tried to move, she would have fallen.

"What are you afraid of, Mademoiselle?" the old voice whispered, rasping, wheezing with the effort to breathe. The invisible hands clasped on the handle of the stick, propping the figure up.

"There is nothing there!" her mind cried. "It is a nightmare. I shall wake, I shall wake!"

"I have come here to be your friend," the whisper said. "Your benefactor. Ask Mr. Mendoza. Do not be afraid, my dear."

She managed to turn her head. The old Jew standing wretchedly, looking at her. "This is not my doing," he said. "But you must listen to him."

Titine's hand feeling its way into hers.

"Little Tit," the shadow whispered. "Mrs. Sullivan's little orphan girl. She misses you, my dear. Oh, dreadfully."

"NO!" Kate cried. "NO, NO!"

"Then come and stand in front of me, Mademoiselle. Listen to me. Let me be your friend. You need a friend, you know."

As though the voice, the whispering, drew her of itself. Step by step. Until she was almost within touching distance of the soft, shapeless bulk. The outline of the wide-brimmed hat lifting, to allow the hidden eyes to peer up at her through the green silk shade.

"If he touches me—I shall die—I shall die."

"I know all about you, my dear. You are in danger. Will you allow me to be your friend?"

Her mouth so dry that her tongue would not answer, would not move. Her lips opening but no sound coming.

"You are to be arrested, my dear. For entering the country secretly, against the law. Do you know what they will do with you then?"

Mr. Mendoza caught her before she fell. "How can you do this to her?" he said.

"But I wish only to help her," the old voice wheezed. "Set her down by me. There." The sound of Mr. Mendoza pushing heaped clothes onto the stone floor, clearing a space on the wooden bench beside the old, crippled man. Kate felt his presence near to her, heard the rasp of his breath. Heard the thick rustling of cloth, as he moved his arm. His hand fell on her knee, a dead, soft weight inside the black glove. Without strength. Without movement once it rested there. Heavy and dead.

"Now we can talk."

She managed to whisper at last, "Who are you? What do you want?"

"A friend. A friend. Who wants to help you. Do not be afraid, my dear. If you do what I tell you, you shall come to no harm at all. I shall protect you. They call me the Squire, do they not, Mr. Mendoza? Because I am able to protect my friends. Is that not so, Mr. Mendoza?"

The old Jew bent his head reluctantly.

"You see, my dear? Now, you are not still afraid?"

"If you truly are a friend," she said, her body rigid under the weight of his hand, the horror of that hidden face beside her, "then—then leave me as—as I am. I want for nothing."

"Except safety, my dear. I have told you. You will be arrested. Within the day. Tonight. Unless—" The hand lifting, touching her face, turning it towards him. Like being held by a soft cushion of wool, no more than padding. She thought for a second that behind the veil, deep inside the shadows under the brim of the hat, she could see the glisten of eyes, and then there was nothing there

[98]

again. Nothing. "It is only just, that if I protect you, you should make me a return. Is not that just?"

She wanted to scream, to tear his gloved hand away from her face. Felt herself growing so weak that even to sit upright on the bench would become impossible, and she would fall against him, slide down onto her knees, fall against those wrapped and bandaged legs hidden now under the folds and skirts of the brown camlet coat. She shut her eyes against him, tried to pray, as if praying could protect her from him.

"My dear, my dear," he wheezed, whispered. She felt that he could read her thoughts, see every shadow of terror passing across her mind. "I want only to employ you. And you shall be well paid. Well protected. No one will dare to touch you. No one will think of arresting you. Now, can you listen? I want you to do no more than be my messenger. A messenger I may trust. Bound to me by gratitude."

"I do not want——"

"But I do, my dear. I need someone like you at this moment. And you need me. Now, is that not a basis for good employment? How shall you like to earn two and three guineas a week? Besides your present employment in the theatre?"

She tried to answer, to understand what he was saying.

"For no more than carrying a parcel here or there. Or a letter. Or fetching one. And always to feel safe! To feel that I—or someone belonging to me—is watching over you, protecting you. You may not know that anyone is there. But you shall not move a step that I do not know of. Now, will not that make you feel secure?"

"Please," she whispered. "I beg of you—what harm have I—"

"Who is speaking of harm? You should be happy. This is a day for you to celebrate. Come, do we understand one another? Are we agreed?"

He pretended to take her silence for agreement, moved her head gently with his hand. A hint of bone and muscle under the padding, inside the softness of the woollen glove. "You will receive your instructions always in my name, but not often from me. A lady, sometimes. Or a gentleman. They will tell you 'The Squire wishes you to do such and such.' And you will do it, and when it is done, you will be paid. What is so terrible in that, eh? Let me see a smile." Patting against her cheek. "And not a word of it, ever. You

[99]

understand that? Because just as I shall be watching over you, I shall be listening too. And those who work for me must be silent. How happy I am that we are so well agreed. Tit? Give me your shoulder so that I may stand up."

Soft whistling of breath, wheezing, the rustling of cloth, the tap of the crutch-handled stick on the cellar floor. Kate stayed sitting where he left her. Titine and 'Ang helping the gross figure to the doorway, Mr. Mendoza standing aside. The doorway darkened. They were gone. Kate heard the slow climbing of the cellar steps and still Mr. Mendoza stood miserably apart from her, looking neither at her nor at the doorway, as though afraid of moving, of being heard if he should say anything. Old, black-gaberdined, helpless. It seemed a long time before Titine and 'Ang came back again. And yet it was only a few moments. Long enough to climb slowly up to the level of the lane; to watch the old man begin to shuffle away into the darkness; to run down. They came running, Titine breathless. She did not ask anything, only stood waiting, as if she were poised to run again, her hands joined together, her eyes huge in the pallor of her face under the hood of her pelisse. Mr. Mendoza came slowly towards Kate and put his hand on her shoulder.

"It was not my doing," he said. "Please, please believe that."

"Who—what is he?" she whispered, not able to look at him. As though the life had gone out of her.

"I do not know. Except—"

"Yes?"

"That—people obey him."

"Why? Why does he want—if it is so simple—if there is no danger, why does he want anyone—"

Mr. Mendoza shrugged again. "How can I answer you? One hears—one hears many things. They may not be true." He smoothed his beard down the black front of his kaftan, combed the soft grey-white hair of his beard with slow, apologetic fingers. He seemed to come to a decision, and sat down on the bench by her. "They say," he said carefully, in his slow Provençal, "that he represents a company of smugglers. When they have quantities of goods, he arranges for them to be sold. For this, he needs messengers. To deliver parcels, to fetch payment, as he has described to you. If a messenger should be caught, he has lost something, but not everything. Not even a great deal. Do you understand? And the messengers know almost nothing. They cannot injure him in any way."

"But—but why me? Why me? Why does he want—?"

"Because you will be in his power, child. He can injure you at any moment, but you cannot injure him. You do not know his name, or where he lives, or even his appearance except his dress. Is that not so? And it will always be so. If you should have a sum of his money, and try to run off with it—"

"But I should not!"

"Of course—of course—but he requires to be sure."

"You know a—great deal of him?" She turned it into a question from an accusation.

"A little," Mr. Mendoza said, not meeting her eyes. "But I swear to you I told him nothing of you. He has many people to tell him what he may wish to know."

"And these—goods? What are they?"

The old, yellow hands spread out, palm upwards. "Whatever may carry a heavy tax. Tea. Brandy. Silk. Tobacco. Tea that here in London costs eight shillings the pound when tax is paid may be bought in Hamburg for a shilling, or a shilling and two pence. There is a great profit in it. And no doubt there are other things as profitable. Since the troubles in France—the war—there must be many things—"

She said nothing, and he laid his hand on her arm very gently. "Poor child. Poor child." He hesitated, and seemed to make up his mind again to go on. "If—it is hard to advise you—but if—you have it in mind to run away from here—"

"To run away?"

"I do not suggest it. I say only 'If.' If you decide on it—"

"Where—where is there to run to?"

"I do not know, my dear. I can offer you little in the way of advice. But money—that I could lend to you—"

Kate put her fingers over his, stared at nothing. "What would he do then?"

"I cannot tell."

"I must—I must try to think—I—" She heard a church clock striking seven. Counted the strokes with a clarity of mind like illness that gives to small things a vast importance. Seven. It was growing late. The theatre. To run away—Titine—And 'Ang.

She stood up. What would they do? Go where? *I must get ready to go out again,* she thought. *The theatre. What shall I do?* Three guineas. To have spent all that money only today. And now—She tried

[101]

to smile. As if it mattered, as if three guineas could make a difference to what had happened, to what would happen.

She went out into the small, rear courtyard, and up the wooden stairs, wet with rain and shining, black and shining. Tea? Silk? Why her? Why her? It had almost a sound of innocence about it. Tea. Silk. Tobacco. Brandy. She thought of the smugglers who had brought her from Brittany. Of the King of Prussia who had given her the handful of guineas, the clothes. Was it he—? Who had told—? Did he send goods to London—to this old man to sell for him? And the young man?

She stood in the middle of her room, looking round it. Bed. Window. Carpet. Stove. Table. To run away. He had seemed so good a man, the King. And the men who had brought her—how could it end like this? An old man wrapped up like—like death. But where could she run? Where? To live day and night expecting, waiting—to think at every corner of the street—at every knock—

She heard a movement behind her, the softest of footsteps. It was Titine. Saying nothing, only watching her.

"We must go to the theatre," Kate said, half aloud, for the sake of breaking the silence. Titine nodded, waiting. Kate wanted to cry out, "What shall I do? What can I do?" And felt for the first time the full meaning of loneliness—that to have the child stand watching her, waiting for what she would say, what she might decide, was lonelier than to have no one at all. And for a moment she was almost angry with Titine that she was there, that she existed, and then in a passion of guilt, of love, of what love should be, she caught the child in her arms.

"What shall we do?" she whispered, again only for the sake of speaking, but no longer feeling so alone, so despairing. Almost wanting to confess how she had felt for that one fraction of a moment; to make amends for it.

"'E don't reely want you to go to prison?" Titine said, her voice half lost against Kate's shoulder.

"No," Kate said. "Don't be afraid. It is only—"

"I tell yer something," Titine whispered. "'E ain't so old as 'e looks. Nor 'e ain't crippled."

"Not—how do you know?" As though it made any difference.

"We was watchin' 'im go off. 'E didn't think we was still there an' 'e started to 'urry. 'E looked back an' didn't see us, nor anyone in the lane an'—an' then 'e went 'urrying like 'e wasn't crippled at all.

What you done, Kate?" Not asking reproachfully, but as if everyone must have done something that merited prison, and she was only anxious to know what it was that Kate was guilty of.

"I have done nothing," Kate said. "Nothing bad—I do not think it is really bad." She tried to explain, and Titine stared at her. It was difficult to know if such words as "France" and "the sea" had any meaning for the child. "And he did not seem truly old?" she said, giving up the attempt at explanation. She was unsure whether that made him more frightening or less. Wondered for a second if the old man—the man—had perhaps meant to be seen hurrying like that.

Titine shook her head, still studying Kate's eyes as if to find the secret there. But even without understanding, it seemed to bring her much closer to Kate; another barrier of her child's unchildish reserve yielding as if she felt now that she understood Kate better, began to understand her. And Kate saw, sensed it, and was half-touched, half-hurt that she must seem a criminal before she could win more of the child's trust.

"We must go," she said abruptly, wanting to be busy, to have something clear and easy to occupy her mind. At least tonight. At the end of it she should have more money, another guinea, twenty-five shillings. And Mr. Mendoza? To borrow from him—And in her mind she cried out in rage, in despair, "Why? WHY? Why cannot I be left in peace?"

She went down the stairs thinking that if it was to be lived through again she would defy the man, would not be weak, and terrified. Let him do his worst. *I am English,* she thought. *How can they really punish me for—?* And checked her steps as she came into the cellar, afraid for the instant that he might have come back, be waiting; feeling her heart beat as if it was truly to be lived through again and her new courage tested. But there was only Mr. Mendoza, avoiding her eyes. She did not speak to him, or to Titine on the way to the theatre, and to collect their baskets of hot pies and cakes, except to bid her to hurry, to keep close. 'Ang followed them with the sack of oranges across his shoulders, his flute in its black, shabby case pushed inside his shirt, one hand protecting it from every possibility of harm.

And during the length of the evening, whenever Kate went to the doorkeeper's room to refill her basket, 'Ang was crouched there, playing his music, and the doorkeeper, instead of reading his paper, was sitting with one elbow on his knee, his eyes shut, listening. Their peacefulness, their happiness, enraged her, and then again made her feel ashamed of her rage. She could have laid her forehead against the walls of the passage and cried aloud, "What shall I do? What shall I do?" Until close to the end of the night's work she had almost made up her mind to go, to leave next day. *For Bristol,* she thought, knowing no more of Bristol than of any other place.

She was in the passage behind the private boxes, wanting to be quiet for a moment, to think. A woman came towards her, tall, thin, dressed in black. A widow's bonnet and veil. Wide black skirts of old-fashioned appearance brushing both sides of the corridor. Kate pressed herself against the wall to let her by. But instead of passing her the woman stopped and pointed at Kate's basket on the floor beside her.

"Give me an orange," she said. "For the Squire."

Kate stopped halfway bent down. Her face close to the black stuff of the woman's skirt, the black cotton glove still pointing. The glove touched her shoulder. "Be quick, my dear. I have instructions for you. Pick up your basket. Offer it to me."

Kate obeyed as though she were mesmerised. Had no will. The woman took an orange, gave a coin in exchange. "Here is a guinea," she said, her voice low, and at the same time cold and clear. "Take a hackney coach tomorrow morning. Use it to collect your oranges from the market. Then go to number three Mecklenburgh Street, and ask for Mr. Thomas. He will give you your instructions."

Before Kate could answer, protest, say that she did not mean to obey, the woman was walking away, down the corridor, her skirts brushing and whispering, her back very straight and thin, and severe. Like the blackness of her clothes, the coldness of her voice. Kate looked at the guinea in her hand and then closed her fingers hurriedly, almost afraid to look at it.

I shall not! she thought. Took a step after the woman, almost called, "Stop! Please!" But the woman was gone. The guinea lay warm in Kate's hand. She went down the corridor in the direction the woman had taken, down the stairs. She was not there. Nor there. Nor— She saw her in the foyer, hurried towards her, "Madame! Ma'am!" The woman turned, an air of cold surprise, displeasure.

"I cannot," Kate whispered to her, holding out the guinea as though she was giving a customer forgotten change.

"Do you see the man by the doors into the auditorium?" the woman said. Kate looked and saw. A man with a thick body and massive jaws. A blue coat that seemed bursting across the shoulders. A heavy stick in his hand. A low-crowned hat. Glancing towards them, towards Kate, his eyes small, deep set under a thick, bony ridge of eyebrows. A face of unthinking brutality, a repressed and waiting anger in it, like a bull in a field getting ready to charge at anything, so long as it moves.

"He is from Bow Street," the woman said. "A police officer. Shall I leave you to him? If I beckon him, he will come."

"No!"

"Then do as you are told. If you are foolish again, you will be punished. Take the change, my dear," she said in a louder tone, "you may keep it." She turned away.

Kate stood, afraid to move, afraid to look at that waiting figure, expecting hands to grip hold of her in the next instant. A man asked for an orange. She could not understand what he was saying, and he had to repeat it. An old customer, who knew her well. Laughing at her for being in love, for dreaming. Giving her sixpence for herself. Patting her cheek. When she could make herself look again, the man in the blue coat was no longer by the doorway.

Chapter 8

Mecklenburgh Street. Number 3. A book-seller's, with bow windows on either side of a white-painted door. A man standing on the upper step, looking about him with an idle air. A gentleman-like sort of man, in a beaver hat, a moderately fashionable green coat and white pantaloons. Looking at Kate's hackney-coach as it drove up. An idle, quizzical air. Of being casually interested in all that passed in the street. He came down the steps, sauntering towards the coach as it stopped, seeming to expect her. Looking in through the glass at her as she sat alone, rigid with fear. Titine and 'Ang left behind, to walk home to Mr. Mendoza's, in case—in case—

"Looking for someone, ma'am?" the gentleman said, raising his hat. His face less gentleman-like than his general appearance. A sharpness in the blue eyes, a sunburn on the cheeks and lowish forehead, a hardness to the mouth. Scars of smallpox like shallow pits in the thickened skin.

"A—Mr. Thomas—I was told to—" All her expectations destroyed. It was not him. The young man.

All the way there she had thought: *It will be—the young man who was with the Squire in the street.* Thought it with rage, with preparations of fury, of the scorn and hatred she would show to him, the contempt. To deceive—to wear that shepherd-angel's face, that mask of purity and courtesy, and to be this! A smuggler's bully, the Squire's tout and creature! Practising in her mind how she would burn him to the soul with her contempt.

"Your sarvant, ma'am." The coach door opening. The man jumping in. Nothing like the young man she had been preparing for. A swift muscularity about his movements. A brutality of confidence that said, "Right, my dear. Sit tight and quiet there, or else—!" Against her will she made a swift movement of fear, almost cried out. Her preparations useless, futile. The man smiled at her, his teeth startling white in the shadows of the coach interior. "No one following you, eh? Drive on, coachman. The Strand."

The coach creaked into renewed movement, the man sitting opposite to her. He leaned towards her, but only to look over her shoulder through the rear glass. Said nothing until they had turned one corner, and begun to turn another. "All clear, seemingly. So you're the new post-girl? Give us a look at you."

He took her chin between hard fingers, turned her head one way and then the other. Looked into her eyes. "Aye, you look honest enough." He laughed, as though struck by the irony of his judgement. "Are you afraid?"

She nodded, unable to do more than nod.

He put his hand inside his coat, drew something out. "Show me your fingers."

Hesitating, uncertain of what he meant, what he wanted, she put out her own hand towards his. Afraid either to obey or disobey, fear growing in her by the second. The man's strength and air of power seeming to fill the coach, dominate her. Her hand on her knee, on the white muslin of her skirt, palm down, fingers slowly straightening. He took her wrist, turned it, turned her palm upward. "Look," he said. His other hand laid something light and cold and hard across her palm. A razor. Open. The blade silver bright. Black handle. Light and cold.

"Are you afraid of that?"

She could not so much as nod. Could not swallow. Could not breathe. She wanted to shut her eyes against the sight of it, and dared not.

"If you closed your hand," he said, "if you jerked it away, it'd cut you. But if you stay quite still, it'll do you no harm at all. D'you understand me?"

She shook her head, wanted to scream, would have given everything she possessed for the luxury of fainting. And at the thought of fainting with that man sitting opposite to her she almost fainted in reality.

"That's your position with us," he said. "With the Squire. If you stay good and quiet, if you do as you're told, you'll be safe. If you try tricks—why then—" He picked up the razor, drew the edge of the blade across two of her finger-tips, very lightly. She felt nothing, almost nothing. But threads of scarlet appeared on the flushed, delicate skin. She swayed forward, felt sick. He pushed her back into her seat, swung himself round to sit beside her. "Now we understand one another, eh? We shall be good friends when we meet again." He laughed. Put her finger-tips to his mouth. "There. The blood's gone. Don't look so white! A man nicks himself worse than that two and three times every morning when he shaves. But remember it." The voice hard again. He drew his finger-nail across her cheek. "Remember it if—you're ever tempted to play tricks. I get down here. Tell your driver to take you to Devon Place. Number eleven. Ask again for Mr. Thomas."

He was gone. Kate sat trying to recover. The coachman, who had halted to let the man get down, waited for her to give him new instructions. She managed to say them aloud, her voice breathless, so frightened that she thought, "He will notice, he will question me," but either he noticed nothing, or in his years as a driver of hackneys he had seen too many strange things to be surprised at anything. He only repeated the address, and whipped up his bony horses into motion.

One bright red drop of blood on one finger-tip. Like a living thing. On the other only the faintest of red lines. She watched the drop grow slowly greater. It would mark her skirt. Kate felt for her handkerchief, closed it round both fingers. It would have been a luxury to cry. She could still feel the man's presence. The nail against her cheek. His lips against her fingers, warm, smooth. The one touch as frightening as the other. And again she felt a rage at her helplessness, a fury that she should be so used. She wanted to beat her fists on something, anything, against the cold leather of the seat on either side of her. And must sit still, in case the coachman should hear her, and think she had lost her wits. Like a hare caught in a net. Caught tighter at every move, every struggle.

If I were a man! she thought. Imagined for a moment being a man. To be strong. To fight. And remembered Callac again. The crypt. The old Vicomte, pacing, pacing. The Abbé. The egg-seller. The man who died in the crypt, lying on the stone floor. And the others. As though some were marked out by—by what? By whom? God? To be hunted. No matter what they did. Or were they guilty first? Of what, of what? She put up her hands against her face, felt the cloth of the handkerchief. The red stain had come through the cambric, the lace edging. Had it stained her cheek?

The coach swaying, turning. An archway. It lay between two houses in a street of which she noticed only the leaning fronts of the houses, a shop window, a hanging sign in the shape of a once-gilded boot, the gilding long ago turned greenish black; an air of decay, of cramped age. The sides of the archway cutting off her view of the street. She was in a courtyard, surprisingly great. Spreading out on either hand, in front of the coach. Like the yard of a large farmhouse. Stables and sheds surrounding it. And more surprising still, a house there, to the right. Very old. White plaster. Black timber. Old windows with diamond panes. Brick chimneys twisting up from the steep roof. Like a country house caught in a network of city streets, its farmlands built on, only the wide farm-yard and the outbuildings surviving.

Kate did not examine her impressions, merely felt them, felt the surprise, the air of countryness, of strangeness. And thought again, without anger this time, only with an ache of wretchedness, *Perhaps he is here.* The young man who had seemed to carry that air of countryness in his clothes and bearing. A dog baying, a brown mastiff chained to a huge barrel that lay on its side by one of the stable doorways. Someone came out of the stable—but not the young man—a tall, stout man in black knee boots and white breeches and yellow waistcoat; boots and breeches stained with muck and straw as though he had been cleaning out. Stout and round-featured and wearing a bob wig that he pushed aside with a big hand to scratch at his scalp. Behind him two other men, rougher dressed in fustian, shirtsleeved, with handkerchiefs knotted loosely round their necks, one of them swinging a heavy cudgel by a thong at his wrist. They leaned in the stable doorway beside the mastiff, while the big man came rolling forward, pulling a great blue and yellow spotted handkerchief from inside his waistcoat and mopping at his face.

Kate let down the glass, her heart beating as if it were trying to escape. "Mr. Thomas?" she whispered.

He came and leaned his hand against the door of the coach, look-ing up at her. "Aye. Aye, little maid. An' who do you be from if I might be so bold as to ax?" His face seemed meant to be rosy, cheerful, as countryfied as the yard and timbered house. But it was London yellowish, like old tallow. She guessed the sense of his words rather than understanding them.

"From the—the Squire."

"Oh, aye, we bin expecting you." In spite of his complexion, he did not remotely have a London voice. "You do ha' come for some paassels, eh? Bob! John! Here's our party. Fetch the stuff out to us."

The dog had grown quiet, but stood watching with lowering suspicion. Its muzzle scarred and misshapen, one ear torn in half. The two men disappeared, to come out again, the one carrying a small wooden chest that seemed to have great weight in it, the other with bales of what might be cloth, one under each arm. Without a word to her, scarcely a look, they loaded them inside the coach, "Mr. Thomas" holding the door open for them. Kate shrank back as far as she could into the corner, the chest touching her skirt, her slipper. The bales on the seat beside her. "Mr. Thomas" looked at her, his eyes shrewd, amused at her fear. The men brought out a much larger chest, loaded it at the back, on the dicky seat.

"There you be, little maid. And still alive, eh? All for the one gentleman this time. Mr. Ed'ard Ponsonby, Esquire. Care o' Jardine's Bank, Cheapside. Can you remember, eh, without that bein' wrote down?"

She nodded, not trusting her voice. Afraid to look at him. Afraid even to seem afraid. To touch the bales. What were they?

"Cheapside," cried "Mr. Thomas" to the coachman. "Jardine's Bank. The far end, you'll find 'em. Wurrdee about wi' em bor."

Phlegmatic in his black, droop-brimmed hat, his greenish-black coat with its double cape, like the driver of a hearse, the coachman jerked at the driving reins, flourished his whip slowly in the air as if to crack it was too much effort for the little he would be paid at the morning's end, and swung the coach about. The mastiff bayed again, seeing the intruding horses begin to move. "Mr. Thomas" saluted Kate, irony in his smile. The two men in shirtsleeves watched without expression, idly powerful. The archway. The grey, aged street. A boy bowling his hoop down the gutter, welcoming spring. An old, bent woman with a basket.

More streets. Traffic. Kate afraid to look at the bales. At the chests. Moving her slippered feet away from the hard corners. One hand slowly moving sideways, touching the rough sacking covers, pressing. Impossible to tell what was inside. Cloth? Silk? Holding her breath, wanting to turn round, to look out of the spy window to see if they were being followed, watched. Afraid to move. The shadow of the coachman's black, impassive back, seen from below through the front glass. Her heart beating, beating. And the chest? If she were stopped? She shut her eyes. Expected at every second that voices would shout, "Halt! Halt there!" What would they do to her? And for a guinea! One guinea, out of which she must pay this coach!

She became so angry that her fear lessened—in a furious corner of her mind she would almost have welcomed being stopped and searched so that they might lose their bales and the chests that they were afraid to carry themselves to their destination. The cowards! The cowards! To force her to do it! For a guinea! Less! The coach halting at a corner, a man looking in the window at her as he crossed the street, smiling at seeing her alone. Or at—was there purpose in his smile? His look?

They are following me, she thought. *They themselves. To make certain—* She clenched her hands in her lap, twisting the blood-stained scrap of cambric between her fingers. Thought of the razor, the touch of the steel against skin, flesh, the sting of it felt only long afterwards. His nail against her face—And she could not help imagining the razor there. As he had meant her to imagine—

The streets narrower, crowded. More halting. Jerking forward. Halting again. The driver banging on the roof with the handle of his whip. "Jardine's Bank 'ere, ma'am."

She must get down. Enquire. No shops in the street. Tall, narrow houses. Stone steps up to the doorways. The windows narrow, dusty, the lower halves of them curtained with green cloth, or boarded behind so that passers by might not see in through them. Tea merchants. Insurance. Jardine's. "Wm. Jardine & Son and Thos. Fordyce Partners. Banking and Brokerage. Foreign Bills discounted." Painted in gold lettering on the black board that muffled the bottom of the high window.

"You best 'urry," the coachman said. "I can't wait 'ere, blocking the way."

Kate went up the steps, through a door. Into a passage. Another door, standing open to her left. Clerks on high stools, scratching of quills, a low whispering of numbers: "Three thousand and eleven, five and seven, two thousand one hundred and ninety-six, eight and four pence ha'penny, four hundred and——"

The counting stopped. She had pushed the door slightly, tapped on it. The clerks turned their heads. Perched on their stools like grey parrots chained to wooden stands. Quills poised. She took half a step inside. Only a small room. She had expected something large, grand. A Bank? This? A youngish, reddish, wolfish clerk, seated not on a high stool but on a chair set on a dais, peered at her, gnawing the end of his grey-white quill.

"Yus?" Judging from her timidity that she was not a customer, a "Miss," a "Ma'am." "Looking for some'un?" Sandy red hair, a skinned and mottled red-white face, as though he had shaved so close that he had removed the top layer of his skin and here and there the blood was visible in irregular patches. Gapped yellow teeth, small and chisel-like as he made the sketch of a smile before resuming his ill-treatment of the pen. "Come in, come in."

"I am looking for—I have a—several parcels for Mr. Edward Ponsonby. I—was given this direction to bring them to."

"Ah!" the clerk—chief clerk? Surely a chief clerk from his chair, his dais?— "Ponsonby, eh? Ah, yus. We been expecting 'em. Where are they?"

He had dropped his quill on the small deal table in front of him and was coming down onto the floor. "Outside are they?"

"In the coach."

" 'Eavy?"

She nodded.

"Pettigrew!" the clerk shouted. "Masters, Sanderson! Outside with you double quick, bring in some deliveries."

Three of the five clerks dropped their pens obediently, clambered down, eyeing Kate, eyeing their overseer, their shoulders still bent as though it would be disrespectful in a bank to straighten up one's back in business hours. But a small air of holiday about them, as they prepared to go out into the street, into the air. "Show us where," the chief clerk said. And eyeing Kate himself he said by way of introduction, "*Mister* Foster. 'Ead clerk 'ere. An' 'ow do you call yourself?" As an afterthought he said "Miss." Like the other clerks he wore paper cuffs, jotted with scored-out calculations. They rattled as he adjusted them, offering her his hand.

"My name is Harriott," she said, uncertain whether she should tell it here.

They were on the pavement, two clerks carrying in the bales and the small chest, the third staggering under the weight of the larger chest, his breath gasping.

[112]

"Let yer coach go," Mr. Foster said to Kate. "We'll 'ave another fetched for you. Mr. Jardine may want to see yer a minute." It was only then that the name reminded her. Madame Pariglia's Mister Jardine also was a banker. Could they be the same? She felt for her purse.

"Allow *me!*" Mr. Foster said. "'Ow much, Jehu?"

"Four an' a tanner, guv'nor."

With a handsome flourish Mr. Foster gave him five shillings. "Keep the differ." The coach drove away.

"If you'll jus' sign a receipt for that afore you goes." A familiar hand on Kate's arm. "An' what brings a pretty young miss delivering parcels, eh? Not but what you ain't a welcome change."

He had the look in his eyes of a young man who fancies his appearance and its effect on young women. A dandyishness about his cravat, his pale mauve underwaistcoat, his beige nankeen pantaloons. Even the creak of his black and glossy slippers had a self-satisfied tone about it. The tip of his nose was gristle-white, quivering, as if he were sniffing her scent. Like a fox.

"The Squire 'as funny ways, eh?" he whispered, winking his lashless eyelids.

She did not like his holding her arm, and tried to think of a way of disengaging herself without offending him. His hand seemed very hot, to be sweating, so that her sleeve grew damp where he was grasping her. He paused with her in the doorway, directing the under clerks as they stowed the chests and bales in a corner.

"Ponsonby, eh? Ha! So you're the Squire's new 'un? Oh, 'e's a cunning ol' devil. A girl, eh?" He pushed her to arm's length, admiring her and the Squire's cunning in one foxy, wolfish glance. "You keep that touch-me-not look an' you'll do all right. Oh Lord, 'oo'd 'ave thought—'oo'd think—?A girl. Come up an' I'll tell Mr.J. you're 'ere, an' the stuff is 'ere. Lord, oh Lord. The ol' devil!"

Still holding fast to her arm he drew her along a brief corridor and up a flight of stairs to a landing. "You wait 'ere," he said. He knocked on a door and, with no more than a token pause, went in. A moment or two later the foxy head reappeared, still triumphant with mottled pleasure, the gap-teeth smiling. Beckoned.

The room behind the door was dark-panelled, a fire burning in distrust of the spring day, a man standing beside it, another man sitting in a great wing chair behind a handsome table. His face in shadow until he leaned forward, half rose at her entry. The old gentleman of the theatre, recognising her in the same moment that she recognised him, the strangest of complicated expressions coming into his face, smoothing away in almost the moment of appearing. Surprise. Guilt. Pleasure. Conspiracy. All smoothing away into a mild and welcoming interest.

"I think that I have had the honour of meeting this young lady on other occasions," he said, his tone conveying that there was no guilt, no conspiracy; only surprise and pleasure. And was even the surprise real? "Do not imagine that you take me at any disadvantage," his tone said, his eyes conveyed. "Mr. Oliver, Miss Katherine Harriott if I have the name correctly? A most industrious young lady. Most trustworthy. Well, well. So you have brought us Mr. Ponsonby's effects? How kind. Let me present to you Mr. Oliver, our Manager."

Mr. Oliver, with markedly less enthusiasm, made a slight bow. "Honoured, ma'am."

Kate had already made her curtseys and stood not knowing quite what to do, what might be expected. She had the feeling that the old man, and Mr. Foster, whatever about Mr. Oliver, were concealing an amusement connected with her that she did not understand. Had it been Mr. Jardine who had told the Squire about her?

"Well, well, well," Mr. Jardine said again. "So all is in order, is it, Foster? Mr. Ponsonby will be pleased." He put two fingers into his waistcoat pocket. "You will need coach fare home, no doubt. Foster will call a hackney for you when you are ready. Well, well." He held out his hand. Kate took it reluctantly. Sensed rather than saw the colour of gold. A guinea. And almost against her will felt a lightening of heart, a sudden warmth towards these three men, or at least two of them, who seemed so pleased with her, and with what she had brought them. She wondered if Mr. Ponsonby existed at all, except in pretence. In case she had been stopped—and the lightening of her spirits hesitated.

But she had not been stopped. And she had two guineas. Two guineas! For one morning! And again against her will, against her common sense, she had a feeling of having done well, of having deserved. Mr. Foster brought her out of the room, down the stairs. A few steps before they reached the level of the clerks' office room he stopped her, turning her round to face him.

[114]

"An' where did you meet the old gentleman before, if I may hask—arsk—an inquisitive question? Eh?" The white gristle of the tip of his nose twitching, the almost hairless eyebrows rising up above the cunningly innocent, muddy-green eyes. The gapped teeth small and yellow and sharp and hungry. Wolfish again, even more than foxy. Kate did not know what to answer for a moment. She wished, belatedly, that she had not given him her real name. But Mr. Jardine had already known it, would have told him. Had told him. And if Mr. Jardine was willing to admit that he already knew her—

"In the theatre," she said. "We—have seen each other once or twice."

"Oh? The *theatre*, eh?" The tip of the nose closer to her, the hand almost kneading the flesh of her arm, hot and damp. As though somehow he was taking possession of her, had already acquired rights. "An' what theatre might that be?"

She wanted to say, "Why do not you ask Mr. Jardine?" He saw her renewed caution, drew her closer to him by the arm so that she was obliged to bend slightly towards him, his mouth against her ear, his breath warm, unpleasantly warm against her skin. "Becoming a sportive old gentleman, ain't he? 'Aving his second youth so to speak, eh?"

Kate's face burned. She drew herself back from him, furious. Even then he did not let go of her, continued smiling. "No offense hintended," he said. "Not a atom of offense." The teeth remained smiling, but not the eyes. "Just the fond interest of a loyal employee, that's all. There ain't anyone in this 'ouse more fond of the old gentleman than what I am. Nor more devoted to 'is hinterests. A friend of yours, per'aps? The hattraction, I mean, at this theatre what we're speaking of? A actress? Or a dancer?"

"You have no right to question me like this! Let me go!"

"Rights? Of course not! 'Oo's claiming rights? Just hinterest. No more than hinterest! What a colour you 'ave when you gets hangry! It suits you, my dear. Velvety. Proper velvety. I flatters myself I 'ave a hartist's eye for a pretty girl."

But he let go of her arm, and in another two or three minutes she was free of him, escaping into Cheapside after signing the scrap of paper to say that he had spent five shillings for her coach fare. He had wanted to send for another coach for her, but she refused, and she was in the street, in the sunshine, two guineas the richer and with a breathless feeling of excitement growing and growing in her mind that perhaps it was not disaster but good fortune that the old man with the green eye shade and the stick had brought to her. Two guineas! Two guineas! And if there was anything so terrible, so dangerous about it, surely a banker, an old gentleman like Mr. Jardine, would have nothing to do with it? The clerk—Mr. Foster—even he— She did not like him, she did not like him at all—but he did not seem the kind of man to risk—The head clerk in a bank—he would not need to risk—

A little danger—there must be a little danger, but— Her spirits rose and fell with her steps as she hurried, now thinking of the danger, that she would not allow herself to become more involved, no matter what they said, what they did—and then of the man who had got into the coach with her—so that she began almost to run, her heart beating, as if there were somewhere safe that she might run to. And next thinking of old Mr. Jardine, of the hidden amusement she had sensed in him; of the guineas. He could not wish to harm her—could not. And the man in the stable-yard—he had not seemed cruel, or bad. Like the smugglers. Had they not helped her, been kind, more than kind to her? Done for her what no law-abiding men would have done? Even the sense she had of being watched—the threat the Squire had made—the proofs of it—were only half frightening—half almost reassuring—like once more being the member of a company. Only a different kind of company. They could not—surely they could not wish harm to her? Why should they? Would it not mean that they would lose whatever they had trusted to her? Even—even the young man was a kind of reassurance. He could not—with that face, that air of kindness to someone so old and ugly, he could not be truly, completely wicked? It was indeed a very wicked business—perhaps—but if there were some—some kind—good-seeming people connected with it, it could not—could not be entirely wicked, surely? Nor too greatly dangerous?

Her eye was caught by a chip bonnet in a milliner's window. On a wax head! A—she stopped to look. Like a real head! With blonde curls and painted features and the most superior of smiles. Such a bonnet! Of straw, with flowers on it, and cherries, and green leaves, and a wonderfully ruched golden velvet ribbon as broad as one's hand. It would not be two guineas that would buy it—nor four—but just suppose! She must not so much as think of it. It would be pure madness, the most dreadful folly. Such a bonnet with a gown such as she was wearing! It would be a laughing-stock. She peeped into the doorway of the shop. A lady and a gentleman talking. She must not think of it. And the lady and gentleman looked so superior, so unlikely to give a kind answer to an enquiry as to the bonnet's price—at least to a young lady of seventeen who could not afford to buy it, or even think of buying it next week—that she did indeed force herself away from the door.

She walked very slowly for twenty yards, thinking of the gold ribbon, the cherries, of whether one could find such things to put on one's own and only hat. Isaac would know. She found herself hurrying again, but with a most happy spring in her step. So happy that she felt almost alarmed at her own frivolity. As though to be anxious, fearing the worst, was the only proper state of mind. But the sun was shining, and she was tired of anxiety, and sometimes, sometimes, good things must happen! When they did, it was surely foolish always to suspect them of bringing evil behind?

"Let me be happy just this once," she whispered to herself. "Just this once." Making a small tune of it that she hummed under her breath. The pavement was of flagstones, each a yard long and she tried to match her steps to the divisions, so that she should not walk on the cracks between the stones. She had to give a small skip now and then to avoid them and for a moment, when there was no one immediately near or watching, she skipped for several paces, unable to contain herself. Until someone turned a corner, a stout woman with a disapproving, frog-like face, her head pushed up in the air by her chin and bosom, so that she seemed to be looking along her blunt, thick nose with astonishment at all before her. Kate checked her pace, walked soberly past the woman, and skipped again. Two guineas. Cherries on a bonnet. And gold ribbon.

And in the strange, unfounded way that happiness sometimes comes, like unexpected sunshine, she walked home almost dizzy, light-headed with irrational joy, thinking, feeling rather, how wonderful it was to be alive, to be here in this street, to see that glistening horse, that old man, that window-pane bright gold in the sun. There was not anything that she could see that was not wonderful—sky, rooftops, people. As if her heart was brimming over with love that must be spent, like a filled purse. Until sobriety came again, and she turned up the market lane with a composed, contented heart. Everything, everything, everything would be right.

Titine and 'Ang waiting for her, sitting on the top step above the cellar entrance. Walking very composedly towards them, as became their guardian.

Chapter 9

April. May. The days so full of happiness that it became difficult to count them, to notice them going by. The coach. The market. Devon Place. Or sometimes another point of departure. Kate's orders from the woman in black, who she learned was the Squire's sister, Mrs. Lammeter, though whether the relationship or the name were true was as impossible to guess as everything else about the business into which she had been drawn. Or else her orders came from the "Mr. Thomas" she had met first, in Mecklenburgh Street, the "Mr. Thomas" of the razor and the pockmarks. Or from someone else she had never seen before and would never see again, a man touching her shoulder in the theatre, murmuring a time and place for her for the next morning. Although never from that young man she had seen when she first saw the Squire without knowing who he was. Did the young man really have any hand in their affairs? Would he one day be the one to give her her instructions?

At times Kate amused herself by imagining how he might come into her life. Jumping quickly into the coach with her as Mr. "Pockmark" Thomas had done. Or in the theatre, buying an orange from her as Mrs. Lammeter had done that first evening. It was an amusing game to play in her mind, driving about London, delivering her "parcels" here and there. Tobacco. Silk. Cigars. Tea. And now and again those heavy, small chests that surely could not contain any of ordinary smugglers' goods. Usually for Jardine's Bank, in the name of Mr. Ponsonby. Looking out through the glasses of the coach thinking, "if they knew! If those people there in the street, that man looking in the gunsmith's window, that woman buying bread—if they only knew!"

Usually she brought Titine and 'Ang with her, and bonnet boxes that Isaac had found for her, so that for all the world they might look like two milliner's apprentices and a servant-boy, delivering urgent orders for their employer. Which indeed was near enough to the truth. Both Titine and 'Ang growing used to riding about, quite blasé and fashionable. But Kate herself did not grow blasé. Always that tremor of excitement like tiny galvanic shocks running under the surface of her skin. "If only they knew!" Even the sense of being watched by the Squire's people, of never being sure what eye was on her. His? That woman's? Someone in that coach following? The shadowy figure in the sedan chair now passing? Even that grew pleasantly exciting rather than frightening, gave her the feeling that she belonged to something greater, more intense and real than ordinary life, like a secret army.

And the money. Not most of all. Not even first of all, once there was enough. But it was still wonderful to be earning more than they spent, more than they could spend, in all reasonableness. The six guineas safely back in her handkerchief, wrapped up in the drawer of her table in their room. Eight guineas. Ten. She could smile secretly at Madame Pariglia who, with her own new wealth, was growing more than a touch condescending: To Kate, to Mr. Benedict, to Mr. Gosport, as lesser creatures who did not have a bank to draw upon for their pleasures. She had removed with Mrs. Bunn to handsome rooms in Great Jermyn Street, where there were now a parlour-maid and a cook and a servant boy, and there was even talk of a villa, somewhere at once fashionable and discreet.

"*Poverina!*" She would say, fingering Kate's curls. "We mus' fin' you someone nice, eh, Bunny?

And Kate could answer her with the uttermost sincerity, "I do not need anyone! I have everything in the world that I want!"

Sometimes her own words would come back to her like an echo, and she would grow afraid again; afraid of so much good fortune. Feel guilty that she was so happy; that she might even seem to have forgotten— "But they cannot wish me to be unhappy? Not forever? And—and I have—have I not done my best to make amends— to—" With Titine? With 'Ang? With Mr. Solomons? Who seemed to have grown younger with his duties as escort and friend and confidant; like a timid, half-ridiculous, half-pathetic imitation of Mr. Jardine. He did not wear cherry waistcoats and lilac gloves as Mr. Jardine did, nor a Brutus wig and gold fobs and a lorgnon, and gold tassels on his half-boots; but he had an air of recovered youth about him, of distant scents of spring.

As for Mr. Jardine, he seemed to be growing fonder of her than it might be quite wise to encourage, she thought. As though, when he asked her to convey a supper invitation to Madame, it was crossing his mind that it might be still pleasanter if Kate herself were to be the guest and not merely the messenger.

Once, instead of a guinea, he gave her a gold locket and thin gold chain, and begged for permission to hang it round her throat himself. She allowed him to and felt his fingers trembling as they touched the nape of her neck. And thought, *I should not accept such a gift—I should not allow—* And thought again, *Why not? Am I not risking something every day in order to make him and his friends richer? God knows how much richer. Why should I not accept a—a little gift? It is really no more than—* But his touching her like that? She turned round and saw his eyes, saw how sad they were behind the excitement, the second youthfulness. "There is so little time left for me," his eyes said. "Forgive me if—" She wished that she could kiss him without his misunderstanding her.

"Thank you," he said, touching her chin, lifting it a trifle. "Are you—are you happy? With—what we are asking you to do?"

"Yes! Oh yes!"

"If ever—if ever you are not—you will tell me? Do you promise me that?"

She did not answer him for a second and he seemed to be searching her eyes for something that he was disappointed not to find.

"I do not need to promise," she said. "I am very happy."

He took away his hand that had been touching her. "I am glad," he said, and sounded as if he were forcing himself to be truly so. He smiled and, with the palms of his two hands, reassured himself as to the careful disorder of his new wig, patting the locks that were more brown than grey, and that did indeed give him a very youthful appearance in the shadows. "And you like my absurd wig, do you?"

"It is very handsome," she said. "And you must not give me such a present again," holding her little gold and crystal locket between her finger and thumb and putting it to her lips, her eyes dancing at him, "or Madame will grow jealous."

"Do not tell her! Pray, do not!" he said, looking a shade alarmed, and then laughing. "It shall be our secret, eh?"

And that too was wrong. Kate knew that it was wrong, but what could she answer him? Walking home that midnight with Mr. Solomons, Titine and 'Ang going tiredly ahead of them, she asked him what he thought of the matter, not because she imagined he could really advise her, but for the pleasure of talking about it. And realised after only a few sentences, a few moments, that what she was really doing was making Mr. Solomons jealous. Or trying to.

I am a monster! she thought. *I am truly wicked! Two such poor sad old men. At least, one is rich—but how sad they both are—and I—*

She felt so young, so happy, so penitent, so ashamed, that she could have kissed Mr. Solomons there and then and wondered at herself for thinking of such a thing—and remembered that she had thought of kissing Mr. Jardine, and was even worse ashamed of herself. And at the same time could have skipped along beside the old man with his stoop, and his thin black coat, and his scarf that she had given him, and that he still wore even though the nights had grown summer-warm.

"You told me once," she said, changing the subject abruptly, "that one must always pay for success?"

"Indeed." They were passing a street lamp, the two globes guttering yellow, letting misty haloes of gold hang in the darkness, like the moon's veil, and he looked down into her face, his eyes and mouth seeming amused rather than jealous, or humbled, or saddened, and she felt even more ashamed of herself for having felt so condescending towards him. She caught hold of his mittened hand and held the cold, rough woolen back of it against her cheek.

"Dear Mr. Solomons," she whispered.

"Are you afraid of having to pay?"

"But I have no success to pay for! I do not so much as think of it—acting—nothing. One day—one day I suppose—but—but truly I am quite content. Just—just to be as we are—I do not ask any more."

They walked in silence for a little. "You said too—" she whispered, not looking at him, "that—that sometimes—people are forced to pay—against their wills? What did you mean?"

"What I said. Some choose. Some are chosen. Some neither."

"And you?"

He looked down at her, smiling again. "How do you know I have not succeeded? Success is not always to own a bank."

She flushed, even in the dark. "I—I did not mean—"

"I have handed music on," he said. "That is a kind of success. But you are quite right," he continued, after another silence, their footsteps echoing in the empty street. "I did not wish to pay too great a price. Only to be quiet."

"And I too!" She said it as though she hoped to be overheard. A carriage passed them, jingling harness, richness of silver lamps, glisten of paint.

"You would be content to be like me?" Mr. Solomons said, his eyes mocking her. She could scarcely see them in the shadow of his old tricorne hat, the dark of the street, but she knew that they were laughing at her.

"Yes! Oh, yes. Of—of course."

He did not answer her and after a few steps she said, "Do not you believe me?"

"What does it matter what I believe? It is what you yourself believe. What you yourself want. But you do not want to be like me, that I am sure of."

He did not sound sad about it as Mr. Jardine might have done. Merely certain. He had the strangest air of certainty, as though he knew things that other people did not, and Kate was even less sure that she understood him than she had been before.

"What do I want, then?"

A shop still lit, the shop-boys putting up the shutters, their faces greenish in the light from the windows. A sedan chair swaying by empty, the chairmen drunk and stumbling, a link-boy running ahead of them, his torch flaming. A footman in a powdered wig walking his mistress's lap dog, holding out its leash in front of him with delicately cocked fingers.

"What do I want?"

"To be good?" he suggested, his voice as full of mockery as his eyes.

"Why—why yes, of course I want to be good! Does not every one?"

"But what does it mean, 'to be good'? Do you know that, my dear? Are not you afraid that it may mean more than you know?"

She looked up at him, feeling a slight pricking of the skin at the nape of her neck. "How could I wish anything else but to be good?"

"Then may God grant it to you, my dear. But that has the highest price of all."

"You are teasing me," she whispered, and hung on his arm for a moment to coax him out of the seriousness into which she had led them both. "I am so hungry I want to think about nothing but what we shall have for supper. I do, do hope that Isaac has had our veal properly roasted for us. And that he has not eaten all the red currant jelly before we get home."

Chapter 10

It began to be a pleasant anxiety what to do with her savings. She had almost forty guineas accumulated. A handkerchief was no longer sufficient to tie them into, and she bought a new embroidered purse and kept her guineas in the old one in the drawer of her table.

There was indeed no one in the house who would steal, but it was still an anxiety, and she found herself going first to that drawer every time she returned to the room.

"Look how rich we are becoming!" she said to Titine. And she would spread out the gold on the table-top, and make small piles of it. Titine would touch a coin with her finger-tip, not really certain that gold was money, that there could be the value of twenty-one silver shillings hidden inside one glistening coin. Five, eight, ten of them in a pile. Four piles like the towers of a castle, and another tower building. Forty-five guineas, forty-eight. A labourer working all the daylight hours like a slave in the fields could spend two years of his slavery and not earn so much. A servant-girl could work ten, fifteen years in a house, and save every farthing of her wages, and have no more than this at the end.

Kate grew almost afraid of looking at so much money spilled out of a purse, and asked Mr. Mendoza to keep it for her. But he was reluctant. No one had troubled the Jews seriously for a long time, not since his namesake, the great Mendoza, had won such fame in the ring. But the bad times could so easily return.

"If they broke in," he said. He spread his hands about the cellar in a gesture of resignation to God's will and men's cruelty. "In the riots of fourteen years ago they stripped these cellars and burned everything."

Isaac looked at the fat red and yellow purse and screwed up his lips to whistle. "You should buy a shop! I'd run it for yer!"

"And what should we sell in it?" Kate said, ruffling his hair, which he was old enough to dislike, and not old enough to desire. His eyes became black-bright with knowledge, like jet.

"Auction stuff! If yer goes to the auctions yer gets stuff for near nothink, sometimes. That table up in yer room we got for a quid. An' that carpet, thirty bob. You goes into a shop to buy 'em, an' see what they'd ask yer. If we 'ad a shop—"

"But you have this."

"A cellar! A cellar ain't no good. Yer got to be up on the street. A good street where the proper flash customers'll see yer winders an' come in 'cause they see something they likes the looks of. If I 'ad all that blunt! 'E's scared," he added in a whisper, nodding his black curly head towards his grandfather. "'E's scared to be up in the daylight, 'case they yells 'dirty yid' at 'im. I'd keep a bull dog in the shop, an' train 'im to go for anyone as yelled anything."

"But I do not think I should like a shop myself," Kate said. She had begun to entertain the most distant, but the most seductive of dreams—of a house. Of a house, very small, but all her own, where she and Titine and 'Ang might live. There would be a kitchen, with a fine, bright window looking out on the smallest, but the sunniest, of gardens, with an apple tree and a pear tree set against a red-brick wall. Old brick. And wallflowers, and climbing roses. And a sun dial. When she went to sleep at night she could see it, detail by detail, as soon as she closed her eyes. And a dining room, and a parlour with a tall clock and coloured curtains, and three bedrooms upstairs, one for herself and Titine, and one for 'Ang, and one for a woman who should look after them all, and be their friend.

She invented neighbours for their house, and neighbourhoods, and in the mornings, as the hackney-coach took them about London on the Squire's business, she would look at this street and that one, and the squares that were new-building, and think, "There. Shall it be there?" Or in one of the country villages beyond Hyde Park? Chelsea, Kensington? Or on one of the old, narrow streets down near the river?

She tried to amuse Titine with the game, but Titine found it impossible to imagine at first, and only stared in amazement. And then withdrew into a secret anxiety of her own, afraid that Kate really was warning her of something; that they must leave the old Jew's house and go away. It took two days for Kate to pry the secret out of her.

"No, no! We do not have to leave! It is only a game! But would you not like a whole house to ourselves? We should choose the curtains, and the chairs. And we should have our own kitchen, and cook whatever we liked. We should have a great black iron pot and make the most wonderful soups, and we should have roast meat whenever we wanted. And a cat—we could have a cat, and he could play all day in the garden, although we should not allow him to chase the small birds."

"Would it 'ave a cellar?"

"A cellar? Perhaps—why—I do not know—do you think we should need one?"

"For Mr. Mendoza an' Isaac. To keep their stuff in."

"But they have a cellar of their own."

The game became lost in complications of reality and they had to interrupt it to deliver a chest to a nobleman's house in Berkeley Square, approaching it by the back lane. One of the small, heavy chests that clearly contained neither tea nor tobacco, and that usually went to Mr. Jardine's Bank, now directed to Mr. Ponsonby, now to the Honourable Someone or other, or Captain So-and-so, but always, until now, in care of the Bank.

The Steward of the house oversaw the reception of the chest, two footmen with green baize aprons protecting their elegant white breeches carrying it in through the cobbled yard and the kitchens. Servant-maids in cotton caps peeping through the windows at Kate. And again the sense of taut excitement came to her—of "If they knew!"—and a compassion for them, that they must pass their lives inside that dull house, peeling potatoes, dusting stairs, bobbing curtseys to the housekeeper, and to this frog-faced Steward with his bulging black waistcoat and his too-tight cravat and his bag-wig with its grey, sheep-curls massed over his ears. *I am free!* she thought. And ran back to the coach, holding the playing card that served for a receipt in all such deliveries. She herself never knew what the card would be, until it was given to her. Two of spades. Ace of hearts. Ten of clubs. That had been arranged beforehand between the Squire and his customer, and all Kate must do was to deliver the card to Mrs. Lammeter, or to one of the "Mr. Thomases" when she next saw them, as proof of her delivery.

"We are finished for the morning!" she said, getting back into the coach with Titine. "What shall we do?"

It was so fine and sunny a morning that she thought of the Park, and had the coachman drive them down to Piccadilly and then to the Mall, as though they were ladies out for an airing.

"Come and let us look for our house!" she said, paying the coach off.

The frog-faced Steward, with a great air of consequence, had given her a shilling tip for her delivery, and she gave that to the coachman as his tip. He brought his whip-handle up to the brim of his hat in gratitude, saluting them as if they were really quality, and drove away whistling.

And there in the Mall, walking with two ladies, was the Squire's young man. Kate stood quite still as if she must hide herself from him, make herself invisible. As if he must know of the day-dreams, the stupid, stupid games she had played in imagination. Imagining what they would talk of, how his voice would sound. She felt her cheeks burn, gripped hold of Titine's arm with such a fierceness of warning that Titine cried out in alarm.

"Be quiet!" Kate ordered her. "Just walk with me quite quietly as if—as if we had not seen him."

"Seen 'oo? 'im? 'im over there with the two old trouts?"

"Sssh!" But they were old trouts, or at least old—quite old enough to be his mother and his aunt, or his mother's friends, and she felt absurdly pleased that he was not—not with two young women instead. It spoke very well for—reinforced the idea she already had of him that, however wrong it might be to do whatever he was doing, he must be very good at heart.

And I am in the same bad case as he is, she thought happily. *We are almost—almost partners of a kind!* And felt an impulse as absurd as her happiness to walk very close to him and catch his eye, to let him know by some secret hint in her expression that she knew him for what he truly was. Did the two old ladies know? Surely not! In their provincial hats and last year's country-dress-maker dresses. One of them quite like the young man—it must be his mother—the same dark, large eyes, and dark, dark hair. But nothing of that—*painting* look about her that her son possessed.

Kate scarcely remembered the ridiculousness of her first image of him—could scarcely remember how it had come about that she seemed to recognise him. But that air of his of having stepped out of a dark picture into daylight remained with him—in the pale forehead, the dark hair, the gentleness of his expression as he bent down and said something to the woman who must surely be his mother.

If he looks at me, what shall I do? Kate wondered, and felt her heart begin to beat unevenly. Five paces, three. They were so close that he must look up—must—must—the other of his two companions looked at them—saw, and her stout, severe expression seemed to say, "two fashionable London chits," as she drew herself up in plump provincial virtue. But the young man did not—and then at the last moment he did, looked into Kate's face with what was surely, surely recognition? But was not. And was gone by, saying something about the coach to Norfolk—the time it left—arrived—but she did not really listen to the words. The slightest of hesitations in his voice, as though for a moment—he had been aware of—had known—

"I am sure he knew us!" she whispered to Titine. Who did not answer her but only stared at her in a kind of wonder, as if she imagined Kate was playing a new game that she did not yet understand. And Kate tried to turn the moment into nothing by laughing, dancing for two steps along the pavement and making Titine dance with her.

"What a wonderful, wonderful day!" she cried. "Just to be alive! Let us go and look at the Palace first, and then we will search for the smallest house we can find, and that shall be ours, looking out at the trees. But it must be a very pretty one, with the neatest of windows. And we shall have to have window-boxes, with geraniums in them. And a bird cage with two canary birds in it to sing in the fine weather."

They walked for half an hour in the sun, turned back into the Green Park, and down into Pall Mall. A group of men, and one or two ladies, were standing on the steps of a house, with an air of waiting for something interesting to begin, and Kate and Titine strolled along to see what it might be.

"An auction!" Kate said. "They are auctioning things as Isaac said they do!" An advertisement beside the door announced the Sale of Genuine and Elegant Household Furniture with some fine-toned harpsichords and a pedal-harp; Table and Dessert Services; Tea and Coffee Equipages; Candelabras; some Antique Marbles and Bronzes and valuable Pictures; all the property of the late Honourable Mrs. James Keeble, from her late house, the corner of—somewhere or other, hidden by a gentleman's shoulder.

"Let us go in and look," Kate whispered. "Just imagine, we might buy the harp!"

"We cannot," Titine said, looking alarmed.

[129]

"Why not?"

The gentleman moved away and revealed, besides the late lady's late direction, that the Auction was being held by Mr. Christie at his Great Room and that they might have the catalogues either there or at the Rainbow Coffee House. Everyone else was going inside and Kate caught hold of Titine's hand and made her come in behind them.

"Why should we not go in?" she whispered. "Imagine if we were furnishing our house!"

But there was no furniture to be seen. Only a large room, middling full of people sitting on benches, like a theatre without a stage: a great empty fireplace with a marble bust on a pedestal beside it; and an old gentleman with spectacles pushed onto his forehead climbing up into a high, enclosed desk like a pulpit. He had a wooden hammer and a sheaf of papers and was saluting people on the benches with elegant half bows and handsome smiles, the ruffles of his cravat spilling out in white cascades above the lapels of his green coat. Titine clung to Kate's hand.

"We have just as much right to be here as anyone else," Kate whispered. "Do not be so frightened. It is very good for you to grow used to company."

No one took the least notice of them. The old gentleman in the pulpit was calling out something about Conditions of Sale. Two men in black aprons were carrying in a small table. A man sitting at a lower desk beside the pulpit was shuffling more papers into order and trimming his quill pen.

But it proved to be much less exciting than Kate had hoped it might be. It was hard to understand what was happening. Men held things up, took them down again, carried them away. The man in the pulpit seemed to enjoy himself enormously, like an actor playing a long-loved role, crying out, "Now, who will do me the honour to say 'ten pounds' for this exquisite piece? Ten pounds do I say? A trifle, the merest bagatelle for such an object! Only observe the inestimable excellence, the subtleties of the design!"

But Kate could observe nothing, not even the object that he was praising, and she was turning away in disappointment when a voice behind her said, "If it ain't Miss 'Arriott! An' Miss Titine! Well, I never!"

Mr. Foster, from the Bank. Looking more like a wolfish fox or a foxy wolf than ever. Very fashionably dressed in a short, dark yellow frock coat and canary-coloured breeches. A look in his screwed-up, muddy eyes that seemed to say, "Gad, ain't I a killer?" His left hand caressing the fobs dangling at his striped brown and white waistcoat, his bicorne hat tilted very slightly forward with a dashing air.

"An' what is the lovely Miss 'Arriott an' the lovely Miss Titine doin' in this dusty 'ole?" he said, casting a look of disparagement at a nearby gentleman whose breeches were of last year's fashion.

"We were just curious," Kate said. She did not know why she did not like him. He had said nothing to her that was wrong since that first morning. Perhaps it was no more than the way he had of catching her by the arm, above the elbow, the way his hands seemed always to be damp, and to leave marks on her sleeves. She felt as if the marks were also on her skin. And his eyes that seemed to price everything that they looked at, and to down-value it. And his sharp little yellow teeth. And his sharp, foxy nose with its whitened, gristly tip. She did not like him at all.

"Rubbish this morning," he said. "Now, las' year when the Doo-Barry stuff was going. Or before that when the Dook of Orleans was being sold up—ah then it was a bit worth-while coming 'ere! Although you'd be surprised what measly stuff them two was getting rid of, as well as a few good lots. 'Allo, Mr. Jefferson, sir. Buying up hanything that's good, eh, sir?"

The man with last year's breeches made Mr. Foster's bow a rather cold return and moved away. "Near bankrupt," Mr. Foster whispered. " 'Is next lodgings 'll be in Queer Street. Probably seeing what chances 'is own stuff 'll 'ave of fetching a price. But you sees that old fellow over there, the one with the ratty coat an' the brown beaver? Now, there's a rich 'un. Mr. Edward Ponsonby, no less, if you recalls the name?" He winked, and massaged Kate's upper arm as though he were kneading cheap butter into it.

She looked up with quick curiosity at the old gentleman for whom she had delivered the heavy chests to the Bank. What had been in them? That had to be delivered in such a manner?

"Not that Ponsonby is 'is real name. Nor Ed'ard," Mr. Foster was saying, a shade nervously. "We'd best get along out of 'ere before 'e sees me an' thinks I might be talking about 'im. You forget what I said, an' what 'e looks like, eh? Give us yer promise on that, now." He was urging her out of the auction room as if he had the right to decide where and when she should go.

"We were just going in any event," Kate said. "But surely you are staying? You have business here—"

"No, no, I saw yer turning in and followed you. Me time is me own at this 'appy moment. A little matter o' confidential business on be'alf of a 'ighly important client—you couldn't 'ardly guess 'ow important." He winked his foxy little eyes, first one and then the other, and bared his teeth. "But don't arsk me what that certain business is, 'cause I haint at liberty to divulge it."

He kneaded her arm all the way down the side of St. James's Square. "If I could offer you ladies a glarss of lemonade, or some such, which I believe ladies is partial to?" He winked again, happy in his success as a ladies' man.

"No, please—do not let us keep you—you must have many things to do—"

"At this very moment," he said, massaging and kneading, "I 'ave nothing in the world to do 'arf so himportant—*nor* pleasant—as what I ham doing just now."

Kate's sleeve had grown quite damp and she wanted to scream.

"Important!" he repeated. "You notice the word, eh? *Im*-portant. Now, Miss Titine, my goldilocks—what would you say to a ice cream an' ginger-fizz and a gaito—to use your native langwidge, Mam'selle—"

"It is not my native language, I assure you," Kate said. But Titine was looking at her with great eyes, and Mr. Foster with masterful hospitality was already guiding them down the steps into a dark, expensive-looking Tea Room with small tables and gilt chairs and an air of velvet hush and gentility.

"I makes a point," Mr. Foster whispered, "of halways going into the best places when I goes anywheres at all. It rubs off, you know; it rubs off. Now, what shall it be, ma'am?" inclining his head to Titine.

I am a monster, Kate thought. *How kind he means to be. How can he help it if his hand sweats and his teeth are that shape? Although,* she thought with the unregenerate part of her mind, *he might clean them more often if he would.*

"If you're going to 'ave anything," Mr. Foster said, " 'ave the best. That's my motto. Hi started my career"—and he sounded as though the very recollection of it amazed him now—"hexactly like them poor fellows you sees in my office. Smelling of poverty like drains in the 'eat. Living on stale bread an' dripping in 'orrible lodgings. Clothes what is a disgrace to a 'uman being. That was my beginnings—" He stuck out his gleaming left foot to compare it to its shining fellow. "Hand in thirteen years," he said, dwelling on the words impressively, "thirteen years—I 'ave made myself what you see."

"It must be a very important position—Chief Clerk in the Bank?" Kate offered, to sound as impressed as he might desire.

"Chief Clerk!" Mr. Foster said scornfully. "Chief Clerk! That's nothing. You'll see chief clerks in banks what you wouldn't wipe your boots on. Fifty years old. Snuffy, scabby, still touching their 'ats to the directors, praying they'll get something worth-while out o' the customers' Christmas Fund. Chief Clerk! Oh no, that ain't yours truly, Mr. Daniel Foster, Oh no. It ain't the title what counts —it's up 'ere!" He tapped his forehead just above his long, pointed nose, his mottled, skinned cheeks darkening with the excitement of self-revelation. "It's what you *does* with a position what counts. You gets 'ints. Tips on what's up. Winks and nods that 'as pages of meaning for them as is sharp enough to read 'em. An' what you ain't told even in 'ints, you finds out. Like what's up jus' now with Mr. Jardine an' your hegreegiwus hemployer the Squire—eh? Heh?"

"I am afraid I do not understand anything of what you are telling me." The bowls of ice cream had come. Titine was already exploring hers with her spoon, as if she did not believe that such luxury could exist, taking out a dark gold walnut, looking at it, and carefully replacing it in its soft, beige bed of coffee ice cream, covering it over again with its white eiderdown of clotted cream, and sighing, her lips slightly parted in dreaming anticipation.

"You don't understand?" Mr. Foster was saying, delightedly. "Of course not! 'Ow should you? Unless"—he laid his finger-tip to the side of his nose—"unless you 'as an investigative type of mind. Like mine. Then, when you investigates, you finds out. And when you finds out—'as it never occurred to you to wonder what was in them boxes an' bales what you delivers round an' about? Of course it 'as. You're a woman. 'Ave you found out? 'Ave you?" He looked at her with triumphant challenge, his spoon poised, a white fleck of cream decorating his mottled chin. He ate with his mouth open, showing all his mouth's secrets, which Kate found distressing. "'Ave you?"

"I think I know," she said, looking away from his mouth. "I—it is not my business to speak of such things."

"Good. Good. I likes that. I does indeed. But them 'eavy chests now. What's in them, eh? Can you tell me that?"

She shook her head, her interest caught unwillingly, and showing in her eyes, perhaps, as she looked up at his face. He crowed in triumph, choked over a fragment of walnut, and had to drag out a large red silk handkerchief from his tail pocket to spit into, and with which to mop his face and eyes. When he was composed again, he stuffed the handkerchief away and took up the silver spoon as if it had a great interest, turning it about to look at it.

"So you don't know anything, eh? Good. Good. That's the way it *ought* to be. But *I* knows. I made it my business to find hout. An' to let it be known in certain quarters that I 'ad found out, an' was still to be trusted. And 'ad to be trusted. If you follows me?" He gave her another cunning look, like a palm print on her skin. "There are them now," he said, "as 'as to trust Mr. Daniel Foster, whether they likes it or not. And they 'as to like it in spite of theirselves, because so much is 'anging on it."

"I still do not understand you."

"No more you should, my dear. No more you ought. Pretty young ladies ain't for hunderstanding matters of 'igh finance an' secret business. Young ladies is for eating hice cream, eh, Miss Titine? Is it to your fancy, Miss Goldilocks?"

"Yes," Titine whispered.

"You must say 'Thank you, sir,'" Kate said, feeling more and more wretched.

"That's all right," Mr. Foster said largely, taking one of Titine's curls and giving it a condescendingly affectionate tug. "Miss Titine an' me hain't on formal terms, har we, eh? An' what a improvement you 'ave wrought in 'er, Miss 'Arriott! Miss *Kate*, if I may make so bold, an' us being colleagues, so to speak, in the same enterprise. And what a enterprise! If you honly knew what you are adding your mite of 'elp to!"

"I do not want to know," Kate said untruthfully.

"Quite right. Quite right." He leaned forward, tapping the tablecloth with the bowl of his spoon, for emphasis. "It ain't—to tell the truth—it ain't a enterprise in what a young lady ought to be involved. In *my* opinion. In fact I 'ave 'ad 'arf a mind to speak to your employer about it." In spite of herself Kate must have looked alarmed and Mr. Foster grinned delightedly. He leaned still nearer to her and lowered his voice to a whisper. "Ho ho! Don't be afraid of Daniel Foster, or imagine as 'ow 'e could want to injure you in any ways. Far from it. The opposite, I promise you, the absolute opposite! I 'ave took a fancy to you, an' I don't mind admitting it." He reached over to take her hand, and she was obliged to make herself busy with the remains of her cup of chocolate to avoid the capture.

"I 'ave a alternative in mind," he breathed, glancing at Titine, who was very slowly gathering the last morsels of clotted cream with her finger-tip. "What would be of *real* benefit. An' safe." He waited for her to show curiosity. She occupied herself with her cup, resolute not to look at him.

"Madame P?" he said, like making an opening move at chess. "Does anyone of that initial figure among your acquaintance, per-'aps? A foreign lady? What sings?" His eyes screwed tight with enjoyment of secrets penetrated. "And among 'er acquaintance there figures a certain elderly party what 'as the initial J? Am I right?"

"Why do you ask me such things?" Kate whispered indignantly. "It cannot be your concern."

"Ho ho ho. But it *can*. Very much so. Ho yes! *Because*—" He laid his finger to his nose again, narrowing his eyes, the pupils small as black knife points in the muddy brown irises, the yellowed whites almost vanished—"because as I told you afore, when we first 'ad the pleasure of mutual acquaintance, I 'ave a deep interest in what my employer does. In private as well as business activities. And the more foolish 'is actions in private life, the more interest I takes. 'E is a very nice old gentleman, my Mr. J. Very kind. Very considerate. And in matters of business, as sharp as needles. Sharper. But outside of business! Ho my word! Like a little child." He shook his head sadly. "Miss Titine there could buy an' sell 'im in 'is private activities. Twist 'im round 'er little finger. Or"— he gave Kate another palm print of a look—"Miss Kate could do it." He paused for her reaction. "*You* could," he said, when no suitable reaction came.

"I?" She did not want to continue the conversation in any way, but felt that she must, in return for the ice cream, and the hot chocolate, and the chocolate cake.

"Yes. An' I am not speaking in a random way, I promises you." His face had grown very serious. She sensed, without understanding why it should be, that he had come to the point he had been labouring towards for the past three quarters of an hour. He twined his fingers together, and lifted one up, with its bitten nail, to em-

[135]

phasize what was coming. "Until larss summer, larss autumn in fact, there wasn't a soberer, better-conducted old gent in the 'ole of Cheapside than my Mr. J. Into the Bank. Back 'ome. Nursing 'is pore mad wife. Looking after 'is daughters. A martyr. A proper Fox's martyr and a example to all. An' then what 'appens? 'Is third an' larss daughter gets married, and off to Scotland with her 'usband, the two previous daughters being already married and unsympathetic to the old gent. An' 'e breaks loose. 'E's sixty, an' 'e's never injoyed 'isself in a 'uman way since 'e was a child. So 'e finds our Madame P.

"Ho, you could 'ave saved me a lot of vexatious trouble if you'd told me what I arsked you, that first day we met. Scouting an' following and watching of 'im where 'e went. Bribing waiters to let me peep through key'oles—"

"What?" Kate cried, scandalised. "You spied on him?"

"'Ush," whispered Mr. Foster, equally scandalised, and darting a look at the nearest other customer, an elderly lady in mauve satin, feeding a cup of chocolate to her pug dog with cooings of encouragement. "'Oo wouldn't keep tabs on 'im in my situation? For Gawd's sake, girl—if Mrs. J. pops off one o' these days from being cured too vigorous of a mad fit, or anythink else, 'e's going to marry that red-'aired, bosomy trollop. Or rather she's going to marry 'im." He darted his investigative look at Kate to see if she would try to contradict him. She looked away. "That red-'aired cow!" he cried furiously, to the alarm of the mauve lady. "An' 'er Mrs. Bunn! That's the one I reely 'ates. That's the one what'll bring them two to the altar. With a marriage settlement what'll drain the Bank."

"But what has any of this to do with me?" Kate said. She knew already what he meant, and was ashamed of herself for asking.

"You knows what it 'as to do with you," Mr. Foster said. "You could pick 'im up like *that*." He took a crumb of chocolate cake from the blue and gold plate and ate it with a smacking of his tongue and lips like a heartily enjoyed kiss. "All what we'd need is to arrange a bit of a coldness atween the two parties—drop a 'int to Mr. J. about some young gent with fluffy whiskers what 'as been seen leavin' Madame's front door in the early 'ours—" His eyes probed Kate's again and this time she could not look away. "But what'd count is to 'ave the alternative ready an' waiting and accessible to the pore old gent's injured pride an' feelings. And that alternative" —he lowered his voice to a still more earnest pitch—"is *you*."

"You cannot mean what you are saying!"

"Ho yes I can. I ain't worked an' slaved an' sweated blood in that there bank since I were fourteen year old, an' climbed up to where I am, to see it all ruined by a cow like that."

"But how could Madame Pariglia ruin a bank?"

She could ruin *me*," Mr. Foster said, all his teeth showing in a snarl of such hatred, such self-preservation, that it shocked Kate into stillness. "Old gents what is left alone in the world," he whispered, "takes fancies into their 'eads. Vagaries. I means to be one of 'is fancies. I means to be a paragraph in 'is Larst Will an' Testament what will lift me out of where I am now, an' set me on the road onct an' for all. An for that I needs a partner. *I* can't go to bed with 'im. *I* can't paddle 'is chops with fat little pointy-nailed 'ands. *I* 'aven't got a bosom like two pillows with powder on 'em. I've just got a brain what 'as worked in 'is service, loyal an' ceaseless these parst thirteen years. An' maybe the nex' thirteen on top of 'em. And I ain't doing it for a gold watch an' a Christmas bonus, I promises you that. I wants my share of the bank, and I means to 'ave it. That's what I'm looking for. An' I needs a partner to 'elp me bring it off."

Mr. Foster looked at Kate with judging eyes, twining his fingers together, chewing at his lower lip as if he liked the taste of it. His skinned cheeks shone with determination. His sandy-red hair seemed to bristle with it, upright on his head like rusty, bitten quills. "I picked you out the first moment I clapped eyes on you. 'There,' I said to myself. 'There's the one. Pretty. Innocent. A 'eart. Not a atom o' greed. Three meals a day for a month, an' the ol' gent could be down on 'is knees to 'er. *If* she was managed proper.' That's what I said. I tell you," he whispered, leaning across the table, and glancing quickly at Titine who, her ice cream and cake and chocolate finished, had lost interest in her surroundings and was staring out of the window, "I tell you, if *I* was the marrying kind—I'd be very tempted by you myself!"

He waited for her gratitude, but she could only look amazed. Some of the horror that she felt of him and of his proposals must have shown in her eyes, because his own eyes grew diamond-hard again. "Don't be 'asty," he warned her. "What I'm offering you is so 'andsome you could 'ardly dream about it. An' you couldn't bring it off by yourself. An' if you tried, I could ruin you in a day. But with me—with me 'elping, managing—an' certain guarantees between us, insurances so to speak against ingratitude or forgetfulness on your part—not that I think you're that kind, but insurances are always good to 'ave—why, it'd be the best stroke o' business done in Cheapside this year or next. You 'eading to be Mrs. J. an' heir to a fortune. An' me, with your 'elp and influence 'eading to be a partner in the bank—well?"

"I have no such wish," Kate said.

"I've warned you not to be 'asty."

"I am most grateful for all your kindness," Kate said, her mouth dry with disgust. "Titine, we must be going. Say thank you again to the gentleman."

Mr. Foster did not stand up as they left, and as they passed the bow-window on the outside Kate saw him still sitting there, staring at his fingers, his sandy eyebrows knotted together in furious thought; wondering, perhaps, how much he had said that she might use against him. She had a moment's temptation to go back and tell him not to be anxious, that she never wished to refer to their conversation again, never so much as to think of it. She felt almost sorry for him, with his pathetic boastings, and his conviction of his own shrewdness. But then disgust returned, and even the chocolate she had drunk seemed to lie sour in her throat, ill-tasting.

"What was 'e talking about?" Titine said. "You ain't—you ain't going to—"

"To what?"

"To marry 'im?" Titine whispered.

"*Mon Dieu*, no!"

"Cause 'e's wicked. 'E's got wicked eyes."

"Do not worry about him. He means nothing to us. Nothing. I am only sorry that I let him bring us into that place at all."

Two mornings later, the three of them coming back from the market, Kate and Titine, and 'Ang carrying their oranges and apples, they found "Mr. Thomas" waiting for them, the "Mr. Thomas" of the razor; dressed like a rat-catcher with heavy, brown leather gaiters, and a blue frieze coat, his hard, slightly pock-marked face expressionless, unwelcoming. Simply waiting. He jerked his head for Kate to follow him, and walked away up the lane.

"Go down to Mr. Mendoza and wait for me," Kate said to the others. She felt her heart beating uncomfortably, she did not know why. Except that always he made her nervous. But this time— She went very quickly after him, almost running. He did not turn round, although he must have heard her. She caught up with him and walked beside him, taking two paces to his one.

"What is it?" she said, her voice breathless. He turned the corner and stood looking down at her. "Is there something today? I thought—"

"There is nothing today," he said. "Nor tomorrow, neither. Nor after that. The job's finished."

She did not want to understand him. And yet she had known that he was going to tell her this. Thought now that she had been waiting to hear it, she did not know for how long. But she said "Finished?" as though she did not understand the word, his meaning. She did not even know what she felt. "You mean—?"

"I mean it's finished," he said impatiently, his voice hard, half-angry. "There's no more for you. He's getting someone else."

"But why? Why? What have I done? What is wrong?"

"Nothing," he said, seeming surprised. "Nothing's wrong."

"But then—then why—?"

"You can't go on forever. You've done it near three months. Isn't that enough for you?"

"But—" She had still not taken it in completely.

"You'll have been seen about by now. Been noticed. Blown. You don't want to get nabbed, do you?"

"No. No, of course not—"

"Then that's it. Oh, an' something else. He doesn't want you to stay round. You're to leave London for a bit. Six months. A year. A year'd be best."

She stared at him, this time truly not understanding, her mouth opening in shock. "Leave—? Leave London?"

"Yes. The sooner the better." He took a long stride back towards the corner they had just turned, and stood looking, as if to see whether any one was coming in their direction.

"But—how can I leave? Where should I go? What should I do?" She had followed him, wanted to catch at his sleeve, beseech him to say it was not true.

"How should I know? Do what you like. Haven't you saved any money?"

"But there are three of us! And my work! At the theatre! How can you say such a thing—how can you think that—?" She had clasped her hands together against her breast as if she were truly going to beseech him for a reprieve, a denial of what he had said. "I cannot go away like that! He cannot mean it! Please—let me speak to him—tell him—tell him I must see him. Have I not done everything that—that he—you—asked of me?"

He came back towards her and grasped her chin between finger and thumb. "And weren't you paid for it? Christ! First you snivelled because you were made to do it, and now you're snivelling because it's over. What the hell did you expect? A pension?"

She could not answer him for the pain his fingers were causing her, his thumb digging into the soft flesh under her lower lip, bruising it against the bone. He let go of her as a man rounded the corner and passed by them. When the man was gone, "Mr. Thomas" caught hold of her again. "What am I going to tell the Squire?" he said. "That you're going tomorrow? Or the day after? It'd better not be longer than that."

"Please," she whispered, "he cannot make me leave. Please. How should we live? I—only ask him to let me stay. I swear I will never so much as—"

"As much as what? As what?" He gripped her so hard that she cried out with the pain and a woman coming from the other direction stared at them. "Mr. Thomas" ignored her, keeping his grip of Kate's chin as though he enjoyed the pain he was causing her. "You do what you're told," he said, "or else—" he put his other hand inside his coat and half-drew something out of an inner pocket— "or else you know what'll happen." He let go of her. "Two days. If you're not gone by then, I'll be back."

He walked away from her, even his walk seeming altered to match his altered clothes. Even more brutally confident. Heavy with indifferent cruelty. He turned the corner and was gone.

Chapter 11

Kate could not tell Titine and 'Ang what had happened. They looked at her as she went into the cellar, at first with no more than an ordinary curiosity as to what "Mr. Thomas" might have had to tell her in the way of the next day's instructions, and then, seeing her face, the two of them struck still, knowing that something terrible had happened.

"What did 'e want?" Titine whispered.

"Nothing. Nothing that signifies," Kate cried, her voice almost angry. Wanting to shout at them, "Leave me alone. Do not stare at me like that!" She hurried through the cellar, up the outside stairs, and stood in the middle of the bedroom with her hands covering her face. A moment later Titine was behind her. Kate scarcely heard her, only knew that she was there, and from wanting her to be silent she now felt a furious impatience with her for staying quiet, for standing there like a ghost. After a moment she had to turn round and face her. Felt as though she were facing an accuser, and grew the more unreasonably angry for that.

"What do you want?" she cried. "Why have you——?" But she could not look into Titine's eyes and remain angry and felt, instead of anger, the full impact of the guilt that she had been trying to force away from her; the guilt as irrational as the anger.

"Tell us," Titine said. She took Kate's hand and drew her towards the bed, made her sit down and sat beside her. "Tell us what's up," Titine breathed. She touched Kate's hair, her hands like leaves. She seemed no longer a child. To be ten years older than the Titine who only an hour before had been dreaming over cake and ice cream. And as Kate looked at her she had a momentary image of herself at exactly that child-woman moment with her own mother, sitting with her like this on a bed in an inn—where had it been? Alençon? Vannes? And a lover gone, her mother desolate. The image was so strangely similar, and the cause so different, that she laughed with the bitterness of the memory, the pain of it, and then, to prevent herself from crying, buried her face against Titine's thin, still childish shoulder. And that too her mother had done. And Kate had stroked her mother's hair as Titine was stroking hers.

"'Ave they twigged us? Is the Runners after us?" Titine was saying.

"No, not that." Kate sat up, ashamed of herself. "It's—we are to have no more work. Nothing. And—we have to go away from here."

"From 'ere? Mr. Mendoza's?"

"From London."

Titine stared at her as though the idea had no meaning, as though there was nowhere else but London. "'Ow?" she said at last.

"I don't know. I don't know!" Her anger coming back, not with Titine this time, but with "Mr. Thomas," the Squire, the Squire's sister, all connected with this business. The young, wicked, wicked man. How could they? How could they treat her so? She began to walk up and down the room in a rage, putting her hands against her face, wanting to tear something. What would they do? Where? And the realisation came that she had no papers, could give no account of herself except the Parnassus Theatre. And Mr. Gosport would have no good will towards her if she—to have to tell him she must leave him within two days! To be given two days to leave London! As if she had stolen from them! He must let her speak to the Squire! He must!

Only that she could not find him—nor any of them. Except the yard! The "Mr. Thomas" of the stable-yard in Devon Place! "I am going somewhere!" she cried. "Where is my bonnet?"

It was on the bed where she had thrown it coming into the room. She did not give herself time to rearrange it, but ran down the stairs again, through the cellar, calling to Mr. Mendoza and to 'Ang, "I do not know how long I shall be. Do not worry about me."

All the way in the hackney-coach, once she had found one, thinking no further than persuading "Mr. Thomas" to bring her to the Squire. He must. He must. And then—Devon Place. The archway. An air—an air of abandonment. The dog—the dog was gone. Everything. She had opened the door of the coach in her eagerness, had her foot on the iron step. The coachman waited.

"They are gone," she said slowly. And to the coachman, "Wait. I will look—" Walking across the untidy yard towards the stables. Nothing anywhere. Even the dog's chain gone. The stables empty. The house! But that too—the door locked, the windows shuttered. Nothing. She stood not knowing what to do or what to think. The coachman impassive, uninterested, earning his shilling. The two jaded horses flicking their ears at flies, twitching their ill-conditioned tails. The horses, the coachman, the worn-out black coach seemed ready to remain forever. She lifted her hands to her breast in helplessness, let them fall. If she were to ask in the street? Someone, surely, must know where they were gone, if they were returning? But they were not returning. She knew that. And if she were to ask questions, draw attention— She thought of the razor, put up both hands again to touch her face. Behind her there was a dragging footstep. She heard it at first without thinking of it, the sound lost in the distant noises of the city, the twitching of the horses' ears and tails, her thoughts. And then it penetrated her conscious mind and she swung round catching her breath, half in fear, half in excitement. But it was not the Squire. An old woman. Small, bent, seventy, eighty years old. Her face seamed with black lines, wrinkles holding dirt; nose, eyes, mouth, black holes in her face; no teeth, no light of intelligence, almost no appearance of life. A black bundle of rags, creeping. Pushed along by something invisible. Kate stared at her, caught with a kind of horror of such age, such dirt, such an appearance of living death, as though the creature had risen out of a grave. Even the smell from her rags had graveyards in it. From her body. Until she was close. So close that Kate could have touched her if she had had the wish and the courage.

"'Oo yer lookin' for?" the old woman croaked. "There ain't no one 'ere."

"Mr. Thomas," Kate breathed. Even the wrinkles of the old woman's eyelids seamed and filled with grime. Hiding her eyes. But suddenly lifting, showing eyes dark as holes in the night sky, with no light, no expression, nothing in them at all. Surely she must be blind, and yet she was looking at Kate. He mouth working, the yellow lips mumbling at nothing.

"Yer'd 'ave to wait," she said at last. "Send 'im away." Her rags jerked, her hand pointed at the coach.

Kate hesitated for a second, a whisper as clear, clearer, than the old woman's raven croak, inside her head and yet seeming real, that was saying, "Go. Go now. Run."

But she had not come so far as this to be afraid halfway. She nodded agreement and went to the coachman to pay him his fare and tip. He wheeled away, through the arch, was gone, the wheels rumbling for a few moments, echoing, fading.

"In 'ere," the old woman said. She had been fumbling inside her rags and drew out a key, old and heavy, rusty iron. She began creeping towards the shuttered house. And again the whisper seemed to be saying in Kate's mind, "Go now, go now!" But she followed her, keeping two or three paces back because of the smell. The lock. The door. "In 'ere. I'll 'ave to lock yer in."

"No!" But she was already inside, and the door was closing, closed. The lock turning. She had her hands on the inner surface, searching for the handle. Heard the old woman shuffling away. "Come back! Come back!" Shuffling. Silence. Dark.

Kate stood where she was, panting with terror, gripping the iron-ring handle of the door so tightly that it hurt her. She began to pray. To pray aloud. The sounds echoing, dying. Covering other sounds? She stood still, not so much as breathing, her mouth half open to listen harder. A footstep? Above? She imagined movements. Shut her eyes against the darkness, and reopened them in terror a second later, imagining someone close to her, touching her—the razor. Why had she come? Why? She would never see Titine again—wanted to cry out for help, and was afraid to make the least sound. Her heart beating so loud that it drummed inside her mind, made her dizzy.

A filtering of light from upstairs, as her eyes grew more accustomed to the dark. The shape of a passage, doorways, stairs. What must be stairs. She could not move. But what was up there to cause light? She had let go of the door handle and was pressing both hands against her heart, trying to make it beat quieter. If there was someone there, she would die of fear before he could touch her, before—imagining "Mr. Thomas"—the razor—the feel of the naked edge against her face—she was going to faint.

No sounds? A creaking? Scurrying? She imagined rats running, scrabbling at the wainscot. What was the light up there? At least—She felt her way towards the stairs, trying to keep silent. Stumbled against the first tread, half fell; screamed, knelt on the naked timber sobbing for breath, for terror. Nothing. The echoes of her scream, the sound of her fall dying. The house seeming to listen. She lay on the stairs, unable to move. If she had heard footsteps coming, she could not have moved; would have lain there with her eyes shut, waiting to be killed. But there was nothing. No sound. Even the scurrying of the mice, the rats, gone silent. Her own heart beating. Her breathing, a shallow gasping in the dark. And still that faint promise of light above the stairs. Clearer now. With a sudden gathering of courage that was itself half terror, she got to her feet, ran up to face whatever it might be. A landing. A door ajar. An empty room into which a few thin fragments of light were forcing themselves through a warped, cracked shutter. The room empty except for a wooden chest. Dust motes floating in the sword blades of light; a grey velvet covering of dust on the lid of the chest, the floor. Carved panelling. She clung to the door she had thrust open, so much relief in her mind that she needed to cling to something to support herself.

An empty room! To be in such terror of an empty room! Of nothing! But the other rooms?

She ran quickly, able to see now, threw open a second door and a third. Flakes of sunlight, through the old, worm-eaten, distorted shutters. Dust. The scurry of a frightened mouse. In one room straw, torn newspapers, some nails sharp under her slipper as she trod on them. Nothing more. In another even the ceiling fallen, daylight through the slates and rafters. An empty, abandoned house, waiting to be pulled down. So much relief that she wanted to laugh aloud, prove to herself that she was no longer frightened. Like a ghost story! That one half believes.

Downstairs the grinding of the lock. She stood with her hands clasped, her knees trembling, giving way. But it was the old woman coming back—or "Mr. Thomas"—the kind one—of the yard outside—or the young— She tried to cry out, "I am here, up here!" But her voice would not answer her commands, made only a whispering sound. She could not move. "I am here," she whispered. "Who—is there?" Slow, shuffling steps, heavy breathing, the tapping of a stick.

"Girl? Girl?" The Squire's voice, wheezing and hoarse. She ran down the stairs as though her slippers had wings, saw his silhouette below, the open door, the courtyard, the daylight.

"It is you!" she cried, as if he were the eldest, the dearest of her friends, wanted to cling to his sleeve. But he was pushing open a door beside him with the point of his crutch-handled stick.

"In there."

[145]

Kate went in soberly. Another empty room, dark, shuttered. His footsteps behind her, the soft, shapeless, gloved hand resting on her shoulder, heavy, helpless-seeming. "What have you come for?" he wheezed. "There is a chair somewhere." He was feeling about with his stick, leaning on her. There too the daylight made its way through the open doorways and she found the chair for him, helped him sit down, and found it impossible to believe for the moment that he was not truly old and crippled. "Well?"

She began to tell him, jumbling up her petitions, her fears, Titine, 'Ang, the thought of having to leave London, begin again, but how, where? If only he would leave her to continue in the Parnassus; death by torture before she would ever betray a word about him, of what she had been doing, an address, a name. Only not to make her leave London, please, please—to do anything, anything that he asked.

She scarcely knew what she was asking by the end, now holding his gloved hand in both of hers, now walking up and down, pacing—turning on him, unconsciously the echo, the image of her mother in that pacing—half wild, half controlled—the sudden turning, the pleading, the tones of her voice; her mother pleading with a young lover who had grown tired of her, frightened of her passion, longing for a younger, docile love. Kate almost knew what her mother was doing, felt as if there was something shameful in it without quite understanding, remembering—hearing those swift footsteps in another room, those tones of voice, deep and passionate, rising to a cry of rage . . . . And she herself now growing furious at the Squire's silence, crying, "You cannot do this to me, you cannot!"

The sounds dying in the room's twilight. She stood in front of him, feeling suddenly ridiculous before his silence, helpless, almost a child. The dark, heaped shape of him on the hidden chair. Broad hat. Green shade, that had no colour in this greyness. Dark, falling coat. His breath rasping.

"You must go," he whispered. "We cannot risk your staying."

"But— I promise! Promise!"

He lifted the shapeless hand from his knee, held it up to silence her. "Suppose—we were to offer you—"

"It is not money! It is not money I am asking—"

"Be quiet, girl. Suppose we were to offer you—another employment? Elsewhere?"

"Elsewhere—?" A tremor of excitement in her mind that astonished her as soon as she was aware of it, and that grew with awareness. "Other—employment?" She had not thought of it—she swore it to herself. She did not want it, could not endure all this again. And yet— Her mother's whisper echoing in her ears—"But my darling, *chérie*, this time—he is different. I swear to you before God he is utterly different. He is good and kind." Growing alive again and wonderful with new hope of real, real love, real happiness at last. And her own cry *"Maman!* How *can* you?" Tears, rage. Jealousy. Foreknowledge of how once more it would end. She had been so much wiser than her mother.

"It is only—" she whispered, "I want only—to stay in the Parnassus. To earn—to earn enough for us—and then—to act again, when—"

The Squire was shaking his head, the folds of his scarf, the collar of his great shapeless surtout, the edge of his green shade, all rustling together. He seemed unaware of the heat outside that was beginning to make itself felt even in that chilled and empty room. "Kneel down by me," he said, his breath rasping. Was he truly ill? Truly old? She obeyed him slowly, unsure of what he might do. Suppose—? "Give me your hand." She placed it between his gloved ones. No sense of flesh or bone or warmth. Cold wool. As if the fingers and palm were wadded out with flock.

"Listen to me, child. You cannot stay in London. Thomas is rough about these things, I know it. I should have come to you myself. But have we broken any promise to you? Have you not been safe from the Runners? Earned good money? Have I not been your friend? As I said I should be?"

"Until—until now."

"It is for your benefit to leave. As well as ours. I did not want to trouble you more. But if——"

"If what? Tell me!"

"If you truly wanted it, I might arrange—"

Her heart beating. That same feeling she had had when she looked into the old woman's eyes. That sense of warning.

"But it is best that we part company," he said. "You have done enough for us. Have you no savings?"

"Yes! But it is not that! It is—" She gripped his glove with her free hand, thought that deep inside the wadding she could feel flesh and bone. Did not know what she was going to say, to plead, or why. Only felt a sense of loss, of lost excitement, emptiness—but it was not that, not that. She swore it to herself as soon as she suspected it. What should she do in Bristol? Or anywhere? Her savings dribbling away— "What else could I do if—if you were to—" She thought, *I am stark mad.* As though one part of her was standing aside, watching, stricken with horror at her madness, her folly. "If you were to arrange it—if I wanted—" "It is only 'if,'" she thought. "Only 'if.'"

Chapter 12

"It is madness!" Mr. Solomons said. "Worse! It is—it is— How could you do this thing?" Lifting his fists in the air, lifting his eyes to the dark ceiling as if calling God to witness the justice of his anger. Kate had never seen him angry before. Would not have thought him capable of anger if she had ever thought of it. He struck his fists against the breast of his old black coat with a hollow sound, like striking rotten wood. "I thought—I have looked on you as—as a daughter! And to commit this folly! This wickedness! When they had set you free—when by the mercy of God——"

"Free to do what?" she said, allowing herself in her turn to sound angry. She had tried laughing at him, cajoling him, reasoning. "Free to starve?"

"You have grown greedy," he said. They were in his room. Even more poorly furnished than hers. A music stand. Piles of music on a deal table. On the floor. His bed. A chair. "There is greed in your eyes!"

"No!" she cried, putting out her hands towards him. "Oh, please, please understand—" She caught hold of his sleeve, put her head down on his shoulder. A strange, dusty scent, of camphor. "You—do you not know that I think of you—as—you and Mr. Mendoza—and Isaac—you are all we have—please do not be angry with me—please." Touching his cravat, winding her fingers into the limp, worn out cloth, almost consciously acting. Not lying. And yet as if she needed to convince herself. And he put her gently away from him as if he knew exactly what she was doing, knew it better than she did herself.

"You," he said, "who told me once that you wished to be good. That that was all your ambition."

"But I do! I do wish it! Nothing else!"

"You believe that this is good?"

"What else could I do?" she cried, hiding her face against his sleeve.

"What can any of us do between right and wrong?"

"But how do you know that it is wrong? It—it is only employment! To be housekeeper to a hotel! In the countryside. By the sea. To arrange meals—see to—How can it be so wrong?"

"What kind of hotel do you think it must be for that man to have an interest in it?"

"It belongs to his friend. I have told you. His friend is buying it."

"And you are to look after it? At seventeen? And this does not seem strange to you?"

"He trusts me!"

"To do what?" He turned away. "To do what?"

"And I am not seventeen. I am—I am almost eighteen."

"Oh wonderful. Wonderful. Who can teach you anything? Warn you of anything? Go then. Go and look after this—this smugglers' tavern. And when trouble comes——"

"It is not a tavern! It is a hotel!"

"Oh child, child!" He came back and caught her by the shoulders. "God forgives all but folly. For the last time, take your freedom. Go away from here, from him, from everything to do with him while it is still possible. Mr. Mendoza has offered——"

"I have given my promise," she said, not meeting his eyes. "And I—I must—"

"Then"—he raised both hands in a gesture of helplessness and let them fall again—"what business is it of mine what you do?" He walked away to the window and looked out of it. "But you are running away," he said. "You know that? You are not running to something. Only away."

"What do you mean? Why are you being so unkind?"

"Do you think that I could wish to be unkind to you? Would it be kindness to say to you, 'Go, go. Do wrong. Run away. All will be well.' Would that be kind? When I know that it will not be well?"

"But how? How do you know?" And she was suddenly afraid that he would turn round towards her and she would see in his eyes how he knew. Could be forced to know herself that it would not end well. But he did not turn. He had begun to drum a tune on the window with two finger-tips.

"Will you not say good-bye to me?"

Mr. Solomons turned then and smiled and held out his hands.

But his smile was so sad that Kate looked away from his face. "I shall come back," she said. "And by then—perhaps I shall get a place in a theatre company and—this is only for a little while."

She kissed his old, worn cheek very quickly, and ran out, and down the stairs to the cellar, where Mr. Mendoza and Titine and 'Ang were waiting for her. Mr. Mendoza no better pleased with her, she suspected, than Mr. Solomons was. Titine standing by the outer door, as still and quiet as a shadow, and yet seeming to be quivering inside with contained excitement. 'Ang sitting on his bundle, their portmanteau and hat boxes beside him, his flute thrust carefully into the breast of his coat. Mr. Mendoza making himself busy about the racks, scarcely looking at her as she came in.

"Where is Isaac?" she said. She wanted to be gone, to put it beyond question that she was going. If Mr. Mendoza began to reproach her—"We must be going at once."

"He will be here in a moment." As he said it, she heard Isaac's boots clattering down the stone steps.

He came rushing into the cellar, breathless, a small parcel held out to his grandfather. "'Ere y'are. I 'ad to go miles——"

Mr. Mendoza took the parcel from him and held it out in his turn to Kate, with a shy stiffness, all his kindness in his eyes, and sadness, and reproach, and self-reproach that he could do no more for her than give her a parting gift.

"Here is something for your journey," he said. "From Isaac and myself. You are not to open it until—" He stopped and smiled very sadly and affectionately, touching Kate's cheek. "Wait until you are somewhere where you may think of us for a moment. We shall think of you often. Shall we not, Isaac?"

Isaac looked embarrassed and turned away to Titine. "G'bye," he said roughly. "G'bye, 'Ang." He ran up the steps again, banging his cudgel against the stone wall. "G'bye, Kate." His voice echoing down, fading.

She held the parcel against her breast. Felt herself on the point of crying. Mr. Mendoza kissed her forehead, drew Titine towards him and laid his hand on her head as though he were giving her a grandfather's blessing. Patted 'Ang's shoulder.

"Go," he said. "All is in God's hands. Let me have news of you."

But I am glad to be going, she thought. *It is only for this moment that—What I am doing is wise—wise— I know it. They have no right to reproach me.* Looking up at the house, at their room under the slates and chimney pots. At Mr. Solomon's window. At the front door that was always locked, that no one ever used. At the lane. That had been so strange and frightening, and had become dear and familiar. Felt tears coming, a tightness in her throat. But at the same time a leap of excitement, an almost trembling. She wanted to open Mr. Mendoza's parcel, but it was not possible there.

They turned the corner, were in a quieter place. She unwrapped a corner of the blue, coarse paper covering. A roll of music. "For Mr. 'Ang. From Isaac." Written with one of Isaac's crayons in his careful print. And two small boxes. Like the boxes that Mr. Jardine gave to Madame Pariglia. Only of cardboard and not leather. "For Miss Kate." And on the other "For Miss Titine."

Kate opened hers. Inside the box a small ebony-and-silver Crucifix. And a note, in French. That Mr. Mendoza must have written in advance of Isaac's purchase. "If you may accept this Holy object from a Jew—let it protect you from all evil." She bent her head over it, began to cry.

"What is it, Kate? What's 'e give you—? What's the matter?"

"Nothing." She held the Crucifix in her palm. Closed her hand on it.

"What is it?"

"A Crucifix."

"What's that?"

"A——" She did not know how to explain, and gave Titine her own small cardboard jewel box. A ring. Silver. Three blue stones. "Remember your old friend." Gave 'Ang his music. But he had no free hand to accept it and she carried it for him. "We must hurry," she said, not letting them see her face. "Or we shall be late."

Chapter 13

Kate had determined from the first moment that she would not speak to the young man, would not look at him, beyond the strictest necessity of cold politeness. How dare he expect it! How dare he look at her as if they—as if he knew nothing of her—had had no part in any of the wretchedness of these past days? Standing in the courtyard hubbub of The Three Crowns, looking at her as she came towards him with no more than an admiring curiosity half hidden by shyness. And she had thought furiously, *At last! At last he has shown himself!* Imagining that he must be the Mr. Gurney she was to meet here. The "Mr. Thomas" of Devon Place behind him, talking to an ostler who was harnessing the lead horses of a coach.

But another man had stepped forward, a heavy-set, strong-made man of middle age and a shade above middle size, with something of that same country air about him that seemed to distinguish all of them, except the Squire. Coming forward with a cold heartiness of greeting for the benefit of bystanders. "Why, my little god-daughter grown into a young woman! And don't you recognise your old godfather, Joseph Gurney, after all these three years? Fi on you, Miss!" A great clasping of hands and show of godfatherly affection. "And this is Mr. Christopher Hatton, m'dear," bringing forward the tall young man. "He'll be our travelling companion, and will be part of your care in Shoreham." Her care?

The young man bowing, flushing slightly. At meeting her? At the knowledge of the wrong he and all of them had done to her, the worse wrong they had contemplated? Very tall, very dark, the hair falling across his forehead as she had seen it already. With the Squire. And in the Mall. Her care? She wanted to ask what that might mean—to show at once that she was not afraid of them. But she was. And scarcely listened to the introductions. "I will not so

[153]

much as look at him," she promised herself. "Mr. Thomas" of Devon Place being introduced as "Mr. Biggins."

The coach that the ostler was harnessing the leaders to now ready. But no other passengers, for this was Mr. Gurney's private coach, only to be provided here with post horses. 'Ang to ride outside with their luggage. Titine and Kate herself squeezed in beside the new-named "Mr. Biggins," who spread himself with easy comfortableness, seeming to take up the space of two ordinary people with his great legs and elbows, his unbuttoned coat and waistcoat, his huge hands on his knees. Remarking on this and that in the streets as if they were on a pleasure jaunt to the country—to the seaside.

What would it be like, Shoreham? The Old Ship Hotel? Kate would not look at the young man, would affect not to hear him if he spoke to her. Made herself unreachable by staring out of the glass beside her, past Titine's bonnet, that now nodded sleepily and next jerked into wakefulness in case its owner might miss a fragment, a moment of excitement.

Streets. Country. A village. The young man scarcely tried to speak to Kate after a first rather nervous couple of politenesses. Perhaps he was no longer even looking at her. He scarcely spoke at all except to answer Mr. Gurney's occasional remarks or questions, or a word from "Mr. Thomas become Mr. Biggins." Now and then she could see Mr. Hatton's half reflection in the glass. Like an ivory shadow. And as the evening grew near to summer twilight and the reflection darker, more definite, the likeness to the picture, that painting of the Nativity, came back to her with a kind of anger, a vexation with herself that she had ever allowed her imagination to be so foolish. A vexation all the greater because she had already been obliged to learn that he was nothing of what she had imagined; not the Squire's son, nor any relation to him, nor any part or partner in any of their undertakings. Was apparently no more than the nephew of the Miss Passover who had sold The Old Ship Hotel to Mr. Gurney. Had that been what had brought Mr. Hatton to share the Squire's coach that day? Talking of the hotel to the Squire's sister, Mrs. Lammeter? Arranging the selling of it for his aunt?

Talk of the guests still at the hotel "—a few old-established people—unwilling to leave"—a clergyman—a sea-captain and his wife, Mr. Hatton himself.

[154]

"You keep the library in Shoreham?" Mr. Gurney said. "That's a quiet business for a young fellow, I'd have thought."

"I like it so," Mr. Hatton said.

"Ah!" said Mr. Gurney.

He did not, Kate had already sensed, feel much drawn to Mr. Hatton. She would have liked to look at both of them, compare their expressions. A difference between them, she had already seen, almost as great, as marked, as between Mr. Hatton and the Squire. Mr. Hatton so—so fine-drawn, his face so full of thoughts that made it seem to change from moment to moment—at least it had seemed like that in the brief instants when she had been obliged to look at him—and Mr. Gurney so heavy-set, an air of such heavy certainty about him as though his mind was long ago made up on all important subjects and could not be changed by any argument.

"Giving out novels to old women, eh?" Mr. Gurney was saying.

"At t-times," Mr. Hatton answered, that slight hesitation back in his voice, together with a dryness hinting at the anger beneath.

"Why do they dislike each other?" Kate wondered, and felt a quick beat of almost sympathy for Mr. Hatton, that he should be obliged to put up with such rudeness for his aunt's sake. Perhaps the sale was not yet complete and he must hold down his indignation until it was. Although he did not look like someone who made calculations of that kind. He was keeping his eyes lowered, the faintest of flushes on his cheekbones, his mouth set.

Why should Mr. Gurney dislike him so? And found Mr. Gurney's eyes on her with an expression that gave her the answer instantly, not by reason or thought, but by an instinct she had not known that she possessed. *Mr. Hatton is young. And I am young. And Mr. Gurney is not.* She found herself blushing, tilted her head so that the brim of her hat should hide her face. *They must think that—that I am pretty enough to be ill-humoured about.* And blushed darker, and stared determinedly out of the window at a field where the shadows of the trees were already losing their definiteness in a golden twilight. But what she saw was the reflection of her eyes, glistening back at her through the coach window. A stranger very pleased with herself, and her new and beautiful hat, and the idea of there being someone like Mr. Gurney ready to be rude to a younger man because of her presence. And of someone like Mr. Hatton—But before she could finish the thought she grew shocked at herself, and whispered to Titine to sit up straight and pay attention to the countryside instead of lolling about and letting her mouth hang open. Then she grew ashamed of herself for that injustice, and was suitably contrite and self-critical for several minutes.

Perhaps, she began to think, *Mr. Hatton is now afraid to speak to me. I was so cold to him in the beginning.* And after another moment or so. *It is just as well if he is, indeed! If we are to live in the same hotel, the last thing I should want—it would be unthinkable to allow him to—to imagine that—that we might become friendly. It is unthinkable. And he is not at all like that painting. He is much older, for one thing. Why, he must be—he must be at least twenty-four. Or even twenty-five. Mr. Gurney does himself an injustice thinking that—if he thinks that—he does me an injustice.* And she flushed again and wished that she might ask how much longer the journey was to last and what time they might arrive in Shoreham. Already they had changed horses twice.

She began to think with a sudden nervousness that in fact they actually would, must, soon arrive—that this journey would not last forever, or even very much longer. That in an hour or so she would be in the hotel of which she was to be housekeeper—would be being introduced as Mr. Gurney's god-daughter and representative— would be obliged to meet the guests, the servants. What servants would there be? What kind? Old? Young? What would they think of her? Of Titine? Of 'Ang?

Another hour. Titine was long ago asleep, her head resting on Kate's shoulder, tiny whisperings of breath fluttering against Kate's sleeve. On her other side Mr. Biggins slept in massive comfort, elbows and knees spreading, mouth open and snoring. Mr. Gurney not asleep but his expression forbidding conversation, his lower lip jutting out, his eyes absorbed in private thoughts—or glancing at the hedges going by as if he were counting them—or, once or twice, looking at Kate with a cold, hard, judging interest as if he were counting her, numbering her qualities for his business, pro and contra. Except that she could not imagine what qualities he might be needing. How could she manage a hotel? And even if she could, how could that be of any benefit to any business of the Squire's and Mr. Gurney's?

She looked, as secretly as she might, at Mr. Hatton, and found that he was looking at her. *He is going to speak to me,* she thought. And waited, making her expression quite calm and indifferent, neither repelling nor inviting. *He is afraid of me!* she thought, seeing his eyes grow shy. Shyer. Lowering them as if he were trying to pretend that he had not been looking at her at all. He had very long eyelashes. Very dark and thick. And that ridiculous lock of hair that kept falling. He pushed it back, glanced at her and smiled, and was so much the shepherd of the painting that her heart seemed to check and then race and then threaten to stop altogether, and she grew so angry at her own stupidity that her mouth and eyes grew coldly furious and he looked away as if she had caught him in the most humiliating of self-revelations. *Now I have hurt him beyond hope of repairing it,* she thought wretchedly. And a moment later was very pleased that she had done it, and so solved all problems of their threatened intimacy in the hotel.

They changed horses for a third and, Mr. Biggins said, waking and stirring himself, a final time. Kate changed places with Titine to make it even more difficult for Mr. Hatton to catch her eyes, and lowered the glass so that she might feel the breeze on her cheeks. The road climbed slowly up a long ridge, and memories came, softly at first, like shadows. Of long roads and hills, and slow-moving wheels. Not swift like these. The plodding, broken-winded horse. The dust, the heat. Or the cold. *Mironton. Mirontaine.* "Oh *maman! Maman!* Is this how young men seemed to you?" And for a long, long moment it was as though her mother was there in the coach, her shoulder against Kate's where Titine's head was again resting, warm and trusting.

"Did they seem to you like shepherds out of a Nativity?" Her mother kneeling by a bed—her hair spread out on the coverlet like the Magdalene's, such a glory of hair that it was like jewels and flowers and dark flames burning. And even in her anger with her mother, even in the depths of her shame for her, Kate could not escape the beauty of that great auburn mass of hair on the grey, dirty cotton. Wanted to touch it, hold it, bury her face in its cool silk. How could any man have left such beauty? And her mother crying as though God had abandoned her.

Kate had not been able to be angry with her. Could only hold her as though again their roles were reversed and she was the mother comforting her desolate child.

Mironton. Mirontaine.

There was a difference in the air. In the coolness of the breeze against her eyelids. A smell of something sharper, salt, raw. The sea. And Kate needed to put up her hand against her heart for a second as those other ghosts came pressing, swiftly jostling in the twilight.

"No!" she breathed. "No! Let me be quiet. It is all finished. Have I not—have I not tried—made amends?" And the folly of that thought made her close her eyes again, feel broken with guilt. Amends? For death? So many deaths? *Amends?* "But I could not—could not help you!" her mind cried out. "You are not ghosts, only my own weakness, only my thoughts, my own dreams! Go away, go away in God's name. Oh please, please!" And had to grip her hands together to quiet the trembling of them. Until she could force herself to say quite calmly, in an ordinary voice of interest and pleasure, "I can smell the sea! We must be—be almost there!"

"Where?" Titine whispered. "What does it smell like?" And then seemed to fold herself inside her mantle as if she were hiding from Mr. Gurney and "Mr. Thomas become Biggins" and Mr. Hatton.

The outskirts of a small town. A church, cottages, villas, a street, a great building with what seemed like a hundred windows looking down on them. Kate felt a sharp terror that this was the hotel.

"Where's the sea?" Titine whispered again. And the next moment did not need to ask. The road tilting steep down. The coachman holding the horses back from slipping, from going too fast down hill. And below them the shore, a great, shimmering distance of sand and mud flats, and beyond all of it, the sea, far out and quiet and leaden grey.

"It is not the same!" Kate's mind cried out. "It is not!" Only the steepness of the road down, the greyness of the small, old houses. The fishing boats drawn up on the sand. It was nothing like! Nothing.

A few moments later they were in front of the hotel, a long, irregular-looking building like three or four private houses clasped together and grown by the passage of time into one. Mr. Gurney pushing open the unlocked door, crying out "Hulloa, there? Porter? Is anyone about?"

An old man, bent as a crab, came shuffling towards them down a long passage from the depths of the house. There were the sounds of women's voices on a stairs. An elderly, weather-beaten gentleman looking out of a doorway beside Mr. Gurney—surely the sea-captain they had spoken of? —the glimpse of the bright parlour behind him, a small old woman in a black shawl, looking nervous at the commotion of arrivals.

[158]

"It is you, is it, Mr. Gurney, sir, back again?" the weather-beaten gentleman said, as though glad to see him. And calling over his shoulder "It is Mr. Gurney, my dear, the new proprietor come back. And Mr. Hatton! How are you, my boy?" And seeing Kate and Titine, becoming instantly alarmed, as if unsure whether his waistcoat were properly buttoned, or his wig on crooked, and looking about him for sea-room in which to beat an escape. But there was none, and there had to be introductions and handshakes and curtseys and "Delighted, ma'am. And a young sister, is it? A friend, eh? Ah, ah, delighted, delighted."

The old porter touching his forehead, making useless efforts to deprive Mr. Biggins of his burdens, although clearly unable to support any of them, let alone all. Turning instead to take Kate's hat box. A stout woman, red-faced, white-aproned, coming out from what must be a kitchen, wiping her hands and bare arms, curtseying; two maids peeping, both black-haired, button-eyed, like sisters. Another girl behind the cook, thin and sandy like a ferret in a shabby gown and greasy apron. Being driven back to her duties by the cook. A gentleman with a book in his hand, and mournful, red-rimmed eyes, appearing from another room. The whole hotel like an ant's nest overturned by Mr. Gurney's—by their—arrival. Not that Mr. Gurney, or any of them, made much commotion, but Mr. Gurney had that way, that Kate had already become aware of, of dominating any place and company.

The maids ran about as they seemed not to have done since they were first employed there, breathless with anxiety, carrying trays, seeing to bedrooms, fetching hot water, declaring that they had not expected them for an hour yet; peeping at Kate, at Titine, whispering about 'Ang who, to Kate's reluctance, had been already settled in the kitchen, Mr. Gurney ordering carelessly that he should be given supper and shown a bed; and that in the morning he should begin to help the old porter John, who certainly seemed in dear need of help. The chief of what he seemed to do was totter about the corridors and kitchens wringing his hands in anxiety. Perhaps he feared that the new proprietor would turn him out of doors, and Kate felt immediately sorry for him, for his worried old peering eyes and his soiled shirt that had gone far too long without being changed and washed, and his darned black breeches and his wrinkled woollen stockings that seemed as old as himself and to have no calves inside them.

[159]

The kitchens full of steam and bustle and smells of supper; the cook, Mrs. Earnshaw, as fussed and harried as though she had not had a fortnight to prepare for them, and all day to cook in. The maids, the two sisters, running in to look at 'Ang, running out to look at Kate, running to the yard door where Mr. Biggins was already striding about, taking possession of the stables that were to be his concern, although what need such a hotel might have of stables was hard to see. Any gentleman with his own horses or carriage would scarcely stay in such a place, and the Royal Hotel, that they had seen first at the top of the hill, was there for the needs of post-travellers. But Mr. Biggins, Mr. Gurney with him for a few minutes, was routing about among the three or four stalls, kicking at dilapidated partitions, scrambling up into the loft above them, and measuring the space for a chaise or a phaeton as if carriage company were expected tomorrow.

Titine lost in the midst of everything, wanting to go into the kitchens to 'Ang, and afraid of the cook, and the porter, and the maids; even afraid of the sandy-ferret kitchen-maid—as thin and nervous-looking as herself, and not even so tall as she was—in a cotton cap that should have been white, and an apron too large for her, and boots too large for her, and skirts too long for her trailing about on the wet scullery floor. The dark stain of damp had spread up to knee height on the faded blue cotton and she seemed to drip as she ran about, wiping her forehead, her sandy hair falling down out of its knot, into ferret tails on her narrow shoulders.

"'Oo's she?" Titine whispered. "The little one?"

"She must be the kitchen-maid."

"She said 'er name's Peg. I think. I can't understand any of 'em."

"We shall learn soon."

Unpacking. Washing. Kate and Titine had a room together at the top of the hotel, smaller than their attic in Mr. Mendoza's house, even quainter-shaped, with wooden beams, and sloping floors, and a lattice window that would not open at first, and that would not shut when the wind blew in the curtains. Cupboards; and an oak table that seemed to have one leg shorter than the others, or perhaps it was the floor boards that made it unsteady; a high-posted, curtained, oak-framed bed that must surely have been made in the room, for how else could so big a bed have been got up the narrow stairs with their sharp corners? A wash-stand and a white basin and great white jug that Peg had carried up to them, staggering under its weight full of hot water; and white towels, rather thin and mended; and on the black timber floor a rug made of pieces of coloured rag stitched together. The walls white plaster gone yellow, and nothing on them but a woollen sampler in a frame: "Agnes Passover Fecit, 1747. 'Who hathe despised the daye of small things?' Aetat 14."

Kate stood looking at it for a moment. Faded red and blue and yellow wool. Had this been Miss Passover's bedroom? Nursery? Fifty—almost fifty—years ago? There was a swift, cold sense of time long past entered into the atmosphere, like the air from a cupboard opened after years and years of forgottenness. Of a child's loneliness, of long grey evenings spent in this small, quiet space, with only the sounds of the autumn, of the winter sea for company. Stitching at that sampler. A young, grey-dressed figure, the ghost of a child in an antique gown, pale and serious and sad. "Who hathe despised the daye of small things?" What did it mean? Kate was suddenly very glad that she was not to be alone in this room. Or anywhere here. She turned quickly towards Titine and kissed her. *Please God,* she thought, *that I have not done wrong in*— she thought that she could hear the sea although that was not possible, it had been so calm. And yet there was indeed the sound of its whispering, like small waves lapping against sand.

"May God protect us," she said and took out her Crucifix. She must find somewhere to hang it up. Where she could look at it as she said her prayers. Long ago, when she and Titine were first together, and she had been kneeling down at night, the idea of praying had amazed Titine, and then intrigued her, and for a time she had imitated Kate, and repeated the words Kate taught her. And then as suddenly had given it up and would not continue, or explain why. But now she touched the Crucifix with her finger and said, "'E doesn't listen."

"But He does! What do you mean? Did I not find you? Are we not safe together?"

"That was you, not 'Im."

"And who made that possible?"

She stood almost in agony at Titine's disbelief, that sense of time gone by. Of fifty years, of echoes and loneliness and sorrow and of lost childhood, and childhood and happiness never found, so strong that she could not move for a moment, could only stand holding the Crucifix in both hands, trying to pretend that she was

[161]

looking for a nail to hang it on. On the bedpost. And there indeed there was a nail as if deliberately driven into the thick oak for just such a purpose. What nonsense found its way into her mind! The child of the sampler had grown into that fat old woman of the Mall, whom she had seen with Mr. Hatton, her nephew. A fat, pompous old woman, nothing sad or lonely or lost about her at all.

I am quite mad, she thought, hanging up the Crucifix.

"It's all stuff," Titine whispered in contempt. "Prayers and that."

"Oh *mon Dieu!*" But there was no time for lessons in religion. One of the maids was calling them, and a moment after they heard Mr. Gurney's voice filling the hotel, or seeming to, asking where the devil they had got to. They ran down to their supper, and to have a more formal meeting with the small handful of guests. Mr. Gurney had suggested at first that Titine be relegated to the kitchens with 'Ang, but Kate had refused that indignantly, and had had her way. Titine was to have no duties in the hotel except at Kate's discretion.

Introductions. Captain Cartwright again, and his lady. The Reverend Mr. Sowerby, the gentleman with the red-rimmed eyes and the book; still with his book, a finger marking his place, bowing; rusty black coat, rusty black breeches, ill-fitting wig, his weak eyes blinking in alarm at the influx of company, at Mr. Gurney's domination of the parlour; in nervousness of Kate and Titine, clearly unused to speaking to young ladies. Captain Cartwright more at his ease now that he had had time to make certain of his wig and his general neatness and meetness for young female company; bluff and hearty and red-faced; a small, square man in a blue coat with silver buttons, his waistcoat looking as though it were cut from white sail cloth, and buff breeches and white stockings and square-toed shoes that might have been made by a ship's carpenter. A half-pay naval Captain, he informed Kate within a minute of this, their second introduction. "Too old for this new war, I'm afraid. Beached. Come and satisfy Mrs. Cartwright that you ain't a young dragon come to shake us all up and make us fashionable."

Mrs. Cartwright tiny in black. A hand like a bird's claw, an eye like a bird's eye, but a bird who sees the cat and cannot fly away. Looking at Kate as though she expected to be sprung upon and devoured. Answering Kate's renewed curtsey with another of her own. "And who is the other young lady?" Mrs. Cartwright whispered. "I fear I did not quite catch her name. She—she looks a very *smart* young lady."

"She is my friend. Her name is Titine," Kate said, amused at the idea that poor Titine was smart, or that she herself might be considered a "fashionable dragon."

"Oh," Mrs. Cartwright breathed. "How—how strange."

Captain Cartwright left them together to join Mr. Gurney. Kate heard "— yer god-daughter—fine young woman—left her peacifying poor Mrs. Cartwright—nervous as be damned, poor woman—any change—"

And on the heels of that Mrs. Cartwright whispering, "I—I do hope that you and—and Mr. Gurney—do not have in mind any *grave* changes? Poor Mrs. Passover—her death seemed so—sudden—although at eighty-four of course—and then Miss Agnes deciding she could not manage by herself and selling the hotel right over our heads, so to speak. Such a shock to all of us. We had grown very set in our ways under their care. And now—and now—" The small, faded brown eyes that must once have been alert as a robin's grew bright with tears. "We have lived here ten years, you know, the Captain and I. And Mr. Sowerby seven. Mr. Hatton has been with us only for this half year, of course. Since—since poor Mrs. Passover died. We—we have been—but it is very wrong of me to seem sad—and on your first evening—and how tired you must be after your journey! We must make your godfather remember that we ladies are frailer creatures than he, and that you must be longing for your suppers and your beds."

"No, please," Kate said, alarmed. But a moment later Mr. Gurney did gather them, and led the way into the dining room where there were cold meats and wine and a dozen other things that Kate was suddenly too tired to identify, let alone sample. And at last bed. Sinking into a depth of feather mattress, down pillows, the linen cold and crisp and smelling of the sea and lavender. That whispering of the sea on sand and shingle, like the blood pulsing in her ears.

The next morning the tide was out and after a late enough breakfast Mr. Gurney took Kate and Titine out onto the sands, stretching for a mile or more towards a horizon that was also the curving line of the sea. He was easier with them than he had been on the journey the day before, and even, in a bluff and domineering way, seemed to be wishing to amuse them as well as to tell Kate things that she must know.

He pointed out the Royal Hotel, although it needed no pointing at to identify it, crowning the cliffs like a rococo barracks, with flags and pennants and candle-snuffer turrets, and row upon row of glittering windows. The Assembly Rooms beside it, where Mr. Hatton's library was, and the Queen's Theatre, and the smart new villas of the Royal Parade along the cliffs.

Below the Royal Hotel and the villas, shrubberies and gravel paths fell and twisted their way down to the fashionable bathing beach, where already the bathing machines were in the water, with their hoods and ladders, their horses long ago led back to the shore. Donkeys were pacing slowly up and down, carrying small children, the donkey-boys leading them. A child's cry of fright or joy came shrilly over the wide glistening of the sands. Couples walked on the driest part of the beach, the coloured parasols like flowers nodding. But all of that quite distant from where Titine and Kate stood with Mr. Gurney, his heavy Malacca cane pointing out this and that to them. The oldest part of Shoreham, the fisherman's cottages and the jetty, away to their right as they faced the shore. And their own hotel, with its name painted in large white letters on the main part of the roof—"The Old Ship Hotel"—presumably so that passing ships might read it, for surely no one else could unless they walked out here, by which time they must have known very well of its existence.

Behind their hotel, and the hidden back road that served its stables and the rear entrances of the neighbouring shops and houses, there rose a more gradual equivalent of the cliffs on which the Royal Hotel and all of New Shoreham stood. Rough and overgrown with bushes, and at the top the remains of a watch-tower. Much farther to their right, to the northeast, the coast grew low and indistinct, sea and land and sky blending in one shimmer of summer brightness; sand, mud flats, the shadow that must be land from its position, but that seemed to float on the sea haze.

"Shoreham Flats," Mr. Gurney said, pointing in that direction. "And out there, Shotton Bank." He looked at Kate, screwing up his eyes with good-tempered amusement. "And what care you for either, eh, Miss? Tell your young friend here to run ahead of us and look for a starfish or a pretty shell, and we will talk business for a moment."

Titine ran on, holding her skirts above her ankles, glad to be free of Mr. Gurney's eye, or at least of having it too closely watching her. Kate clasped her hands against her waist, determined not to show that she was nervous of him. He looked at her, quick and hard. "Ye know how to keep your head on your shoulders and your counsel to yourself, I think? No sorts of young-gentleman-folly, or things of that kind, when it's a matter of business?"

"I hope so, sir."

"So do I, girl. You're wretched young for this, but—well, mark me now, it *is* business, and a damned valuable one too, I hope."

"I shall do my utmost to—"

"Oh, not the hotel! That's nothing but disguise. I don't care a straw if never another summer visitor sets foot in the place. Thank God most of the guests went when the old lady died. There's only one visitor we're waiting for." Mr. Gurney stared out across the Flats and Shotton Bank, holding his Malacca cane poised as though about to point with it again. "Then we shall see something. Meantime it's for you to make it seem that all is *as it seems.* A new proprietor. A young housekeeper learning her trade to help her godfather. Within a fortnight the good people of Shoreham 'll pay no more attention to The Old Ship Hotel, nor to you, than to wonder if you'll wear a new bonnet come Sunday, or if that child there is your sister." He turned on her with a flash of yesterday's harshness. "Damnation, why could she not go into the kitchen with the boy, and there'd be no questions to ask about her? It's any kind of questioning we need to avoid, or prying, or——"

"Titine would cause more questions there in the kitchen than with me," Kate said, flushing. "She—she has had very little teaching, I am afraid."

"Then all the better for her if she learned to scrub. Still, the thing is done. You're a strange young woman," he said, staring into her face with a hard inquisitiveness. He seemed about to say more, but turned away and struck at a wrack of seaweed with his cane.

When he did not continue, Kate said, "May I know what—what kind of business it is that—that this visitor will bring? Is it—smuggling?" She was half afraid to ask, but he showed neither surprise nor vexation, and merely struck again at the sea-wrack.

[165]

"Aye. Of a kind. Ye might call it that. But ye'll know in good time."

"But—but I—what shall I have to do? Must I—will it be as in London—?"

He swung round on her. "Have I not said ye'll know in—" He paused and laughed. "Ye'd like that, would you?"

He flung an arm round her shoulders and made her walk on with him in that way, leaning on her. Not as the Squire had once or twice done, for the support of his supposed infirmities, but with a vigorous possessiveness that did not care whether she minded or not. That seemed to be saying, "I'm twice the man any young fellow of twenty-four or -five could be, and don't you mistake it!" Her question seemed almost to have decided him on something; that she was his creature, to do with as he liked.

"Ye have a hunger for adventure, eh? Like a boy? Ye have half the look of a boy about you at times." Smiling down at her almost kindly. He stabbed his cane towards the horizon. "Out there!" he said. "That's where adventure is. This"—he made a sound between contempt and disgust— "I think sometimes—oh, damme, what's the use of thinking? Look at Cartwright now. Forty years in the service of his King. And stumping out his last days in *that* —" stabbing towards The Old Ship Hotel. "Half pay. Quarter living. Frightened out of his wits that we'll charge him more than he can afford and he'll have to move. He'd be better dead."

"Mrs. Cartwright may not think so."

He stared at her as if he had been talking to himself. "Aye? Aye, mebbe." He laughed again. "Well, we'd best go back on shore, or the town will have us down for lovers. Now, mark what I've said. Behave as if there were nothing in your mind but the Hotel and your own ordinary concerns. Your godfather is a gentleman mostly now in London, but who has travelled previously, and ye know little about him. You—and that child there—are orphans. Make up what tale you like. Give yourself a French mother to account for your accent—it ain't as bad as it was, but ye still sound damned French at times—"

She looked at him in surprise, wondering how he could speak of what her accent had been like any length of time ago.

"The Squire was telling me what ye sounded like," he said, catching her unspoken question. "But no matter. It brings us a greater benefit."

"What benefit?"

He hesitated. "All right, what harm if I tell ye now? It is nothing to be alarmed about. When this fellow comes—he's a Frenchman, and it'll be your business to look after him. Keep him out of the way. Give out that he's sick abed with—oh, toothache—anything. Let the maids do their business about him, candles and hot water and so on; his meals to his room. But you must see to anything that might require question and answer. He claims he speaks tolerable English, but ye'd best report him as a Welshman, say. That'll account for any strangeness if they do hear a word or two from him. And the minute he arrives Biggins'll fetch me to him."

"But in a hotel! With the maids, the guests—is it not the worst place—"

He laughed, as if well-enough pleased at the question. "It is the best place, child. It is why we have chosen it. Where else should he come? To London? With all the dangers of discovery on the journey? Stay in lodgings or an Inn? Or take a private house somewhere, and be spied on as a new curiosity before he so much as comes, with ladies leaving cards and calling, and the Vicar about our ears, and the local gentry wondering shall we keep horses and are we shooting people, or what? Nay, nay. A hotel is perfect for us. Its business is to have strangers about, comings and departures. Who thinks twice of boxes and chests consigned to a hotel? Of a stranger arriving by night and keeping to his bed a day or two, sick from the journey?"

"I—I suppose you must be right," she said doubtfully.

"Of course I am right! Now, listen. When this man comes, ye'll look after him. But ye'll do more than that. We want ye to sound him out. We want to know is he true or false. Has he any aim in the matter but what he tells us? Can he truly deliver what he promises? And to delve the answers out of him in broken French and broken English'd take a hundred years, and there'd be things we could not fathom out even then. It needs someone French——"

Kate began to object, and he waved her protest aside with a sudden sharpening of impatience. "Don't fret at me! Who the devil cares for your being French or English, so long as ye're obedient? It needs someone who knows every shadow of meaning of every word he says. Can read every look, every turn of his eye, every hesitation. More. It needs knowledge of what has been happening these past years in France; the kind of knowledge ye can't get from newspa-

pers, or gossip with émigrés, or men coming over in—no matter—
am I clear?"

"Yes."

"A woman, a young, pretty woman who speaks French better
than she speaks English, who has lived through the same years he
has lived through—ye were made for this business. We thought of
it a dozen times, round and round—ye were too young, too innocent—"

"You—thought of it—?"

"Aye, naturally. It was our first thought. And our last as it turns
out. Don't make us regret it." He had let his arm fall from her
shoulder some time before, and now he grasped her shoulder in
his hand, and twisted her to face him. "We don't ask ye to seduce
him. Only to get the truth out of him. Which ten to one'll be the
truth he's already told us by letter; that he has goods to sell and
needs the payment in good English gold. A great deal of goods, for
a great deal of gold. But if there's a trick at the back of it, we need
to know it. We're searching it out in France as well—but that's easier said than done. Ye're to be our last check on him. If ye hadn't
been there to hand, we must have done without. But ye were."

She looked at him, a dozen questions quick in her mind. But she
asked none of them. Only nodded slowly. And although he had as
good as ordered her not to question him, it seemed not to please
him either that she should remain so silent.

"Well?"

She still hesitated.

"Well?" he repeated, almost angrily. "Ye'll do what we want?"

"Yes. If—yes, I will do my best."

"Good. Then that's settled. Let us gather your wretched little
friend out of that puddle and go back to the hotel."

Titine was crouched by a shallow pool in the sand, watching tiny
creatures dart about like thin shadows in the surface of a mirror.

"Did ye find a starfish?" Mr. Gurney asked her. He had recovered his good humour again and looked as though he was happy to
be out strolling in the sun, on the empty sands. As though there
was nothing weighing on his mind but to amuse his two companions. "Do ye know what they look like?"

"No," Titine whispered. She opened her hand, and there was a
shell in it, like a twisted horn, smooth and iridescent at the mouth,
the outside chalk white and crusted with tiny shells, small creatures

[168]

living on a greater, and the great creature long, long dead.

Mr. Gurney took the shell from Titine's hand and held it to her ear. She shrank away.

"Nay, listen, child. Listen to the sounds in it." He made her stay still while he held the sea-shell close to her ear again. "D'ye hear the roar of the sea?"

She looked her astonishment and Mr. Gurney laughed and turned to Kate. She wanted to cry "No!" but was afraid of irritating him, and had to submit. The shell, warm from Titine's hand and his, touching her cheek and that deep murmuring like blood.

"It is very strange," she said, controlling her horror.

"I used to listen to that as a boy. Took 'em to bed with me to listen to as I fell asleep and make me dream of sea-faring."

"And did you go sea-faring? Afterwards?"

"Aye. Aye, I did." He laughed. "Of my own kind. There's more ways of sea-faring than Cartwright's, although I did a voyage or two for His Majesty as well. But let us go back and begin hotel-keeping in earnest." He stamped along, with every sign of high good humour, stabbing at the sand with his cane, and pointing out a dozen kinds of sea-creatures to them both: starfish, and whelk shell, and cuttle-fish bone; crab, and mussel, and the tell-tale breathing holes of great buried companies of cockles, or their empty shells gone to the surface, smooth as porcelain inside. And the seaweeds, with their black bubbles that he burst for them in his thick fingers, to let them smell at the iodine inside; and the body of a sea gull, half consumed. He seemed truly a different man from yesterday. Even from the Mr. Gurney of ten minutes earlier.

"It is a clean thing," he said. "The sea. It leaves no traces of filth behind."

"That is not my feeling of it," Kate whispered. "It horrifies me." She turned her eyes away from the sea gull's drowned and fretted feathers, its long, gaunt throat.

The sands spread out on either side of them, mirror bright, infinite. The shore still far off, the cliffs dark green against the bright summer sky, the Royal Hotel, the villas of the upper town like bright new toys set out on top of them; the old town huddled under them, straggling. The flower points of ladies' parasols, a flash of mauve, violet, pink, white, as strollers walked near the shore or on the cliff paths. All peace, all brightness. And away to their right, nothing but the shimmer of sand and sky. And the sea.

[169]

Chapter 14

Mr. Gurney left Shoreham the following day, and within another day or so his prediction seemed to be coming true, and the hotel and its inhabitants settled back into their contented, drowsy ways with deep sighs of relief that nothing was to be changed, and only a pleasant new source of gossip and speculation added, in the shapes of Titine and Kate and 'Ang, and what the possible relationship might be between all of them and Mr. Gurney. 'Ang indeed caused much less comment than Kate had feared he might, for several ladies of fashion had brought blackamoor servants to the Royal Hotel or the Royal Parade villas in recent years, and only two years ago a rich old gentleman, a director of the East India Company, had had a Chinese servant-man with him when he came to try the sea bathing for his gout. No doubt behind their backs there was a good deal of wondering as to how godly a godfather Mr. Gurney might be to Kate, and she wished now that he had settled on a less equivocal title of kinship, but it was almost amusing to see the curiosity in the maids' eyes, and the struggle in Mr. Sowerby's between anxiety to conciliate and what she suspected was a natural sourness of disapproval. He was a sallow, bilious-looking man who seemed to live chiefly on milk puddings and white soups.

"Bitter disappointed in life," Mrs. Earnshaw said of him. He had been tutor in a noble family and for twenty years or so had looked forward to a handsome living as his reward for obsequiously swallowed insults. Instead, some alteration of his patron's circumstances had left him pensioned off to end his days in Shoreham, writing a book against the Methodists. But if he disapproved of Kate as being young and pretty and Catholic and French, he kept it to himself and showed her every outward sign of politeness. Only Mr. Hatton kept himself aloof from her, giving way to her on the stairs with a bow and a quick, shy smile, but never attempting a conversation with her; or anything beyond the most necessary of murmurs.

It is because I looked so severely at him in the coach, Kate thought, and felt compunction at first, and then a slight irritation that he should keep up a coolness for so long, for such a little reason. *Surely he does not expect me to approach him?* she thought, with a recovery of anger, and when next they met and he gave her his shy, quick smile before lowering his eyes, she crushed him with a glance of such coldness and hauteur that he looked astonished and so hurt that she wanted to go back and speak to him. But that was impossible. And if they were not on friendly terms, it was just as well. Much the best in fact. "No young-gentleman-folly," Mr. Gurney had said. Indeed there should not be! If such a thing had ever been, could ever be possible for her, it was not such a young man as Mr. Hatton who should tempt her into it. And to satisfy herself of how right she was to ignore him she allowed Mrs. Earnshaw to gossip to her about him occasionally, which she certainly would not have done if she had felt the slightest attraction towards him.

"It is not a very manly occupation surely?" she had said carelessly to Mrs. Earnshaw. "Handing novels to old ladies in a library?"

"His father were a book-seller," Mrs. Earnshaw said excusingly, "and I do suppose he knew nought but books since he were little. He writes poetry too," she whispered, sounding very confidential about it, as though that were a secret not everyone could be trusted with. "But he do fare to have a heart of gold. There een't a scrap o' real harm in him, whatever Mr. Sowerby do say."

"And why should Mr. Sowerby say anything against him?" Kate asked, unintendingly allowing a certain stiffness into her tone. Mrs. Earnshaw looked at her quickly in a motherly sort of way.

"He'd fare to disapprove of anyone, Mr. Sowerby would. Him and his Methodies." She looked round her again in case they were possibly overheard by old John, or Peg, or heaven knew what inquisitive ears. "Although to tell the truth on it," she whispered, "Mr. Hatton do bring it on himself, with his goings on about politics. A proper Jacobin he makes himself sound like when he do get heated up. He'd have his poor aunt, Miss Agnes, scandalised, the things he'd say. Against the King, even. Everything. Nothing pleases him but it ought to be changed. I don't know how the poor Captain do have patience with him. And not an idea o' how to look after himself, let alone other people's affairs. I don't know. It's a wife as he do want, to teach him a bit o' sense." Comfortably unrealistic match-making plans in her eyes as she looked at Kate, before beginning to explain that Kate's ideas of what they might have for the next day's dinner were quite impossible. "You leave it to me, ma'am." She did not say, "Run off and play and don't be bothering me," but her tone more than half implied it. And indeed there was very little for Kate to do, beyond making sure that 'Ang had his breakfast, and dinner, and was not being teased by the maids.

She helped serve the meals, and filled another hour or so looking after Mrs. Cartwright's comfort and listening to her stories of her travels with the Captain; or finding her tatting for her, or the Captain's spectacles and newspaper for him; or fetching Mr. Sowerby some milk or some watered Madeira. Or she would visit the stables that Mr. Biggins was making ready for their own horses and a chaise that he was to buy soon, and try, without success, to wheedle information out of him, about the expected Frenchman. But beyond that she was as much at leisure as if she had herself been a guest and not the supposed housekeeper.

She had indeed more time to think than was comfortable. Of the Frenchman. When would he come? How would she be able to—and what kind of man would he be? Like the men in Callac? The Marats? The Commandant? Until too many memories came back and she thought that she would not be able to face him at all. And what kind of business was he coming to do? Not ordinary smuggling, surely? That did not need this kind of secret visiting, and the huge expense of buying a hotel, and the trouble of employing her to question the man. Mrs. Cartwright had said that the hotel had cost sixteen hundred pounds. Sixteen hundred! What kind of business could justify so much money merely to provide a meeting-place? Unless it was to be more than that? The stables—did they mean to store smuggled goods there? To have other secret visitors? They must need such places, keep their stores somewhere. But from the way Mr. Gurney had spoken—

Kate had guessed long ago, long before Mr. Foster's hints of great doings and mysteries, that there was more involved than tea and tobacco. The heavy chests—so heavy they could surely only contain gold, or something equally precious. Could they be smuggling gold from France and the low countries? Why? Did England not already have plenty of gold, more than any other country? Had it anything to do with the war? With French aristocrats smuggling their wealth to England? But if it was that, surely there was no need for secrecy once it had safely arrived?

And the remembrance of Mr. Solomons's anger and warnings would come back to her and chill her spirits, and make her long for the Frenchman to come and for everything to be done and finished. And then? Afterwards? What then?

If only there was something to do now. In the mornings she would wake full of good resolutions about counting the sheets and learning to cook and overseeing the dusting and polishing and bed-making, and visiting the chandlers who supplied the hotel and looking at their accounts. But she knew so little about any of these things and all was going on so smoothly without her troubling her-self that there seemed to be no point in thinking of interfering. Much better she decided, to spend all this precious interval of lei-sure in educating Titine. Her pronunciation. Her letters that they had begun in London and somehow abandoned again. Arithmetic. Religion. Geography. There were endless things Titine ought to know.

Not the least was what she might and might not say to people, and how she should answer them. Kate overheard her with Mr. Sowerby one morning, Mr. Sowerby's voice rising to a pitch of unc-tuous dismay and horror, Titine's too low and whispering to be un-derstood through the closed door, but with a tone of disdain in it that to any adult must seem worse than the most pert impudence. Kate hesitated between a first glint of amusement and a second, more enduring feeling of anxious concern. What could they be talking of? She opened the door swiftly and heard Titine say with rising contempt, "All right then, 'oo was 'e? What did 'e do?"

"Child!" Mr. Sowerby cried. "Our Saviour? Our Blessed Saviour? You ask me who He was? What He did? Can it be possible that—" He saw Kate at the door and said in the flush of his indignation, "Miss Harriott! I cannot believe what I have been hearing! Such ig-norance, such black depths of—do not you realise that this poor young creature is in danger of Hell Fire, of eternal torment?"

Kate controlled herself with a strong effort of self-discipline, felt almost as if she were becoming someone else in that moment of holding the door open for Titine—someone older, taller, a cold rage in her like ice—ice that burns. How dare he speak like that to a child?

"I do not share your belief that children run such dangers,

[173]

whether from ignorance or from giving impertinent replies to adults," she said. "Although to me the latter is a more serious matter than the former—will you go to our room, Titine? I shall join you in a few moments."

Titine went out, catching Kate's threatening eye at the last moment and making a sketch of a curtsey to Mr. Sowerby as she went.

"Mr. Sowerby," Kate began when she had closed the door again, "I had not thought of asking you to undertake such a responsibility as instructing Miss Titine in matters of religion. You are too generous and unselfish with your time and I must pray you to spare yourself."

She felt her mouth trembling with fury, her hand still grasping the door handle as though she were supporting herself. She could not bring herself to look at him and looked instead at his reflection in the mirror above the mantelpiece, thin and black and yellow and bilious, showing his long teeth in a grimace that was half genuine anger and half the beginnings of a conciliatory smile, an expression almost of fear about it; about his weak, peering eyes that were turning now towards her and now away to the mirror and her reflection, as if he too could not bring himself to look at her directly.

He is afraid of me, Kate thought, and felt disgust suddenly instead of anger and wished she had not come in, not overheard—wished she could wipe out what had happened like a stain of breath from that mirror. But she could not. *What can I say to him?* she thought. *Tell him that his fear is unnecessary? His room, his comforts, his safety here are not threatened by anything I would do to him?* To say that would be worse than anything else she could say and she stayed helplessly looking at the mirror, twisting the thick wooden doorknob in her fingers, all her anger drained away.

"Pray, pray forgive me," he was saying, his lips seeming stiff as he made the words shape themselves, "if I have seemed to intrude. I—I had thought that, like yourself, Miss Titine was of—of the Roman persuasion." He showed a still yellower extent of teeth, and rolled up his eyes as if to demonstrate his willingness to tolerate Popery, showing in the process not the whites so much as the pinks of them, a pale pink rim of inner, watery eyelid that was painful to look at, even in reflection. "—but such a state of darkness—"

"For children," Kate said, recovering her sharpness, "I would think darkness preferable to threats of Hell Fire and eternal punishments. I assure you I have a vivid sense of my responsibilities."

"Oh, no doubt, no doubt."

"Then we need not speak of it again," Kate said. "And now if you will permit me to leave you—"

He bowed, still showing his teeth and the rims of his eyelids, and made haste to hold the door for her. Outside in the hall passage way she took a deep breath and was sorry she had told Titine that she would follow her upstairs. She wanted in that moment simply to be alone, to be free to walk out of the hotel into the open— to—she held her left hand flattened against her breast to quieten her heartbeat, and breathed very deeply, once, twice, as if to draw strength out of the shadows and the still air.

In their small parlour Titine was standing by the table, looking towards the doorway, her eyebrows very slightly raised in an expression of polite surprise at Kate's manner. And something—the barest hint of it, but definably there—of indifference, that stopped Kate in the moment of letting loose her indignation. She had imagined as she came up the stairs how she might find her—angry, half-fearful of a scolding, resentful—but this! Not even indifference— seeming no longer even to be thinking of what had just happened, and ready to be scornfully astonished at any reminder of it.

"Do not you realise—" Kate began, no longer sure whether she was angry or only wishing to be so, thinking that she ought to seem angry rather than feeling it. Titine maintained her look of mildness. "—I *must* speak to you," Kate said, but the possibility had gone. And what, after all, had Titine really done? Given an honest answer to a foolish, interfering old man, an unpleasant bigot who deserved to be shocked? If he had truly been shocked? And what did it matter what he thought of them both, what he repeated? Repeated to whom?

I am as foolish as he, she thought, and caught a shadow of mockery in Titine's eyes, as if she knew Kate's mind and was gently agreeing, her mouth not quite beginning to smile, but ready to smile in forgiveness of Kate's foolishness. For a second Kate was so angry she could not speak. Her heart seemed to swell with anger. And then that moment too was gone, leaving only astonishment at herself, uncertainty. Titine was not even smiling, she had only imagined it—and she held out her hands to Titine as if pleading with her not to smile. Titine took them in hers with an air of tolerance and love, a hint, the merest hint of tolerance.

"You—you did not *mean* to make him angry?" Kate whispered.

She heard the note of pleading in her voice and came close to anger again, at herself, at Mr. Sowerby, at Titine's impenetrable certainties. But in the face of those certainties, that self-containment, what was the use of being angry? And she let her hands be held and wanted suddenly to be held much closer, to be told that nothing mattered, that all was well and safe. As if she were longing for her mother, for the kind of assurances her mother had never been able to provide.

"It does not signify," she said with forced brightness. "I am silly to have become angry. But—oh, Titine, my dear, my dearest, how much you do not know!" And she was able to sigh in a very adult fashion as she held Titine at arm's length and considered her childishness and lack of worldly knowledge. "We truly must become serious about your lessons. I have been thinking a great deal on the matter recently. There is reading—it is truly dreadful that you cannot read. And after that—well, I do not at all agree with Mr. Sowerby, but indeed I must teach you something of religion so—so that you may choose for yourself what you wish to believe. For if you do not know, how can you? We will begin tomorrow. Without fail. Do you promise me?"

Titine nodded, indulgence fading away into watchfulness and the beginnings of alarm at these renewed threats to her liberty.

"And then there is History and—and I could teach you French—and of course before all of those things there is spelling and writing as well as reading." She let go of Titine's hands as if they were to begin being mistress and pupil at once and should avoid too great a familiarity at lesson time. "There are so many things to learn," she said. "We should have begun long ago. Truly seriously begun."

They did indeed begin the following day, and kept their resolution with something almost like firmness, at least for its outward appearances of sitting down to the table with books and pencils and paper between the two of them. But one problem was that Kate herself was not very firmly grounded in many of the things she wished to teach, as she had already begun to find in London, with the alphabet. They would sit, full of strong intentions, at least for Kate's part, at the polished table by the window, in what had once been Miss Agnes's private parlour; papers and pencils carefully arranged, and the copy book, and the book of arithmetic lessons for beginners and an Atlas, with its covers missing, that they had found in the smoking parlour—one that must have served generations of pupils with information about the River Amazon and the Alps and the principal cities of the world—and Kate would try to settle herself to the slow business of turning Titine into an educated young woman. Until the sunshine through the window grew more and more inviting, and Kate's questions and Titine's answers more and more absent-minded, and with a mutual truancy they would decide that it was really and truly too hot for lessons in spite of their resolutions and they should go outside for a little to refresh themselves.

Kate would have liked to bring 'Ang with them on their excursions, and sometimes they did, but in spite of the blackamoors, and the Chinese servant of two years ago, his appearance still caused heads to turn, and it would make it seem as though they were there for no ordinary purposes if all three of them could walk abroad so freely. So poor 'Ang was sacrificed to appearances, and left to help old John carry buckets of slops, and coals for Mrs. Cartwright's fire, she being cold at night despite the hottest weather; and to polish the floors of the public rooms, and the brasses, and help Peg black-lead the stoves and the iron pots.

"We should not leave him like this," Kate said. "He is the only one of us who is doing anything. But what can we do?" And he was being well-fed, and not too put upon, and the sun was shining, and one cannot always be worrying about everything. They explored the town, and the shops, and the Assembly Rooms, and peeped into the public rooms of The Royal Hotel, most of whose female occupants did not look much more fashionable than themselves, to tell the truth of it, although a deal more confident in being out of fashion. Nor was there a very great crowd of people. An air about the hotel, and the rooms, and the new-built villas, and the smart shops, that a hoped-for popularity had not quite materialised. There were shops "To let" and villas for sale, and a sense of urgency about the shopkeepers when they saw anyone passing their doors and hesitating at their windows. The theatre was shut until next month's season of plays.

Down on the sands below the cliffs the donkey-boys were idle as often as they were occupied, and the donkeys, if not grown fat, were at least not overworked. The dippers sat on upside-down tubs by their bathing machines, waiting for courageous bathers to be dipped, and when Kate and Titine ventured near them, gave them inviting smiles and promised them how warm the sea water would be, and how much it should benefit their complexions. Kate forced herself to go down onto the sands because Titine liked to walk there, and find sea-shells, and listen to them. Or hunt through the strands of sea-wrack for crabs that scuttled away from her in terror as she pretended to catch them. Kate even made herself go far out with Titine when the tide was very low; picking their way among the pools; sand-pipers running on quick, stitching feet; gulls drifting; the sea a golden, quiet line still further out. The cliffs so far behind them that they grew low and insignificant, and they could begin to see the countryside behind, green and shadowy—fields, woods, a farmhouse, clouds. A sense of loneliness. No one near them. No sounds but the gulls, the strange small whisperings of the cockles under their feet.

"I loves it like this," Titine said. "I wish 'Ang was 'ere, that's all. 'E could—'e could make it into something."

"What do you mean?"

"Make it into music. Then we could 'ave it always." She had a shell in her hand, and was listening, her eyes looking down, her face absorbed. After a moment she let her hand fall and looked round her, sighing. "I never 'ad any idea," she said. "Could—could we buy our 'ouse 'ere?" She looked at Kate sideways, with a kind of slyness that she had when she was making a joke. A timid offering of the joke under concealment, in case it should not be welcome.

"I do not think so," Kate said, entering into the game. "I have not really seen a house that I liked." She was not even sure that with Titine it was a joke, or a game, and that she did not fully expect her one day to produce a house of their own as she had produced food and bonnets and shelter, all equally miraculous. She wondered if she should explain, and began, and saw that Titine was laughing at her, her eyes dancing with wickedness.

"You are a monkey!" Kate cried and began to chase her, and for five minutes she had no care in the world but to catch Titine and tug her curls, and stand at last, breathless, Titine still out of her reach, thinking, *I am truly happy.* She called out that they should go up on the cliffs and have strawberries and lemonade, and go and tease Mr. Hatton in his library behind the Rooms.

"You like him, don't yer?" Titine said, in an odd way.

"Are you jealous? You bad little thing! Are you jealous that I even speak to anyone? I do not like him at all as a matter of fact. If I did, I should not dream of our teasing him."

[178]

"But we ain't going to stay, are we?" Titine said, still not looking at her. "We got to go away from 'ere."

"Shall you mind that?" and Kate wondered to her own astonishment whether she would mind it herself. "Shall you?"

But Titine had withdrawn into her secret world. And they walked towards the shore, Titine answering no more than "Yes" or "No" to anything Kate said. What did she think of at such times? Kate longed to ask her. And felt hurt that the child could withdraw from her so completely, have an interior life so private that after months of the closest companionship Kate had no idea of what it might contain.

"Could Isaac come and live with us?" Titine said after a long minute's silence, and the question took Kate so much by surprise that she could not comprehend it at first.

"But he lives in London! With his grandfather!"

"When we 'ave our 'ouse, I mean."

"Are you teasing me again?"

But Titine's eyes were serious, looking far away. "I liked 'im," she said.

"But we shall see him when—"

Titine looked at her as though she disbelieved it. "What 'appens to people when you goes away from them?"

"Why! What an extraordinary question! What should happen to them?"

"But you told me all the people what you went away from was dead. Is Isaac dead?"

"No! Oh *mon Dieu*, why do I try to tell you things? It is quite different. That was in France—this is England—and it was—it was quite different—completely different. Those things do not happen here." That chill like a shadow. What had made her say so terrible a thing? "You must not say such things!"

"Why not?"

"Because—oh—" Forcing the shadow away. Trying to laugh, to feel herself as happy as she knew she must be. What did it matter what a foolish, foolish child said? Succeeded in laughing, taking Titine by the hand, forgiving. "Come, we will go and flirt terribly with Mr. Hatton and make him fall in love with both of us and tell us everything that is in all his books."

They had indeed fallen into the habit of flirting—no, not flirting, that was certainly not the word—but of coolly teasing Mr. Hatton at times, so that the idea had seemed to grow quite allowable, and even natural. One could not—indeed in her position as housekeeper Kate positively should not be cold to any one of the guests. If she could force herself to be polite to Mr. Sowerby, and oblige herself to listen evening after evening to Mrs. Cartwright's whispered remembrances of Portsmouth and the West Indies, and of her husband's ships, she would certainly be very remiss if she continued to ignore Mr. Hatton, or let his shyness influence her against him. And so, quite quickly, she had made herself unbend to him a little, had one day answered his smile and bow with the most charming smile she could summon, a smile that had begun as duty and found itself becoming warm and genuine. And had seen, to her amazement, his face grow strangely still, his smile seeming to fade except from his mouth, a kind of wonder in his eyes as if he did not believe what he was seeing. She had left him standing there in the corridor, and when she looked back he was still standing as she had left him, not staring after her, but just as he had been, looking down the stairs as she had climbed towards him. As though he were still seeing her there, in that instant when she had begun to smile at him.

And from that day there was the strangest of alterations in his manner to her, and even towards Titine. At one moment a nervous shyness that seemed to make him avoid them both, made him seem almost willing to run from them. Quite unlike his aloof shyness of before. Now it was as if he were suddenly afraid of them. Of Kate, and of Titine as a warning that Kate might be near. And an hour later he would be making the most transparent of efforts to meet them by seeming accident, to hold open a door for either of them, move a chair, or arrange a lamp or a candlestick on a table. And when he had done it, he would blush and turn away as if to avoid any possibility of being thanked or of commencing a conversation. It began to be a whispered joke between Kate and Titine and when he heard them laughing, he became even worse at ease than ever. Tried to seem dignified, and pushed his hair back from his forehead as if he were pushing all thought of them out of his mind. Only to blush helplessly again as Kate spoke to him at supper, to recommend a dish to him or bid him refill his wine-glass or help Mrs. Cartwright to something.

It really was the most pleasantly innocent of games and very far removed from "young-gentleman-folly." Quite the opposite of it, in fact, her mind was so free of any attraction to him, let alone her heart. A game for Titine, in reality. In order to teach her how to treat young men. To control and torture them into a proper state of fearful deference.

And there was in reality a great deal of that in it, even for Kate herself. To prove to herself that she could control a young man. Could control herself to the last degree of perfection in such matters. Not to be so afraid, so fearful that one dare not talk to a young man in case—in case—it became serious—like the first steps of a slope leading down—to—to—that kneeling by a bed, that desolateness of—

"It is nothing in the world like that!" she cried to herself often. "It is the opposite! I am learning to protect myself so that never, never—" And would force herself to smile again at Mr. Hatton on the first occasion that offered itself, smile with that dancing wickedness she knew was sometimes in her eyes because she had seen it reflected in her mirror. And then she would quieten wickedness to warmth as if Mr. Hatton were a piece of bees-wax and she meant to shape him into a waxen heart and melt him between her two palms.

"Young men are meant to be tormented," she said to Titine. "It is nothing to do with liking them. I do hope he is there in the library with not too many other customers. Or it will not be such fun."

And Mr. Hatton was at once so pleased to see them, and so charmingly, courteously nervous of them; he blushed so deeply, and pushed back his lock of hair so distractedly, that all the shadows vanished and it turned into the pleasantest half hour imaginable. Titine herself entered whole-heartedly into the game of teasing him and asked him to fetch her a book of stories, and then to read it aloud to her.

"But—but, Miss Titine—I—well, if you draw apart with me into the alcove—" They both went with him and appeared to hang on his reading for half a minute until he realised the ridiculousness of his position and cried despairingly, "It would be much better—why do you not read it for yourself?"

"Because she cannot read," Kate said.

"Then—then why does she want a book?"

"I wanted to 'ear you read one."

He stared from one to the other of them, tried to be angry, and succeeded only in looking wretchedly embarrassed. "I think you are making fun of me," he said, his face very young and suddenly flushed as if by going too far they had freed him from the burden and restraint of courtesy. He seemed to have lost ten years of his real age in the last minutes, and to be as young as they and much less wise.

"Oh, no!" Kate cried. "Make fun of you! But we were only saying as we came—were we not, Titine?—how much you must know, what a great thing it must be to have so many books, and be so clever! I do wish that I knew one quarter so much!"

But he would not be cajoled and turned away from them almost brusquely, saying that a subscriber was by his desk and he must go to her. After that he busied himself with a determined air for five minutes until they grew bored with waiting, and went to amuse themselves elsewhere.

That evening, before supper, he managed to come out of his room just as Kate was passing his door. "Miss Harriott?" he said. In such an unusual voice that her heart hesitated for a beat and then went too swiftly to catch up.

"Yes?" she said at last, since he said nothing more.

"I must speak to you," he whispered. "Today—"

He is going to apologise, she thought contritely, *when it is we—I—who should apologise to him.*

"You had—have—no right," he said quickly, "you—"

"I?" she said, drawing herself up to much more than her full, small height. "No right? I am afraid I do not understand you, Mr. Hatton."

He did not exactly wring his hands, but his expression suggested that was what he wanted to do. "I did not mean—oh, Miss Harriott! Why do you treat me like this? You set out to torture me—I see it in your eyes!"

"To—*torture* you?" The word was so exactly her own that she grew genuinely angry as though he had somehow eavesdropped on her. "You do not know what you are saying. Let me go by at once."

"I shall not," he said, in a voice still wretched with unhappiness, but with a quality in it that made her stay where she was. "You have no right to treat me as you do. Nor I— Do not you know how I feel?" he cried, so bitterly that she was sure they must be overheard and wanted to look round them in case one of the servants might be within earshot. "Have felt since—since I first saw you?"

"I do not understand you," she whispered. "If—if I have seemed

[182]

to—to tease you a little"—she felt herself flushing, burning hot—"I—it was very wrong of me."

"It was more than wrong," he said, his hair fallen across his forehead, his hand seeming to be searching for it, his eyes not meeting hers. "It was—and I—it is really I who am at fault. I should never—given the circumstances—the—I think it must be best if—if I leave here—if—I find other—other accommodation now that——"

"Leave here?" she said, a feeling something like pain so sharp in her at his words that it became truly painful; set up a thousand warnings, feelings, emotions in her mind, one jostling and beating against another. "What circumstances?" she cried suddenly. A shadow of his meaning crossed her mind, was dismissed as impossible, returned as certainty. "What do you mean?" she whispered.

"Mr. Gurney," he whispered in return, avoiding her eyes. He pushed back his hair despairingly. "Your—your friendship for Mr. Gurney—I—it places me—you—I must leave at once!" he cried suddenly, and seemed on the point of dashing into his room to pack his valise. But he did not move.

"Mr. Hatton!" she breathed. "How dare you insult me so! It—it—I? And Mr. Gurney? It is monstrous! Monstrous!" She wanted to cry with rage, and was so furious that tears were impossible.

"I do not m-mean to reproach you," he said. "I—how could I? It is entirely y-your affair and—I—I quite understand that—I *must* go," he cried sharply, as if she were holding him there. Behind her there were voices, Captain Cartwright's, one of the maid's.

He will see us like this! she thought. And before the thought was complete Mr. Hatton had caught her into his room. She was not even certain how he had done it, it was so swift. The door shut. The two of them standing breathless, close. Captain Cartwright's loud voice calling, "Miss Harriott? I swear I heard her a moment since— Did ye see Miss Harriott gone by, m'dear? I wanted—" His voice receding as he went down the stairs.

Kate wanted to lean against the inside of the door. Her legs threatening to give way. Although why? Why? As if she and Mr. Hatton were secret lovers, almost caught.

"I do—do beg your pardon," Mr. Hatton said. "But I—I feared—he is such a man for taking up wrong notions."

"I cannot stay here," she said, without moving. Looking not at his face but at his shoulder, the line of his coat, his sleeve. She had almost forgotten that she was angry.

"Miss Kate"—he was whispering—"do not you understand how I have felt? Seeing you—day after day—thinking—I do not reproach you," he said again. His voice so miserable that she was forced to look at him.

"Reproach me for what?" she said, trying to make her voice very cold and adult, the voice she had used for Mr. Sowerby when he had threatened Titine with eternal torment. But she did not succeed.

"For your—y-your friendship with Mr. Gurney," he whispered, avoiding her eyes. "Do not think I am so innocent—ignorant—that—that I do not know how such things can—*must* sometimes—come about. Any—young woman—alone—w-without p-protection—w-without money—"

Kate had collected herself now, had gathered the completest control of her mind and voice. And allowed him to go on, his voice stumbling lower and lower into a morass of stammers and circumlocutions.

"Yes?" she said at last, raising her eyebrows with an air of such amused disdain, such condescension of grown, sophisticated woman towards callow, ill-minded, stammering young man, that it was as though she had shot him in the leg. He leaned against the wall beside him for support, and put both hands over his face.

"I—I—" he said uselessly.

"No doubt you have gathered evidence?" she said, beginning to enjoy herself. Like bees-wax in her hands. "You have questioned the servants? Watched through keyholes when Mr.—my godfather—was here? What dreadful things you must have heard and seen to make you so—convinced of my character."

"Miss Harriott," he whispered, "please—"

"I thought you better-minded," she said. Looking about his room that before she had only seen when he was out of it. The bed that he had managed to make untidy again despite all the maid's neat efforts of that morning. The miniature of his mother on the chimney piece. That same severe, dark woman she had seen with him in the Mall. Young in the miniature, and with a look of her son that caught Kate's mind every time she saw it. Books on his table, papers, quills, an inkpot, a pounce box with the pounce spilled about. *How untidy he is*, she thought affectionately, without even wondering at the affection. It was as though he had walked into a net and bound himself about with it and laid himself helpless at her feet. How could she not feel affectionate towards such stupidity? She looked up into his face, smiling at him with her new-found sense of ownership—an ownership that would cost nothing, that created not the slightest obligation from her towards him. Where all the obligation, all the apologies and efforts and stammered excuses must be on his side, and all the offerings of his heart, and she need not even return him a glance of recognition. He certainly must not be allowed to escape by leaving the hotel.

"Are you not ashamed to think such evil? Of anyone? Without the least fragment of evidence?"

"But—but—"

"But what?"

"Everyone—I—I saw—in the coach even—you did not—"

She could have cried out with joy at such imbecility in an opponent. It only presented the problem of which of his mistakes to use against him first.

"In the coach?" she prompted. "I did not what? I did not seem sufficiently overwhelmed by the privilege of sitting opposite you? Such a handsome, eligible young man?"

"You know I did not m-mean that," he cried. He seemed to want to take hold of something, to take hold of her and shake her perhaps.

Let him dare! she thought happily. Instead he pressed his two fists against his forehead.

"What *did* you mean, in that case?" she asked him.

"I—I—"

It was nearing the time to deliver the coup de grâce. She felt as if she were settling the hilt of her sword more firmly in her hand.

"You are too foolish to be angry with," she said. "I will not say you should be ashamed of yourself. You will know that without being told."

"D-do you"—he opened and closed his mouth, held out his hands beseechingly—"Is it—are you—"

"You want to ask me am I telling you the truth?" she said, with infinite condescension. "What a child you are! What possible right do you imagine that you possess to ask me such a question?"

"But is it true?" he shouted. "Is he nothing to you? Except—except your godfather?" Without her knowing it, quite allowing herself to know it, he had reached out and captured her two hands.

"People do have godfathers," she said mildly. "Would you like to let go of me?"

He dropped her hands as if they had burned him, and she

sighed in contempt. "What should I have done if he had tried to kiss me?" she asked herself. And felt a shadow of disappointment that he had not made the attempt so that she could crush it.

"Suppose someone were to hear you shouting at me?" she said. "Or to see me leave your room? What might they not imagine—if they were like you?"

She thought he would kneel down and grew almost tired of playing with him. It was too easy; there was no need for effort, even. Titine could have destroyed him in half a minute, without thinking of it.

"I must go," she said. "Let us hope none of your informants have overheard us."

"I will leave to—tonight," he said. Standing helplessly, as though waiting for the sword-thrust in his heart.

"So that you may multiply all the damage you have already done? So that your gossips may say, 'He would not stay in the same house with her because of her character'? How wonderful to be a man and have no need of a reputation. Or even common sense."

"You t-twist everything I say! You—you are enjoying it!"

The sun was lying in a pool of gold on his table, his books and papers. And beyond the gold, the pool of light, dark shadow, his mother's miniature—so like himself in that shadow, that all Kate's sophistication fell away, and she put up one hand to her heart, not looking at him.

"Do you think that I enjoy such insults?" she whispered. "You do not know much of women."

And behind all the playing the hurt was there, sudden and fierce as an open wound. That he had delivered to her, not she to him. Turning her sword. Her eyes seemed to grow blank with the pain of it. She could see nothing but the pool of gold, the shadow, the distant ivory pallor of the small painted face. Wanted to be alone—alone—and at the same time to have him take her hands again—hold her—felt on a sudden that longing to have pain healed that her mother must have felt so often—going from wound to wound, pain to drive out pain. Felt that in that instant, at last, at last, she understood. Understood the young men, the desolation, the Magdalene agonies of loss and longing.

And I denied her, she thought, and felt her heart break in two. If Mr. Hatton had touched her then—she looked slowly into his eyes, searching for knowledge. But only abject misery was there, contrition, humility. No possessiveness. No strength to take. Or if there was strength there, he dared not use it.

"How can you—is it possible—to—to forgive?"

"It is possible to forgive anything," she said, almost forgetful of all that had gone before. He did kneel down then, took her hands and pressed her knuckles against his lips. So hard that they must have bruised his mouth.

"I am not used——" he whispered. "I could cut out my tongue."

"You must get up," she said. "Suppose someone were to come in?"

But he did not get up. And she looked down into his face as he knelt in front of her and it was like looking into a child's face, a child's great, dark eyes. Younger than Titine. Younger than she herself had ever been. She wanted to smooth his hair, lift the lock of it away from his forehead, touch the line of his eyebrow with her finger-tip. But he had imprisoned both her hands and continued holding them, against his mouth, his cheeks.

"You are so—so beautiful," he said. "I thought—your—you looked so coldly—so—and here you have—you have tormented me so—"

Like lovers who talk in the dark of their first meetings, the expressions of their eyes.

"Let me go," she breathed.

What would he do now? Her heart beginning to beat so fast that he must hear it, know how weak she was. She would have liked to tell him of the shepherd in the painting. Of seeing him that day in the street, getting down from the coach to help the Squire. Of seeing him in the Mall. Of all she had imagined. Of the games she had made up about him. To have knelt down facing him, here in this shadowy, sunlight-shafted room. To have—

She drew her hands away, slowly at first and then sharply.

"Someone will—you are forgetting yourself utterly," she said. "Let me go at once."

He opened his fingers to release her.

"Will you—I cannot hope that—that you can— Why did I say anything?" he cried despairingly.

"I hope you are thoroughly ashamed of your evil-mindedness," she said. "I could expect it of Mr. Sowerby. But of you!"

He gave a low, miserable whisper of pain.

"Now it is over," she said. "We will not speak of it again."

"B-but you will th-think of it," he said. "I cannot—hope that you would not."

"That will depend on your behavior," she said, beginning to feel lightly happy once more, like a child putting away a toy that she knows she may take out again whenever she pleases. "Now I am going."

No one in the corridor. Nor on the stairs. Nor calling her. She found to her astonishment when she looked at the grandfather clock in the hall that scarcely ten minutes had gone by.

But they are ten minutes he will remember a long time, she thought. And had to go outside in order to be able to skip across the road. Even the sea-shore, the sea-wall and the rocks had no power to darken her happiness. *What would I have done if he had tried to kiss me?"* she wondered, taking another skip, and checking it as a fisherman went by in his great oilskin boots, carrying a basket of cockles. *What would I have done?* Something very cool and wise.

How simple, how foolish and childish men are, she thought. *It is quite true that they are like children. There is nothing to be afraid of at all if—if one is sensible. There is no need for it—for it to be like—"Oh Maman!"* her heart cried with pain and love. *"Why could you not—be as sensible as I am?"* And even to her momentarily exalted mind the thought seemed unwarrantably arrogant, and she tried to alter it for something that meant the same thing yet appeared more becoming. *Perhaps it was different in France,* she thought generously. But the skip had gone out of her steps, and she walked along soberly, looking across the empty sands to see if she might spy Titine anywhere.

"I will be very careful," she promised herself. "And I shall not allow Titine to be naughty to him at all. I shall be very prudent."

And she kept her promise so carefully that a few evenings later Captain Cartwright said, in the middle of helping himself to some Hottentot pie, "By Gad, Hatton, what have ye done to offend Miss Harriott? She treats you as cool as a cucumber and I had ye both marked off as sweethearts."

"Alexander!" his wife cried, in tiny horror.

Mr. Hatton blushed scarlet and Kate was thankful to escape out of the dining-room with some empty dishes.

When she came back, they had fortunately turned to other subjects—the theatre company that was to arrive within the next days, and the two chief members of it who were, by long arrangement, to stay in the hotel.

"Ye should go to see them," the Captain said. "They always give us free tickets and although I'm no judge of playacting I hear them well spoken of. Shakespeare and that stuff. For me I'd rather have a good farce any day, but you young people—eh, Hatton? Ye might bring Miss Harriott?"

"Alexander!"

"Dammit, ma'am, what have I said now? Eh, Sowerby? Have I said aught I shouldn't?"

Mr. Sowerby gave his yellowish smile that made him look even more bilious than usual. "Miss Harriott must answer you for herself, Captain, but no doubt like all young people she will wish to be at the plays."

"If I have the time," Kate said, her voice sharper than she had intended. And the sharpness as much for herself and her own uncertainties as for the Captain, or Mr. Sowerby. She did not know how she felt about the players coming. One moment excited, as if her old life were returning to her, and the next, almost afraid. Almost guilty? As if in the mere thought of their coming there was a reproach. As if all her folly of thoughts about Mr. Hatton were no more than self-deception, a running away as Mr. Solomons had told her.

"Time?" the Captain was crying delightedly. "Ye must make time. Eh, Hatton? Will ye not invite her, man? It might take your mind off your damned politics for an evening."

"If you did not provoke him," Kate said, growing truly vexed at being pursued on the matter, "he would not speak half so much about politics, and he would certainly never quarrel about them."

"I?" the Captain said, pretending to be both wounded and amazed. "I provoke him?"

The Captain had a way of reading certain items aloud from his newspaper that he knew would drive Mr. Hatton into a fury: the arrest of a radical journalist for criticising the Government, the whipping of a chapman for selling copies of *The Rights of Man* in a market-place.

"Serve the cur right!" the Captain would shout, if Mr. Hatton was slow to rise to the bait. "And these damned Corresponding Societies! If every man jack of a traitorous rascal in them was given the same medicine—!"

"For wishing that poor men might have votes?" Mr. Hatton would cry furiously, goaded at last out of his inarticulate shyness.

"For wishing that we might have a Parliament that would serve the people instead of itself?"

"For treason, man! High treason! Against our Sovereign Lord the King, God bless him! Whipped? Hanged drawn and quartered and their heads on Temple Bar, by God, that's what I long to see."

"I know that you do not mean it! You are only trying to make me—"

"Trying to drive sense into your head, boy. And dangerous nonsense out of it. Reforms! Does France not teach you where reforms end? In murdering your King! In monstrous ruffians like this Robespierre. In the guillotine! There is your true reformer. The guillotine!"

Mr. Hatton growing still more furious, crying death to all kings and priests and every sort of tyrant. "An English Robespierre might bring us some j-justice—at long last! After seven hundred years of slavery to N-Norman insolence!"

And the two would be at each other's metaphorical throats like bull dogs. Except that the Captain fought for the sheer pleasure of annoying his adversary while Mr. Hatton burned with a generosity of spirit that to Kate's ears was at once courageous and yet destroyed all reason and common sense in him. *If he did but know what such talk can lead to!* Kate thought, sometimes with a wise, adult condescension towards childish folly, and sometimes with a shiver of remembrance.

She played with the thought of telling him—trying to tell him—what the reality was like of those things he spoke of with such fierce easiness. But for all her feelings of wisdom and condescension, her certainty that in all matters of "young-gentleman-folly" she could mould Mr. Hatton like wax, she sensed already that there was another side to him, or rather, an inner core, that could not be shaped at all, by any furnace at her command, or perhaps at any one else's. Like Damascus steel. Quivering with tension, with concealed strength.

Not the Captain's blunt, oaken strength, nor Mr. Gurney's power of command, nor "Mr. Razor Thomas's" force of brutality, but something different to all those, and bewildering—a force of mind that would go to the stake for an ideal. And stay untouched, unchanged, even when the body became ashes.

Once in his room she had found rough scrap-sheets of poetry, drafts of lines and trial verses, words and phrases scored and re-scored out into such a palimpsest of alterations that it was not possible to make out a meaning, let alone a poem. And yet in a phrase, two words together, here and there a whole line, there had been something like the flash of sun on distant weapons, hinting of strength hidden there; the image of a chained man; of waking, of the pain of waking to that weight of slavery; the soul crying out to the bright sky, "I was born free!"

Those words had echoed in her mind for days. "I was born free!" She had not thought that poets made verses about freedom, and had once or twice looked to see if the completed poem might be lying on his table, among his heap of papers, so that she might discover what became of the chained man. *We are not free,* she thought as she was searching. *Nor have we ever been since Eden. How could he think that we were born free?* And searched again for the poem. But she had not found it.

Since then, when she had heard him arguing, she had told herself that he did not really mean what he was saying, but was no more than turning his poet's fancies into weapons to hurl at the Captain's obstinate, weather-beaten head.

The Captain was beginning exactly that kind of argument now, at the supper table, as if to prove to Kate that it was Mr. Hatton and not he who was at fault. And when she returned to the dining-room with a dish of preserved plums and Spanish cream, they were shouting at each other about the King's supposed attacks of madness, and the Prince of Wales's fitness to act as Regent.

"What a—a choice for us!" Mr. Hatton was saying, stammering with passion instead of shyness. "T-to be ruled by a libertine instead of—of a lunatic!"

"Have a care! Have a care, Hatton! There are some of your radical friends in prison at this moment for saying scarce more than you are saying."

"The more shame to—to England, then! Thank God there are those brave enough to—to speak the truth and—and speak it aloud! I wish that I might t-truly call them my friends!"

"Do ye? Do ye so? Scoundrels like Horne Tooke and Hardy! Men that want to do away with our Constitution! Bring in French villainy? By God, Hatton, if Sowerby or I were to take ye seriously and report such traitor's talk to the magistrates, as we ought—"

"Report what you like and—and—I am no traitor and you know it. Nor are those poor wretched men in prison." Mr. Hatton saw

[191]

Kate's amused eye watching him and pushed back his chair so violently that it fell. "Report that to that drunken booby Marjoram, if he's ever sober enough to listen."

"Boy! Boy!" the Captain cried, but Mr. Hatton was already striding out as though a firing squad were waiting for him.

"You are wicked," Kate said to the Captain, and he had the grace to look slightly ashamed. Mr. Sowerby merely looked grave and yellow.

"Aye, aye," the Captain said as if to make amends. "He's in the right of it about poor Marjoram. It's a damned disgrace to have such a fellow for a magistrate. Go and tell poor Hatton I am sorry and let him come back and eat his plums."

But Mr. Hatton had already slammed out of the hotel and was vaulting the sea-wall to go striding across the sands.

"Promise that you will not provoke him like that when Mr. Otterley and Mrs. Dundas are here," she said, "or I do not know what they will think of us."

"No fear of that," the Captain said, helping himself to more cream in spite of Mrs. Cartwright's whispered protest. "No fear of any of us talking of anything when Otterley is here, eh, Sowerby! Eh, Jane? I never knew a fellow to talk more and say less in all my life. It's a wonder to me the others on the stage with him ever get to saying their parts."

The theatre company's visits had been annual events for the past five years, ever since the promoters of the "New Shoreham Development Scheme" had begun their attempts to create a rival to Brighton and Margate. The promoters had hoped that within a year or so the visits would give way to permanent residence, and that Shoreham's Theatre Royal would be open the year round. But these hopes had been disappointed like many others the promoters had entertained, and Mr. Otterley continued to bring his company for no more than July and August.

"Even then he don't fare to do so well, poor gentleman, from what I hear," Mrs. Earnshaw said. "The people round here een't the theatre-going kind, not really, and there een't never enough gentlemen and ladies staying to fill the theatre for him."

Kate tried to feel at once sorry for the unknown Mr. Otterley, and glad for herself that she was no longer living that life. *I am right,* she thought, over and over again. *I chose right to come here instead of*—Instead of what? What else could she have done? If there had even been a theatre that would have offered her any place—any chance—*I was quite, quite right.* As if she were talking to Mr. Solomons, beating down arguments he had never propounded.

But perhaps in compensation she made herself very busy preparing for Mr. Otterley's and Mrs. Dundas's coming, seeing to their bedrooms and their private sitting-room, where they might study their parts, avoiding Mr. Hatton as though telling herself she could not waste the least moment, afford the least distraction; tormenting the maids with unnecessary instructions, tormenting Mrs. Earnshaw with suggestions for late supper trays, until she said with great patience, "Lord save you, little ma'am, they've been here five times and nothing ever went amiss for them. You leave it to me."

The afternoon of their arrival Mrs. Earnshaw as good as ordered Kate out of her kitchen and out of her way. "If you must be doing something, take Mrs. Cartwright her tea and cake and sit quiet with her, the poor body, and leave me get on with the baking."

Kate did as she was told, and for a quarter of an hour listened again to stories of Mrs. Cartwright's son, who had died of yellow fever in the West Indies when he was thirteen years old, and such a paragon of virtues as the Navy had rarely seen in a midshipman. The letters he had written, the thoughts he had had for his mother, the shawl that he had bought for her out of his pocket money, the opinion his Captain had had of him.

"Oh, my dear Miss Harriott—if you could but have seen him! He was scarce eleven years old when he went away from us! How small he looked! And so brave at parting! The Captain scolds me for crying when I think of him that day, but how can I help it? Oh, dear—oh, dear, you will think me such a foolish old woman, and it was so long ago. But for mothers it is never long ago. It is always yesterday. And your own dear mother dead? Oh, my poor, poor child!"

Kate had told the guests as near the truth as she could, that she had spent much of her childhood in France—and only left it indefinite as to the year of her return. Mrs. Cartwright, once her fears of Kate were vanished, had become timidly affectionate, and professed to find Kate's accent no more than made her attractive. She sat now, drying her tears with a miniature scrap of lace handkerchief, saying, "How kind you are—it is so rare nowadays—young people—they have no patience with—with—and indeed, how should they understand such sorrows? God forbid that they should. These dreadful, dreadful wars! Oh, dear—oh, dear, I am so foolish. I tell myself that if—if my son were still alive—he would be at sea now, and in such dangers—and I should not sleep at nights." She began to cry again.

Outside there were the sounds of wheels and hooves and harness, a voice shouting, "Whoah. Hup."

"They are come!" Kate said. Not wanting to leave Mrs. Cartwright to her tears, and yet urgent to run out and see. "Do not cry, ma'am. Listen, the theatre people are coming! You shall not like them to find you crying, shall you? Let me make you handsome to meet them." She took Mrs. Cartwright's sodden handkerchief out of her fingers and patted her cheeks with it, not to much effect.

"Oh, I could not meet anyone! I beg of you, do not desire it of me!" And in terror Mrs. Cartwright gathered herself up and pattered out of the room and up the stairs to safety.

The new guests were already in the hall-passage; deep bell tones that must be Mr. Otterley's crying: "Old John, I declare! And younger than last year upon my soul! You have the secret of eternal youth, has he not, my dear? And who is this Oriental lad before me?"

Old John's quavering voice explaining—Mrs. Passover dead—Miss Passover gone—new proprietors—Mr. Gurney—Miss Harriott—the assistant porter—dumb—

"Poor fellow! Poor, poor creature!"

Kate was already there to greet Mr. Otterley and Mrs. Dundas and in spite of Mrs. Earnshaw's declaration that there was no need for any extraordinary fuss for the simple receiving of two additional guests, the hotel for a good ten minutes was full of such scurrying and running and opening and shutting of doors and calling of orders and greetings as might have done to welcome the entire theatre company instead of its two senior members. The Captain declaring Mrs. Dundas to be even handsomer than last year, and Mr. Otterley to be the picture of himself, not a whit changed; and was he come to bring them a decent farce or a burletta instead of all that tragic stuff? Mrs. Earnshaw needing to be complimented on the promising scents of her baking, condoled with over the loss of her late mistress, and congratulated—this with a handsome Shakespearean leg and a bow for Kate—on her acquisition of such a handsome young new mistress as she now had. "And Mr. Sowerby, sir! How goes the Treatise? Have you destroyed the Dissenters yet?"

During most of which Mrs. Dundas preserved herself from over excitement by lying down in her room and calling for the best Bohea, and her toilet case, and the curtains to be drawn. "My head! Hand me the sal volatile, there is a good child." Her hand held out with elegant resignation for the crystal bottle of smelling salts.

"You are very young to be housekeeper," she said, lifting slightly pouched and folded eyelids to look at Kate.

"My godfather—"

"Ah yes," said Mrs. Dundas, her tone containing all-sufficient knowledge of godfathers and young women, and closed her eyes again.

She is not going to like me, Kate thought, *and I am not going to like her.* And she felt rather foolish at the thought of all the excitement she had felt, and the preparations she had made, and the stupidity of them, and went out with Titine for a walk.

By nightfall—under the soothing influence of Mrs. Earnshaw's supper, and the best claret, and tobacco pipes for the Captain and snuff for Mr. Sowerby and Mr. Otterley—the hotel had returned to its usual quietness except for the continuing sonorities of Mr. Otterley's voice in the morning-cum-smoking-room, rising to great carillon climaxes as he told the Captain and Mr. Sowerby and Mr. Hatton of the triumphs and disasters of his company during the past year.

"And then in Belfast! Every basket of costumes, every piece of our scenery misdirected! Gone to Cork, we discovered at the last! And there we were, with *Hamlet* promised for that night, and not so much as a skull or a grave-digger's spade to help us. When who should come to our aid but Lord Antrim himself! 'By God, Otterley,' he said—we are the oldest of friends, you know—'By God,' he said, 'if we have to set every seamstress and carpenter in Ireland stitching and hammering for you, you shall be fitted up by tonight as though you were back in Drury Lane—'"

Mr. Hatton let himself stealthily out of the parlour, and saw Kate, who assumed a look of not having been listening, but of merely passing by.

"He is insufferable!" Mr. Hatton whispered, and blushed, beginning to stammer apologies for criticising her guest.

"It does not matter," she said, scarcely thinking of what he was trying to say. She had for a moment, as he was closing the door, seen his face in the light from the room, before he had seen her,

[195]

and it was as if she had been looking at a different man. Not the stammering, blushing young man whom she and Titine could reduce to helplessness in two minutes of teasing, nor the near-lover she had so utterly destroyed in that ten minutes in his room, nor even the idealist whom the Captain could as easily drive into an equally helpless rage. Another self behind that again. Graver. Older. As he might be in ten years time, and she had the strangest, fearful sense of nothing being as it seemed.

And I? she thought. *Does he look at me and see two, three different Katherine Harriotts? Does he see me as I shall be in—in ten years time?* And she had the most foolish of impulses to take his hands and say, "Please! Please tell me! What do you see when you look at me?" Not for coquetry, not remotely for anything so vain. But to know. As though someone else could tell her who she was. Who she ought to be. And she thought, *If Mr. Solomons was here now*— and grew instantly afraid. *He will imagine I have gone mad,* she thought. But the moment had been so brief he could have seen nothing in her face except that she was looking at him with unusual gravity, and he began redoubling his apologies.

Ever since that evening he seemed, whenever he and Kate were alone together, metaphorically to be kneeling in front of her. She found herself growing quite tired of so much contrition and once or twice had wondered what she might do about it. As if she longed to bring forward that other, secret Mr. Hatton she only guessed at, had seen only in the shadow of his present self for that one moment. What would he be like, that hidden man? And she was drawn, and fearful, and drawn again. Fearful not of what she might find in him, but in herself. And yet still drawn.

"Please," she said, coolly enough, but ready to be conversational, "I do not in the least mind what—"

Someone was calling her. Mr. Biggins from the far end of the passage.

"I must go," she said. Mr. Hatton, looking at her as if he had detected a difference in her voice, was himself still that different man who had come out of the smoking-parlour a moment ago. A man who might not be at all so easily tormented, so effortlessly destroyed.

"Miss Harriott, ma'am!" Mr. Biggins's voice urgent, commanding attention.

"I am coming." Following Mr. Biggins through the kitchen and the scullery, into the stable-yard. There was no moon, and in spite of the brightness of the stars and its being no more than a day or so past Midsummer's Eve it was dark enough at that hour of the night.

"He's comin' to us tomorrow," Mr. Biggins whispered, "him as we're expectin'. He did land up the coast less'n an hour ago, an' is to lie up safe somewhere till morning. I'll be fetchin' him here to you afore noon."

Chapter 15

He came with his head swathed up in a cloth, groaning with pretended toothache. Rather too dramatically, Kate thought, but she had never suffered from a toothache herself, and every one else aware of his arrival seemed convinced, and was duly sympathetic. He was brought in a strange chaise driven by Biggins, who announced him as a Welsh gentleman he had come upon by enquiry as willing to sell his chaise at a fair price, but for the moment only anxious for anywhere quiet to rest his toothache. No, there was no need for a sugeon; for the moment all he required was a bedroom, and some brandy, and maybe a cup of broth. Miss Harriott might be the best to see to him, if she would, since in any event she must make terms with him for both the chaise and his accommodation.

"Whatever he asks," Biggins said, "cut him down by a good third." The Welsh having a reputation as great rascals in matters of buying and selling, but the chaise was a good one. He himself needed to go off at once on some business of Mr. Gurney's, he said, and might not be back until the following evening. He should not be surprised if Mr. Gurney and a friend were to return with him.

His heartiness in the matter sounded at once so natural, and so full of double meanings to Kate, that she half expected to find a real Welshman upstairs with a real toothache. She sent 'Ang up with two great cans of hot water, and Mary with towels and fresh soap, following close on their heels herself with the brandy and the hot broth.

As the stranger came in with Mr. Biggins she had seen no more than a tall, thin man with a swathed head under a wide-brimmed, high-crowned hat, and a surtout that seemed too big for him, and was wrapped round him like a dressing gown, as if he had just got up from his sick-bed to make the brief journey. He had, Biggins had pretended, been staying at an inn some fifteen miles inland.

He planned, as soon as he had sold his chaise, Mr. Biggins had added, to return into Wales.

'Ang and the maid set down their burdens and Kate dismissed them. The man was sitting on his bed when they came in, still holding his head in both hands, and groaning at intervals. He had taken off his surtout and was sitting in his shirt-sleeves and breeches, his boots thrust off his feet and lying untidily in the middle of the floor. He had a hole in the toe of one stocking, Kate noticed, and in the heel of the other. Nor was his linen very fresh-seeming.

"You may stop groaning now," Kate said in French. "And take off that cloth so that we may see one another."

She thought that he must hear her heart beating, and the unsteadiness of her voice. He unwrapped the cloth slowly, and looked at her.

"You are French?" he said, his voice as unsteady as hers. Young. Less than thirty, she judged, not greatly older than Mr. Hatton in years. Until she looked into his eyes and saw that he was a thousand years old, that he had such an age as Mr. Hatton would never reach, nor anyone in this quiet country. A bad complexion, as though he had been often ill fed and had lived much by candlelight. His black, ragged hair receding from a high, pale forehead; hollow cheeks marked with three deep, purplish scars of long-ago boils or carbuncles—two on one cheek-bone, one just below the other, like the scars of bullet wounds—a narrow, pointed chin. Only his teeth still handsome enough, white and regular, giving the lie to their story of his toothache.

"I am not French," she said. She put down the tray near him, irrationally afraid of him, of his touching her, as though he were a prisoner she was guarding who might attack her at any moment. She could not look away from his eyes. So deep a blue, so full of dreadful knowledge that they drew her like a cliff's edge. What had he seen to make them look like that? And she thought of Callac. "Here is brandy," she whispered. "And food."

He was sweating. She could see it on his face, like tallow melting. More than that, she could smell it. And knew that he was sweating as much from fear as the warmth of the day. He was in terror. Not of her. Not of the hotel. Not of any immediate danger. He suffered from terror as he might have suffered from the pain of cancer; something that dwelled inside him, gnawed at his liver and his stomach, incurable. And sweated from his indwelling terror as he

[199]

might have sweated from the pain. She had heard it said that gifted people can smell those who are soon going to die. She thought that she could smell death in him. And it did not make her less afraid of him, but more.

He ignored the tray. "Then who are you? I know you are French. Why are you deceiving me?" His hands twisting themselves into the white cloth that had been wrapped round his face. His eyes fixed on hers, trying to beat down her resistance. He must have seen it done, but he did not know how to do it, and merely stared at her, revealing his own depth of terror rather than finding his way into hers. "This is not a good beginning," he said, turning his eyes away from her at last.

"I have lived in France very long. I was a child there. My mother was an actress."

Extraordinarily he seemed to draw reassurance from that irrelevant fact. "An actress?" he said, looking at her again with a different expression. He lifted his two hands, linked by the cloth. "I thought once of being an actor. Long ago." He laughed without humour. Dismissing "long ago" as something belonging to another life, unimaginable now. "When am I to see the people I have come to see? I thought they would be here."

"How could they be? They are in London. They will be here soon." What should she say next? How should she question him? And surely she must not stay too long alone with him. "I—shall come to you again—in an hour. Now you will want to wash—to eat—"

He looked as though he was amazed at both suggestions. But he picked up the brandy in both hands and tasted it. "In an hour?" His eyes filled with suspicion, calculations, of what she might be intending during that hour, what trickery, betrayal.

"And do not you need to sleep? You look tired."

Perhaps a note of kindness in her voice reached him. Perhaps it was very long since he had talked like this, alone in a quiet room with a quiet girl. Although his own voice was low, she sensed that he was more used to shouting; a hoarseness in it, from hour upon hour of shouting in crowded, stifling rooms where the air was poisonous, and he looked suddenly stricken, all his bearings astray. It might have been no more than that he realised his helplessness; that no matter what she intended he could not prevent it. Only fear it. And he looked for a moment as he might have when he was really young, before all the blood he had seen had run down onto the stones.

"Yes, I am tired," he said. He seemed to know it only then. To be sitting without strength. Not even the strength to lie down. The brandy set aside. His hands fallen into his lap, twisted again in the cloth as if they were bound.

"Then sleep," she said. "I need not come to you until evening."

"I cannot sleep."

"I could fetch you laudanum. I would say it is for your toothache. It would make you sleep well."

"No!" The dark blue of his eyes seeming to turn black with horror at the thought of it. His whole body shuddering. "I do not want to sleep!"

"I know," she said. She did not know why she troubled to speak kindly. She did not feel it. She felt as though she were looking at something dreadful, an animal wounded in an ugly, piteous way. A dangerous, cruel animal, that would turn on anyone who tried to help it.

"What do you know?" he was saying furiously, furious in contempt. "How can you know?"

"I have felt that too," she said. "That I did not want to sleep. I have been afraid of what would come if I slept." She said it like an accusation, and as she said it, the shadows did come, one after the other in the curtained room. As if he had brought them. He sat staring at her. "How could you?" she whispered.

"How could I what?"

"All the people that you have killed."

"I have killed no one," he said. She had expected him to be angry, but he said it in the strangest way, painfully, like a man begging to be believed, trying to persuade himself. "No one." He looked down at his hands.

"Shall I fetch you laudanum?"

"No."

"But you must sleep. You must sleep in the end."

He shut his eyes, and rested his face in his hands, his elbows on his knees. "Leave me alone."

She went out and heard him lock the door on the inside.

An hour later, and two or three hours later again, when she tapped on the panels and called the name by which he was to pass with them, "Mr. Evans? Mr. Evans, sir?" he did not answer. Yet she knew that he was not asleep. He was not moving about; she could hear no sounds, not even his breathing. But she could see him as clearly as if the door were glass, lying on his back, staring at the ceiling, his hands still twisted into the napkin.

It was more than strange, it was unpleasant, the certainty she had. She felt she knew more of him in those five minutes of talk than she knew of—even of Titine. She stood holding the door-handle, thinking of that and looking down the corridor without seeing anything at all. Knew him to the depths of his soul. Knew him. Disliked him. And yet felt drawn as one might be drawn by the sight of blood. A kind of longing to put out one's hand and touch, and see the stain, and shudder, and want to touch again, until one's whole hand was crimson.

I am mad, she thought. And went away to make some arrangement about dinner and a tray for his room, and came back to stand outside the door again, and tap, and call, and listen, and hear nothing. She thought, *He is like a stain. Like an infection.* She wanted to run away, and could not.

After a minute or so Mary came up with the tray and Kate banged on the door with emphasis. "Mr. Evans! Your dinner is here. You must open the door and eat something."

He opened it, but only to allow the tray to be put inside, and went back to the bed to stay obstinately silent. Mary went away, and Kate arranged the tray on a table, and set a chair for him.

"You must eat," she said. "And then you must talk to me. Or both at once. I have questions to ask and you must answer them."

"I shall answer nothing. Go away."

"I have been ordered to question you."

She thought that she might as well be straightforward about it. He would have to be a great fool not to guess what she was at. She felt a childish vanity at having so much appearance of authority over him, and with it the same shuddering, unwilling attraction. Not by reason of his person, God knew, but—her mind hesitated, trying to think why—but for what he was—what he represented. As though it had been he who had ordered those deaths at Callac, and she was drawn to him because of it. Like a victim drawn back to her attacker, step by unwilling, yet fascinated step, knowing what the end must be. She knew that it was madness, a sickness of soul, and revolted at herself for feeling it, and felt it still. *So rabbits must feel with snakes*, she thought. *But I am worse, for I am seeking to find the snake pitiful, with his broken back. His semblance of a broken back.*

She said, "I am to find out certain things from you," lifting her chin a little and looking down at him, like a small schoolmistress at a great, slovenly pupil forced to stay in school until his piece is recited.

"What things?" he said contemptuously, not bothering to look at her. His flashes of interest in her seemed to have disappeared.

"Such as whether you are telling the truth to my employer," she said.

He looked up at that and laughed, for the first time with something like genuine amusement. He had strange manners. In part the ordinary Republican manners that she remembered, that would rather spit on the floor at a woman's feet than show her any courtesy, for fear of being thought uncivic-minded, and less than egalitarian; and that cultivated brutality in conversation as earnestly as the old regime had cultivated politeness. Perhaps with no more meaning in the one case than the other. But beneath, behind the brutality and coarseness lay something else, almost prim and puritanical. It did not lie in any particular word of gesture, but in his atmosphere, and she knew it was there as she knew that he was frightened, could almost have drawn a portrait of his background.

"What were you before?" she said.

He began to say "Before what?" with the same coarse indifference, and then smiled and said, "A schoolmaster. An Oratorian. I taught Logic and Theology to young boys. What did you do?"

"I was an actress."

"Like your mother." He sat up, swinging his feet in their worn socks onto the floor, and scratching his armpits as if he disliked the feel of them. "What was it like?"

"Very hard."

"We were not supposed to go to the theatre when I was in the Seminary. We used to borrow clothes and climb out of the windows." He looked at her, his face changing again. "Well, ask me something. Find out the truth about me."

He gave his humourless laugh and stood up, still scratching. It seemed to give him a remote pleasure to behave like that in front of her. He sat down and looked at the food she had brought him. She had had to say in the kitchen that he had fasted so long he must eat well or be truly ill. There was game pie, and cutlets, and some slices of roast veal, and some of the preserved plums, and flummery, and a bottle of claret.

"Are you not going to serve me?" he said, his voice with a sneer in it that was only half unpleasant, and the other half no more than mockery. He tasted the game pie, began to thrust it away contemptuously, and was suddenly overcome with hunger. He pulled the dish back to him, and began to eat. The precise, neat, starved eating of the ex-Oratorian, a swift yet niminy-piminy play of knife and fork, the lips primmed and nibbling.

"I do not like to be watched while I eat."

"But you do not mind it while you scratch?"

He turned to look at her, his fork poised. "I did not think actresses were so delicate-minded."

She flushed, not knowing how to answer him, and furious with herself for not knowing. She felt as if in a moment he had reduced her to nothing again, to childishness. She would have liked to say something tremendous, to show her importance in the affair, and could not think of anything. He seemed to sense it, and smiled as he ate. He stopped eating for a moment and sucked at his teeth with a smacking sound and then picked at a recalcitrant shred of meat with a prong of his fork. He succeeded at last, and sucked the fork, absent-mindedly.

"How did you come here?" he said, taking up his wine.

"It is not you, it is I who am to ask the questions."

He laughed again, good-humouredly, savouring the wine.

"You do not know what to ask me. Your employer must be a fool."

But there he was misled. Perhaps for the very reason that she did not know what to ask, perhaps by mere instinct, young woman's inquisitiveness, she got more from him in the next half an hour than an interrogator might have done. Not facts, which really could have had no importance for her without the means to verify them, but a sense of what his life had been, and was, and why he was there.

"I hate him," he whispered, his lips almost white with passion. And fear. The smell of fear in the room was like that of an animal. And again, not the immediate, almost trivial fear of pain and danger, but a fear that had become part of him, that cancer-growth in his mind. "He will kill all of us. One by one."

He spoke of Robespierre more to himself than to her. Of Robespierre's way of not answering when one tried to plead with him; not seeming even to listen. While he examined himself in his looking-glass, finicking-neat about his dress, like the provincial *petit-maître* that he was.

"Christ's curse on him!" he whispered. "I begged him. On my knees. When I think of it—" The sweat stood on his face like an ugly film of grease. "But he has done it to all of us—Barras—Tallien—Fouché—He means to kill us one by one. Tallien's Spanish whore—He watches us all with those lizard eyes—and we run and scuttle in the shadows—"

"But why do you not stay here then? In safety."

"Don't be a fool," he said. "What safety? In England? There is no safety until he is dead. And France. The Revolution. Everything." He had his eyes hidden by his hands. As he said "France" and the "Revolution," his voice took on, for her actress's ear, a false note, like someone who recites a part so familiar he can no longer put his heart into it. It was neither of those things that troubled him.

"What do you hope to do here, then?"

He looked at her, without really seeing her. "To get money to bring him down, of course. Half a million would do it. A million, to be sure."

"Pounds?"

"In gold. It must be in gold. They will trust nothing else."

"They? Who are they?"

"Other deputies. Enough of them. Barras to stiffen his courage. Some of the commune leaders. The National Guard—some of the leaders there. It is only a matter of gold." He laughed savagely. "Only! And Tallien has three millions in treasure that is useless to us."

"I don't understand."

"What does it matter whether you understand?"

"Because my employer wants to know."

He said something so coarsely terrible about her employer that she did not know what some of the words meant, although she had thought she knew all the words of that kind anyone could say. "If you speak like that," she said, "I shall leave you, and you may as well return to France."

Again he tried to beat her gaze down, and showed her the weakness that lay at the back of his own eyes. That snake's injury that

[205]

crippled him. The fear. "Your people want what I have to sell even more than I want to sell it," he said, attempting carelessness.

She shook her head. "They do not," she said. "They are very afraid of this business. They would be relieved if it came to nothing."

"Did they tell you that?" He made to catch hold of her arm and she drew back towards the door.

"Yes. And it is only reasonable. They have everything to lose. They could go to prison—"

"Prison?" he cried scornfully. And then, with almost a hiss of fear, "What do you think *I* have to lose?" He put up his two hands to his throat and looked at her. And in his eyes the steps of the guillotine, the basket, the blood.

"I do not understand what you are selling to them."

"Christ Jesus! You and what you don't understand! I am selling treasure. Jewels. Plate. Gold watches. Diamonds. Chests full. The loot out of Orléans, Toulon—everything that Tallien and his doxy Fontenaye laid their hands on in Bordeaux—some of the Crown Jewels from the Garde Robe—for a million pounds! They are worth three, five. You could not count their value. And then there is everything from the September—" He broke off, and looked away.

"From the massacres? In the prisons two years ago?"

"You know of them?"

"Yes," she said. What he had been saying took slow shape in her mind. "And all this that you are selling—" she whispered. "It is from—from people you have killed—"

"I have killed no one!" he shouted. "How dare you say it? How dare you accuse me?"

"Be quiet! For God's sake, hush!" She laid her ear against the door and listened. But there was no sound outside.

"And it is not true," he said, whispering now. "Many were not—it is ransom money—they paid to escape—Tallien, the Fontenaye woman. That is why Robespierre has turned on them, for letting so many escape. And the Crown Jewels—they were simply stolen— officially stolen so we could have bribe money. I swear to you I have never injured a living soul. My hands are—" He looked down at them. And to Kate's eyes the palms of his hands seemed to have grown dark. But it was only shadow. "And where did they get their jewels?" he sneered. "Whores in satin." He touched the palms of his hands very gently together, rubbed them, the one barely touching the other, still looking down at them.

"But why must you come here?" Kate kept herself as far from him as she could, her back against the door, her eyes too on his hands. That quite certainly had never used a knife, or a club, to get the treasure he was selling. "Why must you sell them in—in England?"

"For English gold! For God's sake, what can you understand of any of this? You cannot bribe these men with diamond necklaces! They do not know diamonds from glass; they are as ignorant as pigs! And they do not want gold watches—they have five or six apiece, stolen and hidden under their floor boards with God knows what else. They want gold coins, gold Louis, gold guineas, that they can recognise. For a handful of gold now you could buy a house, a farm, where diamonds would scarcely buy your dinner. Christ above, I am putting a fortune into your hands—"

"Not mine." She put the palms of her hands behind her against the wood of the door.

"You! You little prim émigrée! What do you matter in this? Let me talk to your employer as you call him. Your lover. Whoever the devil he is."

"I have no lover."

"I am not surprised." He had pushed his plate away from in front of him with a gesture of contempt and now he went and threw himself on the bed. "Get out. Leave me alone."

She left him. Halfway up the corridor she met Mr. Hatton, coming out of his room with an air of manufactured surprise.

"Oh—I—and how is Mr. Evans?" he said, trying to sound natural and only succeeding in sounding like a bad actor reciting an ill-learned part. "I—we—missed you at dinner. We—I—we were wondering—"

She would have liked to touch him, to convince—remind herself that she was still in England—that nothing had altered beyond recall. Would have liked still more to tell him the truth—tell him everything. And then?

I do not know what I want, she thought.

"Are not you well?" Mr. Hatton said. "Is that why you were not at—at dinner with us? I had thought—"

"I am quite well," she said, her voice growing almost angry, so that he looked startled.

"I did not mean—"

"Be angry with me in return!" her mind cried at him. "Take hold of me! Shake me into reason!"

Why did he look so kind, so gently courteous, so—so young and innocent and unlike—as though Mr. Evans stood beside him in the shadows, drew all the strength from him like a dark and wicked spirit who can suck out the life from living men.

"I know you did not mean any wrong," she said swiftly. "Forgive me." And put up her hand to touch his coat with her finger-tips. Let them rest there for a second. And slowly, unbelieving, Mr. Hatton put up his own hand to clasp hers, keep it there against his heart.

"Do you—have you—forgiven me?" he said in a very low voice. "Truly forgiven me?"

She wanted to say "Yes," to make no games or mysteries or torments out of it any longer. But she could not entirely surrender such an advantage over him.

"I am not sure," she said.

"What must I do for you to be sure?" But his eyes were already certain of forgiveness. They looked at her in a different way, and all that advantage was gone from her, like snow melted in the sun.

"It is I who am giving the advantage to you now!" her eyes tried to tell him. But he could not see so much, and only continued pressing her finger-tips against the cloth of his coat for another moment before footsteps threatened them and he released her with a swift and guilty look. But a look that made them friends—lovers.

"Lovers?" her mind cried in protest. "No! Oh, no!" And yet she felt a warmth of pride in the thought, the accusation, and was almost content to look guilty beside him as Mrs. Cartwright came pattering by, full of tiny compliments about the dinner, of reproaches for Kate's absence, and more compliments that she should be so self-forgetfully kind to the poor Welshman. When Mrs. Cartwright had gone, it was as if a promise had been made and sealed between Kate and Mr. Hatton, in the presence of the innocently unseeing old lady.

"I must go and fetch Titine for our dinner," Kate said. It seemed strangely pleasant to explain to him what she must do.

"You are very good to her," he said.

She looked down, and swiftly up at him and he smiled uncomfortably, as if he was unsure whether he might presume to pay her such compliments or not. And she wanted to say, "And you, you were so good to the Squire, so unashamed of him. You did not know I saw you that day!" Wanted to tell him of seeing him like that. Imagined that someone else was coming and that now—now—he must draw her into his room again. But no one came.

"I must go," she said. And he still did not move, did not try to prevent her, and of a sudden she was gripped with something like rage—not at him, but at—at the Squire, Mr. Gurney—at God knew who—at all of them—every shadowy threat that surrounded her—and terror behind the rage. That someone would go into the Frenchman's room, discover who, what he was. Or that he would try to leave—escape.

"I must go at once!" she cried, turned and began to run, run the five foolish steps to the Frenchman's door, and stopped, knowing that Mr. Hatton must still be there behind her, watching her, half-astonished at her running away from him. She wanted to knock—to throw open the door and see that the Frenchman was there—still there lying on the bed, his boots thrown off—and could not. Could not so much as stay to listen.

She looked back, saw Mr. Hatton watching her as she had known he would be, and wanted to stamp with fury, to shout, "Go! Go! Do not spy on me like that." And managed to control herself. Turn away again, go down the stairs, look for Titine, arrange for their dinner to be brought up to them. Behave as if Mr. Evans was not there. Like death. Like a dead man lying behind the locked door of his room. A dead man who had brought plague with him. That was already corrupting the air they breathed.

Chapter 16

Mr. Otterly and Mrs. Dundas were out at their rehearsals, or seeking for patronage, and the supper table had the air of a family party released for the moment from the presence of guests and the need for a degree of ceremony.

"And how is the poor Welsh gentleman tonight?" Mrs. Cartwright ventured, toying with her collared veal. She had a way of prodding at dishes with her fork that was most exasperating to watch, and Kate felt her nerve ends quivering as a piece of meat was pushed slowly towards the edge of the old lady's plate.

It will fall off the edge, Kate thought. And she longed to seize the tiny, helpless fingers, make them grasp the fork in a sensible fashion, and thrust the prongs into the meat with one stab. But Mrs. Cartwright continued finicking. *I shall cry out with vexation,* Kate thought. The Welsh gentleman? She had to capture her thoughts before she could make sense of the whispered question.

"Oh—I—I think he is a trifle better, but—"

"Is he a handsome young fellow?" the Captain asked with pretended carelessness, his eyes glancing sideways at Mr. Hatton, who was treating his supper in almost as irritating a fashion as Mrs. Cartwright.

"I have not considered him from that point of view," Kate said, setting more wine by the Captain's place with a slight bang of the bottle on the mahogany.

"La-la!" the Captain cried. "That means he is vastly handsome," he confided to Mr. Sowerby. "But she does not wish"—a sideways glance—"to arouse any"—his voice falling to a dramatic whisper—"jealousies."

Mr. Hatton's cheeks burned and he set his knife and fork against his plate with a finality far from justified by the amount he had eaten.

"No appetite, sir?" the Captain said innocently.

Kate took an opportunity to leave the dining-room. She had already seen to the Frenchman's supper, and she hesitated whether to go up to him again. But she did not, and went instead to have her own supper with Titine. And she let two more hours pass before she tapped at his door.

"It is I," she whispered. "Let me in."

"What do you want now?" he said, relocking the door behind her and returning to the chair he had placed by the window. He sat, disregarding her, his elbow on the sill, his chin resting on his hand.

"To see if—you have all you require."

"When are they coming?"

"Tomorrow."

"What will you tell them?"

"It depends upon what they ask."

"An actress!" he said, sneering. "All this to depend on a little actress's opinion!"

"You are too flattering. They will make up their own minds."

He swung round on his chair. "Come here. Stand in front of me so I can see your eyes." She came forward and he put out his two hands and gripped her waist, his fingers almost meeting round it. "So soft!" he said, sneering again.

There was something like hatred in his voice and his expression, as though he wanted to break, to hurt. As though the sensation of soft, girl's flesh under his hands offended him. He dug his fingers in like talons, not hard enough to hurt, but to promise the possibility of hurting.

"You dress like a whore," he said. "Without stays—scarcely with underclothes from the feel of you. If my sister—"

"How fortunate your sister must be," she said, not attempting to free herself.

"What do you mean?"

"To have such a protector."

He let her go at that, his nostrils white at the corners. "Did you sleep with the actors?"

"No. Is that why you dreamed of being one?"

"I told you that?" he said, seeming surprised. "Are you not afraid of me?"

She did not trouble to answer, merely smiled as if he were being childish. He looked at his hands again, at the palms, rubbed them

[211]

slowly together, like a man rubbing off a stain. "You are very strange."

"So I have been told before."

"Why did you come to me now?"

"To see if you wanted for anything."

"It was not only that, I think?"

"What else?"

He had turned away from her and was looking out of the window once more. "Tomorrow? What time tomorrow?"

"I cannot tell."

He put his two elbows on the sill and his two hands to his face. "Go away."

She hesitated. She scarcely knew—did not know—why. Where his hands had grasped her round the waist she could still feel the impress of his fingers, like bruising, at once an aching and a half-painful warmth.

When she did not leave, he swung round again. His face was twitching, his eyes hidden by the shadows cast by the remaining light at the window behind his head. "Do you want to stay with me?"

She backed away from him, one step, another. He did not move, merely watched her, his expression once more sneering. Perhaps it had been sneering all the time. "Why did you come?"

"I have told you," she whispered. She felt a shivering of fear and horror, thought that if he moved towards her she would cry out, she would not be able to help herself. Her two hands touching the door behind her, the key still in the lock. She had only to turn it. Open the door. Go. He had not moved. His expression hidden from her by the shadows.

Now, she thought, her mind in a strange state of separateness from her body. *He will get up. He will—* She seemed to be watching herself. With a kind of horror. And at the same time an almost cool, an almost distant interest. As if she were watching someone else. Watching someone on a stage. As if what might happen scarcely mattered.

And the girl, that other self of hers, stood not moving, not able to move, not able to cry out. *Now*—she thought again. Closed her eyes against his silhouette. Heard the rustling of his clothes, the small movement of his chair as slowly, slowly he stood up. *If he touches me, I shall die!* she thought. Her hands flattened against the door, her left hand beside the lock, the key. *I shall die.* She dared not look at him. Felt his presence close. Heard his breath, the sound of his moving.

"What will you tell them?" he said. His hand touching her face. Her shoulder.

"I will—will—" She could not move. Could not speak. His hand no more than brushing against the thin nainsook of her sleeve. And that light, light touching more frightening than if he had gripped hard, torn.

In another moment he will—he will— She felt herself swaying forward. Falling. Caught at the key to save herself, and the cold metal seemed to wake her, startle her into life again—and she did cry out "No! No!" Tore at the key so that she hurt her hand, twisted it in the lock, pulled at the handle as if it were the bar of a cage. Felt the door opening—was outside. And he had not touched her again, had not tried to prevent her, keep her. Seemed to have stepped back into shadow, nothingness. She leaned with all her weight against the outside of the door, her forehead against it, her eyes shut. Unable to control her breathing. Breathing as hard as if she had run a race, escaped from terror.

A minute dragging by. His voice whispering against the door. Against her forehead. "Are you still there?" She did not answer. But he could—must—hear her breathing. Hear her heart.

I am not only mad but wicked, she thought. Looked at herself in horror. As if she were a crawling thing. *What will become of me?*

"Whore," he whispered. "Little whore of an émigrée." Like an endearment. Cajolery. She imagined his fingers touching the smooth wood. There and there. By her forehead. Her cheek. An inch of mahogany between his fingers and her mouth, her throat.

"Come to me now," he whispered. "I will take off your clothes for you." A seminarian's day-dream in his voice, a prim lasciviousness. "Little breasts," he whispered. "Soft skin. I will touch you between your thighs. Until you cry for me." A seminarian, dreaming of whores in his dormitory, of actresses, of rich women in silk dying of love for him.

And I? she thought. Wanting to answer him, insult him, threaten. *I am Bedlam mad,* she thought. *If he were even handsome—* And Mr. Hatton's image came to her closed eyes and it was as if she had been struck with a whip across her back. Like fire.

"O God!" she breathed. "O God, forgive me. Mother of God—"

[213]

But she could not pray. And she had dared to condemn her mother? If she could kneel down. Slide down here by the door, kneel, lean against the wood. Be still.

"Tell me who first took you," he was whispering. "Was it an old man? Or a young actor? Tell me how it happened. Answer me. Are you remembering? How he touched you? Unfastened—stripped you—threw you down on the straw so that the straws pricked your flesh—pricked your naked buttocks, between your legs? Was that how it was?"

"Christ have mercy on me," she breathed. "Christ forgive me." She tried to make the sign of the Cross, but her hands could not move themselves. "Mother of God—"

As though his voice was flesh, was touching her. Her own flesh sick and shivering with horror, and yet—and yet—

"Holy Mary, Mother of God—"

On her knees. As if she were truly praying. But to that locked door. That hidden whisperer. Drawing her through into the dark, the secrecy, the warmth of—If he should open the door. Catch hold of her arms.

It is my punishment, she thought. *It is they who have brought him here. So that—so that—they may see me damned.* And then she thought, *Perhaps it is an expiation—because I denied my mother—and I must—I must destroy myself so that—* like a sleep-walker who dreams of suicide and walks nearer and nearer to a cliff's edge.

"I order you to come to me," he said, his voice altering. "Now!" And she found herself standing up—scarcely able to stand—touching the door-handle—

"I will not," she told herself. "I—" And heard footsteps coming. Thought, *I must hide, hide! Inside his room. I must, there is no choice for it!*

And almost without knowing it found herself not opening the door, but running from it. Running like the wind, soundlessly; the corridor, the stairs, into her own room where Titine was already in bed, half asleep, looking up startled at the rush and swiftness of Kate's entry. Kate standing, listening, one hand lifted to her lips as if she had been followed, was being hunted.

"What is it?" Titine said. "What you doing?"

"Hush!" Kate breathed. And of a sudden threw herself down beside the bed, dug her fingers into the coverlet, buried her face in it.

Felt the tears come. Slowly at first and then like a storm, a flood, burning. Burning her eyes, scalding.

After a moment she felt Titine's arms round her, and she thought she would die of pain, the arms were so thin, so innocently loving, so unquestioning. Titine saying nothing, not even telling her not to cry, not to be sad for anything. Only holding her.

Chapter 17

Mr. Gurney came the next evening, bringing "Mr. Razor Thomas" with him, under the name of "Johnson," both of them brought by Mr. Biggins in the chaise, round by the back road, into the stable-yard with a clattering of hooves and wheels, a snorting and jingling; old John and 'Ang running; all the bustle that Mr. Gurney seemed to create and dominate without conscious effort. He summoned Kate with a word as if she were a servant-girl.

"Well?" he said, as she made him her curtsey. And "We have a new visitor?" he said aloud for the benefit of old John and Elizabeth and Peg, who were struggling with a heavy chest between them until Mr. Biggins came to their rescue, 'Ang being already loaded with two portmanteaux and a dressing case. Lowering his voice Mr. Gurney said, "You have talked with him? And formed an opinion?"

"Yes, sir." Wanting to look away, as if he might see in her eyes what had—happened?—and she herself hesitating in astonishment at the word, the thought. As if already it was nothing, part of the dreams that had come after, as she lay in Titine's arms, shivering, and at last growing quiet. And at the same time it was so great and terrible a thing, that there were no words for it at all. As if she were utterly changed from the young girl that Mr. Gurney had last seen—had become so different that he might scarcely recognise her.

"Well?" Mr. Gurney was repeating. "Have ye lost your tongue?" He glanced round them as if thinking that she was afraid of being overheard and said roughly, "All right, all right, come to us in my room in a minute or two. Bring us some sherry wine and biscuits and order a cold supper for us. Make it a sufficient one. We shall be late enough tonight, I imagine."

Five minutes afterwards she was setting the decanter and biscuits in front of him, the newly-named Mr. Johnson staring out of the window, ignoring her, his hands clasped behind his back, whistling softly through his teeth. When Mr. Gurney said, "Now, girl. What do you think of the fellow?" Mr. Johnson swung round on her, his movement powerful, like a boxer's, balanced and threatening.

"He is—"—she gave a shiver—"There is something—he is evil," she whispered. "He is like someone damned." And did not know herself if she was pretending as she shivered.

Mr. Gurney laughed.

"Did he try to seduce you?" Mr. Johnson sneered. "It's not his soul we care about. Now—tell us. Is he what he claims to be?" He made to grip her by the chin with his thumb and forefinger as he had done once before. She put up her hand to protect herself.

"I am trying to answer you!" she cried. "How can I until I understand what—" Making an enormous effort to be rational, to drive that whispering out of her mind. *A poor wretched, frightened thing,* she thought. *No more than that.*

"Keep your voice down, damn you," Mr. Gurney said, lifting his head to listen for sounds outside the door. "Until you understand what?"

"What you want from him. He is afraid. If you want courage from him, he has none; he will break." As if she were making herself brave by telling how afraid he was.

They stood and looked at her. Mr. Johnson let himself sink slowly into a chair and rested his pock-marked chin on his hand, still looking at her. "Go on."

She shrugged, trying to seem indifferent. "There is nothing else in him. He is like a snake that is dying."

The two men looked at one another, and seemed, astonishingly, to be pleased with what they had just heard. She sensed that they too were afraid. Not in the way that the Frenchman was, not that sick permanence of terror. But afraid. And were relieved that he was even more afraid than they were. They would be glad when this was over.

"You sound like a poetess," Mr. Johnson said, stroking his lower lip with his finger-tips. The pock marks showed dull white against the London-grey of his skin. His eyes very pale blue. "What is he afraid of?"

"He is afraid of the guillotine. Of Robespierre. Of the things he has done."

"What has he done?"

"How should I know?"

"Why must he sell to us and not in Germany or anywhere else?"

"You did not ask me to ask him that. How can I possibly tell you? He wants English gold he said. That was all. The people he wants to bribe will trust it. Perhaps the Germans have no gold."

They looked at each other again. Mr. Gurney leaned forward, his elbow on one knee, his forefinger lifted. "Good. So far so good. Don't be afraid of us. You have done very well, but now you must think hard. Does he really possess the things he has offered to us? Or is part of his fear—not all, but part, even a small part—because he is lying to us? Trying to cheat us in any way, and fears being found out by us? Think hard."

She shook her head in irritation, and despair of being able to answer. And thought with a renewed wonder, *His life depends on what I say in the next moment. If I say one thing instead of another, they will kill him. They will drown him like a rat in a barrel.*

She did not know how she knew, but she was as certain of it as of the time of the evening, of the twilight outside. She had kept away from the Frenchman all day, except to push a tray of food to him through the half-open doorway, her heart beating so hard she could not trust her voice to speak to him. And he had not spoken to her. Had not moved from where he lay on the bed in the curtained, shadowy room. But she had sensed in him a growing fear as the day progressed, a different kind of fear to that cancer of his—an urgent, immediate one—a fear of these two men or of whoever was coming. Of never leaving that room alive.

"No!" she said. "He is not afraid of anything like that!"

"You said that very quickly," Mr. Johnson murmured. "Too quickly for my taste. Has he touched your French heart, perhaps?"

"Quickly?" she whispered. "I—I have answered you as I—as I think."

Mr. Johnson came smoothly out of the chair, in one easy movement, like an attack. This time Kate had no chance of protecting herself. He had his hand on her throat, loosely enough, one thumb pushing up into the soft underside of her jaw. He seemed to know exactly where the least pressure of thumb and finger-tip would hurt most. If he altered the angle of his forearm in the slightest degree, she must stand on tiptoe or suffer increasing pain.

"Have you been touched?" he said. "Or bribed?"

Mr. Gurney sat watching them. She felt that he would have sat watching as quietly while she was killed.

[218]

"You are hurting me—" She had to stand on tiptoe to be able to say anything, and felt the humiliation of it worse than the pain that in reality was almost nothing. Merely the threat of pain.

He let go of her and stroked her cheek. "You were growing too pleased with yourself," he said. "Now, tell us again. Does he possess these things?"

"I—how can I know?" She felt tears in her eyes and that too was humiliating. "Why do you ask me such questions? He says he has treasure—jewels—he says they are worth millions of pounds—three—five—how do I know what he has?"

"Did he describe where this treasure comes from?"

"Yes."

We are talking of murdered people, she thought. She was looking at Mr. Gurney's face and it seemed to disappear, and she was looking at a dark courtyard, torchlight—men kneeling, and being clubbed as they knelt, axed, struck with butchers' cleavers, hatchets, until there was so much blood the yard turned scarlet. Men running, screaming—their voices thin as echoes—like watching a stage from so far away that all is in miniature. Small figures dying, and the murderers running from one victim to the next, rifling, stealing, stripping pockets and throats and fingers. So much blood they slipped in it and fell, and went on killing. The courtyard of the Abbaye prison two years ago. She knew it as if she had been there. She would have fallen if the vision of it had continued another second. She put up her hand to her head.

"He has the things he claims to have," she said. "That is why he is so afraid." She no longer cared whether they believed her or not. "They have some of the crown jewels, he says. And they sold people their lives. Hundreds upon hundreds. That is where most of it comes from. And murdered men's houses. They went to the houses afterwards and stripped them to the walls."

"You must have had long conversations with this charmer," Mr. Johnson said. "He should have brought you something for a keepsake."

She did not bother to answer him.

"She is telling the truth as she knows it," Mr. Gurney said. "Good. You have done very well. Now we will go and talk to this gentleman ourselves and you may leave us alone for a while. Make it understood that I am closing the business about the chaise with him. In half an hour or so you may call us both to supper, and I shall tell you that we have taken such a fondness for our Welsh friend and are so sorry for him in his lonely convalescence that we mean to sup with him in his room. Eh?"

She left them, unable to think for the pressure of that vision she had had. As though she had been there. Beside him. She wanted to run to his room and scream at him, "Murderer!" and knew at the same time that he had no more killed anyone in that courtyard with his own hands than she had done. Than she had drowned anyone at Callac. And the comparison struck her mind so hard that she stood still in the corridor and could not move for a second, pressing her hand against her heart.

There is no comparison! He ordered—he was one of those who ordered— he—I did nothing evil, nothing.

"You did nothing," a voice seemed to whisper in the dark of the corridor. "When you might have cried out. You might have saved—might have saved even one."

"It is not true! It is not true!"

She expected to hear her voice echoing, a scream. And there was no sound at all. She went downstairs like a sleep-walker, gave her orders about their supper, went out into the yard. Mr. Biggins was rubbing down one of the horses, 'Ang rubbing down another with handfuls of straw, looking small and thin against the great dark flank of the animal. She thought, *How wonderful to be him. To be so innocent.* She imagined that she would give up the power of speech joyfully if only that weight of guilt could be lifted away from her. "But it is not true," she whispered. "How can I be guilty? There was only a moment—I had no time to think—it was too late." She twisted her hands together.

Mr. Biggins smiled at her and beckoned. "Come an' lay your hand on his neck, little ma'am—ain't he a beautiful fine animal? An' how do he fare to go on today, the poor Welsh gentleman?" He winked and laughed, his face as innocent as 'Ang's, laughing like a man whose sleep is never troubled by dreams.

"Did you ever kill anyone?" Kate whispered, knowing that the question must sound like madness, and unable to prevent herself from asking it. But Mr. Biggins did not seem to take it as madness. He only looked mildly surprised for a moment, suspending his rubbing of the roan's neck. The horse nuzzled at him, already his friend.

"Aye. Mebbe I did, a few. Here an' there. What makes you ax that, for God's sake, little one? Ist you feeling blood-thirsty?"

"Do they not come back to you?"

He was truly astonished now and turned to look at her fully. "Come back to me?" He laughed as heartily as before. "Nay, there's summat! What would they come back for? More of t'same?"

"I am thinking of the Frenchman," she said. "They come back to him."

"Did he tell you so?" He had looked round him as she said "Frenchman" and now began leading the roan horse into the stables to join the two horses already there, rubbed down and waiting for their food. "Finish 'em proper, 'Ang bor," he called out to 'Ang. And to Kate, in a whisper, "Dunna be callin' out wrong names an' words like thaat, my dear. You never knows who's listening. So he do fare to have bad dreams, do he, friend Evans?"

She would have given five of the guineas hidden in her mattress upstairs to be able say, "And I too." To tell him the story. But he would only have stared at her with his small, innocent sea-blue eyes, in kindly amazement at anyone's feeling guilt for anything, let alone such a contortion of guilt for nothing, such self-torturing.

"He is near to going mad, I think," she said. *And I. And I.*

"A poor sort o' wretch I reckoned 'em, the minute I did see 'em."

"Mr. Gurney asked me to question him, to find out things about him. Why did he need me to do that?"

" 'Cause he's a new 'un to us. He ann't the old kind, decent smugglers an' robbers, as do have been sending stuff to us for years. He must have heerd of us from some o' they an' he sent messages as he did fare to have a powerful stroke o' business to do with us if we had a mind to it. A stroke as 'ud make us all rich as Crissus. So nat'-rally we were interested; an' just as nat'ral we did feel suspicious. So you, being like a French maid as 'ud worm things out o' 'em if they was there to be wormed, you fell in right handy for 'um."

"And did they mean me to come here all the time? Even when the other Mr. Thomas—Mr. Johnson—told me I could no longer work for you?"

He laughed heartily, smacking his great hand on the brown crupper in front of him. "Now there's axing. You go an' ax Mr. Johnson thaat."

"But why? Why did they do it? In such a cruel way?"

"I ann't sayin' they did."

"But you know it."

"Go on away with you, little one, an' have a bit o' meat an' ale set out for me. I ann't a Frenchy as has to have things wormed out a' me."

When she continued questioning him, he merely picked her up, one hand under each of her elbows, as if she were a child, and set her outside the stable, with amused gentleness and at the same time impatience. "You go an' see to my supper, little pretty, or I'll set you up in t' loft above there, with the rats an' mice, an' take away t'ladder."

She was obliged to obey him, and to spend the rest of the evening sitting in her small private parlour. Outside in the courtyard she could hear 'Ang playing his flute for Titine and the maids and Mr. Biggins. Mr. Biggins whistling a tune and 'Ang catching and following. He could imitate anything, play birds' songs so perfectly the birds would answer him, hear a tune twice and play it back again like an echo. He was playing a dancing song now. She could hear the steps in it, almost see them—forward and back, forward and back, round and round and round. The sounds very thin with distance, almost the ghosts of sounds. Through an open window at the back of the house, overlooking the courtyard. Through an open doorway, along a corridor.

She went to the window to look as well as hear. Mr. Biggins was teaching the dance steps to Titine, and the maids were dancing opposite one another. Only Peg was not dancing, keeping in the darkest shadows by the scullery door, her white face staring towards 'Ang as if she were afraid of him and his music. The beginnings of moonlight, candlelight from a window, the shadows of the dancers, the tune now sad, now swift. It gave Kate a feeling of piercing loneliness. She thought that her heart would burst with it. She did not know why, nor what was in her heart to make it so full that a touch could injure it like that.

She would have liked to go down to them and take Titine's place in the dance. She felt the steps in her feet, the tune in her blood. And yet something held her where she was, as if she were so cut off from them by—by all that had passed—that she could no longer do anything so natural. So innocent. The moon near full, not yet above the black ridge of the stable roof on that side of the yard, but the sky grown hazy with the light of it. Titine bending her head to one side as she danced, with her child's gravity of concentration, her hands held out to touch Mr. Biggins's great hands, her foot pointed forward with a lightness that made Mr. Biggins's shadow seem like a bear's. And yet he danced very lightly too for all his bulk and height. Forward and back, forward and back on the cobble-stones and the straw. *It could not make a very satisfactory dance floor*, Kate thought.

She turned away from the window and went back to her parlour. But there through the window the moon lay on the sea and she could neither bear to look at it nor make herself look away. She thought she could see the silhouette of a boat sail into the white path. She took the stockings she was mending for Titine and went down the stairs with them. But Mrs. Cartwright had long gone to bed. Mr. Otterley and Mrs. Dundas were still out, and the Captain and Mr. Sowerby and Mr. Hatton were in the morning room that they used as a smoking-parlour. She could hear Captain Cartwright's voice, loud and confident. "Damned ruffians—I wonder at a young fellow of your education—"

Mr. Hatton's reply was too low to hear the words of it, but she thought she could hear the beginnings of exasperation. She felt a temptation to go in and interrupt them with enquiries about their comfort, but instead she sat herself in Mrs. Cartwright's chair in the parlour, where the lamp was still lit, and forced herself to attend to her work. How could Titine make such tears and holes? "The next time she shall mend them herself." No wonder she tore them dancing on cobble-stones, with a great monstrous fool like Mr. Biggins. And the maids—they would not be one quarter so lively in the morning when they were beginning their work—and Peg should have been in bed an hour ago. And 'Ang. She had a mind to go out and tell them so. Had Titine any idea what stockings cost to buy? Nearly three shillings for this pair, and she could not have worn them six times. Even her anger a pretence, an attempt at naturalness. An escape from—

She threw the mending down on the table, and lay back in the chair with her eyes closed. What were Mr. Gurney, Mr. Johnson and the Frenchman doing now? She had half-expected to have been called on already as interpreter. She wondered what kind of French Mr. Gurney spoke. Or did the Frenchman speak enough English? He had said he knew a little, but the three words he had tried for her had not sounded very intelligible. Not that she wanted to be called on. God forbid it. She felt so restless she could not stay sitting down. Got up, went to the window, drummed her fingers on the glass. Went out into the passage.

"What is the most important part of the population?" Mr. Hatton was crying. "Twenty dukes? Four hundred lords? Or—or ten million honest men and women who earn their livings and—and create the wealth those four hundred and twenty leeches f-fasten on?"

"Ten million rascals!" the Captain shouted. "You cannot have a ship without officers!"

"It is God's will that one man should be set above others for their guidance," Mr. Sowerby said. Kate could imagine his hands folding, his pale yellow lips pressed together.

"But—but—but you belong to the ten million! Both of you!" Mr. Hatton said, his voice breaking with desperation. "If—you were my Lord Cartwright—do you think you would be rotting on half pay—like—like an abandoned hulk? You would be in the Admiralty, drawing your five thousand a year, and making as much again in bribes from purveyors. You would—"

"Silence man!" the Captain roared, stung at last into using his quarter-deck voice. "How dare you!"

"You are blind!" screamed Mr. Hatton, losing all traces of stammer in his fury. "Deaf and blind! The only Admiral we ever treated as he deserved was Admiral Byng. If we shot another twenty admirals and as many generals and field marshals alongside them, we might win this war, not that we ought to be fighting it. We make boys of twelve and fourteen into officers to lead men in battle, and wonder that we lost the American colonies! We have majors and colonels not yet twenty, scarce older than Miss Harriott and knowing as much about soldiering, given the right to lead five hundred men to slaughter! Why? Why? Because their fathers are rich men and can buy them their commissions as they might buy them a pair of horses. And how did those men get rich?"

"You are questioning God's will—"

"And you!" Mr. Hatton shouted. "Twenty years grovelling to my Lord someone in the hope that he would present you to a fat living, and he died or changed his mind, or—"

"Grovelling? Sir!"

"Grovelling! And someone who grovelled better did you out of it. Was that God's will? God help the poor sheep who get such shepherds!"

"I shall not stay to be insulted further. I trust it is the three large glasses of brandy punch I have just seen you consuming, and not your true mind that has been speaking—"

[224]

"Hatton, man! Apologise dammit, ye have gone too far this time. A joke's a joke, but this is scoundrel's talk—"

"Do not disturb yourself, Mr. Sowerby, sir. I—I am sorry. I cannot speak on these things in a calm way. My—my apologies—I must go out and walk myself calm—"

Kate had scarcely time to withdraw into the doorway of the parlour when Mr. Hatton came out of the morning room. She heard the front door bang behind him and ran to the parlour window to watch him. He strode across the road to the sea-wall and leaned there, wiping his forehead with his handkerchief.

She thought, *If I were to go out—to—to find him there by—accident—* and she was already shaping excuses in her mind—the heat—the moonlight—but he had turned, and was looking at the window where she was standing, the lamplight behind her. He could see her as clear as she could see him and they stood like that, looking at one another, the window, and the width of the road, between them. And seemed as close as though they were touching hands.

He could not possibly see that she was smiling. She must be no more than a silhouette to him, against the light behind her, but he straightened, and crossed the road again towards her. Not to the front door beside the room where she was standing, but to the window. She opened the casement and they stood facing one another, the road outside that trifle lower than the floor she was standing on that brought their eyes to a level.

"Were you—did you hear our"—his fluency of passion lost, and replaced by his ordinary manner—"our quarreling?"

She nodded. "I could not help it."

"I am afraid they are both—I have made both of them very angry."

She laughed and he smiled, as if he had been afraid that she too might be angry with him.

"I saw you standing at the window," he said unneccessarily.

"I know."

"I wish—"

She waited for a long time. "What do you wish?" she said at last. They seemed to be quite alone in the world.

"I do not know what I wish. That the world were different. That—impossible things." He smiled again, his smile so full of wished-for things for others that she wanted to touch his hair, push it back from his forehead. Touch his mouth with her fingers as

[225]

sometimes she touched Titine's. Make him perhaps think less of those indifferent others, and more of—

He will ask me to walk outside in the air with him, she thought. *Or else he will ask if he may come and join me.*

And felt suddenly as if she were hideously crippled. As if her face were scarred by wickedness, and he must see it. Must know what she was. She needed to hold on to the window frame, look away from him.

He will see! He will see! And would have given her soul to escape from him. "But there is nothing to see!" her heart cried. "O God, please let me—" and did not know what she wished that God might let her have or do. Only to be good. "Let me be good," she prayed. "Only let me be good."

His goodness shines in him, she thought, and lifted her eyes again, and smiled, half in gladness because he was so good, and half in fond compassion because it made him so defenceless.

"Miss Kate. Kate," he said. He seemed to have trouble in pronouncing her name. "I—"

She did not help him. Only smiled. Her smile gathering power and losing its humility.

"I wondered—the plays—are to begin next week," he said with a rush of effort. "I—I was thinking that—they say that Mr. Otterley's Othello—and even his Romeo—are—"

"And is Mrs. Dundas to play Juliet?" Kate asked with sudden innocence, all her heart, her soul, in her eyes.

"Why—I suppose—" He began to laugh, and stopped, looking at her. "Will you—?" he said. "Will you let me bring you to the theatre?" As though he meant to say much more than that, tell her much more.

"I should be most honoured," she said, trying to sound light-hearted, mock-romantic. Trying to sound anything but what she felt.

"If he should—if it had been him, and not—if he should touch me now, touch my face—" Felt her body shivering, trembling. Knew that he must see it, almost—almost wished—

"You are cold," he said. "I have kept you standing here." But he did not move to let her close the window.

"I am not cold," she whispered. "It is hot—so hot that—" Stood. Feeling her heart beating. "It is so hot that one can scarcely breathe."

"It is," he said. Smiled. Took her hands in his so naturally that he did not seem to be thinking of what he was doing.

He must see, she thought. *Must see in my eyes, my face—must feel in my hands what I—must know that I—*

As if she had no remembrance of what virtue was. As if last night, all the horror of it, were wiped away, and there was nothing in the world beyond themselves. His touching her.

"Touch my face," her mind begged of him. "Touch my—my heart." Wanted to draw up his hands until they were against her breast. Shook in that instant with such a force of passion that it was like lightning striking a tree, terrifying, blasting all her girl's coquetry and playfulness and childish temptations as the lightning blasts leaves and branches, shrivels them. Made her in that one fraction of a second from girl into woman, and such a woman as frightened her herself, unrecognisable. A woman who would take and burn, turn a man to charcoal. Then the flash was gone and she was herself again, ashamed, drawn, half-frightened, longing. Safe.

How safe I am with him, she thought. And wondered what he would think if he could see into her mind, and smiled at the idea, like a mother with a child. They heard voices. Mr. Otterley's voice, declaiming something. Perhaps he was only saying that he was tired and hungry, but he made it sound like King Lear. He and Mrs. Dundas were upon them before they could separate.

"Aha, Miss Harriott—how sweet the moonlight sleeps! But we do wake! Eh, Mr. Hatton, sir?" His eye was filled with the excitement of rehearsals, and perhaps with wine, and he looked at them both indulgently. Mrs. Dundas drew her silk shawl round her shoulders and passed them by with a nod. Mr. Otterley followed her, obedient to unspoken disapprovals.

"I must go and see to them," Kate whispered. "Their suppers—their lamps—I—"

"Juliet!" Mr. Hatton whispered, and they began laughing, as if neither of them was older than Titine.

Chapter 18

The next morning, with all the precautions necessary for ill-health, "Mr. Evans the Welshman" left The Old Ship Hotel as he had come, his face wrapped in the large white cloth, his groans almost as loud as when he had arrived. Helped into the chaise by an attentive Mr. Biggins, Mr. Gurney and Mr. Johnson attending the process like old and solicitous friends. When he was safely inside, Mr. Gurney joined him, Mr. Johnson mounted a saddle-horse brought round for him earlier, and the party set off to a flourish of Mr. Biggins's whip, a crunching of wheels on cobbles, a peeping of maids' heads from windows and doorways, and the clatter of hooves. Until all faded, leaving the stable-yard and the hotel extraordinarily empty-seeming.

Kate, who had helped to see them off, went back into the house, feeling at the same time relieved and flat, scarcely knowing what to do with herself, or at least with that part of herself that was not concerned with Mr. Hatton. And she was not sure, very far from sure, how great each part was in relation to the other, or how great she wished the one and the other to be. She went up to look at the Frenchman's room, to make sure that nothing untoward had been left behind him, before giving orders for it to be cleaned out and aired. There was a strong smell of tobacco smoke and brandy, not yet dissipated by the open door and window. Not the ordinary untidyness of a man's bedroom after he has left it, but an extra, brutal slovenliness. She wrinkled her nose in disgust at smell and appearance and went to lean on the window-sill.

What had they arranged? Something positive, for they were all three to return within a week or so, and at breakfast Mr. Gurney had taken pains to prepare everyone's mind for their returning. He and Mr. Johnson, with some others, he had told them, were to commence building a Public Baths on a nearby site, just along the Hard, and Mr. Evans was to be a leading shareholder in the project. The whole of breakfast had been taken up with talk of hydro-therapy, and the attractions of such a venture.

"It is the one thing Shoreham lacks!" Mr. Gurney had said. "Eh, ma'am?" to Mrs. Cartwright. "Is it not a capital idea? May not we count on you for our first lady visitor in the Baths?"

"Oh, I do not think that—oh, dear—oh, dear! You will make Shoreham so fashionable and smart—"

"And why not, ma'am? Imagine if His Majesty was to visit our Baths for a treatment!"

Poor Mrs. Cartwright was so overcome at the thought of what might follow on such a visit that she could not finish her toast, and twice in the next hour waylaid Kate to ask her did she truly think that such dreadful things might happen. "We could not possibly afford to stay in such a case! Oh—oh, Miss Harriott, even if you should be indulgent to old guests and not put up your rates quite out of our reach, I know what the shopkeepers would do—and I should be afraid even to step into the street for looking so shabby and old-fashioned."

"You do not look at all old-fashioned," Kate had tried to console her. "You look just as you should. And I am quite sure that none of it will happen as Mr. Gurney says. It is just a pipe-dream."

"But the Welsh gentleman who is to put his money into it? And the bricks? Mr. Gurney says he shall have even the bricks and timbers delivered soon!"

"I beg of you not to be troubled about it."

But the old lady clearly remained very troubled, and Kate felt that she had gone as far as she dared in reassuring her. And perhaps Mr. Gurney did intend, for some queer purpose of his own, and of the Squire's, really to construct a Baths. *They were capable of anything,* she thought. And the idea—not of the Baths in particular, but of that capacity for *anything*—was a pleasing one. It gave her again a sense of strength, of belonging to something hidden, but great and powerful. That could buy a hotel here, and construct a Baths there, and send secret messages and receive disguised visitors, and spread its web between towns and countries.

And I am a part of it.

And Mr. Hatton?

She stood very still at the open window, staring out at the exposed, bright sands, the tide a line far out against the edge of the sky. Some fishermen's wives and their children dotted across the mud flats, small black figures bending down, gathering mussels and cockles into baskets. *Mr. Hatton.*

"He is a fool, that boy!" Mr. Gurney had said, his face angrier than she had ever seen it. Indeed, she had never seen him angry before. "Damned Jacobinical ravings! I have a mind to kick him out of here this morning and let him find lodgings where they'll tolerate his rubbish. Did you know he spouted such stuff?"

"I—I have heard something—"

"You should have told me before. Good God! A damned radical agitator here in this very house! Calling the attention of the authorities down on us at the very moment we can least suffer it. Damned puppy! Tell him to—"

She had found herself holding her breath, expecting the next words to be an order to tell Mr. Hatton to leave. But Mr. Gurney swallowed his anger and said, "No—the least fuss the best, perhaps. It is only another week or so. But tell him—tell him I am not pleased at what I hear of his talk and of his insulting my guests, and I'll have no more of it. If the rascal was here—But we must be off in an hour. Mind now, tell him."

She had already rehearsed it several times, like a game. Like the game she had played long ago with his likeness, before she so much as knew his name. Of his riding with her in her hackney-coach. Of what they might say to one another. And now? What should she truly say to him? "Mr. Hatton, I have something of great seriousness to say to you. Mr. Gurney is shocked! Shocked at your conduct!" How could she say anything so nonsensical? And yet—and yet she must say something.

I shall be very gentle with him, she thought. *Very indulgent and understanding. And yet I shall make him understand that—that I too really consider—feel—that he has gone beyond—but I shall be very understanding! Very kind to him!*

May I clean t'room, ma'am?" Elizabeth, behind her, with broom and duster.

"Yes, yes do. What a smell there is, I must send up 'Ang with some lavender polish when you have done."

She went down the stairs, her mind still occupied with Mr. Hatton. And it remained so for much of the day. She would, she decided at last, go to his room as soon as he came back from the library. And found her heart beating strongly as the time drew near. His shape passing the window of the parlour. His voice greeting someone. His tread through the hall-passage, light and quick. Running up the stairs. Apart from herself and Titine he was the only person in the hotel who ever ran anywhere, ever. Even poor little Peg never ran, but trudged about in her too-large pattens as if she were behind a plough.

"Now!" Kate said to herself, and began running up the stairs after him, composing her opening words as she ran. Altering her pace to a most dignified housekeeper's tread as she neared his door, knocked. His face showed surprise and pleasure at seeing her in the doorway.

"Miss Harriott!"

"Mr. Hatton—" She had forgotten what she had just composed. "Mr. Gurney—"

"He has gone?" He looked as though Mr. Gurney had weighed on his spirits and his going had left a holiday mood behind.

"Yes." Mr. Hatton's room also was untidy. He had but a moment ago come in and it was untidy already. His hat thrown on the bed, books dropped on the floor, a drawer pulled open. But nothing of the Frenchman's atmosphere about it. The difference between light and dark, good and—*I need not be angry with him,* she thought, half nervous and half amused again. *Only—only the least shade severe.* She felt her mouth threatening to smile at him, and drew down her brows in a severe expression.

"Mr. Gurney is very angry with you," she said. He stared at her in amazement. She nodded confirmation. "With your Jacobinical talk. And upsetting Mr. Sowerby and the Captain."

"Oh. Oh, dear!" He looked once again about fifteen, as he might have done as a school-boy brought up before the master for grave misdemeanours.

Kate raised herself slightly on her toes to give weight to her words. "You are never to say such things again in this house or"—she struggled to retain her severity, with not much success— "or—or Mr. Gurney says—that—that you must find other lodgings."

To her surprise the severity seemed unneeded. Mr. Hatton looked utterly defeated without it. Very slowly he sat down on the bed, still looking at her with that school-boy's face, one hand at his hair unconsciously. "Find—other—" As though it was ten thousand, a million miles from his mind that not so very long ago he had suggested that very thing himself. "Find other lodgings?"

"Yes indeed."

"And you?" he said.

"And I?" she echoed him, suddenly unsure of just what kind of game she had entered on.

"I thought—" he said, "I thought that you—that you agreed with—that in such things you agreed with me?"

He no longer seemed childish, unless sincerity is always childish, or at least childlike. His eyes were searching hers as though for an answering sincerity. One hand still thrust into his hair, the other resting beside him on the untidy, disordered coverlet.

"How—can I know anything of such matters?" she said. All her power lost. Standing in front of him as though he had summoned her to answer him. They looked at one another, and the reason that had brought her there faded into nothing. Vanished. There were only the two of them. Even the conventions seemed to fade like mist. As if there were no hotel, no maids, no guests, no one in the world but their two selves.

He smiled at her, an odd, self-conscious smile, that began with a half-embarrassment, and became self-mockery, and then irony—as though moment by moment he put off his appearance of gaucherie, of being incapable of dealing with the ordinary world, and the man he would become showed himself, as had happened that night downstairs—a man who knew himself very well, and knew the world he lived in, and was not willing to make terms with evil, but understood now why it was there. Understood the world much better than quick and easy "men of the world" can ever do. Or perhaps all that was only in her eyes. Because she saw him differently.

I have not really seen him until now, she thought. *Only the things about him that do not matter. What does he see in me?* And for a second she wanted to stand in front of him utterly without concealment, like a soul at Judgement Day, as if she had nothing to conceal. Only gifts to offer. Wanted to extend her hands, hold out her arms, lift herself up like a gift. And then the shadows came and she wanted to hide herself, wanted to cover her face. *If he knew!* she thought in a swift rush of pain. *If he could see—the things I have done—thought. How he would turn away from me! How he would look!* But he could not see, and without knowing what she was doing she took a step towards him, and another, until her hand was able to touch his shoulder.

"Mr. Hatton," she whispered. "I am to be very angry with you.

You know that?" Smiling at him so dearly that it was as if she were crying.

He did not answer her, but put up his hand to cover hers. She touched his hair with her free hand, stroked it. Slowly drew his head against her body. "Very angry," she whispered again. "Are you not afraid of me?"

He had moved his hand, put his arms round her waist. His forehead against her breast. They stayed like that, and the seconds became a minute, longer, became so quiet, so still, that they ceased to have any length of time about them—became so filled with love that it was not possible to imagine they would end, that anything could change.

She wanted to bend down her head, put her cheek against his, but even that might spoil this still depth of happiness, like throwing a stone into a deep well. She wanted to whisper to him, hear his voice. And yet nothing could add to what she felt. Wanted to sit by him on the untidy bed, hear him tell her how she looked to him, hear him tell her that she was beautiful—for him—for him— Until the need to move, to hear, to touch, to lift his face up so that she might see it, to bend down her own face close to his, became so overwhelming she could not hold the stillness any longer. Like water spilling from one's cupped hands, no matter how one clasps them close, makes them one.

"Are you not afraid of me?" she breathed, bending down, putting both hands under his chin, lifting his head. And to her astonishment he seemed to be crying, tears in his eyes, making them dark-bright. "What is the matter?" she whispered.

"I did not think—" he was saying, "I did not think I could be so happy."

She sank swiftly down onto her knees in front of him, her hands finding his, holding them against her face. "And I," she said. "And I."

Somewhere, somewhere, there were sounds, the clatter of a jug against a basin. Voices. Steps. As if the world were jealous, making itself heard. She knelt up, looked round. The door was open; she had left it open.

"Did you not see the door was open?" she whispered, pushed his hands from hers, got to her feet with a swift dart of near anger, real anger, that she knew was unjust in the moment that she felt it, and that seemed the more justified for its injustice. "Are you gone mad?" she said, her voice trembling with the fear that it was she, she herself who had gone mad. To kneel in front of him—risk being seen, heard; to let him—to let him think—what had she said, done? His arms round her! If the maids—anyone—Mr. Sowerby— had gone past—*I shall die, I shall die if anyone has seen us,* she thought. *Die!*

He was standing up, so much the Mr. Hatton of ordinary times that she could have struck him dead where he stood. Worse than the Mr. Hatton of every day—a Mr. Hatton in helpless, lost confusion, his hair falling forward, his cravat half untied, his clothes, his manner, his expression all looking as though he had fallen from the clouds. She wanted to run at him, strike him awake, re-fasten his cravat, button his coat, straighten and mould and re-order him until he no longer looked like a poet in love, but like an ordinary, unnoticeable hotel guest who has just been soberly reproached by the housekeeper for offending another guest.

She backed away to the door, listened, looked for a swift second into the corridor. Not a movement, not a footstep. Only the distant sounds of ordinary things. She felt her heart quiet again. Looked towards him and was so filled with contrition and tenderness that she could have died herself. Very gently and swiftly she closed the door. Took three swift steps towards him and held his face in her hands.

"I forgive you," she whispered. "But you must never, never be so wicked again. I have your promise?" And before he could promise, or even imagine what he was being asked to promise, or why, she had covered his lips with her fingers, preventing him from answering.

"Until the theatre," she whispered. And was gone. To meet him a few hours later with the most innocent, the coolest of friendly expressions, as if nothing had happened between them at all and she had only agreed to come to the theatre as a means of giving Titine and 'Ang a trifle of excitement that she herself was far too adult and sophisticated to share.

Indeed she did not have any particular expectations of the play except that it would be an opportunity for her and Titine to put on their very best gowns and bonnets, and to be gently malicious at poor Mrs. Dundas's expense. But the play was *Macbeth,* and Mrs. Dundas, who might be ridiculous enough as Juliet or Desdemona, had in Lady Macbeth a role that suited her into her very soul. From the first scenes she made it felt and spread a conviction through the audience that here was something they must attend to. She was not a good actress, and it was not a good audience, and in a strange way those two limitations helped. For the most of the audience were not used to good playing, and would not have recognised as fine anything that did not have broad strokes and tirades and overemphasis.

But just as at times a plain woman may seem beautiful because she is in love, Mrs. Dundas seemed to act well, and through the evening built up a majesty of evil that held even Kate in subjection, until she forgot that she was watching a woman she despised and disliked, and watched only the play and the playing. A turn of the head that made her think, *I would not have done it like that and yet*—A fall and hissing of the voice that reminded her of her mother. A sudden turning on Mr. Otterley's Macbeth that was clumsy and yet powerful, so that Kate kept thinking, *If only she knew how to do it rightly* and at the same time recognised with humiliation that she herself might not have achieved as much.

Mr. Otterley's playing was of much the same order as Mrs. Dundas's; a professional bag of tricks absorbed over thirty years of theatre, from childhood on, with that much of natural talent in it that a player must have to continue for thirty years. But it was clear, at least to Kate, that he had long ago been better than he now was, and that for the past ten or fifteen years must have been playing the same parts worse and worse, with no one to correct him, and Mrs. Dundas or her similar predecessors quite content for him to play below their standard.

Kate had seen it a hundred times in companies in France, and sat in a growing strangeness of feeling, as if at once she had gone back five years into the past, and ten, twenty years forward into the future—so that she was seeing again her mother acting with someone who made her seem more wonderful than she truly was—and seeing herself—herself doing what? Doing what in ten years time? And she sat between Mr. Hatton and Titine, twisting her hands together in growing uneasiness, unhappiness.

"You are running away," a whisper seemed to echo. "Running away!" From this? And she wanted to touch Mr. Hatton to make sure that he was there. And in the next instant was almost furious with him for being there, for being so comfortably uncritical, so accepting of Mr. Otterley's wooden clumsiness, so innocently pleased to be there with her in the audience, to be no more than a spectator.

I am wicked-mad, she thought, and touched his hand for a moment. But would not allow him to hold hers, even for an answering moment.

"You have promised never to behave wrongly again," she reminded him, and turned away from him to ask Titine if she was liking the play. But Titine was incapable of telling. From the beginning she had sat in a gathering concentration of amazement, holding 'Ang's hand in hers. Once she whispered to Kate, "That ain't never 'er? Mrs. Dundas?" And again, early in the second act, "Ain't the giant coming yet?" But after that she kept quiet, her eyes seeming to grow greater and greater, and when, after the play was over, they went to have strawberries and cream and lemonade in the small tea-garden behind the assembly rooms, she had nothing to say at all except, "Thank yer" in a very small voice.

'Ang put the palms of both hands together and bowed his thanks to Mr. Hatton, his face revealing none of his thoughts about *Macbeth,* or Mrs. Dundas, or Mr. Otterley.

"They have never seen a real play before," Kate said. "Only *Jack and the Beanstalk* and things like that." Trying to sound indifferent, conversational. And the Parnassus Theatre, Mr. Solomons—all of it there like a pain under her heart. As if even the Parnassus was like a lost Golden Age, and she was desolately in exile.

"I expect they would have preferred *Jack* to *Macbeth,*" Mr. Hatton said. He smoothed Titine's hair and she permitted it with so distant a politeness that he dropped his hand swiftly away and flushed, looking at Kate as though appealing to her for something. "If we could be alone together," his eyes said. And in Titine's manner as they walked to a table in a corner of the garden there was something grown watchful, aware. As though the play itself had set up echoes in her mind, taught her something she was half sorry to have learned. Not about murder, or revenge, but deeper again than that. Her eyes considering Mr. Hatton so gravely that Kate longed to order her to look away, concern herself with her strawberries and cream and lemonade.

And Mr. Hatton trying so hard to be the host, the man at ease with young women. And failing. But Kate was no more at ease with him than he was with her or with Titine. It was as if they had leapt over that ordinary time of courtship, of small looks, of smiles, of hands touching momentarily, of half words, of whispers, and were in a country where there were no maps, no guide books to tell them what was necessary or conventional.

It is certainly not love, she thought. And looked at him as if he were a stranger. As if he had never put his arms round her, she had never held his face in her hands. And he turned his head, smiled at something, and her heart seemed to die of pain.

"But he is not even handsome!" she cried out in her heart that seemed to welcome pain. "He is not wise, nor—nor anything that I could love!" She watched his hands touching his dish of strawberries, his lemonade glass. The fingers long and beautifully shaped. *I could not think of him at all if he did not have fine hands.* And remembered how they had held her for that moment, and bent down her head, feeling the blood run dark and burning from her throat to her forehead. Titine watching her, her eyes very serious.

I shall die, Kate thought. *My heart will crack with too much feeling and I shall die of it.*

And that night in bed she lay beside Titine afraid to speak to her in case Titine might ask—might say—

"It is not true!" she wanted to cry out. "I do not love him. I do not love anyone." And in the next second had to put her arms round Titine to show that that was not true—not remotely true—that she loved only Titine—as if Titine might have guessed her thought—as if some spirit of the air might have heard her and determined to take the child from her in revenge for such a foolish, wicked ingratitude.

"I love you!" she whispered. Held Titine close, imagined— imagined—that it was not Titine in her arms but—drove the imagining away with horror—with fear and at the same time longing, until Titine seemed to guess her treachery of feelings. Sat up and stared at Kate in the moonlight filling the room through the open window, its curtains drawn back for coolness.

"You—you ain't going off with 'im?" she whispered. "You ain't leaving me be'ind?"

"No!" Kate cried. "No! Never! I shall never leave you! Never! How could you—I do not love anyone but you!"

"And 'Ang," Titine whispered. "Don't yer love 'im too?"

"Oh, yes. Yes." She put her hands to her head. Thrust her fingers deep into her hair as if she wanted to tear at it. Sitting up in the bed, her elbows on her knees.

He is asleep now, she thought. *Is—is he dreaming of me? Suppose I were to—to go down—look into his room?* and saw him lying in the moonlight—dark hair; pale, shadowed face. The shepherd's face. Reached out to touch, so softly he did not wake. Only dreamed that he was being kissed and smiled, still asleep. *To kneel down beside his bed,* she thought.

"'E's going to want to take yer away," Titine breathed. "Will you go with 'im?"

"Never!" Kate whispered. "No one shall take me away from you. I swear before God that no one in the world shall take me away from you. Now go to sleep."

And she made herself bend over the child, no longer a child, grown so grave, so thoughtful—smoothed her hair gently away from her eyes, closed her eyelids, held her finger-tips there for a moment, kissed her, lay down. As if she were lying beside him. In such purity of heart. She folded her hands on her breasts. "O Mother of God, help me to be good."

But there was no answer. Only Titine's soft breathing, deepening into sleep.

I am not good, Kate thought. And held up her hands, open, so that the moonlight laid shadows on the palms. Dark ivory. Rubbed the palm of one hand slowly against the other. What was the doctor's line as he watched Lady Macbeth? "What is it she does now?" And then "Look, how she rubs her hand." Mrs. Dundas had rubbed her two hands together with ferocity, as though to tear the skin away along with the imaginary stains. But the Frenchman had touched—not quite touched his together very softly and wonderingly, as if he were afraid of them, afraid even for one to touch the other. She held hers as he had done. Almost touching, so that the stains of shadow joined together, made a darkness. Like dark blood. "No," she whispered. "I have killed no one. No one." Who had said that? Tried to pray. "God have mercy on me, a sinner." The dark shape of the hulk in the sea, sinking deeper and deeper.

Felt herself lifted beyond that ordinary sense of guilt into a cold darkness of terror, like the dark space between the stars. As if she were dead, and damned, and wandering forever. In Eternity, always to be frozen in the knowledge of evil. Without light. Without forgiveness. Nothing, nothing, nothing. Echoing.

"I am lost," she wanted to cry out. "Lost." But she could not cry. Could not move. Saw a procession of faces that did not know what evil was, and yet were touched by evil, touched it unknowingly like children touching fire.

Like me! Like me! I did not know! O God, I did not know!

Held out her hands, crying to the people—"Listen! Listen!" Scarcely knew what they must listen to, what she could tell them— only of the terror of death, of darkness, of those infinite dark spaces beyond the last of the stars. Telling, holding out her arms to them, who had become an audience—an audience bound into quietness, chained by horror—by the fear of that image she was making for them. Only the deep, deep breathing of the pit.

Chapter 19

In contrast to the nights the days seemed so quietly beautiful that it was almost frightening. Like something that cannot last. So filled with gentleness—so still—so loving. They would meet sometimes on the stairs and touch their hands together for a moment. Nothing more than that. Or their eyes would meet.

Dear love, she would think. *Dear, dear love.* Without any thought of what might follow. Of what does usually follow when two people love one another. It was enough to love. To see him for a moment. Even when the others were there. Know that he was thinking of her.

He had grown so quiet that Captain Cartwright pretended to be anxious for his health. "Ye're turned downright yellow man, bilious. And I amn't surprised. I never knew a Radical yet that wasn't as bilious as a ferret."

But Mr. Hatton only smiled at him distantly as though he had scarcely heard what he said, and the Captain looked almost alarmed, and then, glancing up at Kate as she stood serving him, gave her a look of such sly understanding, of such knowingness, that her blush seemed to burn her entire body, beneath her clothes, like running fire, and she had to go out of the room and scold Elizabeth for something in the kitchen.

They went to see *Romeo and Juliet* that same night, and even Mrs. Dundas's and Mr. Otterley's inappropriateness for the parts could not spoil it, and the play seemed to have been written that day for them, for Kate and Mr. Hatton, the lines echoing, saying themselves again and again in true lovers' voices, young and wonderful and dazzling. Lovers who would never die, nor grow old.

Only Titine cast a slight shadow on the evening for Kate. Not by anything she said or did. Not truly by any detectable difference in her manner, so that Kate at moments must tell herself "it is my imagination, I am creating shadows," and in the next moment thought, *It is true, she is drawn away from me, drawn back into herself again.* Holding hands with 'Ang as if he were her—*her only true friend*, Kate thought, and was half angry and half stricken. "She is only a child," she told herself. "She does not understand that—that grown-ups— If she shows the least trifle of jealousy towards him, I shall be very severe with her. She must, *must* understand—" And wanted to hold her again and cry, "Nothing is changed, nothing!"

And yet that withdrawnness of Titine's, that shadow of—of distrust—had always been there—had never quite vanished away. *It is only that I have brought it back more strongly*, Kate thought wretchedly. And was half angry with Titine, and half with herself—and then determined to be so loving, so kind and good to her—even to be a little distant with Mr. Hatton in front of her—not always, not all the time, but now and then—that Titine must see—must know beyond doubt that she was more dearly loved than ever, and always would be.

"And she will love him too," Kate told herself. "How can she help it?"

And certainly Mr. Hatton treated Titine so beautifully that she ought to love him—might even, Kate thought once or twice—love him too much. Too much for a child—he was so kind to her, so courteous, as if she were not a child but a young woman.

It is I who am jealous now! Kate thought, with a kind of horrified delight. As if every emotion were precious, even those she should not feel. *I am even jealous of Titine!* And was then truly horrified, and promised herself a thousand penances and mortifications—of luxuries of thought and dreaming that she would deny herself that night—and tomorrow night—to pay for such wickedness.

But for the most her mind was too filled with happiness to torment itself very much. Each daylight, every evening moment like a gold coin, shining and heavy in her palm.

Mr. Hatton had banished himself from the smoking parlour and Captain Cartwright's and Mr. Sowerby's company, with the unanswerable excuse that, if he joined them there, he would inevitably quarrel with them and distress Mr. Gurney. And Miss Harriott.

"Oh, aye. Aye. We'll not want to distress Mr. Gurney, will we?" the Captain said, glancing and winking and screwing up his eyes. But Mr. Hatton was beyond the reach of such clumsiness, and even the Captain seemed touched by some memory of his own youth and did not pursue the matter too far, with too much heavy-handed jocularity. So that Mr. Hatton was left free to come into the small sitting-room and make the evening splendid.

Mrs. Cartwright crocheting a lace collar at one side of the table, Titine at the other side, slowly spelling out words in a book Mr. Hatton had brought her from the Library, the lamp between the two of them. And Mr. Hatton and Kate by the open window, looking out at the sea, and the last of the evening. Telling her of his home in Norwich, of the book-seller's and small printer's shop they had owned before his father died.

"He read more books than he sold," Mr. Hatton said, smiling at memories. "He read Voltaire to me before I could read myself. Translating as he read. He was a strange man."

And your mother? Kate wanted to ask. *Was she—of your father's mind in such things?* She would have preferred to hear about his mother who was still alive. But again and again she had been made aware of that part of him that was beyond her reach or her questioning. Not as Titine sometimes was, withdrawn into an inner privacy, but like someone who has climbed a steep hill, and by effects of the clear light seems still very close. Yet in reality is far off, high up beyond the reach of anyone's ordinary voice.

In one way he still seemed—seemed more and more—so close to her that he was almost like another Titine, almost younger than herself. And in the next moment his eyes would alter their expression, looking towards things she could not see and could not understand if she could. So that she grew part jealous, and part afraid, and—and part pleased, that he was not just the nice Mr. Hatton of the Library, that there was so much more depth in him than merely the kindness to old people, the gentleness and the stammer and the ridiculous, handsome lock of hair. *But what lies behind that changing of his look?* she wondered. *What is he thinking of?* As though he were looking across immense distances—just as a man might who has climbed a mountainside, and sees landscapes, and sea-coasts, and cities hidden from those who have not climbed.

That look was in his eyes when he spoke of his father. An amused affection that belonged to the day-time Mr. Hatton, but also much more than that. Much more. And she remembered again the shepherd in the painting, and seemed to remember things about him that she had not known she had noticed at the time. A look in the eyes of—distance. Although the Child was so near. *Is all goodness so far off?* she wondered, with a kind of pain.

[242]

"My father wanted to be a soldier when he was very young," Mr. Hatton was saying. "In the Jacobite Rising of 'forty-five. He was seventeen, and he walked all the way to Derby from Norwich, although he was lame from birth, and he fought in a skirmish of some sort, and got a wound that lamed him worse than ever. They left him behind when they retreated up to Scotland, naturally enough, and he was lucky not to be hanged. But I think that cured him of princes and generals. Afterwards he did all his fighting in print, against the idea of having any princes at all, Stuart or Hanover. He wrote pamphlets and printed them himself, and went to prison for it, twice, or three times. He was a notorious man in Norwich."

Kate wanted to question him and could not. Wanted to tell him that she too—she too had been in prison, and in a way—a strange, accidental way—also for an ideal. Although not his father's, not his ideal. And again she wanted to cry to him, "It is not as you think! Not as your father thought. Liberty—equality—these things are not just a falling away of chains from wretched men. They are death, they are cruelty. They are old women bound in a cart being stoned. They are men, women, drowning—drowning as they scream for mercy. It is not as you think!"

But it was beyond her power to explain to him, or beyond her courage to attempt it, and she liked so much to listen to him that it was easy to stay silent. To listen, see his childhood take shape there in the twilight by the window—the dark bookshop, the candlelight, the books, an old man reading, a boy listening, arms clasped round knees, dark head bent down, both shivering with that intense inner cold that comes at midnight when one is in a deep excitement of ideas; dreaming of a world free of tyranny, free of superstition, free of cruelty and privilege, of too great wealth despising the poverty it makes.

"There is no need for hunger! There is food enough for all mankind! No man or woman need go naked, or begging for bread or work. Men have rights! Rights! Did you never hear of Thomas Paine? There is a man worth all the kings that ever were."

She had not heard of him, but it did not matter. Only that she might listen. Now tenderly, as if she were much older than he. And then again with that almost fearful stillness, unsure of what he meant, what he saw. Yet held. Until the happiness itself grew almost unendurable and she must do something, anything, to mark its surface; bring it back to reality; to ordinary, endurable happiness.

"What is the book you have brought for Titine?"

"*Romeo and Juliet.*"

"What? But she cannot read such a thing! She could not understand three words together in it!" And she made to stand up as if to take the book away.

Mr. Hatton laid his hand on her arm. "Leave her," he whispered. "Why should she not understand it? She is not—not quite a child any more, you know. And it is the—the best way for her to learn." He became aware that he was touching her and took his hand from her arm very quickly. "You are very fortunate," he whispered.

"I?"

"To have s-someone to look after. Who loves you."

She looked at him, not knowing how to answer. Nor wanting to.

"I envy her," he said.

She turned away, blushing, to look at Titine and Mrs. Cartwright, and that night and the next day the image of the room returned to her again and again as something so beautiful that it was almost painful to remember. The old woman, and Titine. The lamplight. The white lace. The book. The darkness of the panelled wall behind them. Such quietness.

And I have looked after her, she thought. *If it were not for me—* And she felt very humble and wanted to cry, again and again, as she thought of it, as though it were something she was in grave danger of losing. Went outside to the stable-yard to be alone, to be quiet with her happiness. But Mr. Biggins was there, come back with the chaise and two extra riding horses, and had again appropriated 'Ang as his helper.

'Ang seemed to love the horses and they him and Kate played with the fancy that they recognised his dumbness and had compassion for it, nuzzling at his black hair with their black velvet nostrils, blowing against his neck with a heavy fluttering of their great lips. And 'Ang groomed and fed and watered them like an attendant spirit serving princes turned by witchcraft into noble animals.

I have looked after him too, Kate thought, and wanted to embrace him. The sun was turning the loose straw to gold, shining on the polished cobble-stones, filling the air with magic. She loved 'Ang, she loved the horses, she loved Mr. Biggins, stooping his great bulk for a moment to lift a horse's hoof and examine the shoe. *If this*

[244]

could continue forever. Nothing ever to change. Her love for Mr. Hatton seeming to brim over like a cup, to fill the world with love.

"Bricks an' timber do be comin' shortly," Mr. Biggins said, finishing his inspection of the horseshoe.

"What are they really for? Surely he is not truly going to buiid a Baths?"

Mr. Biggins winked. "Ann't you a curiosity box?"

"But I want to know."

"Go away with you."

"They—" She thought suddenly of her own journeys by coach in London. "You are going to hide things inside the load of bricks!" And was half-excited, half-afraid, as if any change, any novelty must threaten happiness, and yet by being new was wonderful.

He stared at her, the humour draining out of his expression, leaving it very thoughtful. "You do fare to be worse'n a curiosity box. Least you do know about them bricks t' better. If I catches you prying—"

But she was no longer afraid of him and stroked his flannel shirt sleeve as if he too were a great animal she was soothing. "Of course I won't pry. And if I knew all about it, I should not need to be curious, should I? Is the gold coming hidden inside the loads?" Her heart beating. All the London excitement coming back to her.

"What gold?" he said roughly, shaking her off. "You was my darter, I knows what I'd give you."

"Those small chests I used to carry in the coach. Did they have gold in them?"

"Some on 'um. Leave me be, girl. I do have to take Rose here to t' smith."

The next evening the loads arrived; a long dray piled with new bricks and another with new timber, both drawn into the yard and backed into the empty stables with a vast stamping of hooves and shouting of drivers. Kate recognised both the drivers as men she had seen in Devon Place, but they gave her no recognition, drinking the ale she brought out to them and leading their horses away again with scarcely a word to anyone.

When they were gone, she stood by the entrance of the stables looking in at the drays. Huge piles of darkness. And inside them, gold. She tried to imagine half a million guineas. A million. How many chests would they fill? Perhaps the ones she had carried had been payments for the smuggled goods she had also carried. Like threads crossing. Or stolen things from Germany or France? Loot from the wars? Stolen by the "decent robbers" Mr. Biggins had spoken of. That the Squire's customers would buy for half their value? And now it was to be not just one or two chests of loot, but—? Like trying to understand a tapestry picture seeing only a few inches of the back of it, the coloured knots.

Her heart beat very fast and she went and laid her palm on one of the bricks. If she lifted it out? And another? But the brick was too large for her fingers to grasp, and too heavy. And the beams of timber might have built the keel and ribs of a ship, let alone the roof of a sea baths. It was only after she had stood there for minutes together, thinking of what must lie hidden in front of her, that she thought of what the gold was really payment for. And that image came back to her of men running, running, in the courtyard of the prison. And the tiny, puppet figures falling and dying, flinging out their arms. She laid her forehead against the bricks.

Mr. Biggins's voice roused her, gave her such a start that she jerked herself upright and found herself pushing against his unyielding bulk, he had come on her so close, and so softly.

"I told you not to be prying."

"I am not! I—"

"What was you doing, then? Counting t' bricks?"

"When will they come back?"

"Mister Gurney an' t' other? Soon as our friend Mr. Evans do. Two, three days. Let me catch you peerin' an' pryiпg again an' I'll larn you summat as you'll remember a bit."

She left him indignantly, too indignant to remember what she had been thinking of before he spoke to her. But the memory returned. And she woke in the small hours of the morning, thinking of it, listening to Titine's small, soft breathing beside her on the pillows. Watched the window grow pale, and finally slept again.

When she woke it was late, and the house was full of its morning sounds, from the yard, from the rooms downstairs: someone filling a bucket with hard, ringing gushes of water from the pump; breakfast sounds of china plates, of pans on the iron stove, now louder as doors opened, now lost in the depths of the house. Sounds from outside, from the roadway, the sands. She should have felt light and happy, and felt truly so for an instant. And then remembered. And felt not unhappy, but a tension of nerves, of expectancy that was neither pleasant nor unpleasant, but had the possibility in it of becoming either. Her mouth, her upper lip, almost trembling with that taut anxiety that had no rational foundation to it, but that she was almost conscious of creating for herself. As if she needed to be anxious, without knowing why.

She became aware that Titine was gone, up already and crept out. How quietly she must have gone! And she was half pleased at the consideration behind the quietness, and half displeased, as though it were another indication of secrecy. Why had she got up so early? It was usually she who lay late and had to be made to get up and wash and who clung to her warm pillow until the last moment possible. Kate felt Titine's pillow and it was quite cold. What was she doing downstairs? And the thought of Mr. Sowerby questioning Titine again made Kate get up very quickly, and wash and dress herself much more hastily than usual. Titine would be playing in the yard and ruining her stockings again—But she was neither in the yard nor with Mr. Sowerby, nor anywhere in the house. Nor was 'Ang. Old John looked vague, and Peg only mumbled that "They did have fare to have gone out t' front." She did not know how long ago. "An ower, mebbe, m'm," and no, she did not know where, or to do what. No, Mrs. Earnshaw had given them no errands to the shops or the chandlers.

Nor had Mrs. Cartwright seen them. And her elderly alarm at the idea of children being lost under any circumstances, no matter how ordinary and safe, added to Kate's irrational fears and made her feel that her anxiety at waking had been a warning of something, of something terrible. Like a punishment! And against all common sense she ran out onto the road, imagining—she did not know what she was imagining, only felt her heart beat and stop her breath as if it were a bird beating its wings inside her breast.

The tide was far out and the sunlight turned all the sand and sea to a great sheet of silver, dazzling, almost painful to look at, and yet with subtle areas of darkness underneath the silvery, mirror surface; dark mud, deep water, piles of sea-wrack. And half a dozen small black figures far out at the sea's edge; far, far away against the brightness of blended sea and sky; thin black silhouettes, four, five of them, running, stopping, bending, chasing one another. A faint, faint echo of their voices, their laughter reaching the shore. Or perhaps it was only imagination that she could hear them. She narrowed her eyes against the sun, the sky, trying to make out from

[247]

those stick shapes, thin as blackened sea gull's bones with their silvered edges of light, whether two of them might be Titine and 'Ang. And the others? Fisher children? One of the silhouettes seemed to be carrying something, a dark sack, a basket. Fisher children gathering cockles? And Titine and 'Ang with them?

It must be them, she thought, and she leaned on the sea-wall, careful not to look down at the rocks just below, not to think of the sea that had lapped there a few hours ago, and told herself that she was glad if it was them. If they were playing. 'Ang for an hour or so free of the hotel, his polishing and carrying, Titine—

She felt very wise and generous, unconscious of her left hand pressed against her heart, forcing herself to smile as if there were some observer who might know her thoughts if he were not carefully deceived by her expression. In her mind there were images of quicksands, of swift, treacherous depths of water running like sea-rivers between the mud banks, sudden, deep pools where Titine— But the other children would know. They would be wary, would warn her—*I am so foolish,* she thought, *I search for terrors.* And smiled more firmly and deceivingly for that non-existent observer. "Children are so careless of one another!" her terrors cried.

"Titine!" she called uselessly, across the mile of wet sand and mud that was now black and softly hostile, now inviting bright, sun-brilliant. "Titine! 'Ang!" Her voice like a sea gull's cry, like any of a dozen sounds fading and lost in the immensity of shimmering, reflected distance, of empty, turquoise sky. "Titine!"

I shall go in, she decided firmly. *And leave them to play. She will be quite safe. I am only seeming foolish standing here like this—* If anyone was watching her from the hotel— But instead she looked swiftly round, and seeing no one at any window, nor in the roadway near her, she perched herself on top of the low wall, swung her legs up and over to the far side of it with a white flurry of muslin skirt, and let herself down onto the rocks. Half a dozen careful steps from rough rock surface to other white barnacled space between the slippery blacknesses of seaweed and sea-anemones, and she was on the sand.

She made herself walk very composedly, very slowly and easily out towards the moving, running silhouettes, looking about her as if she were walking for her pleasure, taking the air. But her pace quickened without her knowing it until she was walking swiftly, almost running; the silhouettes becoming child shapes, the flash of

[248]

bare legs as a boy jumped over a rivulet, and back again, splashing his feet in it. Another carrying what had become the clear shape of a cockle basket, making his thin body bend to one side with the weight of its contents. Shrill voices calling, laughing, one of the figures taller—she had tucked up her skirts—Titine? It was Titine, her skirts caught up round her hips, her legs long and thin as a tall bird's, like a grave heron bending his delicate neck and head to search the mud for precious morsels rather than for mere food; here, there—her legs silver-wet, delicately bared—and a fisher-boy running behind her, pushing her so that she went stumbling, almost fell into the stream she had been inspecting so absorbedly.

"Titine! Titine! Boy! Leave her alone! Stop that!"

Running, breathless with anxiety. And then anger. The figures turned to look at Kate, five of them: Titine; 'Ang with his basket; three little boys—ragged, too-large trousers rolled up above their knees, hair yellow in the sun, whitened with dried sea-salt, their faces alarmed at Kate's sharp cry of authority. One of them began to run away as if by instinct he knew that he should not have pushed Titine, treated her like a sister.

"What are you—I have been looking everywhere—" Kate cried. And "I must not be angry," she told herself. "I must seem—must be—" Not even with the boy who had pushed Titine. "O God, let me be wise." She tried to smile, to seem as if all was quite well and natural and she had been no more than mildly concerned at where they might be. And indeed, what did it matter if they—if Titine— played with some fisher-children for an hour or so? It was only— only the quicksands, the wet—and sand in all her clothes—her hair—but it did not matter.

"Where are your stockings?" she said, coming close.

Titine looked about her, with a shadow of guilt in her eyes, but also as if she expected to see her stockings lying just there. Or there.

"And your slippers?"

'Ang came to Kate, with his small, obedient smile, his gladness to see her.

Like a good dog, she thought again, with a sort of anguish, *sure that he has done right by guarding Titine—by following her, by ensuring that she did not go anywhere alone.* But he had done more than that, and dug among the mass of cockles in his basket to find Titine's slippers and limp, sodden stockings.

"*Mon Dieu!*" Kate cried, almost glad to have found an excuse for anger, for being honest at last. "What have you done? You must be quite mad! They are ruined, ruined!" She took a slipper from him, held it up in furious contempt, an urge to fling it away from her struggling with economy, the knowledge that it was not really ruined, that it could be washed and dried and restored to something like its original appearance if she took enough trouble with it. She wanted to cry with rage and that feeling of loneliness, of being tragically misunderstood that they both gave her whenever she saw them together. 'Ang looked worried, and Titine came quickly beside him and put her arm round his shoulders. Protectively, as if she half-expected Kate to strike him, or take hold of him and shake him.

And I could, Kate thought. *Both of them. O God, let me be patient, let me be wise.*

"Come back at once to the hotel," she ordered, truly glad now to be legitimately, wisely angry. "You shall wash these yourself, at once. There must not be a stain, not a mark left. And you, little boys, go away, go home. Go off with you. How dare you push her like that!"

The three fisher-boys had already backed away from her and now grouped themselves twenty yards off, not quite touching one another for mutual support and safety, but almost so. They backed farther off as Kate waved her hand, the slipper dripping sea-water and wet, fish-smelling sand onto her wrist and sleeve.

"It's their basket," Titine whispered.

And for no reason, or none that she could think of, Kate began to cry. Felt the tears gathering, swelling uncontrollably, her throat filled with tears, her eyes glazed, half blinded with them. "Give it to them," she said. A tear ran down her cheek, warm, almost consoling, and she was part furious, part relieved at crying; wanted Titine to see, to realise how she felt, and at the same time wanted to hide her tears from her, wanted to feel hurt because they remained successfully hidden.

"But some of the cockles is ours," Titine said, poised but not moving from where she stood beside 'Ang, her arm still protecting him. "Couldn't we keep our 'alf of them?"

"I do not care!" Kate shouted. "I do not care what you do!" She began to run again, back towards the now distant shore. Remembered her dignity and forced herself to walk. Walking quickly, scarcely able to see where she was going for the tears. *I shall die,* she thought. *How can she? How can they—?*

She felt a dampness against her breast and saw that she was holding the wet slipper against her gown. The fish smell of it came to her and she held it away from her body like something unclean and horrifying, a dead creature. *I will not look round,* she thought, and looked, and saw them following. 'Ang still carrying the basket, the three smaller boys close to him as if in concern about the basket and its contents and their eventual division. Titine walking a trifle ahead of them, picking her way with her bare, silver feet, lightly and at the same time thoughtfully, as if each step had its significance.

They saw Kate turn towards them, and stopped, Titine's expression grave and watchful and—and *withdrawn,* Kate thought again, as she had so often been forced to think. Withdrawn into that inner fastness of privacy and self-certainty, of a self-containment that defeated all Kate's efforts at mastery and loving conquest. "Only on my own terms will you possess me," the expression said. "Even though I love you. They are my terms of love." And tore Kate's heart. She held out her hands, the slippers; wanted to hold her arms wide with longing. Forced it to be no more than a gesture of holding out the slippers, and with that gesture a hint, the merest least overture of love and forgiveness for Titine.

Titine came very quietly to take the offering, and at the last moment smiled. "Dear, dear Kate," her smile seemed to say with adult understanding. "Poor, loving Kate." Or so Kate thought. *Or is she afraid?* Kate wondered. *Afraid in spite of all that one day I will abandon her? Be taken away from her? And is preparing for it even without knowing?* And the day seemed to grow dark for a second. The bright sea and sky turn threatening.

Chapter 20

They came two nights later—Mr. Gurney and Mr. Johnson. Very late in the evening, barely greeting anyone before they went to their room.

They were up the next morning early and away on the riding horses, ordering Kate to wait up for them however late they might be, and to make sure, if she could, that everyone else in the hotel was abed before midnight.

That in itself was not a problem, for Captain Cartwright considered it an evening of dissipation if he sat up beyond eleven o'clock, particularly now that Mr. Hatton had deprived him of politics, and Mr. Hatton himself would go to bed or at least to his room as soon as Kate bade him good night and took her candlestick upstairs. By midnight the hotel was full of sleep and silence. Kate brought her candle down the stairs again and sat by the window, waiting and listening. Her heart beating so loud that it seemed louder than the grandfather clock outside in the hall. Louder than the sea. Why did they want her to sit up for them?

Thinking of the gold, the Frenchman. Now excited. Now guilty at her own excitement. That she should have any such feeling in such a dreadful business. Dead men's stolen treasures. Murdered men.

It is wicked, she thought. *I should have no part in it all, not the least, least share. Suppose he knew?* Imagined his eyes, shocked with horror. And felt almost a wickedness of joy that he did not, could not know. And felt guilt at that. That she should not only have secrets from him, but be pleased by them.

But when this is over, she thought, *then I will never, never have any secret from him again.* And sat imagining him sleeping, imagined she could hear his breathing. But it was her own.

She heard Mr. Otterley and Mrs. Dundas coming. Welcomed them and lit them to their rooms and their waiting, napkin-covered supper trays, and returned downstairs. Sat at the open window with her elbow on the window-sill, half asleep, dreaming. Of nothing so definite as marriage, or of what they might do when—if—they should be married—only of small things—how a room might look that she would arrange for him. And Titine with them—and 'Ang—dear, dear 'Ang. She would learn to cook properly, and to sew—but such details began to take away from perfection, and she brought Mrs. Earnshaw, or someone like her, into the background of her picture—imagined a garden, full of roses—and a lawn—and there should be a tree with a great spread of shade—a chestnut tree—not a very large garden—but with a walk where one might be in secrecy with—with one's lover. "How I shall love him!" her heart cried out—almost as though it were answering a denial. "I shall! I shall! Nothing shall prevent me." What could prevent her? Nothing, nothing in the world.

There were the sounds of horses' hooves. The chaise. She went to the door and Mr. Biggins jumped down from the box and caught her by the arm.

"Is't any'un about?"

She shook her head and he whispered for a moment at the door of the chaise. To her surprise three men got out, who must have cramped themselves if their journey had been a long one, for both Mr. Gurney and Mr. Johnson were big enough men. The third was the Frenchman. His face ghost-white. Mr. Gurney in such a rage that his body seemed to shake with it as he got down, his lower lip thrust out, his eyes almost vanished in his cheeks, like small coals buried in a bank of ashes, still burning.

"I'll open for Biggins," Mr. Johnson said, making to go through the house to the stable-yard, and the great, bolted yard doors. He touched Kate's shoulder, not roughly, as she had expected, but with something like comradeship that astonished her. But she could tell that he too was angry, although not with her. "You go up with them," he said. "Is there wine upstairs?"

She nodded and followed the Frenchman, Mr. Gurney already leading the way. The Frenchman hung back for a second and whispered in French, "I insisted on seeing you. For God's sake be truthful to me—"

Mr. Gurney turned, hearing the whisper, and jerked his hand for them to be quiet and swift. In his room he flung himself into an arm chair without bothering to speak to either of them or bid them sit down.

The Frenchman went to the window, drew the curtain aside an

inch or so and looked out as if afraid of watchers. When he turned round again to look at Kate, standing in the middle of the small room, with its table and three chairs and side table, and curtained bed in the deep alcove, his fear was pitiful. And yet it was not direct and simple fear, of arrest, of being in an enemy country at the mercy of such men as Mr. Johnson and Mr. Gurney. But still that inner, crippling terror, grown even more savage. All his nerves strung tight as harp strings, quivering, on the point of breaking. Such fear and such taut control of it as gave him a kind of dignity against Mr. Gurney's blunt anger.

Kate watched him and waited. She had thought as she came up the stairs that she would be bitterly ashamed at having to face him, had braced herself against it like another penance. But there was no need. Even in the few days that had passed he seemed to have changed in a way that took him beyond ordinary judgements. It showed in the details of his face, grown almost spiritual in waxen haggardness, the small, purplish scars in his cheeks grown darker, like fresh wounds.

He is dying, she thought. *He is dying of fear.* There was death in the ghost-whiteness of his face. Death in the way he stood.

Mr. Gurney kicked his heel at one of the firedogs, and it fell with a small clatter of iron and brass in the grate. The noise was a relief in the silence and the Frenchman looked at the fireplace and lifted his hands in a gesture of impatience.

"Does he not come?" he said, in English, his accent heavy and raw. They heard steps, and Mr. Johnson came in, closing the door very softly behind him and staying with his back towards it, like a guard watching a prisoner. His eyes narrowed and dangerous, but his anger much more controlled than Mr. Gurney's.

"Well?" he said. "Speak to her." He looked at Kate. "He has taken a fancy to you," he said, his eyes half-amused. But behind the amusement reawakened suspicion. "He does not quite trust us. But you! *La petite citoyenne,* oh, she!"

"He wants to see the gold first," Mr. Gurney said. "Tell him whether he can trust us."

"Have you yourself seen it, the gold?" the Frenchman said to her, his voice shaking slightly. "They want simply to put the chests on board tomorrow night without—Can·I trust them?" His voice rising, and she sensed that it was not this question that worried him, but something quite different, for which this was no more than a mask, behind which his real terrors could hide.

[254]

"You can trust them," she said. "They are honest men."

"Honest!"

"Of their kind. They would not cheat you. And the gold is outside, in the stable-yard. Hidden among bricks."

Mr. Gurney and Mr. Johnson watching her face, and then the Frenchman's.

"How can I believe you? How do you know? You are only a—only their girl."

She did not answer him.

"And you have seen the gold?"

"I know it is there. But they cannot unload it here. It is too dangerous; it could be seen."

The Frenchman sat down then, and poured himself wine from the bottle standing on one of the tables. He drank it as if he were alone. Kate would have liked to touch him, his shoulder, his hand, offer him some kind of comfort, as one does with people who have little time to live. "It is all right," she said, "I swear to you it is all right."

"I could not wait at the boat alone," he whispered. "I had to come here with them."

"I understand."

"Would you come back with us? Tomorrow?"

"I cannot."

He nodded, accepting what she said, a strange, strange expression in his eyes, and she thought, *It was to see me that he came here. Beneath all else. To see me.* She seemed to have known him for a great length of time. To know him as she did not know, would never know, these other two men watching her. As she would never know even Mr. Hatton. And the pain of that was sudden and terrible, so that she wanted to hold her heart.

The Frenchman continued for another five minutes, asking to be reassured. But nothing would reassure his true fears and he spoke only for the sake of hearing her answer him, again and again in different words. "It is all right. They are honest men as this kind of business goes." Until she thought of a last argument: "They could not dare to cheat you. Suppose you were to tell the smugglers they always deal with? All their reputation would be gone."

"And I could have them informed against," he said slowly in French. "I have already thought of that. A word to their authorities."

"For God's sake!" she said quickly, in his own Auvergnat dialect.

"Do not say such a thing, they may understand it." And Mr. Johnson seemed to be listening with a keener ear, his face grown harder still.

The Frenchman shrugged, and laughed his bitter, humourless laugh. "Do you think I have not taken my precautions?"

"What is he saying?" Mr. Johnson demanded.

"He says the same things over and over. It is only that he is afraid, not really of anything here, but of things in France."

It was the Frenchman's turn to look at her with a new expression. But he said nothing.

"And is he satisfied yet?"

"Yes."

"Then leave us and go to bed. We will be gone before you wake, since we have this hero with us."

Mr. Johnson followed her out of the room, caught hold of her and swung her round in the dark passage. "He has a tenderness for you, eh? Our dancing master?"

They heard soft, slippered steps, a door closing. He tightened his fingers on her shoulders until they hurt her. "What was that? Which room?"

"It must be Mrs. Dundas," she said. "And Mr. Otterley."

He laughed and let go of her. "It is nearly over," he said. "You're a good small creature." He caught her chin in his familiar, painful grip. "I could have a tenderness for you myself, I think. Maybe afterwards? In London again?"

She could not tell whether he was serious, and was afraid to show how angry she was. But he let go of her and she ran up the stairs to her room. To stand for a long time inside the door of it, simply standing there, the small window a pale square of moonlight through the thin curtains. *It is nearly over.* Titine's breathing. Softly stirring in her sleep, her hand searching for Kate, her voice murmuring, "Where—Kate—?"

"I am here." She went and knelt by the bed, and held Titine's hand. "O God, please protect us both. Help me to look after her." She prayed also for the Frenchman, and found that she was praying for him as though he were already dead.

She woke the next morning to the sound of a great rumbling of carts and horses' stamping, and running to a corridor window saw that the two great drays were leaving the stable-yard, Mr. Biggins guiding them out, the two drivers from Devon Place cracking their whips, shouting, "Whooah, hup, hup!" The maids running out to see, 'Ang darting under the wheels of one of the drays to lift a fallen brick out of the way. One gone. The other. The sounds echoing for a long time from the back road, fading. Done.

At intervals through the morning consoling Mrs. Cartwright, reassuring her that nothing would change, the hotel would not be rebuilt around her, nor would Royalty be soon invited to open the Baths, nor anything else happen to destroy her tranquility. Mr. Hatton coming in at dinner time with a box, a present for Titine.

"For me!" Titine whispered. Looked at Kate almost in alarm. And out of a cloud of tissue paper a doll, a girl doll. Dressed in velvet, a tiny velvet cap with beads sewn to it, like seed pearls.

"'S like Juliet!" And turning to Kate again in disbelief that anything so wonderful could exist. And be for her.

"It *is* Juliet," Mr. Hatton said, blushing very red. And Kate made herself feel as glad as she should feel, and then did feel glad, for Titine, for Mr. Hatton, for herself, who had a lover so kind, so thoughtful.

"It is beautiful!" she said. "Wherever did you—"

"It is from Norwich. My mother sent it—I—"

He has told his mother of me, she thought. And kissed Titine and told her to kiss Mr. Hatton. But Titine's kisses could not be commanded and she stayed holding her doll and looking down at it with gravity.

"She'll be lonely," she said at last.

"But she will have you," Mr. Hatton said.

"Lonely for Romeo." She lifted her eyes to Mr. Hatton's face. "'As she got to die like that?"

"It is only a story!" Kate cried. But when she went up to their room after dinner she found the doll laid out on the dressing table with two tapers burning, one at her head, one at her feet, and Titine watching, absorbed.

"You must not put her like that!"

"You got to. She's dead." And she laid the doll in a drawer as though it were Juliet's coffin. It gave Kate the strangest of feelings and she went quickly away and left Titine to her macabre game, if it was a game.

The day passed, and the night, and the next morning. *Mr. Evans*

[257]

is gone, she thought. *He is almost in France.* Must have reached the coast. Was landed. On the road to Paris. What would he do? How would he transport his fortune in English gold?

The days going by. The same perfect days as before—before the Frenchman had come back. Only—remembering him. Now and then. Thinking of him. Why? Why? What did he mean to her? All done. Her share done.

On the fourth day Biggins came back, riding one of the saddle-horses, and stayed for two nights, telling Kate nothing. Not even by a nod, a glance. Five days. Six. The sixth morning he saddled up again and asked her to walk out onto the back road beside him, for a few yards.

"I'll come back for you with the chaise," he said.

"What do you mean? When? Why?"

He bent down to make certain of a buckle. "Dunna shout, girl. A fortnight. Three weeks, mebbe. I'll be bringing summ'un else to look arter t' hotel."

"Someone else? But—?"

"You do have done your part, li'l maid. Dunna fret you'll be paid for that." He straightened, and swung his heavy bulk into the saddle with a creak of leather, a snorting of his burdened horse. "You keep yourself quiet an' still. All's gone well an' smooth as silk. Three weeks time you'll have a wedding portion. Mebbe I'll ax for you myself!" He tapped her cheek with his knuckles and laughed at her, riding away heavily, like a man more usèd to driving than riding.

Kate stared after him until he vanished from her sight round a long bend of the road, was hidden by the backs of houses. Come back for her? Bringing someone else? She stood very still in the roadway as if she were obeying him. The sunlight seeming cold.

It cannot happen like that, she thought. Three weeks? Someone—someone else?

But I cannot leave him! They cannot make me go!

A wedding portion. The irony of that was like the feel of the razor, laid across her hand. Three weeks.

"It is not possible!" her mind cried. "They cannot!" She held her hands together there in the quiet roadway, wrung them as if they were wet with something and she were drying them. As if—she looked at her hands and tried to think what she was doing, where she was. Three weeks.

I will have money, she thought. And—and the wedding portion. To add to her fifty, more than fifty guineas. Surely that would come to a great deal? Enough—enough to—marry on? And he must have— his salary. His—his mother would—might— She wanted to run to him—now—this instant—throw herself on her knees beside him—tell—tell everything. Beg—beg him to—forgive what? What have I done? That I was not forced to do? Nothing—nothing bad! I will tell him now—now— She even began to run. And stopped. "What will—he think of it?" she whispered to the doors of the stable-yard. The straw motes in the sunlight. The windows of the hotel that overlooked the yard. "Suppose that—he—thinks I have done wrong?"

She went slowly into the hotel. She must find Titine. Tell her— that—that perhaps—that certainly—one day soon—as if that might be a preparation for telling—Mr. Hatton.

"Titine?" Looking for her in the parlour. In their room. Hearing her voice through the half-open door. She seemed to be whispering to herself, in a strange fashion—so strange that even at that moment it struck Kate into stillness, made her listen. Titine whispering aloud, to herself, lines from *Romeo and Juliet*—in an empty room, as though she were listening and *judging*—judging the sound of what she said, the feel of it—like—like an actress studying her sides at half-voice, rehearsing. She could not be reading—she still could not read beyond a word or so—she must have learned the passage by heart, from Mr. Hatton reading to her.

Very softly, Kate went into the room—not knowing what she thought—what she felt—only astonished. And saw Titine standing—one hand lifting to her cheek as Mrs. Dundas's had lifted, but with so much more grace that it gave Kate the strangest feeling, almost of jealousy—and then a swift rush of tenderness—Titine's head slightly tilted to the left, her mouth half-smiling. And she became aware of Kate, the smile remained, as if her mind was still dwelling on what she had been whispering. An expression in the smile, in her eyes, that Kate had never seen before, or not consciously. An adult's thoughtfulness as though she was turning over some matter in her mind and finding new subtleties of humour in it, layer upon layer of them, and was considering them.

She is grown up, Kate thought. *She has grown up while I have—* And felt an astonishment that overcame her urgency.

"What are you doing?" she said, and heard a movement behind

the opened door and looked quickly round the edge of it in surprise, to find 'Ang there. Kneeling in the corner of the room holding a polishing cloth against his thin chest, a block of bees-wax beside his knees. A foot or so of one floor board was clouded with wax that he must have been intending to polish bright again when Kate's voice had interrupted him. Or perhaps before that when Titine had caught and held his attention.

"What are you doing?" Kate said again, a vexation in her voice that she had not meant to be there. That they should be playing here when—when she was so borne down by everything!

"'E was listening to me acting," Titine said. "'E's Romeo."

Kate did not know whether to laugh or not, and managed to hide her astonishment. An astonishment half that he should be Romeo, and half that both he and Titine should not know, feel, what had happened, was threatening to happen—that they could seem so apart from her, so untouched. Titine had lost her adulthood and was looking down at her book that Mr. Hatton had given her, picking at the cover with nervous fingers. "I was just playing," she whispered, hanging her head even more, her face shadowed. 'Ang had bent down and was rubbing at the stretch of waxed board.

"Oh, leave that!" Kate cried, almost in despair. "I—I must—tell—I must talk of something with Titine. Go down and help old John—please—quickly."

Titine was by the window now, pressing her forehead against the glass. And Kate could see that even the side of her long, delicate throat had reddened with a dark flush of embarrassment. *I have made her angry,* Kate thought, and that too was strange, and almost frightening, that Titine was so much grown up without Kate seeing it, that she could feel that kind of silent, adult anger.

"I—I came to—to tell you something—something important—" Kate whispered, almost appealing to be understood, forgiven.

"Why did yer 'ave to send 'im away like that?"

"But—but it was only so that—oh, my dear—" She turned helplessly from the accusation, stared at the window in her turn, out of it at the summer sky. "I love him too," she said, still not trusting herself to look round. "But—we may—we will—have to go away from here!" she cried at last. Bitterly, as though Titine knew it already, and had not cared. Had not cared enough to—

"Away?" Titine repeated. Turning towards her. "From 'ere?"

"Yes. In three weeks time. It—it is all finished here."

"And 'Ang?" Titine whispered.

Kate stared. "'Ang?"

"'E'll be coming too?"

"Of course," Kate said. And thought, *That is all she cares about. Not me. Not what it means to me—Mr. Hatton—only—*

"But you didn't want 'in to know." Not accusing her. Only stating it. Her eyes of such a clear, clear blue that they were like reflections of the sky, showed every change of thought, every shadow.

"It was not that!" Kate said. She wanted to hold out her hands to Titine, beg her to understand. As if Titine—even 'Ang—had drawn utterly away from her. As if she must lose everything. And Mr. Hatton? What would he—how would he hear the news—if—if she could find a way of telling him? Suppose he does not—does not mind so much? And the thought hurt her so cruelly that she held out her hands to Titine. And Titine took them, with her cool instinct for silence, for gentleness. Forgiving.

It was that night that Kate dreamed of the Frenchman's death. She dreamed that she woke up. She could see the pale curtains blowing in a heavy breeze from the sea, and there was a shadow that was like a man standing by the open window. She was so frightened she could not move, nor cry out. And the moonlight came from behind a cloud and showed his face. He was saying something she could not hear. Trying to warn her of something. And at his throat a red line, like a fresh, still bleeding scar.

The shadow faded, and she was truly awake, the curtains really blowing in the wind. She was soaked in sweat, her shift, the sheet under her. The pillow. *He is dead,* she thought. And at last crept out of bed to strip off her shift and dry herself. And knelt down to pray for him.

Chapter 21

She must tell him. And she could not. It was as if even her dream of the Frenchman's death played a part in it. Made the confession still more difficult. Impossible. Confession?

"But what have I to confess?" she demanded. "Only that—that I must leave here—that my—my godfather—"

She practised ways of telling him. At night was quite certain that the following day she would be able to. Would find the perfect phrases. The perfect moment. But when day came, it was impossible again. There were people nearby who might overhear. Or they were so alone that what she said would sound too serious, too full of mystery, and it would seem as if she had needed to be alone with him to tell it.

And all the while he was so happy, the moments they were together were so wonderful, that it was like the thought of wounding herself with a knife, with a razor, to think of telling him. Yet it must come to an end. Soon.

But why must it? Why? She could simply stay—beg Mr. Gurney—or take—take lodgings in the town if they would not let her stay in the hotel. Take rooms and—she counted her guineas again—fifty-five—why it was a vast sum! Tried to guess how much more they might give her. A hundred guineas more? It would not be too much for what she had done for them. If they gave her five hundred guineas, it would be little enough out of their profit.

And the Frenchman dead. She knew it as if she had read it in the Captain's weekly *Gazette*. And asked the Captain with elaborate indifference if there was any news from France.

"Only that villain Robespierre making worse wickedness."

"They—they have not—there is no story of people—plotting against him?"

"Against Robespierre? Plots? He'd have a short enough way with plots, my dear. Aye, maybe there have been plots—but he has 'em

[262]

all in the cemetery." He was delighted with his joke, and repeated it to Mr. Sowerby, and again to Mr. Hatton and the rest of them at dinner. "Plots in the cemetery! You get the point, eh, Jane? Burial plots. Aha! Oh damme, if one can't draw a laugh from even the worst o' things, where'd we all be?"

Mr. Hatton finding a polite smile, seeking Kate's eyes. They were to go that night to *Othello*.

I will tell him in the theatre, she determined. *I will send Titine and 'Ang to fetch lemonade in the interval.*

But when the interval came, it was he who had something to tell her.

"I—I have heard—I have heard from my mother—" he said. "In—in answer—to—"

She stood very still, afraid to look at him. "Yes?" she said at last, trying to sound indifferently interested, merely polite.

"She—oh, Kate! Kate! You know what I am trying to say to you!"

She wanted to pretend that she did not, and could only look down at her hands. How small her hands were beside his. And yet his, when they were by themselves, looked almost too fine to be a man's. But they were strong enough. They held hers now so that she knew she could not have freed herself even if she had wanted to.

"I want you—Kate—help me! I—"

The crowd round them—chattering about *Othello*.

"He kills her in t'end of it—oh, aye—I saw it two years past in Urnford when the players was there from Lunnon. He strangles 'er."

Someone else tittering at such provincial simplicity. Titine and 'Ang finding their way towards them with four glasses of lemonade. Why must they come back so soon? The chandelier winking its forty candle flames. The ushers in near-white gloves and shabby velvet coats. An old man—one of the candle-snuffers—tottering towards the chandelier with his long stick and its small metal hood. Mirrors. Battered gilding on the frames. Playbills for next Saturday's *King Lear*. As though she were taking stock of treasures. Answering the pressure of his hands. His eyes dark with anxiety—and at the same time with happiness.

"She will let us marry," he was whispering. "I am certain of it—"

"Let?" Something echoed in Kate's mind. "Let?" As if he had become young again. Too young. Too gentle. But the thought was overwhelmed by other thoughts, other feelings—and as if there was no such echo she drew herself up on tiptoe so that her eyes were level with his chin and said with mock severity, "But there is someone you should need to ask even before your mother—you have not asked me yet!" And must laugh, and wanted to cry, and there in front of the ushers, and the crowd, and the candle-snuffer, and the stout shopkeeper who knew how *Othello* ended, and the mirrors, and Titine and 'Ang, she lifted Mr. Hatton's fingers to her breast, and then to her lips, and kissed them.

"But if you do ask me—" she said, "I do truly think—that I might say yes."

And if she had not known already how *Othello* ended, she might have been grateful for the information, for she saw none of the rest of the play, but sat seeing and hearing almost nothing, thinking about nothing, so filled with happiness that she felt at moments she must die of it, that no heart could withstand such fullness without breaking.

Afterwards—how long afterwards? Ten years? Two hours?—they were standing in the small sitting-parlour—in the dark—by the open window—as long, long ago they had stood there. But that time he had been outside, the window-frame between them.

"My mother thinks of me still as twelve years old," he said, his arm round Kate's waist, holding her as if she might slip away from him, vanish into mist if he did not hold her. "And she is not well just now. But—she wrote very kindly—I am all she has, you see. It is very lonely for her sometimes."

Kate did not answer him. Scarcely listened, except to the sound of his voice. Only felt the pressure, the strength of his arm. Three weeks? Long, long before three weeks could be over—they would—three weeks were an eternity—and she tried not to calculate how many days of those weeks had already gone by. But what did it matter? What could they say to her if she was to be married? What could they do? And if they tried? They dare not do anything if she withstood them. She knew too much—had seen—*They dare not do anything!*

"And I must speak to your godfather," he was saying. She shivered uncontrollably. "Oh, my dear—and to think that—that I—how can you have forgiven me? Was anyone ever so good—so wonderfully forgiving?"

He lifted her chin very gently, trying to make her look at him.

[264]

And she did look at him. Seemed for the first time in all her knowledge of him to be really looking. Traced his hair. His forehead. His dark, curving eyebrows. His dark, dark eyes that were reflecting light from somewhere, although where could it be coming from in that almost moonless night? His face a pale, beautiful shadow. Like ivory. His mouth. His chin. She wanted to touch his chin. Touch his mouth.

He does not know anything about me, she thought. *If he did—* But she felt that she knew him to the soul. Clear as crystal. As ivory.

"I saw a painting once," she whispered. "You were a shepherd in it. Watching by the Crib."

"The Crib?"

"By Our Saviour's Crib. On the first Christmas Day."

"I have told her that you are a Catholic," he said, trying to sound easy. "She—she is a little old-fashioned of course—"

That severe face in the miniature, young and certain of everything. And now old and still more certain.

"Oh, Kate," he whispered, as if unable to contain his knowledge, must share it or die. "How beautiful you are! There is no painting where I could find you."

"And I saw you—I have never told you this—I saw you one day in London—with—the—" She stopped. What did he know of the Squire? Anything at all?

"Yes?" he breathed, only wanting to hear her voice.

"With two—elderly—not very elderly—two ladies—in the Mall—Your mother? And—"

"My aunt Passover! You saw us in the Mall? Why yes! Yes! I knew—I knew that I had seen you somewhere—somewhere—as if—oh why did not you tell me? If only we had known one another then! If I could have introduced you to my mother!"

"Do you think—do you think that she will—like me?"

"Like? How can she not? She will love you! If only for my sake at first. And then in the next moment for yours! Oh, Kate!" And he could no longer restrain himself and bent down and kissed her mouth. As the shepherd might have done. With such tenderness, such love, that it was no more than a caress.

She felt herself trembling, lifting her face towards his, her arms finding their way round his shoulders, holding him, drawing him down towards her littleness of height. Pressing her mouth to his as if he were a honey flower and she must drink and drink and drink from him, empty him of sweetness. He seemed to be trying to escape and she held him tighter, felt his body trembling, his mouth softening, softening, growing greedy in its turn. Fastening. Like two flowers joined, melting their honey wells together, becoming one sweet, drained helplessness. Her breast crushed against his, until he was kneeling, pulling her down to kneel beside the window-seat. His hands touching her hair, her eyes, her throat, her breast. Her clothes an imprisonment. His. Her hands finding their way under his coat. Feeling the beating of his heart.

"Kate—Kate—we must not—Kate—tell me to be good."

"It is good," she whispered, breathed against his eyes. "There is nothing in the world but goodness." His hands unfastening the throat of her gown, button by tiny button—down to her waist. All the warmth imprisoned there escaping like a scent, like drunkenness. Holding her breast through the warm, thin cotton of her chemise. His eyes shut as if he were at the one time in pain and in a shivering of joy.

"Hold me," she breathed. "I love you—love you—"

"You do not know—know—what you are saying—doing to me— You do not understand."

He tried to free himself and she caught at his shirt. A button, a fastening, tore from it as he drew back. She saw the shadow of his skin, no darker than the white linen of the shirt. Pulled him towards her. Pressed her face against his body.

"I belong to you," she breathed. Tasted a kind of cleanliness. Seemed to taste his skin. And with a small cry of pain, almost of despair, he had taken her gown in his two fists and ripped it downwards. Gown. Chemise. Left her naked to the waist. And the moon that they could not see came out from a cloud behind the hotel, threw its reflected light on the sea, the road, seemed to fill the room with the palest memories of light. Both of them half-naked, kneeling by the open window. Very slowly he touched her breasts, smoothed his palms over them, under her armpits. Drew her towards him like an offering. A gift. His face twisted in despair at his own weakness—and then in something quite new to him—a strength of passion that she had not thought it possible to see in that shepherd face.

He got up, still holding her, lifting her, bent suddenly and caught her with one arm behind the knees, lifted her completely from the ground like a doll. Carried her. She said nothing. Did not breathe. Out of the small parlour. Passage. Stairs. His room. As though it must happen. Must. Had always been meant to happen. From the first moment of—seeing him—Her eyes not shut, but watching him. Watching his face. Dark room. Dark bed. Dragging at her clothes that would not answer to his fingers. So that she must help him. Her own hands shaking so much that it was long seconds before she could lie naked.

And then such pain as she had not imagined could exist. Not sweetness. Pain. Like a knife twisting in a deep, deep wound. And yet she welcomed it. Lay still as if she were dead. As if he had killed her with the pain and she was happy to be killed by him.

"Oh, my love," she breathed. The tears running. "Oh, my love."

He lay on her as if he too were dead. Hands on either side of her face. His body heavier than she had dreamed it could be. She thought too that he was crying.

"Don't cry," she breathed. "My love. My dear. Don't cry." As sometimes Titine had comforted her. Dear, dear Titine. Dear love. Dear pain. Smoothed his bare shoulders with her hands. His back. So astonishingly strong. She felt the muscles, ran her finger-tips on them. An athlete's muscles. The kind that do not show well in clothes. *He should always go naked*, she thought, smiling at the imagining. Shepherd bare. In a fleece, thrown over one shoulder. A goatskin for breeches. A pipe to play.

"Dear, dear shepherd love."

Chapter 22

It took all her strength and tenderness to help him afterwards. Lying together. Holding him. Stroking his face, his body. He seemed in one moment to have become the young boy of his mother's imagining—shocked in his innocence—and at the next to have become again the Mr. Hatton of ordinary days, who thought that he could never, never forgive himself for what he had done to her.

"But it was I," she whispered, "it was I" and was afraid for a moment that he might believe her. But he was too innocent for that. And too masculine in vanity—even so timid a vanity as his—to believe that it was not he who had taken her.

"My dear," she whispered, stroking his eyelids with her lips. "My sweet love." And felt very old beside him. She did not want him to hurt her again like that, and yet she wanted to belong to him completely forever, wanted to feel him master her. To guide him like the beautiful strong creature that he was and make him think that he was taming, taking her. Forcing her to submission. And she succeeded and he grew passionate again, accusing himself of brutal selfishness, covering her throat, her breast with kisses, kissing her eyes to taste the tears, holding her, hurting her, such a sweetness of pain as made her cry out, bite her lips until the blood came. Cling to him. As though she were winding her body round a young tree. Giving, giving, until there was no more to give and she lay limp, crying, smiling, her eyes open, seeing nothing but his face, her tears running as he bent down to catch them with kissing.

He lay beside her at last. Dawn showing a flushed promise through the window. The sea breathing on the sand, whispering and lapping against the rocks. Like the whispering of their blood. She could hear his heart, laid her ear against it, listened.

All our lives together, she thought. *It is not possible to be so happy!* And thought she heard footsteps, the creaking of a door, the sound of day beginning.

"It is too soon!" she cried. Even Peg could not be up. Not for an hour yet. Two hours. Titine! Titine awake and looking for her! Frightened, calling out!

"I must go," she breathed. "At once! Oh, my love." Held to him as if someone were trying to tear her from him. "I must! I must!"

But it was another hour before she went. On tiptoe, carrying her clothes, making him go back into his own room, leave her. Going swiftly in the shadows, up the stairs. Stealing into quietness. Only the softness of Titine's breathing—the gentlest stirring of the white muslin curtains. Lying down beside her with infinities of care not to waken her. Lying naked. Even the sheet a burden. Touching where he had touched. Remembering. Sleeping. So deep, exhausted a sleep that all dreams were lost in the depths of it. Waking to find Titine leaning over her.

"Where d' you get to last night?"

"What do you mean?" she said, smiling, longing for Titine to know how happy she was. Thinking, *how different I must look!* No one could fail to know what had happened to her. How happy she was that they should know! And came fully awake, sat up—cried, "What do you mean? You were not—you were asleep when I came in! Fast asleep!"

"I din't go to sleep for ages. Waiting for yer. You was with 'im, weren't yer?"

"And if I was? For—a few minutes?" Quietening her sudden anger. "Would you mind that very much?"

"But you said we was going away. Does 'e know?"

They stared at each other. "I am going to marry him," Kate whispered. "We shall not need to go away." She caught Titine's hands. "You and 'Ang—you shall stay with us forever. Do not be afraid! We shall be so happy together! I swear it! I promise you! Oh, Titine, I love him so!"

"What about Mr. Gurney?" Titine said. "An' the Squire? Won't they mind?"

"I don't care! I don't care! I love him and he loves me, and nothing in the world can stop us loving one another."

Titine looked at her for a long time, kneeling up in the bed. "'Ow does 'e tell yer?" she said at last. "Does 'e—does 'e kiss yer?"

"Oh, yes, yes! A thousand times!"

"What else does 'e do?"

"Nothing else. What else is there? What a question to ask! You should be ashamed to ask it!"

"In the cellar—with Missis Sullivan—when I was with 'er they did other things. They wanted to do 'em with me, but I screamed too much and they was frightened."

"Oh, *mon Dieu!*" Holding her. Smoothing her hair. O God, why must there be such evil?

"He is not like that," she breathed. "He is so good—he is like an angel—it is as though he truly came to me out of that painting I have told you of."

"An' won't 'e never want to do anything like that?"

"Never! Never! Do not think of it!"

"Then you won't never get married. Yer can't 'ave babies without that."

"Be quiet! You don't understand—and promise me—promise you'll not breathe a word outside this room—even if you think we're alone—about—about him? Not even to 'Ang?"

"But I tells 'im everything. An' 'e can't tell back."

"Oh, my love. Only to him then. Life is going to be so wonderful!"

That afternoon they went for a long country walk. *I will tell him about the Frenchman,* she thought. *And about the Squire.* Everything. As if the least stain, the least shadow, must be smoothed away from their love. As if the Frenchman had been a moment of unfaithfulness—as if the Squire were something she must tear out of her heart. What happiness to cleanse herself so totally—make confession—receive absolution. And if he were jealous? Angry? If he thought as Mr. Solomons had done? *He may give me any penance that he pleases!* And that too would be a kind of happiness. Complete happiness. *I am his. All his.*

But she did not tell him on the walk. *Not now—not quite now. Soon. When we reach that tree. When we are sitting in a quiet place and*— Titine and 'Ang too near to them. Some girls in a field, mowing. Blue skirts and red bodices. Like flowers in the deep yellow harvest. An old horse resting his grey chin on a gate. Rooks flying, cinder dark.

"They—they are in love like us!" Mr. Hatton whispered. Pointed secretly towards Titine and 'Ang. Who walked ahead of them, Titine's arm round 'Ang so lovingly, so tenderly, her golden head bent so gently towards his dark one, that love was written there, like a song.

"They cannot—cannot be—they are only children—" Kate whispered in answer. Did not know how she felt. Angry? Amused? Jealous? And then so full of kinship that it did not matter how young they were, how—inappropriate. The whole world must be full of lovers. Hedge. Field. "Let all the world be lovers!" her heart cried. She felt tears coming. Wanted to cry with love, as if only tears could give her heart relief. Walked leaning on his arm, holding it.

"I heard you singing once," she said. "What was the song? About liberty?"

"Plant, plant the tree, fair Freedom's tree—"

'Ang caught the tune from his singing, answered it on his flute. Titine sang in her strange, sweet, husky voice.

A ploughman passed them, lifted his broken hat, smiled. They smiled at him. Kate wished that she had her purse with her to give him a guinea that he might be one fraction as happy as she was.

Mr. Hatton's voice lifting, ringing. He sang very well, and Kate held his arm and listened to the sound, without troubling about the sense. Patriots? Blood? How well he sang! And the afternoon became evening.

He is grown different again, she thought. Older. As he was that night coming out of the smoking parlour. *I do not know him at all,* she thought, and thought again, *Every day I shall be discovering new things about him.* Watched Titine and 'Ang as though she were watching the reflection of herself and Mr. Hatton. Strange, strange reflection. Time going by in a dream of happiness.

They rested in the corner of a field, ate a basket of strawberries that he had brought for them. Lying back, their heads resting in deep grass and wild flowers, their minds half asleep with the heavy warmth of the evening, the last power of the sun. A deep murmuring of insects in the hedge behind them. 'Ang playing his flute, very softly and strangely.

"There was a queer cove in the yard this morning," Titine said drowsily. "Asking questions." Kate did not answer her for a second. Could not.

"What sort of—questions?" she whispered finally. The sounds of a cart rumbling along the road a long way off. A man's heavy footsteps behind the hedge. Stopping for a moment as if he were listening to them. The notes of 'Ang's strange music. Mr. Hatton watching her, his eyes full of love. The sounds of bees searching for honey in the hedge flowers. "What questions?"

"Oh—I dunno—if any 'un strange 'ad been staying with us. 'E was asking Peg."

"Why did not you tell me?"

The heavy footsteps had begun again. Were going on up the road behind the hedge, invisible. Kate felt as if a cold breath of wind had surrounded her.

"I only jus' remembered."

"What did—what did Peg tell him?"

"I dunno. 'As there bin anyone strange? Mr. Gurney ain't strange, nor Mr. Johnson, are they? She jus' said about Mr. Evans an' 'e give 'er sixpence. 'E said she was a clever girl an' went off with 'imself."

Kate could not say anything for a long moment. As if everything she was looking at was very far away, enclosed in glass. Unreachable. Controlling her face so that he could not tell what she was feeling. Her mouth stiff. And then the trembling of a nerve at one corner of it.

"What are you two whispering about?" Mr. Hatton said idly, lovingly. Reaching out his hand lazily to touch her, to put his fingers against her bare wrist. As if for a moment a stranger was touching her—and then a sense of loss, of danger, so fierce that she wanted to catch hold of him, cling to him. It could not happen, could not be true. God could not let it happen! But what? What was it after all? Only a man asking—if he was asking it was because he did not—did not know. Or—or it was the Squire's spy! Had he not said—that—that she would always be watched—guarded? That was what it must be!

"How did he look?" she asked carelessly, forcing herself to sound careless.

"Jus' queer. A big sort of cove. Rough."

There was nothing to find. The carts—the gold. Nothing at all.

"Does it matter?" Titine was whispering. Her eyes grown anxious.

"Does what matter?" Mr. Hatton said. Not as if he really wanted to know, but for the pleasure of hearing her answer him, of being part of everything about her.

"You must not be curious about women's secrets!" Kate said, not knowing where she found the strength to deceive him. "We are talking of our lovers, aren't we, Titine? Things that well-conducted gentlemen would not want to hear about."

He laughed and opened her palm as if he were a gypsy reading it. Shook his head.

[272]

"There is no lover here," he said. "Only a dark stranger. And a journey. No. Not a trace of a lover anywhere." He lifted the palm towards his lips. Looked at her over it. "A lonely old age," he said, his eyes longing to kiss her.

"Do not say that," she whispered, the trembling at the corner of her mouth growing stronger, harder to conceal. "Not even as a joke. Please."

The rumbling and creaking of a cart had come close. Was entering the field by the gate. The mowing girls—or others like them—walking behind it, their scythes on their shoulders. Like red poppies and blue cornflowers. Their talk and laughter sharp in the fading sunlight.

"We must go!" Kate said. Suddenly unable to stay still, needing to be moving. To question Peg—see if—if the stranger had come again. To be sure of what Peg had told him—to see if there were any traces in the stables—in Mr. Evans's room.

"There is nothing! Nothing to find!" her reason told her. But she was beyond reason, and if she had been with Titine and 'Ang alone she would have run—run until she reached the hotel, or dropped breathless and gasping on the road. But Mr. Hatton being there she was obliged to walk, to walk like a lover, allowing him to hold her hand, to walk slowly, while Titine and 'Ang went ahead of them, also holding hands, Titine gathering flowers out of the hedges, making a coronet of them for 'Ang's black hair. And then a necklace. Until he seemed like a strange woodland creature dressed in flowers.

And when Kate reached the hotel at last she no longer wanted to question Peg. Was almost afraid of what she might hear from her. Could not settle to anything.

"Come to my room," Mr. Hatton whispered. "It is the only place we can be quite private."

She looked at him and he flushed crimson. "Not—you do not think—it is only *about* that that I wanted—I could not talk of it this afternoon—it did not seem right—"

"I will come when I can," she said. Longing suddenly to touch him. And half an hour later, Mrs. Cartwright settled to her crocheting, Titine safe with *Romeo and Juliet*, the Captain and Mr. Sowerby in the smoking parlour, the one with his milk and a *Commentary on St. Luke*, the other with a glass of Hollands and his *Gazette*, Kate

[273]

stole up the stairs to find Mr. Hatton waiting for her. Her heart already beating, half in terror, half in excitement—and behind both feelings another terror, as if it were for the last time.

He was standing by the window, fully dressed. Almost as if he had dressed himself especially, combed and brushed his hair afresh since supper. She stood by the door, closed it slowly behind her. Her heart beating, beating. Even if she were to die of it—if this were the end of everything—she would give herself.

"I thought all morning—all afternoon—how—that I must—must say this—"

Her heart grown cold as a stone. "He does not love me! He despises me! Despises me for—for giving—giving myself to him!" Thought she would die. And found such a strength of pride in herself as astonished her. Seemed to herself to grow tall as she stood there, her face grown cold and distantly surprised, disdainful.

"What must you say?"

"That I am ashamed," he whispered. "How—how could I have—" He turned away from her.

"You are ashamed of me," she said flatly. "You think very poorly of me now. I am not someone you would bring to your mother."

"No!"

But it seemed a year of seconds before he moved. Came swiftly then. Knelt down.

"Little Kate!" he whispered. Buried his face against her dress. She touched his hair. "It is just that—we must not—I must never—never—not until—until we are married. It was so wrong of me—"

He is only a child, she thought. She lifted his chin until he must look at her. *Still only a child.*

"I want—our love to be—to be perfect—" he breathed. "You do not know how I have fought with myself all day. If we had been alone this afternoon—"

"Yes? If—"

"I do not know what I might—might have—"

"We are alone now," she said gently, bending down.

His eyes grew wide with something almost like fear.

I will make him ashamed of me, she thought with cold determination. *And then—then—if it must end—if—if I must go away—he will not—will not mind so much—will not be so terribly hurt as he might have been.*

"We must not!" he was saying.

She loosened his cravat, slowly. Undid his coat. He did not try to prevent her.

I am worse than Maman, she thought. Her fingers shaking. *Worse!*

"We cannot!" he was whispering. "Not now—not—"

And as though a sheet of ice were breaking in her, breaking on a frozen river, she cried out in her mind, "It cannot be over! It is only beginning. I must make him so pleased to be my lover that—that he cannot think of anything in the world but possessing me. Night and day. In dreams. When he is with other people. Only me—only I will be there—inside him—inside his heart. I will make him share my soul."

Touched his face. As if she were smoothing away doubts, fears, all thoughts of shame and conscience. As if even conscience, even thoughts of right and wrong took something from his love for her.

"Love me! Love me!" she breathed. Saw his eyes grow adult, felt his hands grip her, and ceased to be the stronger, became like a captured creature—and yet seemed to be two people—that captured, supple, small and delicate body that he was undressing, lifting up, loving. And someone else. Like steel. Making this happen. Governing it. As though by sheer force of will she could change everything, prevent—As if by this surrender she was annihilating something else, something terrible. *They cannot take me away from him now,* she thought, that steel-strong self. *God will not—cannot—* And the small, soft creature cried out, had her cry stifled by his fingers, the palm of his hand. "Hush! Hush! Oh, my love! Oh, Kate!"

Dressed again. Slowly downstairs. Her face and heart full of pure content. Helping Mrs. Cartwright with her crochet work. After a few minutes Mr. Hatton joining them, reading for Titine.

"Sin from my lips? O trespass sweetly urg'd! Give me my sin again!"

He caught Kate's eye and she looked demurely down, a piece of crochet delicate ivory between her fingers.

"You must teach me how to make such pretty things, ma'am," she said to Mrs. Cartwright. "Although I do not think that gentlemen appreciate them as they should."

Like building a shield, a wall of small safeties between herself and—terror. *It cannot happen! Cannot!* Without even knowing what it was that she feared. Tomorrow night they were to go to *King Lear. And tonight, tomorrow night, and every night I shall go to him. Un-*

til he cannot live without me. We will leave no possibility that anything can separate us. The lamplight. Titine's golden, golden head. His dark beside it. *My heart will burst,* she thought. *How can I live until—until I—until he can hold me again?*

Chapter 23

Kate was in the parlour, tidying it. Her mind half-dreaming. Half-asleep as she moved about, set candlesticks and ornaments in their places. Picked up a scrap of Mrs. Cartwright's crocheting, smoothed it out. Put away Titine's book. *In a few hours I will see him again. Only a few hours. And then the theatre. And then—*

"Ma'am? Miss Harriott, ma'am?" Mary. Calling her.

She stood not answering for a moment, her head lifted. As if in Mary's voice there was already something—a warning—a threat.

"Miss Harriott? Oh there you do be, ma'am—there's some 'un as is asking fer you—out in t' yard."

"Someone? What—what does he want?" Holding the piece of crochet against her like a protection. Holding it against her heart. "What—what sort of man?"

"I dunno, ma'am. He didn't say. A sailor sort o' man. Rough."

Titine's word. *I cannot go out to him,* she thought. She would not have the strength to move. But she must. Must move. The girl looking at her. Already staring at her strangeness, her expression.

"I—I will go at once—yes—yes. I—I will go out and see him now."

The man was standing some way off from the back door, seeming to take his ease and be interested in the yard, the sky overhead, anything. A man dressed like a sailor or a fisherman, a flannel shirt and a neckerchief tied loosely round his throat; a glazed sailor's hat, canvas trousers, canvas waistcoat and serge jacket. He turned to her, his face mahogany-tanned with weather, a white scar showing strong and clear above one eye and down the cheek almost to his jaw-bone.

"God save ye, ma'am. Walk a bit up t' yard with me, if you please."

"What is it? What do you want?" Ready to fall. Her legs trembling.

"I do have come to fetch you off, soonest as ye can come with me. Now'd be best."

They were by the open doors of one of the stables. She put her hand against the timber to support herself. "To—fetch—what do you mean? You cannot—"

"Keep yer voice quiet, ma'am—fer God's sake!" He looked round him. "Didn't they tell you as I'd be comin' fer ye?"

"No!" It was a trick. A trick to make her betray herself—to—"I do not know what you mean!"

"There's trouble," he whispered. "Trouble from France. The whole lot of 'um is run for it. One of 'um, a pock-marked gentleman, said as he'd warn ye as how I was to come an' fetch ye off."

"What do you mean? Fetch me off? I cannot go anywhere!"

"Ye'll go soon enough. With me, or with the Runners. For pity's sake, little maid, dunna you believe me?" His eyes honest behind the sailor's swarthiness, the savage scar. "You dunna fare to have more 'n an hour, at most, they said."

"An hour?" As if she were unable to do anything but repeat his words.

"If we' to catch t' tide, you do have less. I'm to bring ye off away to t'other side. There's a house there o' Black Peter's, him as deals with 'um—you'll be safe there a bit."

She would have fallen if she had not been supported by the frame of the stable door.

"Dunna look so frit, lil ma'am. There's women there as 'll take care o' ye. No one as'll harm you."

"I understand nothing," she whispered. "What trouble from France? What can there be?"

He shrugged, beginning to grow impatient. Or to show the impatience he already felt. "They did say you knew all as had happened." He dragged out a great metal watch from somewhere in his soiled white canvas waistcoat. "I tell you, ye han't as much as an hour. An' that's speaking o' t' tide—not o' them as is comin' to arrest ye. 'Tis a while back they said an hour."

"Arrest?" She began to fall. He caught her and held her up. "I—I—" She could not speak. Could not make one thought connect with another. She must go to him. Titine, 'Ang. An hour. Arrest. The other side. Stared at the sailor as though she did not know what he had been saying.

"Best to come now," he said. "Fetch your bits an' pieces an' lie up

[278]

safe for a half hour with my missus whilst I get things in trim, and get my lad ready. 'Tis no but a short, fair run in this weather. Dunna look so white, m'dear. They says as how you speaks French like a Frenchy."

"I cannot go to France," she said, as though that were all the trouble that there was.

" 'Tis not France, 'tis the Low Countries. An' Black Peter's bit o' it that no Frenchy or anyone else 'ud get into or out of without his saying they might. Dunna you fear nothing, m'dear."

He set her upright, held her steady. "Go an' fetch your things good an' quick, and I'll be down on t' Hard, waiting for ye. Five minutes, no more'n ten now. No titivating."

She did not answer him and he must have thought that she agreed. Would run to her room and pack her life inside five minutes. Abandon what could not be packed. Leave her love as if he were no more than Mrs. Cartwright's crochet work. That was still in her hand. She looked at it without recognition, let it drop.

"Yer handkerchief," the man said, restoring it. "Five minutes now." Pushed her gently towards the back door leading to the kitchen.

She reached it and turned round. He waved and turned away himself, went swiftly with his sailor's rolling walk out of the yard, waved again from the roadway outside, holding up five fingers meaningfully, and disappeared.

She went into the small parlour as though she were sleep-walking. Nothing that she had just heard made any sense. The words turned and turned about in her mind like leaves in the wind. Meaningless. Five minutes. The other side. The Low Countries. Black Peter's house. Arrested.

The last word shocking her awake like a door that slams in the night.

I must tell him, she thought. *Find him.* And Titine. She must find Titine, 'Ang. Still half-stunned, her mind not grasping anything properly. Arrested? Bow Street Runners coming to—

"Titine!" she cried. " 'Ang!" Ran to look for them. And they were both out. Titine buying ribands in the town, 'Ang with her for escort. Peg frightened at the way Kate questioned her, wringing her wet hands in nervousness. "A good two hours gone, m'm. About. I dunno when as they do mean to be back—"

Kate running up the stairs—down again—the sailor a long way

[279]

off, down the Hard, waiting, leaning against the sea-wall, smoking his pipe. Up the hill towards the new town. Running, running. But she could not go to him like this! The people there in the Library, watching, listening— "I am to be arrested!" How could she tell him that? Oh God, what should she do? What was there possible to do?

It is only a trick, she thought. *He is only—perhaps he is the man Titine saw, asking questions. That is it! That is it! A spy, trying to trick me now into admitting something! If it was true, they would have come themselves, sent word, a note—something—*

Almost a relief to think that that was the answer—so much a relief she could stop running, stand holding her side where there was a pain under her ribs like a needle stabbing.

They were coming down the hill towards her. Titine and 'Ang, dawdling slowly, arms round one another—and in some last, untouched corner of her mind Kate thought *They should not—must not walk like that!* And almost made up her mind to scold Titine. As if—as if—

"Titine! Hurry!" she cried. "Run!"

The two of them running towards her, their faces startled. Someone turning to look.

"Hurry!"

They came to her and there was so much to say she could not find the words to begin. Had they seen Mr. Hatton—had they— had he—

"The man," she said, gathering her breath. "The strange man you saw—did he—was he dressed like a sailor? With a scar on his face?" Drawing her finger in a long curve from her eyebrow to her chin. "Like—this?"

Titine only stared, shook her head slowly. "I don't think—I don't remember 'im 'aving a scar. 'E could 'ave been a sailor—I don't know. 'As 'e come back?"

"I'm not sure." Walking back down the hill, trying to think, to plan.

A man standing by the sea-wall across from the hotel. Seeming to pay no attention to anything but the rocks and sea below. A big man. The sailor a long way off beyond him. Beginning to walk quickly away. As if—as if he knew—She could not continue holding herself upright.

"If—something happens to me," she said, her voice unsteady, "you and 'Ang—must look after one another." Her lips trembling. Uncontrollable.

The man's shadow large and heavy at her side. His hand touching her shoulder. "I am a King's Messenger," he said. "Are you Katherine Harriott?" Another man advancing on them across the road, from the doorway of the hotel. She did not know what she answered him, but he took it for admission of identity. "—a warrant—arrest—search—" She could not hear properly. Her heart made such a beating in her ears. Could not see. Only shadows. Titine and 'Ang staring, Titine's mouth opening. She wanted to cry out to her, "Run, run, do not let them take you too." But they had no interest in Titine. Nor in 'Ang. Brought her past them, into the dark of the hotel. Mrs. Cartwright coming out of the parlour, saying, "Oh, Miss Harriott—have you seen a piece of my crochet work anywhere? I think I left it in the parlour last night."

Brought past her staring face. Mary backing away from them. Old John—voices whispering—up the stairs. Her room. Forced to sit. One of them standing with his shoulders against the closed door. The other searching. Drawers. Corners. Bed. The Crucifix taken down. Lying on the searcher's hand, turned over, laid carefully on the table. A book, Titine's *Romeo and Juliet*, the leaves ruffled through. The mattress. Felt with experienced, careful hands. The man took out a pocket-knife, slit the stitches where she had concealed her guineas. Drew out the purse, emptied it onto the table beside the Crucifix. Counted the coins. Fifty, fifty-five. Saying nothing, only looking at the man guarding the door. Searching under the mat, probing crevices between boards, behind the panelling. In the heavy timber of the bed. Nothing more.

"Have you a portmanteau?" one of them said. It was the only time they spoke in the course of an hour's search. She said "Yes" and the King's Messenger opened the door to call for it to be brought. 'Ang there on the landing, shrinking back into the shadows. And Titine. And behind them other faces, that vanished like shadows. 'Ang bringing her valise. Titine trying to run to her and pushed back. The door shut. She did not ask the men where they were taking her. Only as they scooped up the gold, pouring it carefully back into the embroidered purse, she said, "I want to—give that to—someone—" To Titine. To 'Ang.

They took no notice and put the purse and book and Crucifix into the valise, thrust her clothes in with them, fastened the lock and straps.

"Now you. Stand up. Lift your arms." They searched her body as though she were made of wood, their faces impersonal as their

[281]

hands. Emptied her skirt pocket of the shillings there, her thimble, her needles in a tiny wood and leather case, a twist of thread, a handkerchief. They gave back the handkerchief, but nothing else. Opening the door again, summoning 'Ang, who was still on the narrow landing, with Titine. The sense of all the others watching, listening, whispering. The horror spread through the house like a disease. Like plague. 'Ang carrying the valise for them, down the stairs, the faces vanishing, reappearing behind them, the whispers. A cry from Mrs. Cartwright, "Miss Harriott! Oh, my dear!"

Outside. A coach drawn up. A driver. Hands forcing, lifting her inside. The smell of old leather, straw, stifling. Dark. As though each step was already known to her. Even the sounds the coach would make. The glimpse of the sea. It was so bright in the sun it seemed to be made of polished silver. She had known always it must happen. Always.

Chapter 24

London. Evening. The swift, jostling traffic of the streets. In all the eight hours of the journey they had scarcely spoken to her. One brief twenty minutes' halt for a meal she could not eat, brought to them in a small, private room by a staring man servant. They had manacled her hands in the coach, and before they got down to eat they had also chained her ankles to an iron ring that they locked round her waist. When they continued the journey, they left the additional chains fastened and the iron ring chafed her at every movement of the coach. And that too she seemed to have known beforehand. Like a dream that one has dreamed already. Prison. And she could see the walls of it. Like Callac. Heavy, grey. Echoing.

But it was not to a prison that they were taking her first. A handsome street. Chairmen waiting outside a house that seemed even more imposing than its imposing neighbours. The sound of her chains as they made her get down onto the pavement. The chairmen watching, staring—as though the world were walled with eyes. A servant in dark clothes and powdered wig, grave-faced, unastonished at a chained prisoner and her escort.

Footmen. Stairs. Deep carpets, dark mahogany, great portraits whose eyes too followed her, followed and stared. A room full of evening light and shadows, long, slanting shafts of sunlight touching a great table, papers, men's hands. She saw the hands before she could see the watching faces. Dark sleeves, ruffles. The hands of gentlemen, white and cared for. And then the faces. Three old. Three younger. One of the younger three standing behind the others, his back to the empty marble fireplace. Thin and tall and waiting, his eyes impatient, on the edge of anger. One man old and heavy, his face in soft grey folds under the grey, heavy wig. One man handsome, indolently leaning back, his eyelids drooping, lazy, almost caressing. A clerkish gentleman with pen and inkpot and a sheaf of empty paper at the far end of the table, his back to the light. Darker, stiffer dressed than the others. Thinly precise.

"Sit her down there," the indolent man said.

They looked at her, and she saw them through a veil of strangeness. Not even wondering who they were, what this place was. Her two guardians standing behind her, not bidden to sit. She felt in some way drawn away from them, almost from herself. That sense of dreaming, of knowing what would happen.

"Are you French, or English, child?"

"I am English," she said. Even her voice sounded far away to her.

"Be careful about such answers," the old, soft-featured man was saying. His voice old and soft. The man standing by the fireplace starting forward, saying, "What? What did she say?"

"That she is English, William. Do you know the meaning of High Treason, child?"

The watchfulness increasing, only by a shade, but sensibly. Like a ring that tightens.

"I think—High Treason?" Moistening her lips. That too they saw.

"It is to conspire against your lawful Sovereign, the King."

"I have not done that."

"The French man who came to the Old Ship Hotel?"

She looked down at her manacles, at her hands that lay in the lap of her white dress. The chains had soiled the skirt of it, marked it with grease and rust. And the iron ring. What was *he* doing now? Thinking? He would have heard long ago. Did he believe that— that she was guilty of anything? Who were they talking of? The Frenchman. Of course. The Frenchman. She was not astonished. Did not betray anything in her face. Scarcely thought of how they knew. The old man continued, his voice as soft and gentle as his features. Like an old man speaking to a wayward child, persuading her to contrition.

"It is no use your concealing anything," he said. "We know most of what we need to know already. About your employer, Mr. Gurney, for example. And the man you all refer to as 'the Squire.' Where are they now?"

"What does she say? What does she say?" The young, thin, impatient man seemed deaf, cupping his hand to his ear with a gesture half angry, half contemptuous.

"She says nothing, I am afraid.—It will not serve you to remain mute, my dear. You know the penalties for High Treason?"

She shook her head very slowly.

"If you are found guilty, you will be hanged."

And that too she had known. But she could not answer in words. The old gentleman looked at her with what seemed truly like sadness. His lips shaped themselves. Very delicate in the soft, heavy face. Shaped into a bow. "Your friend Mr. Hatton," he said. "He is your friend, is he not? You do not wish to see him hanged?"

She stared at him, not understanding. "Mr.—Hatton—?" And then, half-understanding, still not believing, she cried, "What do you mean? What are you saying? He has nothing to do with—"

All of their eyes on her. Their stillness. When she did not go on, the indolent man said, "Ye-es? Nothing to do with—?"

"But he has confessed, my dear." The old man's voice as tender as his mouth, pouting a little, sweetly delicate. A mouth that forty and thirty years ago must have kissed many women. "How do you think that we are so well informed?"

She stayed looking at his mouth, unable to take in what he was saying. The words echoed and re-echoed in her ears. Confessed. Informed. Mr. Hatton. Hanged. Took new patterns, each as meaningless as the last. "It is not possible," she whispered.

The old man sighed gently. "Alas, child. You have much to learn."

"It is not possible! You are lying!"

A hand grasping her shoulder, holding her in place on the chair, although she was not aware of having tried to stand up.

Another of the men leaned forward, into the slant of sunlight, the last brightness of the evening. Even as it touched his face, the thin, yellowish lines of it, the fine bones, the sunlight vanished into twilight. All grey in the room. "If you were to turn witness for us?" he said, his voice dry as sand in an hour-glass, falling as gently. "Did you wish His Majesty to be killed?"

They were lying—lying—that they had arrested him. It was not possible. Lying.

His Majesty? Killed? Her mind lost to their questions, to their words that seemed to go further and further from reality. The thin, pale, youngish man crying again, "What? What? What is she saying? Tell her to speak up!"

"She does not answer us, William."

He had gone to the far end of the table, was looking over the clerk's shoulder, turning to the window to tug at a curtain, to stare out. The others seemed to wait on his return to them. "Tell her if she does not turn King's Evidence, she must be charged as one of them. Do not let us waste more time on this."

"Do you hear, child?"

"Mr. Hatton—" she whispered. "What have you—you cannot have arrested him?"

They looked and waited. When she said no more the old man lifted his hand in a gesture of resignation. A dark green sleeve. The white lace at his wrist fell very elegantly. He had a great red seal ring on his forefinger. How could they have arrested him? Behind her, hands were lifting her by the elbows out of the chair. "You have not much time," the old man said. "When you are next questioned you must decide. Either you turn witness for us, or you face hanging. You are very young to hang, my dear. Think on it these next days."

Being brought out of the room, down the stairs. Into the waiting coach. Their words like echoes. Hanged, hanged, hanged. Arrested. Arrested him. And "he has confessed." She shook her head again and again in the coach, and the two men with her eyed her in a strange way as if they thought she was maddened by fear, and looked for some violence from her.

"It is not true," she said aloud. Lifted her manacled hands and looked at them, but what she was seeing was his face, his hands manacled. It could not be true, They were lying, tricking her. Confessed? Confessed? And the fear came like a flash of lightning out of cloud that they had tortured him, and then she did throw herself forward, struggled to reach the handle of the coach door. They forced her back into her seat, and threatened her.

"They have tortured him!" she cried, They did not understand what she meant and exchanged fresh glances of distrust. Until they reached the prison and she was brought inside and consigned to other keepers. She could not think of where she was, of what was happening to her. The smell of damp stone. Another, fearful smell, a stench growing in the stone passage as they walked, her chains heavy, chafing her ankles. A thick, sweet, stifling smell like decaying flesh. Iron gates. Iron doors. Someone unlocking her chains, thrusting her through into a courtyard, the sounds of screaming. Shadows in the twilight of the deep, narrow yard, running towards her. Iron clangour behind her back, locks. Bolts ringing.

"'Ere's a new 'un! Garnish, garnish!"

Mouths screaming, faces, hands. Hands held out, naked arms, naked breasts. Dragging at her, dragging at her clothes. Surrounded, screamed at. Hell's voices screaming. The stench so dreadful she could not breathe. Hands finding her locket, Mr. Jardine's small gold locket, the gold chain that the searchers had not found, wrenching it away in triumph.

"'Ere's something, 'ere's 'er garnish."

Still clawing at her, searching, searching. A girl with a ravaged handsomeness, pock marks like deep pits in her face, red hair, rags of velvet and satin, elbowing her way through the mob, striking left and right with her fists. "Shut up, you 'ores! Let me see." Reaching for the locket and chain. When the woman who held it seemed reluctant to surrender, the red-haired girl drew her fist back and hit the woman in the mouth. Examining the booty in the remains of twilight. "All right, she's in. Leave her alone, curse yer." Lifting her fist again, clearing a circle round Kate. Grasping Kate's throat with her left hand. Her fingers like a man's, hard and powerful.

"I'm the ward woman," the girl said. "When I tells yer to do anything, you does it. Understand? 'Ave yer got blunt?" When Kate did not answer, the girl rifled her pocket. "'Ave yer got anyone outside to feed yer?"

Kate shook her head, held by the girl's fearful strength of eye rather than her hand. Like a lioness. "I'll 'ave this," the girl said, taking Kate's neckerchief. She twisted it round her own half-naked shoulder, challenged the circle of women with her eyes, a contemptuous jerk of her head. "She's mine," she said. "Any scabby 'ore as touches 'er gets 'er crutch kicked in. Understand?"

The women backed away. Old women. Young. Children. Thin. Starving, hideous in rags. Filth. Blind eyes. Sores like dark mouths. Dark mouths like sores.

They have tortured him, Kate thought.

The girl leading her somewhere, through the crowd of women, through a doorway, up stone stairs, into a long, stinking room. "You can sleep 'ere. Beside me. 'Etty, you bitch! Fetch 'er 'er rugs."

Kate looked at the girl as though the answer might be in her face. The deep scars. The fierce lioness's eyes.

"They have tortured him," she whispered.

A woman with one eye, an idiot's smile, spreading out two rugs for her. Grey with filth. Stiffened. "That's yer piller," the idiot was saying, laughing, moping with her head this way and that. "Lovely piller for yer." Pointing to the beam of wood that ran along the sloping floor. "Ain't she a pretty 'un, Dolly love?"

"'Ave yer 'ad any grub?" the red-haired girl was saying. "My name's Doll. What's yours?"

"My name?"

The girl caught her by her shoulders, began to shake her violently, until Kate's head rolled back and forward, and she could scarcely see. Trying to protect herself with her hands. The girl stopped as suddenly as she had begun, and with great care, like a surgeon preparing to operate, measured her hand against Kate's cheek, and with a sharp chopping of her wrist struck Kate very hard on the face, on one side and then the other.

Kate's eyes filled with tears, her head swam. For a second she lost consciousness, swayed and buckled at the knees. The girl caught hold of her.

"Yer got to come out of it," she said. "Yer don't want to go like 'er, do yer?" She jerked her head towards the idiot. "You ain't never been in gaol before, 'ave yer?"

"But I have," Kate whispered. *I have come back*, she thought. *They have brought me back.*

"They just nicked yer today, though? Sit down 'ere with me. Poor rat." She sat on a mattress beside Kate's rugs, and pulled Kate down beside her. "Where was you in gaol before then?"

But the kindness in her voice was more than Kate could bear, and she began to cry, the girl pulling her head against her breast, holding her as a man holds a woman, but only if he is very kind, very gentle. Mr. Hatton. The tears running. The big, raw hands smoothing Kate's hair, the voice whispering above her head, "It'll do yer good. It ain't that bad, my duck. We ain't dead yet."

Asking her name again, what she had done, who her friend was that they had tortured, not bothering greatly about the whispering, broken, unintelligible answers, but only for the sake of talking, until Kate was almost asleep against her. The idiot brought them food, bread and cheese and porter. "Yer'd die of the grub they gives yer 'ere. Yer got to get it from outside. Ain't yer got no one?"

The girl made Kate eat. Threatened to strike her when she refused. Held the can of porter to her lips and forced her to drink. "You ain't the same as these lot. Poor rat. Maybe we'll go on the lagship together. I'll look arter yer."

"They are going to hang me," Kate said.

"Garn away with yer. They tells yer that. Eat yer bread or I'll give yer another clout."

Until it was night. The girl making her lie down, holding her hand. And the long darkness beginning. Out of the dark the faces coming like marsh lights, drifting by, bowing in mockery. "We have never lost sight of you, Mademoiselle. Never."

The mother of the child, in Callac, beckoning. Mademoiselle Blanche. The Vicomtesse. The nuns. "Did you think we had forgotten?" And in the wood the heaped leaves, stirring in the fingers of the wind. Leaves rustling, rustling. And under them—"How could you think that you could go on living, when we are dead? How could you think of happiness?" And they were torturing him.

The sounds of prison. Sleepers. Crying out in sleep. The smell. The stones. She had thought Callac had been the depth of suffering. But it had been sweetness to this place. Depths under depths. *And when I am hanged?* she thought. She put her right hand to her throat. It was as though they had already prepared it for the rope. Taken her chain and locket. Her neckerchief. "We will be waiting for you," the shadows whispered. And Titine? "Titine!" she cried out, only realised then that she must have been not asleep but half unconscious.

The girl touched her face, was leaning over her. "Shurrup!" Her hand threatening, caressing.

Let it be quick! Kate thought. And then, *I am glad. Now there is nothing to fear, any longer. It has happened.* Until she thought, *They will hang him too!* and cried out again.

The tears ran down her face, onto the girl's hand, and the girl smoothed them away, whispered, "Don't cry, don't cry. I'll look arter yer."

Kate must have slept, because Mr. Hatton came to her, his eyes bewildered. "What have you done to me? I—I am innocent! I don't—understand." And Titine, in a lonely place with 'Ang. An empty road, a hillside, and the two thin figures walking, walking, and her own voice calling them. "I am here! I am here!" But they did not turn their heads, went on and on in front of her, while it grew dark. If she could catch up with them before it grew too dark to see. But they were drawing ahead, their figures smaller and smaller in the distance, in the shadows, in the dark.

Morning. She was brought to another building that day, wearing her chains again. Made to stand in a kind of dock, listen while they read things out to her. Meaningless, gabbled things. An old man in an untidy wig, sitting on a dais beneath a clock. Another man, thin, shabby, his wig unpowdered, clerk-like, reciting. To the old man? To her? "—that contrary to the provision of the Act for Establishing—*Anno Tricesimo Tertio, Georgii Tertio Regis*—that being an alien she did in a private and clandestine manner come into this country—"

Afterwards they brought her back to the gaol and unchained her. Night. Another morning. She lost count of time. In the day she stayed in the courtyard, sitting on a stone, walking about, waiting. Trying to think. To understand. High Treason? The King? It was only smuggling! But there was no one to tell. And again and again, *They cannot have arrested him! They cannot! For what? What can they imagine he has done?* But they would have discovered their mistake already, long ago, released him. She almost expected he would come to find her. And sat half-waiting to be called to the grating where the prisoners saw their friends.

The others left her alone, partly for fear of Doll, partly from fear of Kate herself, of the whisper "Treason. Going to be 'anged." Only the idiot coming near her, moping and gabbling, touching her clothes with filthy, claw hands, cackling with sudden shrieks of laughter. "Pretty clo', pretty clo'." They did not stay pretty long. Morning. Night.

The fourth morning someone did call her to the grating at the far end of the yard. And for the wild moments of running there she knew that he had come. Could see him. See his eyes. His hair falling. His smile. Very sad for her, but very loving. So loving that she cried out to him with the pain of it. "They did not torture you? Thank God, thank God!"

It was Mr. Foster there. His face twitching with fear, his small eyes glancing this way, that—at the other visitors beside him, over his shoulder, at the street, at every shadow and movement.

"Mr. Fos—"

"No names, for Gawd's sake. No names. John. I'm John, remember? John." Twitching with nerves. "What 'ave yer told 'em?"

"Nothing. Where is he? Mr. Hatton? What have they done to him?"

"No names!"

"They know all the names."

"Oh, Gawd! Not me? Not my name?" he whispered. "Not—not

[290]

Mr.—'im as you knows, my—employer?" His voice sinking still lower, his mouth close to the rusty grating, the rough iron. The freckles, the waxy skin, the white tip of gristle at the point of his nose framed in the grating like a trapped animal's.

"I don't know—Mr. Gurney—"

"Quiet, put yer mouth close—" Sweating with terror. Trembling. "Tell me what yer've told."

"Nothing. Nothing at all. They know."

"They can't. Not everything. They've took your friend Mr. 'Atton, they think it's politics."

"What have they done to him?" Almost a shriek that made the other women turn their heads, stare.

"Sssssh. Nothing. I don't know. 'Cept it shows they're on the wrong track. Thank Gawd for it."

"Tell them he is innocent!"

"Are yer mad? I don't dare go near anyone. It's only to know what you've told that I'm 'ere. Swear you've told 'em nothing."

"I swear it! But they know!"

"Not about me? About Mr.—about us—?" His voice pleading to hear her confirmation, hear her oath. "Oh, Gawd! Oh, Gawd. An' what I told yer that day—about 'im, the 'igh up person—" His lips pressed between the bars, whispering, urgent with terror. "Why did I say anything to yer? I was mad, mad. Yer can't do yerself no good by telling that! They'll 'ang yer worse!" His eyes darting, full of tears of self-pity. "Yer wouldn't do me 'arm, would yer? Nor Mr.—'E was yer friend, 'e would 'ave—oh, why didn't yer do what I begged yer to? That slut, that fat 'ore, she 'as 'im, now. You don't want to see me 'anged along with yer? I'll give yer money. Look—" He held his closed fist against the bars, thrust it through. "Open your 'and."

Coins. Hot and damp. She took them without thinking. He sighed, a kind of relief that she had taken them, that perhaps he had bought her silence.

"Listen," he whispered. "They don't know everything. I been thinking it ain't possible, they're 'aving you on. A couple o' names, something. Not any more." His eyes quick as a rat's, thinking, scheming, sliding sideways. "Someone 'as blabbed a bit, but not much. If yer keeps yer mouth shut—" Looking this way and that, pressing his mouth against the bars again, whispering. "They knows 'oo was in the 'otel, they just 'ad to ask. But nothing else. An'

[291]

if you tells 'em nothing—swear you won't tell 'em anything. Go on, swear! I'll 'ave grub sent in, money—"

She could not swear, could not make herself say anything to him. Looking at him as if she were looking from one world to another, as if already she were a ghost, looking at the living, far away. Too far away for her voice to reach. Filled with pity for his terror. Someone behind her, touching her. Mr. Foster looking worse frightened still, backing away from the bars, his lips writhing the word "Remember!" Turning his head so that his hat should hide his features. Hurrying, gone.

"Is that yer friend? Is he ah't again?"

Kate turned. Doll there. "No, he is—only someone I—I knew."

"What's 'e give yer?" Opening Kate's hand. Three guineas in her palm. Three gold coins. Doll taking them. "I'll look arter these, my duck. Yer'll get robbed of 'em. We'll 'ave a bust, eh? Some 'ot beef, an' a couple o' bottles o' something good, an' I'll get a bed in for yer. Come an' tell me what yer'd like fer your dinner."

That evening Kate was taken away and questioned again. For three hours. This time by two men in a shabby office, the stamp of policemen about them. But all she would tell them was that Mr. Hatton was innocent. And she began to sense from their questions almost without thinking, troubling about it, how much and how little they knew. Nothing of the gold. Only a garbled idea of the jewels, of the treasure that had come in. They seemed to believe that it had come in to pay for something in England, for a conspiracy. Asserted that they knew everything about it. There were to be weapons collected. A landing. Bribes. A great personage involved. Who? Who? Do you know what it is like to be hanged?

But she could think of nothing but his innocence, of what he must think of her, how he must feel, must be suffering. And of Titine, and 'Ang, and what she had brought on all of them. And all that she could determine on was to say nothing, nothing that could worse injure him. She begged them to let her see him. But as for Titine she was afraid even to mention her name, ask what had happened to her. She should have asked Mr. Foster to find out. But he was too afraid for himself— Only half her mind on their questioning. Less than half. "We know. It is useless to conceal. We know." But they did not know. Even that one part of her attention that she gave to them told her that. At last they gave up the attempt and had her taken back to the gaol.

"What did they do to yer, pet?"

In a strange, remote way Kate had grown almost to love the red-headed girl. To love even the idiot. As if they were part of her love for him. Part of her suffering. The women who dragged themselves about the yard, quarrelled and fought over pennies, cans of porter, pieces of bread and rags. Over lovers, lies, crimes against one another, treacheries. Kate sat in the August sun in the yard as though she was already dead, watching and loving shadows who belonged to a world she had already left behind. As though she could see in them things that were not there for living eyes. As if by love she could at least a little appease the Furies who were waiting for her. So that they might leave him free. Not a love that makes one happy. Like a pain in the soul, that deep sense of loss that the souls of the damned must have.

"Yer got to come out of it," Doll said, catching hold of her in the yard, shaking her, not violently, but like someone waking a sleeper. "Yer got to fight or yer'll die before yer even gets tried. They ain't going to 'ang yer, I swears it. Fourteen years. I told yer, we'll go on the same lagship, maybe."

"Fourteen years?" Kate said, and smiled at her.

"That's better. Yer got to 'ave guts. Sod 'em all."

She heard her name being called "Kate? Kate?" and went to the grille. Mr. Foster come back? She would ask him about Titine—to find out—surely we must be able to do that much? She wondered how she could make him less afraid. But it was not him. An old woman in black. With a basket. A basket of small cakes. The old woman from Devon Place. Kate was almost certain of it even before the blank eyes lifted, searched for her through the grille.

"What 'ave yer told 'em?" the old woman breathed. The eyes like death.

"Nothing! I shall never tell anything!" And what was there to tell? Names that they already knew.

"There's a fine girl," the voice croaked, whispered. "'Ave a cake, my dove; 'ave one of granny's cakes. Yer won't be 'ere long, my sweetheart. They'll see yer gets aht safe an' 'appy. They won't see yer 'anged."

"Have you seen them? Have you seen Mr. Hatton?"

"Sssshhh. Names! Give 'em a couple o' days, my duck. Just a while an' you'll be so 'appy." The old, knotted hand fumbling the cakes in the basket, choosing one with a red cherry on it, white sugar icing like snow. "A fairy cake, my sweet'eart. Granny's own baking." Holding it through the bars.

"You are very kind to come."

"God bless yer, my pet. Eat it up. Let granny see yer eat it up."

But she could not. She put it to her lips to please the old woman, pretended to be eating.

"There's my good girl. Keep yer 'eart up, my dear." Shuffling away. Looking back. Lifting her hand. Calling out in her raven's croak, "Eat every crumb, mind."

Kate held the cake in the palm of her hand, thought of Titine. The idiot was there behind her, gibbering and crying, "What yer got? What yer got in yer 'and?"

"You take it," Kate said.

"For me?" Touching the cherry, the poor twisted face, the one eye, laughing with happiness. "Good Kate. Good Kate." Making a swift, clumsy snatch, running three steps away with the prize. The small cake crammed into the dribbling mouth.

She heard her name called again. "Harriott! Harriott!" To be taken for more questioning.

Chapter 25

"Leave her with me," the man said. "We shall be an hour or so."

They had chained her before they brought her here, to the top of an old house by the river. Grey house. Grey people. Clerks in naked-seeming rooms, naked corridors. A glimpse of another prisoner in chains, sitting with head hanging, not even lifting his head as she went by. But it was not him. Pushed into this small room. Table. Two chairs. Small, grey window. Grey with dirt. The glimpse of a mast through the grey glass. Rigging. Made to sit. To wait. A fly buzzing, caught in a web on one of the small window-panes. Buzzing. The table bare wood. No papers. Nothing.

"It is useless," she said to the two men who had brought her there. "I shall tell them nothing."

They did not answer her, and after a few minutes footsteps came, heavy and slow. A big, shambling man, with cavernous eyes under grey eyebrows, a head so cropped of hair it seemed almost shaved. A grey stubble on a bony skull.

"Leave her with me," he said to the two men. "We shall be an hour or so." A French accent. Sitting down when the two men left them alone. Heavily, the chair creaking. Rasping a great bony hand against his skin, over his cropped skull, sighing. Saying nothing, not even looking at her. Opening a drawer. Rattling inside it as if he were searching among a dozen unwanted things for something trivial that he needed. Taking out a short, narrow piece of wood. Two lengths of thick cord attached to it, through holes bored in the wood, one at either end. He put it on the table in front of him, arranged it so that the cords lay stretched out. His fingers playing with it, his lower lip thrust out thoughtfully. And still he had not looked at her. Black clothes hanging loose on him, large as he was. A something of collapse about him, of a great chest slipped down, of huge shoulders grown stooped. Heavy cheek-bones. Heavy jaw.

"You say you are English?" he said in French.

"Yes." She would say nothing, answer nothing, until they let her speak to him.

"But I am French," he said. "You were in prison in France, I think? Why?"

She started, tried to shrug away the look of fear, of unreasoning guilt. Forgot her determination. "I was in La Vendée—the Blues came—"

"Ah yes. And your companions? In prison? What happened to them?"

"They—they were drowned," she whispered.

"But you were not?"

She stared at him, and for the first time he lifted his eyes to look at her. So deep-set under the overhanging brows that they had no colour, were no more than points of light in shadow. "What bargain did you make with them? To save your life?"

"None! *Mon Dieu*, none!"

He looked down at his piece of wood, touched the cords with slow, careful fingers, rearranging them into a new pattern. "The money that you had when you were arrested. The fifty-five guineas. How did you come by them?"

"I—I—"

"Yes, Mademoiselle?" Touching, rearranging, pushing the cords until they made an exact and satisfying curve, each equal to the other, the wood between. "Go on."

"I saved—saved them—It is not what you are thinking!"

"No? Where is the man they call the Squire?"

"I have been asked that before. I do not know, I tell you. How can I make you believe me? I want to see Mr.—"

"We shall come to that. Who is the 'great personage' we have heard about?"

"I know nothing of any of this! Nothing!"

"I would like to be able to help you," he said, still looking down. His fingers pushed at the two cords until their free ends touched one another, made a circle with the piece of wood, only the wood flattening its perfection. The fly buzzed in its web. Outside the window the mast of the ship seemed to move an inch this way, and then, slowly as the earth turning, an inch that. "If you become our witness," he said, "your life will be saved. You might receive money, too. A great deal of money. Would you not like that?"

"No!"

"To be free again? To walk in the streets? Buy pretty things?"

"I know nothing, I tell you. Where is Mr. Hatton? What have you done to him?"

He ignored that. Rearranged his device of wood and cord. "We know that you know a great deal. We have a letter. From your friend Cauvillier."

"I have no friend Cau—Cauvillier. I never heard that name."

"You called him 'Mr. Evans.' He had toothache, or so he said."

She could only stare at him, her mouth opening. Closing again.

"He has been unfortunate, Mademosielle. He was guillotined on the fourteenth of last month. Did you know it?"

She shook her head slowly, and he smiled at the admission. He had great yellow teeth like a horse's teeth, ugly and powerful. "But before he died he wrote a letter. He does not seem to have trusted any of you, Mademoiselle. He thought that his death might come about through some of you. And this letter was to avenge him."

"I have taken my precautions," he had said. She did not answer. The piece of wood and the two cords had begun to hold her eyes.

"I cannot tell you anything," she whispered. "I know nothing to tell."

He had picked up the cords in his two hands, twisted them round his fingers so that the wood was held between his fists. He leaned his elbows on the table and looked at his hands as if he were playing cat's cradle, his eyebrows drawn down, his lower lip thrust out thick and heavy. "I think you do. The London Corresponding Society, for example. Mr. Hatton was to be your avenue to them, was he not? And to the other Jacobin groups in England?"

"He had nothing to do with anything! I swear before God he knew nothing, nothing, nothing!"

"Mademoiselle. That cannot be true. We have found letters, books. He has been overheard."

"Overheard?"

The man had got up from his chair and was coming round the table, heavy and tired, sighing. He came to stand in front of her, resting himself against the table's edge, looking down at his piece of wood.

"He has spoken openly of the King of England's death, of desiring it. Of fomenting mutinies in the English Navy, in the Army here. Of a republic. He has praised Robespierre. He has been very indiscreet."

"He is young! He is—he says these things—"

"Yes?"

"He knows nothing of anything that you have asked about. I shall not say one more word to you until you believe me about that. Let me see him, Monsieur! Please! In front of you! Anywhere! And you shall see then—he is completely innocent."

"Where did the money go that Cauvillier brought in?"

"He did not—" She stopped, tightened her lips, looked away from him, away from the piece of wood.

"Go on."

"I shall say nothing more. Let me see him. Bring me to him."

"Where is the money now?"

She did not say anything. Did not look at him. With a sudden reach of his left hand he had caught her face, was holding it between finger and thumb. "I do not want to hurt you," he said. But his eyes told her that that was not true. "For the last time will you answer me willingly? Or must I force you to tell?"

It is going to happen, she thought wonderingly. And was surprised that she had not known it sooner. She could not shake her head because of his hand holding her. She closed her eyes instead. His finger and thumb tightened, forced her teeth apart. The wood slipped into her mouth, greasily smooth. The cords twisted round her neck, tied tight. He must have done it many times before, he was so swift and practised. He rested himself against the table's edge again, took her hands in his. The chains made a soft rattling as he lifted her arms from her lap. The fly buzzed.

"I am going to hurt you," he said. "When you are ready to tell, nod your head." His thumbs feeling the bones at the backs of her hands, arranging them, pushing them inward, his hands closing round hers. "For the last time?"

She shook her head. And in the next second arched out of the chair, her mouth trying to scream, the pain from her hands like burning wires thrust up to her shoulders through the length of her arms. Sweat broke on her body, ran down from her armpits.

"That is only a beginning," he said. And closed his hands again.

When she fainted, he brought her round with water that he fetched from somewhere. Until at last she broke, soaked with an agony of sweat and the water he had flung on her, not knowing what she was doing, wanting to kneel down in front of him, lie on the floor, die.

Told of the jewels, the meetings, everything. "But he is innocent," she kept repeating. "He knew nothing, nothing, nothing!" Would have fallen out of the chair again if he had not held her there. And Mr. Jardine's name. She did not tell that. Perhaps it was easy enough not to tell it because he did not ask for it, did not believe her story of gold to pay for treasures—of Tallien and Barras and Fouché and plots to bring Robespierre down.

"Robespierre is dead," he told her. "Like your friend Cauvillier. They do not need gold to kill each other. Must I continue?"

She would have kissed his feet if he had allowed her to lie down. When he began again, she fainted before he could ask another question and he was unable to bring her round for so long that perhaps he grew afraid. When she came to, the room was empty. The fly still buzzing. She was lying with her face against the table-top. Could see ink stains, the grey grain of the wood. The pain in her hands made her think that all the bones must be broken, and she was afraid to move them, to look at them.

What have I told? she wondered. It seemed far away. She felt sick. Tasted it in her throat, the remains of vomit. The mast and rigging rose and fell and swayed in the window, inch on slowly-stirring inch. Her two escorts came to take her away.

In the prison she lay down, saying nothing, unable to use her hands, staring up at the ceiling, with its grimy plaster, its cobwebs. Unable even to cry. *I have betrayed them,* she thought. *Please, God, let me die soon.*

The idiot too was lying down in the ward. She had been taken ill and was groaning and crying out. Hour after hour. "I'm burning, burning!" she kept crying. "Give me water, som'un! Me throat is burning!"

None of them slept that night for the idiot's screams, until five o'clock in the morning she rose up on her knees, grasping and tearing at her throat with her finger-nails, and threw herself about the floor, against women's legs, against the walls, tearing and tearing. After another hour she grew quiet and they put her back on her rugs, cursing and exhausted.

When the gaoler came that morning, he found she was already dead. Her face had turned blue black and her mouth was locked open in a last attempt to scream.

"She's bin poisoned," the gaoler said. "'Oo done it? Which of you bitches done 'er in?"

[299]

No one answered him, and Kate was scarcely aware of what had happened, lying still sleepless, unable to use her hands for anything. Afterwards, when Doll brought her something to eat and drink, and held her up to feed her, she asked about the idiot. What had happened to her? Was she really dead?

"She must 'ave ate some of the gaol grub an' died of it, poor bitch."

"I gave her a cake. Someone brought it to me." She stared at Doll. "It could not have been that? It was only a little cake—"

"It was enough for 'er," Doll whispered, glancing round. "Don't say anything to these 'ores about it. Maybe it wasn't nothing to do with it. Is there som'un outside as wants to knock yer off?"

Kate shook her head slowly. "Who could do such a thing?"

"Someone done it. If they asks yer, don't say nothing at all."

But no one asked her anything. The victim was only an idiot waiting to be tried for theft. And there had been poison set down for rats in the drains. She must have found some and eaten it. She ate everything, the filth, everything. After another day or so Kate was the only one who remembered her, and the idiot joined the ghosts who haunted her at night. Her mouth like a wound, crying. But it could not have been the cake? Please, God, let it not have been my doing.

Three days after the idiot died they brought Kate to the magistrate again, and charged her with High Treason, "that being a subject of our Sovereign Lord the King, not having the fear of God in her heart nor weighing the duty of her allegiance but being moved and seduced by the the instigation of the Devil—"

They did not seem to be speaking about her at all, nor even paying much attention to her. The stuffy room full of people, coming and going. The same thin, shabby man in his unpowdered wig, gabbling the words like a prayer he was in a hurry to have done with. The same old, untidy man on the dais listening. The clock ticking. The two men who had arrested her also there, staring at nothing.

"— compassing or imagining the death of our Lord the King, levying war against our Lord the King in his realm or in adhering to the enemies of our said Lord the King in his realm giving to them aid and comfort in his realm or elsewhere and of all misprisions of such High Treasons—"

She wondered if she must answer anything, but no one told her that she should. The thin, clerk-like man stopped reciting as suddenly and unintelligibly as he had begun. One of the men who had brought Kate from the gaol touched her arm, made her step down from the dock and go through the crowd again.

People stared at her and whispered. Drew back slightly as though she had gaol fever and it was written in her face. Even her guards treated her with a kind of distance—not respect, but a sort of wondering contemplation, that such a depth of vice could be contained in so small a frame. Her gown and body had grown filthy in the gaol and she wondered if it was because she smelled dreadful that they looked at her like that.

"It is not possible to wash there," she said. "Could you give me a piece of soap?"

They did not answer, and brought her back to the courtyard, and the familiar women, and Doll. Like coming home.

"What do they mean, 'Igh Treason?" Doll said. She had bought a meat pie and wine and shared it with Kate, as though Kate were her lioness cub, making her sit down on the mattress, breaking off portions of the pie crust for her, making her drink the wine.

"I do not know," Kate said. "They say I made war against the King."

"You!" Doll laughed, opening her mouth wide, her splendid teeth ruined only by two that had been broken and had turned black. "You! If it was me! I'd make war against 'im, the ol' bastard. If I 'ad the chance." More days. Nights. Growing thin. So thin that Doll could lift her like a small child. Laid her in bed, covered her with a clean blanket she had begged or stolen somewhere in the prison. Fed her. Threatened her. "Don't give them bastards best. Yer got to fight. Yer got to stay strong. We'll go to lagland together. Yer never knows what'll happen. Drink yer broth, duck."

September. October. Even the memory of the idiot fading. Becoming no more than a shadow. What had they done to him? Did he lie like this, remembering her? Remembering—?

They brought her to be questioned again, but this time by many people. She did not try to understand what was happening. Only shook her head when they spoke to her. One day they told her there had been an attorney appointed for her defence, and that she must come and speak to him. And she went as listlessly as she had gone to be questioned, thinking that it was the same matter again, holding out her wrists, then one ankle and the other for the chains, being brought down corridors, through empty rooms. But this time not into the street, a coach. Only into a room. A bench. Chairs. A table. A window with iron bars. A stone wall close to it outside. Made to sit. Left there. Five minutes dragging by. Footsteps.

Mr. Hatton.

So changed, so ruined in appearance that she thought she had imagined him. Standing where the turnkey had pushed him, inside the doorway, staring at her. His hair gone grey. His face hollowed like a skull, eyes sunk, spent. Skeleton thin. But not filthy as she was. Almost trim. Clean linen. Clean coat. Shaved. Yet like a ghost inside a coat. Like a skeleton in clothes that have not decayed. She could only open her mouth. Not speak. Not smile. Tried to lift her hands. And he looked at her as though she too was almost unrecognisable to him. Trying to smile at her. Like a ghost smiling. She held out her chained hands, but the turnkey pushed him away, towards a bench a few steps from her and sat between them, picking his teeth.

A dozen times she shaped phrases, chose words to say. Said none of them. What could she say, sitting chained like that, the turnkey there? "I love you. Love you." Or to say, "I am sorry. Can you forgive me for—for this? Can you—do you?—Is there any love still left?"

Like a ghost. "And I have done this to him!" Yet how? How? She wanted to ask him that too. Wanted to look at him again, reach out and touch him. But nothing was possible. And they sat there and the turnkey sucked his splinter of wood with satisfaction, and eased his position on the bench.

"The attorney is coming," Mr. Hatton said at last. Even his voice had changed, grown hoarse. "And counsel. We are to—to be tried together—if you agree." Trying to tell from his voice if—if—there was still love there.

She began to cry helplessly. "How can this have happened?" she whispered.

"That is what you are to tell us." His voice seemed to have no expression, no life in it. "I cannot understand any of it."

"I have told them again and again that you are innocent." And she cried out with a sharp agony of remembrance, "They tortured me to tell." She lifted her hands as if he could see in them what had happened.

The turnkey shifted uneasily, took his splinter of wood from between his teeth as if he were going to contradict her or at least make some remark. But he said nothing. And neither did Mr. Hatton. She wondered if he had understood what she said. She looked at her hands, at the manacles. The tears ran down her cheeks.

More footsteps, voices. Loud and confident. Laughing. A turnkey opening the door with a different air, obsequious. Their turnkey standing up, taking his splinter out of his mouth and holding it respectfully between finger and thumb. Two gentlemen entering, one tall and heavy and florid-faced, one spare and able and quick; old-young, young-old. The florid man handsomely dressed, not dandyish but rich. Gold fobs and snowy ruffles and cravat, flowered waistcoat, handsome wig, a smell of cleanliness and scent. He held a silver vinaigrette to his nose. A large, purplish nose. The spare man had a sheaf of papers in a leather folder, an air of judicious bustle. Of many appointments waiting.

"I am Mr. Deering," the spare, youngish-old man said to the room at large. Glanced at Kate. "Your attorney. This is Mr. Mays. You may leave us, man." There had been someone else in the corridor behind them, who now beckoned and murmured. The turnkey took his splinter away, closed the door. Locked it. Mr. Mays, the florid, heavy man, spread out the skirts of his coat, looked distrustfully at one of the wooden chairs and gently eased himself down on it. Mr. Deering shuffled with his papers, put on a pair of silver spectacles. They made him look younger rather than older. As if he were trying to look old.

"Now," he said. Tapped the end of a silver pencil on his papers. "Miss Harriott. This is a bad business. Eh, Mr. Mays? A very bad business. You understand we are acting for you almost in the way of charity? If we—" he coughed—"if we succeed, you have money that will be returned to you, since you did not attempt to fly. In that case"—he coughed again—"you will be in a position to discharge some of your debt to"—he bowed towards Mr. Mays—"to counsel. I do not speak of myself."

Mr. Mays inclined his head to Mr. Deering, and sniffed at his vinaigrette.

"Now, come," Mr. Deering said. "You have told a strange story. Jewels. French plots. It is very unfortunate. Very unfortunate. You should have told them nothing until you saw us."

"They tortured me!"

"My dear Miss Harriott." He tapped his pencil again and shook

[303]

his young-old head in its narrow, elegant wig. Felt the edges of his papers with precise fingers. She thought of the man who had tortured her, playing with the wooden gag, its two lengths of cord. "You have evidently a vivid imagination. You—ah—were an actress, is that so? In France?"

"She was first charged with being an alien, illicitly entered into England," Mr. Mays said reflectively, looking at his vinaigrette. "There is a point there, Deering. She can't be both alien and traitor."

"Indeed so, Mr. Mays. But they have withdrawn the lesser charge as you know. Subject to your further consideration." He inclined his head to Mr. Mays, "I am not sure that we would be wise to press that very far."

They talked between themselves for several moments and Kate tried to see in Mr. Hatton's face what he might be thinking. But he was looking down at his own manacles. His hands and feet chained like hers.

"I am not sure that her story is so ill-considered as you think, Deering," Mr. Mays was saying. "It is quite a clever story, you know." He looked at Kate as if seeing her in a new light, almost approvingly. "A girl with a criminal past, in France."

"I have not!"

"Be quiet!" Mr. Deering said in a shocked tone. "Listen to your counsel."

"But—" She closed her eyes against him. Almost closed her mind.

"A criminal past. The associate of smugglers. Illicitly entered into the country. I think there is a point there, you know, Deering, I should not like us to dismiss it without farther thought. No, no, I have a feeling about it. The associate of smugglers, involved with a smuggling gang in London and in Shoreham. One of their French confrères feels betrayed, denounces them in a letter to the Government here, a letter calculated to do the maximum of harm to them—it would be a quite usual trick for this sort of ruffian—hints at politics, plots—and in the present atmosphere they would create conspiracies and treasons out of a mousetrap and a piece of cheese. No, no, I think that I like this idea, you know." He looked towards Kate and nodded. "Her associates get wind of the denunciation, and decamp. Abandon her. There is even a touch of pathos there, do not you think, Deering? The seniors in crime escape with their loot. This poor young creature is abandoned by them to her fate."

[304]

"But all her story about Robespierre and—and—I forget the names, but they have a damned political ring." Mr. Deering also looked at Kate, with much less than approval. He drew out his own vinaigrette and sniffed at it.

"That was injudicious, certainly. You should not have embroidered your story, girl. We shall have hard work undoing that portion of it. But we can make some play with the fact of her having been an actress. She has heard these names and created a tale out of them to give herself importance. Something of that kind."

"But Hatton here. I do not see how—" Mr. Deering gestured with his precise white fingers as though Mr. Hatton were no more than a piece of furniture.

"Why—an innocent bystander! Seduced by—you told us she was a lovely creature, eh, Hatton? When you met her?"

"I—I—did not say—I said she was beautiful." Looking at Kate for the first time as though they were still lovers. Flushing. In his eyes a thousand things that could not be said, could not be explained there.

What had happened to him that day? That night? Kate had tried to imagine it a thousand times. The arrest. Like hers? Being searched? Chained? Taken to London to be questioned by those same men? How must he have felt? Out of nowhere, a clear sky, thinking of the theatre, of the night to come, of making love. Had he felt longing, guilt, joy at the thought of her? Imagined her nakedness as he sat at his desk in the library giving out chaste, dull novels to talkative old ladies? And in the midst of all that to be arrested—chained—what wonder if he had said—if he had cursed her. It would have been too little.

"I understand," she cried to him silently. "It does not matter what you told them. Curse me now if it will help you! Cry out against me!" But he had looked down and was clasping his hands together, the manacles clinking in his lap, the knuckles showing white with strain. His face grey.

"Only let him be free of this," she begged for him. "Then if he struck me, spat on me, I should still be happy. It would not be enough punishment for me. Only let him go free." And she dared not look at him, for fear of what she might see in his face now, if he should turn to her. *There is a curse on me*, she thought. *They do not want only to destroy me, but everyone I have loved. Everyone I have known.* The idiot seemed to be whispering in the room. Laughing.

"An innocent bystander!" Mr. Mays repeated, pleased with the image. "A young idealist. Foolish. Yes, foolish as you like. Hot-headed. Wrong-headed. Choose your epithet. But a traitor? A conspirator?" Mr. Mays gestured with his vinaigrette as if the jury were already assembled to be convinced. "A lover! Lovers do not conspire! Seduced by this girl. Ignorant of her true character."

Mr. Hatton lifting his head. Trying to interrupt. Mr. Mays sweeping over him. "Pooh—as for that—she is not being tried for her morality as a smuggler's doxy. A pair of young creatures in love. I think this is our line, Deering, depend upon it. Blow their case to pieces with ridicule rather than reasoned argument. We should be very weak there. For how can we reason against a case that only exists in the most shadowy outline? A conspiracy whose details are unknown? Conspirators who are not in custody? No, no. They have no real case against us unless we create one for them in attempting to answer their charges by detailed argument. If we commence arguing that this French fellow never came, that Hatton was entitled to have a copy of *The Rights of Man* because so and so, and to subscribe to the Corresponding Society because he did not know such and such about their intentions, or that he was entitled to say this or that because Pitt once said a similar thing in the House—if we try any of that we are lost.

"No, no. The line is that the Government is seeing shadows and creating bogeys out of them. Smugglers with a cargo of brandy become an invading force of Frenchmen. Lovers on a country walk become plotters against the King. Pitt is so eager to strike terror into the country that he has struck it into himself. We shall ridicule them into common sense again."

"I wish I shared your faith in the jury's likely sense of humour," Mr. Deering said. "I do not like this story of Robespierre."

"But it is true," Kate said.

Mr. Deering cast up his eyes. "You see? If they get hold of her, the case is lost."

"Then we shall not let her speak. Do you understand, girl? If you say anything that we do not advise, you will be hanged. Nothing can save you. And Mr. Hatton will be hanged and quartered alongside you. All your duty in this business is to keep silence. No matter what temptations you have to speak out, to contradict—no matter what the prosecution says, what I may say—you are to hold your tongue. Do you understand that?"

"But—"

"You are to hold your tongue! Look at Mr. Hatton beside you. You see into what case he is reduced? By you! By your wickedness, your folly! In danger of the gallows, of the most dreadful death a man can suffer. Hanged, cut down alive, disembowelled—"

"Mr. Mays! Mr. Mays!" Mr. Deering was pleading. "You forget—Mr. Hatton is here—"

"Why, yes; yes, indeed. Of course. You understand, Hatton, I must impress on her—Good God! How did you come to take up with her? You, an educated man, a gentleman?" He shook his great fleshy head in wonder at youth's astonishing propensities for self-destruction.

Mr. Hatton tried to answer again and was again silenced by Mr. Mays's oratory. The talk continued, lost itself for Kate in discussions of things she did not understand, did not even wish to understand. It was only at the very end that she had the chance to beg them to get news of Titine. And 'Ang. But they already had it, such as it was. Looked surprised that such a matter was worth mentioning.

"The two young persons in the hotel? Oh, yes. Yes. They were consigned to the parish. As being without means of support. As paupers."

"But they were not! They—they could have stayed there. Who—who drove them away? I wanted to give them money! I would have—where are they now?"

"I think—" Mr. Deering said, shuffling his papers again, finding the one that referred to the matter. "A Mr. Sowerby brought them to the magistrates. A clergyman. Yes. That is the name I have here. A witness against you, incidentally. Against you both."

"What will happen to them?" Wringing her hands together, wanting to catch hold of him, shake him from his calmness, make him aware.

"What will happen? Why, they will be cared for, naturally. Set to work as apprentices."

"Set—?"

"In the mills, most likely. In the North. They have great need of labour up there, young people's labour. I should say almost certainly that they are safe there already. You do not need to worry about them." He looked in astonishment at her tears. Mr. Mays coughed impatiently, pulled out his beautiful gold watch and raised a commanding eyebrow at the turnkey.

[307]

The turnkey quivered into obedient life. "All right, up with yer," he said to Kate. "On yer feet! And you!" to Mr. Hatton.

And as they both stood up, they were for a moment left facing one another. Within hands' touching distance if their hands had been free to reach out and touch. His eyes looking down into hers, his mouth suddenly smiling, but not the smile she remembered, shy, and loving, and afraid to love, afraid of how her smile might answer his. Grey, and grown old with a kind of sad irony, almost as though he was sadly mocking their condition, the room in which they met, the lawyers' busyness and self-conceit, the turnkey, their own love that had brought them there. An irony so much older than the young man she had known that it was like a ghost, like a love letter in faded ink, from half a lifetime ago. So long ago that it is hard to read the signature, remember the sender's voice, the look of his eyes.

"My poor Kate," the smile said. Pity in the smile. Even love. But not belief.

She tried to answer him. Although he had not said anything.

"You do not believe what I have told!" Tried, failed. "You do not believe in me. You only pity me." And it was as though something still alive in her until then was dying. As he looked at her. Her hands chained. Wanting to go out to him. Her hands that still hurt as though they were broken whenever she tried to hold anything, her bowl of soup, her bread.

And yet there was love there, in his eyes, in the grey, worn smile.

Yet even love is not enough! You must believe in me!

As though they had both grown old. Not in years only, but in knowledge. Eaten of the Tree of Knowledge. Grown grey and sick with it. Searching his eyes for the youngness that had been there and that she had once condescended to, thought of such little value that she had longed for it to grow wiser, older.

"Can not you believe in me?" she cried, as the turnkey began to thrust her roughly away, as the other turnkey entered to take Mr. Hatton to his own place in Purgatory. "Tell me!"

But perhaps she had not said it aloud. And he was already gone.

Chapter 26

Kate knew her—recognised her instantly as his mother, the woman she had seen with him in the Mall. Dressed in black. Black veil. Her face hidden, and yet she knew her. By the way she sat, very still, her head turned towards the dock. A half-hour together, not moving. Sometimes watching her son. Sometimes Kate. And Kate knew too the moments when Mrs. Hatton's eyes were on her. She could feel the cold pressure of her hatred, and she would have to close her own eyes against that black figure, force herself to look away. At the judges. At Mr. Mays. Mr. Deering. At the other men whose names she did not know, whose purpose there she could not so much as guess. A great, cold room. Square pillars. Ranks of benches. Galleries. Huge windows reaching up to the shadowy ceiling. A dais for the judges. A sword hanging above the head of one of them against the grey wall.

Was that the jury? She felt so ill that it was difficult to concentrate. She could not hear a great deal they were saying. A man would stand up and recite something, gabble it very fast, sit down. Two or three men would argue. There were so many people there. Whispering and rustling. That endless whispering. Sometimes a burst of shouting. Quickly hushed.

All their eyes on her, on Mr. Hatton. If she looked up, they whispered, caught her eye. Sometimes excitement, sometimes hatred there, anger. Or a greedy questioning as they looked at her. Small, sickly pale. Filthy. Smelling of the gaol. They had spread sweet-smelling herbs all about the floor of the court in front of the judges' bench, and on the ledge of the dock in front of her, and on the long desk in front of the judges. But the prison odour conquered the rosemary and rue and thyme. Not her smell alone. That of all the prisoners who had passed through that dock, impregnated it. She felt them there. She was not aware of the stench; she had grown used to it. Was scarcely aware of the gaol fever that was already in her thinned blood. Only of the misery that had sat there before her. A voice seemed to whisper, "I was starving. The children was starving. Christ, 'ow could I see them die like that?"

And that echo of the judges' whispering, "—to be hanged by the neck until she is dead." Once she had put up her two hands to her throat to ease it, and such a rustling sound ran through the court that it was like a field of corn in the wind. Someone cried, "Silence." Someone else shouted, "Liberty! Down with all Tyrants!" Ushers tried to reach him, and there was an ugly murmuring, more shouts of "Liberty, Death to the Tyrants!" One of the judges banged his wooden hammer, threatened the gallery.

If I could speak to her, Kate thought. If I could tell her that I would willingly have died rather than bring him to this. But when she looked at her, tried to send that message with her eyes, only the black veil was visible. She began to have fancies about the veil. That behind it lay an old, old woman with blank eyes that seemed to have no pupils, and yet could see. Once when Kate leaned forward to look at the judges' bench, the old woman from Devon Place seemed to be there with them. She had her baskets of cakes in front of her, resting on the bundles of herbs. The gaoler behind Kate reached forward and pulled her back onto her seat.

I must listen, she thought. *I must know what they are saying. It is very important to know what they are saying.* But it was so difficult to understand. She wondered if he understood. But she would not look at him again. She had already seen it in his eyes that he could not believe in her. That he was only pretending belief. Pretending love.

"Believe in me!" her eyes had cried out to his. "I do not ask even for love. Only believe in me! Stupid, wicked, greedy—let me seem all that you wish! But believe I love you! Believe I never betrayed you, never meant you to come to this, never dreamed that it could happen!"

And his eyes had tried to show belief—but in them she saw mirrored only pity. And he had sat looking at nothing. Never at her. Never with belief in her, even when they described what they imagined she had done, had been. And all her soul there waiting to show itself to him. "You know! You must know that at least those things are not true!" But he would not look round. Perhaps he could not, for the pain of hearing such lies. *Oh God, let this be over,* she thought. And then—*If he is to be hanged too!* She swayed and had to be held upright, and that whispering ran and ran, rustling of grass. She thought that it was the sound of the wind in grass, in a field, and that she was walking there with him and Titine, and 'Ang.

"Titine!" She must have said the name aloud because Mr. Mays turned his heavy, florid face towards her, drawing his eyebrows down in menace. Mr. Deering laid his finger against his lips and frowned. He had told her a month ago that they had run away. She had begged and begged him for more news of them, to find out where they were. And weeks later he had told her that they had run away. From the mill. They had only stayed there a day or so. Mr. Deering had sounded shocked. And at the time Kate had almost laughed aloud at the news. The two of them escaping. Titine and 'Ang. And imagined them creeping out of a great building in the dark. Out into the night fields. The hills. And the anger of someone when he found them gone.

For nights after she had hugged the news round her like a shawl. They have escaped, escaped. Imagined a long, empty road, white between green hedges, turning brown with autumn. Red berries and birds singing. *They are free*, she thought. *Please God 'Ang still kept the flute, and he will play when they are tired.* She lay in the ward in the dark making up fancies of their happiness. Firelight in a wood. Fairy stories of two children in a wood. Playing music. Holding one another against the sounds of the night. Coming to a farmhouse, being given milk. Oh surely, surely, the whole world must be kind to them, must love Titine?

"They'll find something," Doll said. "It ain't poor people what's wicked. Some'un 'll give 'em a bit to eat, don't you worry, pet. You'll see 'em 'ere in Lunnon one o' these days, laughin' at yer."

But it was November. And cold. And then December and someone told her that in the north of England the snow came in December. And her fairy stories turned to nightmares. Of two thin figures in the snow. She could see the tracks of their feet stretching across white hillsides into a leaden immensity of distance. Feel their shivering. Feel their hunger. "Oh God, let them only be safe and warm." As if they might somehow make up for his love and hers. That there should be something left. Some love survive.

Mr. Sowerby was there in the court. Reciting the oath. Being questioned. "He spoke against His Majesty in the most dreadful terms. I was deeply shocked. He praised the French system and the French murderers and said he should be very glad to see such a system introduced into England, and then we should see true justice.

[311]

He spoke once of the guillotine as the surgeon's knife that should amputate the evil and gangrenous members of Society."

"What did he mean by that last, sir?"

"I took him to mean His Majesty, and the Lords."

She looked at Mr. Hatton then, and his face was like grey stone. Answer them, she begged him in her mind. "Tell them it is all lies, that you did not mean such dreadful things." But he did not move a muscle, did not speak.

"And the woman Harriott. Did you form any opinion about her?" Mr. Mays attempting to say something and being hushed. Sitting down murmuring and angry. Pretending to be angry. He looked secretly at Mr. Deering as if he were quite pleased.

"A most immoral young woman. It was notorious that she was the kept woman of the new owner of the hotel, Mr. Gurney."

Mr. Mays standing again. "My Lords! I protest most earnestly. It is not the prisoner's morality that is in question here. I beg that you direct the jury—"

One of the judges saying something to the jury. She herself longing to cry out, "It is false, it is false!" Only Mr. Deering's eye upon her keeping her silent. How could they say such things? And Mr. Mays seemed pleased by it behind his protests? She dared not look at Mr. Hatton, for fear of seeing that pity in his eyes.

Someone describing Mr. Hatton's books and papers. *The Rights of Man*. A copy of *A New Constitution for England*. Pamphlets about reform. "Young man's nonsense!" Mr. Mays was crying. "Do conspirators act in that way, leave their secret papers lying about in unlocked desks, on open tables?"

A countryman, lost in the court, twisting his best hat in his hands, staring about. As lost as Kate. Directed to swear an oath. "I were paassing along the road t' mill to see Maister Sevenoaks an' I did fare t' hear singing an' music. Very sweet it did sound, beggin' your pardons, sirs. Singin' about Liberty. An' I did fare to come round t' corner, by Maister Sevenoaks's big field, and there in t' road comin' face to face with me were a man an' two little maids an' a queer strange lad with a pipe, playin'. If that had been t'wards evening an' night I should have thought it were fairies playin', that sounded so pretty—"

The laughter rustling.

"'T' Liberty Tree' they were playin', and the two little maids laughin' an' singin' too."

"You knew the song?"

"Aye, sir. I have heard it many a time in t' Crown Inn. They do sing 'eet when they do be tipsy a bit an' merry."

Laughter again, like a relief from pain. A shout of "Liberty—the Liberty Tree!"

"And you knew this to be a most wicked and seditious song. What did you do then?"

"I did tell Maister Sevenoaks."

"You did quite right."

A shout of "Villain!" from the gallery. Other shouts. Hushed and threatened into silence.

Another countryman, a fisherman. Who had seen white signal cloths spread out on a window-sill of The Old Ship Hotel. He was crossing the sands late at night and saw them clearly and wondered about them. A ship could have seen them from far out. Kate could not understand what he was telling until after he had stood down, and then cried out, "They were our clothes! Our shifts that had got wet when we were playing! We had spilled our ewer of water and mopped it up with our shifts! We laid them there to dry!"

Great laughter, and Mr. Deering leaning towards her, his face pinched with anger. "Be quiet!"

Evidence beginning from one of the two men who had arrested her. Of how they had arrested her. An argument between Mr. Mays and the judges. Saying that the man should not be allowed to give his evidence now, so far into the trial, no matter what duty had taken him from London until this moment. Being ordered to sit down. The King's Messenger continuing. What he and his colleague had found. The Crucifix. The guineas. A book. *Romeo and Juliet.* Pencil marks under certain words in the first pages. The appearance of a cypher. A great sum of money for a young woman to have concealed in her mattress. A French accent. No. Not pronounced. No. She had not seemed surprised at her arrest. Not shocked. She had not cried out or screamed. Young persons being arrested usually showed great fear and horror. The prisoner seemed to the witness to be both bold and hardened.

Mrs. Dundas. In a new velvet gown and fur-edged pelisse. A green velvet bonnet also trimmed with great elegance. Oath. Questions. Dates. Her voice full of drama. Deep with horror at the idea of such fearful treasons.

"On that night did you hear anything that surprised you?"

"I heard a conversation in French, between a man and a woman."

"Did you know the voices?"

"The woman's voice was the housekeeper's. That woman's." Indicating the prisoner's bench, Kate, with scornful, condemning gesture of the silver pomander. "The man was known in the hotel as Mr. Evans. A Welsh gentleman she told us."

"And his face was always concealed from view by a cloth? For the toothache, it was explained?"

"Yes."

"But you heard him speaking French? Like a Frenchman?"

"Yes."

"Did you understand what they said?"

"I am not accustomed to remain listening at doors, sir."

"But you remained at least some small length of time there? In understandable surprise?"

"Yes. Although I was not so much surprised at hearing the prisoner speak French. I took her to be such from the first. I have an ear for language and I should never have taken her for an Englishwoman. Voices are a part of my profession, my art."

"Of course, ma'am."

She seemed willing to stay much longer but they made her step down and give way to Mrs. Earnshaw. To Mary Deakin. To Elizabeth Deakin. To Margaret Stone known as Peg. To John Hobhouse, old John the porter. To Captain Cartwright who grew red with anger and embarrassment as he was questioned, and could not look at Kate or Mr. Hatton.

"A foolish young fellow," he said. "Not an atom of harm in that lad that a year at sea would not have cured. Why yes, an argument now and then. But no more than— Mr. Sowerby is an old hypocrite, sir. A damned canting old humbug. And Miss Harriott is a fine young woman. I should be proud to have such a daughter."

The man questioning him very angry at that, very contemptuous. And the Captain roaring out, "By God, sir, you are a damned impudent villain, and I should be glad to meet you anywhere if you was gentleman enough to know how to fire a pistol."

An uproar, great cheering from one of the galleries, shouts of "traitor" from other parts of the Court. The judges scandalised, banging of wooden hammers, crying of, "Silence, silence!" Someone warning the Captain that he was in danger of going to prison for such an outburst, that he must apologise to the Court. Only his long service to the Crown—his gallantry— more cheering, furiously silenced. Counter-shouting of "Jacobin! Jacobin! God save the King and Constitution!"

Mrs. Cartwright. Timid as a mouse, twisting her black-mittened hands together, almost weeping. "Such a kind young man—only wrong-headed. Truly it was often her husband's fault, he teased him so. And teased poor Miss Harriott. So sweet a young girl, so kind to an old woman. And to see her—" She looked at Kate and wept, and they had to bring her away.

Mr. Mendoza then. Mr. Mendoza? Kate leaned forward, astonished, wanted to catch his eyes, to ask him why he was there. Mr. Mendoza in his long, green-black gaberdine. His skull cap. His beard. Lost and blinking in the great crowd of gentiles. Made to stand up before them. Bowing. His eyes lost and frightened. Trouble about the oath. Christian. Jew. A Jewish Testament. Reciting something with his eyes closed. The Court full of whispering. Jew. A Jew.

Yes, he kept lodgings in that house. Yes, he knew her, knew her well. Had hired a room to her. A most excellent young lady, most kind and good. She had taken in two orphan children and cared for them although she had scarcely enough to feed herself. Yes, she had gathered money over a period. Earned and saved.

They asked him about the Squire and he answered reluctantly, word by word dragged out of him. He knew very little of the man they spoke of. Only by hearsay. He had heard of criminal acts, but only heard of them. Of smuggling. Of selling smuggled goods. It might be that the prisoner had been involved with such things, he could not tell.

"You are upon oath!"

He could tell only what he had seen with his eyes, heard with his ears. Did they wish him to invent, to lie?

"Do not be impertinent! Do not dare to trifle with this Court! Answer, did she work for this gang of criminals?"

"They forced her to. They have means of forcing the innocent."

"And this was how she gained her money?"

"So I understand, sir. She gathered small sums every week, and saved them. They may have come from such a source."

Mr. Mays pleased at that. The other questioner grown angrier still. The day had become evening. Night. Almost midnight. The judges standing, going through their door. All the court full of noise, shuffling, loud talk. Someone shouting. "The Jew should be tried with 'em!" A huge uproar of shouting and counter-shouting. Men seemed to be fighting somewhere. Arrested. Taken away.

Kate herself taken back to the gaol.

The next day she heard that Mr. Mendoza's house had been attacked by a mob, and all the clothes in his cellars dragged out and burned, or stolen. The mob had chased him through the streets, and daubed him with filth and tried to hack off his beard with a butcher's knife. Forced him to eat pork while they mishandled him. The turnkey who told the story to her enjoyed the details enormously, and laughed very much. "Them as is shoutin' Liberty so loud ain't 'aving it all their own way, eh? Traitors!"

Now I know that there is a curse on me, Kate thought, and longed for the end of it.

She felt so ill that she understood almost nothing of what went on. Men were making long speeches now. Mr. Mays among them. They seemed to be telling Mr. Hatton's story all over again, and then again. And hers. The Frenchwoman. A Catholic. Spy. Sums of money. Cunning. Seduction. Books of cypher. Innocent lovers. Nonsense. Two young foolish creatures, crushed between millstones of—Idealism—smuggling gangs—who may lay hand on heart and swear that he has not enjoyed a cup of smuggled tea—a glass of smuggled brandy—oh, gentlemen—it is not to try a case of morals that you have been brought here—not a case of smuggling, heinous as that too-general crime may be—shall those two poor wretched young people suffer a most dreadful death because our poor Prime Minister has seen bogeymen in the shadows and had a fright? Every so-called Treason Trial this winter has ended in acquittal! Why? Why? Because they have been trumped-up trials, built of nothing but ministers' fears and the vile work of agents provocateurs. And juries have seen their emptiness, their profligate folly. As you, gentlemen, can clearly see the emptiness and folly of this trial here before you. Let us take the so-called evidence, piece by piece, and examine it for what it truly is— Shouts of "Liberty" and "Jacobin Traitors," like a chorus, two rival choruses. A great murmuring sound outside the building as if a vast crowd had gathered.

Kate could feel Mrs. Hatton's eyes on her, and looked down at Mr. Mays who was growing mocking in his speech, making wide,

[316]

scornful gestures, scratching under his wig with mock-bewilderment. The judges watching him, their eyes narrowed, hooded. One seemed asleep, in spite of all the uproar. She thought that he was fortunate to be asleep. She could not remember how long it was since she had slept. Sometimes a kind of darkness came and time went by very quickly. Perhaps she was asleep then? But not at night. Then she knew she was awake all the hours of the dark. Waiting for them to come for her. And most of all the woman with the child.

"You knew that we were going to be drowned," the woman would whisper. "You knew, and kept quiet, so that you yourself might be saved. And my little boy died in my arms. Why should you have lived, when he died?"

"Nothing could have saved you. Nor him! Nothing!"

"But you were saved."

And Mademoiselle Blanche, her hair pale as the sea. "We have brought you here. It is we who are trying you. It is our deaths that accuse you."

The little *cocassier*, the egg-seller, still crying his innocence, holding up the stumps of his wrists. "They cut off my hands!" His eyes still shocked by death. "I tried to climb out of the hold and they cut off my hands with axes. And I was innocent, innocent!"

"My child, my child," the abbé would come whispering. "Do not you know that you are damned?" She would lie quiet while the ghosts whispered. "Kill me," she would say to them. "Take me now." Sometimes she would pray that her mother might come to her.

"But she too is damned," they whispered. "For all her lovers. All the men. She cannot save you."

They cannot come here, she thought. *Not in the daytime into this court of people.* But they were there. She knew that if she looked up into that gallery she would see one of them. And another there by the pillar. Until she covered her eyes with her hands and the whispers ran again through the great room. The shouts had died. Mr. Mays himself had begged for silence. Only deep, hornet murmuring outside the building in the street.

One of the judges speaking. Mr. Mays had sat down. Kate seemed to be floating. Not to be touching the wooden bench. And yet, when she looked, she was still sitting there. How strange she looked. Like a ghost already. Grey. Grey rags. Grey skin. Her hands so thin now that the manacles fell off if she was not careful, and it was a pretense between her and the turnkey that she was still safely chained by the wrists.

But the chains on my ankles are still fast enough, she thought. *I could not run away.* And she thought of Titine and smiled and seemed to float farther from that small, grey figure with the dark tangle of hair and the chains. She was floating higher. Only a silver chain still holding her to the grey bundle on the bench. *They have not seen me escaping,* she thought. *They believe that I am still there.*

And saw him sitting stooped, ill. As if he too were dying. But was not yet free. "Oh, my love," she called to him. "It does not hurt—oh, look at me, look up, come with me! They cannot see us escaping!" But he did not move.

"Please, please! Oh, my love, I will tell you everything, you will see, you will understand. We will love one another again; we will be free!"

But he did not move from where he sat. Did not seem to hear.

I must go down to him again, she thought. *Touch him. He must hear me then.*

The silver chain tugging at her. Dragging her down. Not towards him, but to her own hunched, small body. The turnkey shaking her. All the shuffling in the Court that came at each of the intervals. "Come an' get yer broth," the turnkey said. "You was asleep!" He said it reproachfully. He seemed to have grown almost fond of her in the past days and to need to remind himself at every moment what a monstrous criminal it was that he was guarding.

She and Mr. Hatton were separated at such times. She wondered if his mother was allowed to see him and comfort him. *If I could go to him,* she thought. And was then afraid of what he might say to her, fail to say, how he would look at her. Of what might be missing from his look. She was even afraid to remember how he had once looked at her, in case even in memory his eyes should change.

"You ain't drunk yer broth. Yer got to keep strong for the verdic'."

"The verdict?" It was a strange word.

"Yer'll 'ave it tonight. 'E won't go on much longer now."

Back into the Court. The judge speaking again. Mr. Hatton seemed to be truly ill now. Sitting in a kind of daze, drowsily. His head nodding. When Kate looked at him, he did not seem to notice. Even his face had changed. Seemed to have swollen, grown darker, as though all the blood in his body had come there, given the grey skin a dark blue colour, like a great bruise. Now and then he raised his chained hands to his forehead, rubbed at it as though he was in pain, his head nodding slowly from side to side, in a kind of puzzlement. He looked about him as if he did not know where he was, opening his mouth. He seemed to be trying to lick his lips. But his tongue was brown and thickened, like an old stuffed woollen glove. A dark scum had stained his teeth.

"He is ill!" she cried. "Someone must help him!" But the turnkey shook her into silence and Mr. Deering glared up at her ferociously from where he sat. The judge continuing. His voice seemed very far away. Flat and whispering. And then it stopped. Without any kind of warning. At least, to her.

Just coming to an end.

Then the judge speaking again. "—that the Country may be satisfied—true deliverance made between the King and the prisoners at the bar—sorry to have to remark—the dignity of a Court of Justice violated—improper behaviour within and without doors; men who must wish to dissolve all government and the bonds of all Society—I trust we shall hear no more of such uproars—you will now withdraw, gentlemen, and consider of your verdict."

One of the jury asking for something, a document. Saying that they did not wish to take any refreshment before they retired, they would not have occasion for it. Kate and Mr. Hatton led away, all the sounds of the Court behind them.

She sat looking down at her hands. Grey with long-ingrained filth. Dark grey. Her gown and shift were torn and she needed to arrange them carefully so that her flesh might not be seen through the rents. And that flesh too was grey. She shivered as she sat. Sometimes she sweated in the cold. Sometimes shivered. *If it could be only I who should be hanged! Oh, please, please!* She would have liked to ask them how long it was between verdict and execution, but they might think that she was afraid. She leaned back her head against the wall. Fell asleep.

Her mother was beside her. Bringing her a new gown. It was made of autumn leaves. The leaves wonderfully stitched together, rustling.

"I have been making it for you all this year. It was very hard."

"Are you damned, *Maman?*"

"Try on your new gown, my love. The colours match your hair."

She dreamed of when she was a child, of the roads. Of riding on the cart. Jolting, jolting, the great baskets of properties and costumes surrounding her, the countryside going by. And the nuns were in the cart with her and the people threw stones at them, and screamed with hatred. One by one the nuns died, vanished, and she was alone once more, alone in the empty cart, and the gallows were at the top of the long hill. She could see the noose. Nearer. Nearer. The crowd screaming, "Whore, whore! Hang the French whore!"

The turnkey woke her again, a sense of wonder in his square, yellowed face that she could sleep at such a moment.

"They're coming back in," he said.

All the whispering in the court. A deep murmur, barely dying at the cry for silence. Mr. Hatton being called forward. He was so ill now that even the turnkeys were aware of it and held him upright between them. His head lolled, and he gave no sign that he knew what was happening. "Christopher Hatton, hold up your hand." A turnkey raised his hand for him, as though he was already dead, and must be manipulated.

"Gentlemen of the jury, look upon the prisoner. How say you? Is Christopher Hatton guilty of the High Treason whereof he stands indicted, or not guilty?"

"Not guilty."

Roaring and stamping of the crowd like a storm breaking and he was being lifted, half-carried, half-dragged away by the turnkeys. Vanishing out of her sight.

But he is ill! Do you not see? What has happened, what—?

"Stand up at the Bar, Katherine Harriott." She could not hear for the roaring of the crowd, had to be pushed forward, held. "Gentlemen of the jury, look upon the prisoner. How say you? Is Katherine Harriott guilty of the High Treason whereof she stands indicted, or not guilty?"

"Not guilty."

The tumult growing, monstrous, threatening. Men fighting, a window breaking with a great crash of glass, ushers shouting for silence, silence in the Court. What were they shouting? That she should be hanged?

The turnkey striking off her chains, clapping her shoulder, bending close to her ear to shout, "Are yer all right? They've give yer 'not guilty!' Don't yer understand?"

She could not. Mr. Deering there. Mr. Mays. Mr. Deering leading her to a table, pushing a quill into her hand. The noise deafening, beating in her ears.

"Sign here! Quickly! It is for your possessions. And here—the fee. You are a very fortunate young woman and I hope you are duly grateful."

Mr. Mays nodding, going. Mr. Deering shuffling his papers together.

"He is free? He will not be hanged?"

"As free as any gentleman in England. And you too, girl. As free as any woman, as the air. But you had best make a swift escape from here. Do you not hear them?" Another window crashed its great panes into the court. Stones struck and rolled. The noise outside was like the sea.

"Can I go to him?"

Mr. Deering hugging his leather folder beneath his arm, tightening his lawyer's gown about him. "I should not advise it. I do not think his friends would welcome you. Run, girl!"

A trampling, doors bursting, shouting. "Hatton, Hatton! Liberty! Death to tyranny! Hatton and Harriott! Where are they?"

"Run, you fool!" Mr. Deering cried, and ran himself, like a sleek crow running between the benches and the tables, vanishing. Someone catching hold of her arm, yelling, "Here's the girl, here's Harriott! Liberty! Liberty or Death! Bring her along!"

Dragging her outside. Fighting. Voices screaming "Whore! Traitor! Hang the French whore!" Other voices shouting, "Liberty or death! Hatton and Harriott! Death to tyrants!"

They are going to kill me, she thought, and prayed that it would be swift. Lifted up, carried, surrounded by screaming faces, cudgels waving, men singing.

"Plant, plant the Tree, Fair Freedom's Tree,
Midst dangers, wounds and slaughter,
Each Patriot's breast its soil shall be,
And tyrant's blood its water."

They smashed windows as they ran, gathered a greater and a greater mob. She was half-naked from their handling, tossed about like a bundle of rags, a Guy Fawkes doll. They hurt her and she cried with pain and they could not hear her crying. Only held her aloft like a banner. They came to a noble-looking house and smashed its railings down and all its windows and tried to set fire to it.

"Tyrant! Judas! God save Liberty! Hatton and Harriott! God save the People's rights!"

There was a drinking shop and they brought out barrels of ale

[321]

and brandy and tin mugs and gave one of the mugs to her, tried to make her drink so that the liquor ran down her rags, soaked her.

"Let me go!" she wept. And at last the men who were holding her grew tired or drunk and let her fall to the ground. She began to crawl away between their legs and someone kicked her by accident, someone stepped on her hand, someone else fell over her and cursed her. She crawled and crawled until she was on the fringe of the mob, could struggle upright against a wall. Began to run, stagger. She had gone twenty yards before the cry went up of "Harriott! The girl! She's gone! Gone away! Gone away! Tally-ho the Liberty whore, tally-ho!"

Feet running, clattering behind her. Screams of laughter, curses, singing, a stone flung after her that bounded and rebounded and struck her in the back like a heavy fist. A scream of triumph from the throwers. "The Liberty whore! Catch her! Tally-ho!"

She ran like an animal, mindless with terror. Twist, turn, stumble, hide. Crouch behind the broken door of a yard. A dog barking, rattling its chain. Chain. Chain. Shouts and cursing. Liberty. Not Guilty. Free. He is free. Oh, thank God, thank God. He is free. Lay down on a pile of filth and mud. Mob running by, shouting. All going by. Last staggering feet. The shouting far away. Dying. The dog still barking. Frantic with the excitement of the shouting, the running feet, a stranger in his yard. Face down on the heaped mud. *Do not let him die.* The same fever shaking her that had gripped him in those last hours in the Court. "Let him live," she whispered through swollen, burning lips. "Let me die instead, and let him live."

Chapter 27

The cold crept into her body. She seemed to herself to be growing brittle, like water turning to ice. When the dog barked the
sound was sharp and brittle in the air. *I am dying,* she thought, and
was very glad of it. "You have taken me at last," she said aloud to
the mud and straw and filth that she was lying on. To the shadows
round her. There seemed to her to be leaves under her hands and
that she was in the wood. And then the shadows brought her to the
crypt.

"I have been asleep," she said to the abbé. "I have been dreaming
of my home."

"It is time to confess," the abbé said. "They are to kill us soon."

"I have been afraid, Father. I have feared for my own life when
others were dying, and I might have saved them by crying out."

"That is a grave sin, my daughter. What else?"

"I have brought good people to their ruin. A poor idiot died."

"Go on."

"I have betrayed my friends." He did not answer her.

"I have been in love. Have loved. Given my body to my love." He
turned his face away.

"Absolve me! Please! Please! Will you not absolve me? Is love so
great a sin?"

But he had drawn far away from her, his face closed, his eyes
grown blind. She stumbled to her feet to catch hold of his soutane,
but he still drew back from her, made the sign of the Cross against
her as though she were evil. Turned and ran. And the shadows
cried out at her, "Judas! Betrayer! Whore!" And she too ran. The
dog barking, rattling his frozen chain. Out of the yard with its broken door, into the lanes, the streets, the shadows following. She
stumbled among people who thought she was a drunken beggar
woman, and either laughed at her, or drew away in disgust—or,
once, when some boys found her, threw stones and filth at her and

tripped her up, until they saw her face, and grew afraid of what was in her eyes, and ran from her.

She did not think of where she was going, did not know where she was. But she came to a half-familiar street, and another more familiar, and old habit made her turn one way rather than another, until she was in the Market Lane. Empty of people. Midnight.

Mr. Mendoza's house. And she remembered then what had happened there, what had been done to him because of her, and stayed sitting against the wall opposite the cellar entrance, trying to think. Whether to go away, or to try to tell him that she had not meant— not meant— Not meant—was that enough? Not to mean evil? She almost laughed, and heard a strange whispering sound.

I must not die here, she thought. But she could not stand up. *I must crawl.*

She began to move, very slowly, on hands and knees, but there was no feeling in her hands and it was very difficult to move. She remembered there had been someone else crawling **here** once. Another woman. Who had it been? But she could not remember. They had kicked her, she remembered that.

"You should not have kicked her," she whispered. "Have you no pity?"

Someone touching her, trying to lift her up. "Let me go! Let me go, I beg of you."

"But you will die of the cold," a voice said. "Are you ill?" And then, as he succeeded in lifting her, seeing her face in the starlight. "It is you!"

She stared at him, trying to remember who he was. Hung in Mr. Solomons's grasp like empty rags and, frail and elderly as he was, he supported her with ease to the head of the cellar steps, and down them into the cellar. Candlelight, and Mr. Mendoza, and Isaac. She could not stop crying. Lay on the table where they put her first and cried with weakness and shame and grief for what had happened. When Mr. Mendoza tried to take her hands she put them against her face and hid her eyes from him.

"My dear, my dear," Mr. Mendoza said, covering her with something, tucking a woollen shawl round her feet. "All is well. You are home." He caught her hands, chafed them slowly between his.

"How can you forgive me?" she tried to say. Perhaps he understood her whispering. He smoothed her hair that was full of vermin, touched her cheeks. She looked at him, looked away at the shadows of the empty cellar. Stripped of everything. Even the racks for the clothes had gone, the benches. Only the table she lay on had survived, too heavy to drag up the steps. Mr. Mendoza's face still bruised from their fists.

Between the three of them, the two old men and Isaac, they carried her up the outside stairs to what had been her room. There had been another lodger there, but he had been frightened by the mob, Isaac said, and had gone away.

"Hush," his grandfather said to him. "Such things do not matter. It is very good that her room is here for her. Fetch hot water and do not talk so much."

They laid her down on the bed and whispered between themselves. She did not understand what they were saying, but after a while—she did not know how long— a woman came into the room, an old woman with grey hair and black eyes and gold rings on her knotted fingers.

"Mrs. Reuben will look after you," Mr. Mendoza said. "Be good, my dear, and do everything she tells you. She is a fine nurse for sick people."

They went away, leaving the old woman with her, and the candlelight, and the stove burning. "We must get clean," the old woman said. "Oy, such dirt!"

Pulling off her rags, that seemed to disintegrate as they were touched. Making her lie down on a sheet spread out on the familiar rug. Lie naked while the woman washed her with warm water. The smell of sulphur as the old woman cleaned her hair, sucking her lips with horror at the filth, the sores. Where the chains had been round her ankles for the days of the trial the flesh was raw, and the water and soap and the washing hands hurt her so much that she screamed once, and was ashamed, and bit her lips against screaming again, until the blood ran in her mouth, tasting of iron.

Being dried. Like a child. She began to think it was her mother there. Lifted up. The bed. The covers drawn close round her. The taste of warm milk.

"Sleep, my dear, sleep."

Dark sleep. And among the nightmares, the Squire, as if he had drawn all evil into himself—as if he were no longer a living man, but the image of Death itself, and all the phantoms that had haunted her were no more than his missionaries.

She woke in tears. Mr. Mendoza there. Mr. Solomons. Slept

[325]

again. A strange man who felt her pulse. He had spectacles and a black medicine case that he rested on the table. Herbs burned in the stove, filling the room with a scent of countryside. Mr. Hatton. The summer fields. *My love, my love.* Lying very still and quiet. The old woman knitting. Mr. Solomons coming up from his room to sit with her. He had been at her trial each day, he told her, until the time came when he must go to the theatre. "The people loved you," he said.

"The people? They threw stones. I ran away away from them."

He did not seem to understand and it was too much effort to explain. She was so weak. *Oh my love. I will give up even the thought of him, even the remembrance of him, as penance. So that he may live. And forget me. And all of this. Be happy.* Promised. Prayed.

Sometimes in the mornings she heard Mr. Solomons's music, and she would cry, thinking of 'Ang, of Titine. Of all the memories she could no longer remember clearly. And the Squire. Those curtained, invisible eyes searching for her. Sometimes she was afraid to eat, for fear he would try again to poison her. But she could not tell this to the old woman, nor to anyone. They would think only that she was afraid of dying. And she could see the shadow of the Squire waiting, waiting for her to die, there—there, in that darkest corner of the room. And then? She tried to pray, to cross herself, and the poor idiot caught at her hands, pulled them aside, mowing and gibbering so that she could not remember even her Rosary.

Only Isaac knew all that she was suffering. Perhaps he had heard her whispering in her nightmares. Or if not all, at least that terror of the Squire.

"'E's gorn," he told her. Patiently, over and over, until she must pretend to be quieted. "Gorn off to America with the others. All of 'em. I 'eard it down the Market, everyone knows they're gorn, 'an good riddance to 'em. They won't be coming back, neither, you can lay yer last quid on that. Not unless they wants to do a Tyburn jig, they won't. Yer got to believe me, Kate. You won't never 'ave to clap eyes on none of 'em, never. I'll lay yer me tray to arf a dollar on it."

He patted her hand as if he were a grown-up comforting a sick child, and in pretending to be comforted she did somehow find if not comfort at least a lessening of her fear. Forcing it back into the deepest shadows of her mind. Although that seemed only to make room for other fears. For Titine. For 'Ang. And above all that he— he might be as ill as she was. Suffering.

"You are not getting stronger," the old woman said. "You are not trying."

"You must get well," Mr. Solomons said. She had told him of Titine and 'Ang. "They will not have come to any harm. That Titine, she knows more than you do. And 'Ang will protect her. Maybe they will come back here one day. Who can tell? Maybe, I am saying? It is not even maybe. They must! Where else should they come? Like two clever little dogs that know how to find their way home through anything. And you must be strong and well to greet them."

"But I should only do them harm again," she said.

"How can you say that?"

"There is a curse on me." She hid her face from him.

"You have said this before. You have cried it out in your sleep. It is only wickedness to say such things. It is to believe that God is Evil. No one is cursed by God. God is our Father. You have a life to live. He desires you to live it. That is why He created you. No one is cursed, unless they curse themselves."

"Was not Judas cursed?"

"That is a Christian story. I cannot speak of it. But I will tell you another story. It is an old, old story from the marshland where I was born. There is nothing there but the sky, and the marshes, and the reeds. Would you like to hear it?" He stroked her damp hair away from her forehead. "My grandfather told it to me when I was very small."

She turned to look at him because she loved him and wanted to please him if she could.

"Give me your hand," he said.

She let him take it, and stayed looking at him, her head turned on the pillow.

"Once upon a time?" she whispered, trying to smile at him, to show him that she loved him, that she was grateful.

"Once upon a time," he agreed, "long, long ago, a reed stood in a lake in the marshes, and day and night she sighed with unhappiness that she was only a reed, and set in such a place forever. Can you imagine such ingratitude?" Mr. Solomons said, stroking her hair again. "To be set in such a quiet, lovely place, the sky above her, the stars at night? And be unhappy? But so it was. The little reed only sighed more because everything round her was so beautiful. The fish came and spoke to her of the deep water of the lake, and the dark mud, and said, 'We will bring you there, if you ask us.

[327]

We will gnaw through your stem and bring you there, and you may forget everything, all your unhappiness.' "

Stroking her hair. His voice old and gentle as old music.

"'But it is the sky that I long for,' the reed sighed to them. Can you imagine such a reed? The stars that move in the Heavens, she cried for. And the sun and moon. And she wept to the birds passing that they might take her and lift her up into the sky, above the wind. Can you imagine such ingratitude as that little reed was showing?

"'You are too strong for us to pluck,' the birds answered. 'And too hard for our nest. You are only a reed. Stay there. It is your destiny.'

"'What is destiny?' the reed cried out to them. 'Can this be all that there is, forever? This emptiness? This sighing? Or else the dark mud, and forgetfulness? Shall I never know the stars and the moon?' Oh, little reed, little reed," Mr. Solomons whispered, smoothing Kate's damp forehead. "And then one day it happened that an Angel of God was walking by the lake in the brightness of the morning, and he heard the reed sighing.

"'Small reed,' he said, 'thin reed. Those are nothing but God's bright toys that you are sighing for, and longing to know. Would you not like to know God himself, who created them?' Such a tall, bright-shining angel!

"'Dearly would I love to know God,' the reed said. 'Tell me of Him, that I may know why I am set in this lonely place. And why I am so unhappy.' And then do you know what?" Mr. Solomons said, his voice growing deeper.

"The angel took a golden knife and cut the reed down. Such pain she felt! Unimaginable pain. And she such a thin, small reed.

"'Is that pain God?' she cried in her agony. But the angel was drawing out her heart.

"'This is not God, but death!' she cried. 'Let me die now—without more pain.'

"But that bright angel only smiled, and notched the reed for his lips, and cut holes for his finger-tips, and with each stroke of his knife the poor, poor reed cried out in the depths of her heart against the terribleness of God. Until—until—can you guess it? Can you guess what had happened?" He touched Kate's cheek, brushed her tears of weakness, of illness, away from the wax skin, the wasted flesh. "That little reed had become a pipe for the angel to make

[328]

music on, and the angel walked by the border of the lake and played on it.

"'Holy, Holy, Holy,' the great angel played. 'Lord God the Highest.' And the song of the little reed pipe rose up into Heaven among the stars." Kate looked at him, her hollowed eyes like shadows.

"Do you seek to understand God?" Mr. Solomons whispered. "One may only praise Him."

"I do not know how."

"Have I not been telling you? Out of our sufferings we are made instruments of praise. You should thank God that you have suffered so much. My child, my child! You have been cut very deep by the knife. But out of such pain may come the sweetest singing if we are strong enough to bear it. Did not you tell me once that you wished to be good? God listened to your prayer."

"But I am not good!"

"Who can claim to be good? But maybe you are on the path to it. God at least has shown you that the path is there. Lie still. Get well. God is merciful."

It was not long after that that he told her Mr. Hatton was recovered. There had been an item in a radical newspaper about it. About Mr. Hatton the patriot, who had caught gaol fever in Mr. Pitts's dungeons and almost died of it, another martyr for Liberty. But God had spared him to fight again for the cause of right.

"It does not mention you," Mr. Solomons said indignantly, "but at least you know now that your friend is well. All that remains is for you to be as sensible and also get well like a good child."

Now I can be content, she thought. And her promise to herself that if he should only be allowed to live, she would not allow herself to think of him again, that promise lay on her heart like a stone.

Another day Mr. Solomons came to tell her that he had been to see Mr. Jardine and that Mr. Jardine had given him money for her. "He wishes to help you," Mr. Solomons said. "There is a cousin of Mr. Gosport's who has a theatre. In Bristol. He will give you a trial there once you are well again."

"He is very kind." But she could not grow well. She lay striving to keep her promise. "Do not think of him. Do not think of where he is, of what he is doing. Do not think that he will come to you. Do not wish for it. Do not!" Making herself think instead of the reed, of what Mr. Solomons's story meant. Of being good. Thinking of Mr.

Jardine. "At least I did not betray him." And was ashamed to the depths of her soul that she should try to find comfort in one betrayal not made, one friend not ruined. Thought of Mr. Gosport. Of the theatre. Bristol. Tried to imagine acting again. And dreamed that night that she was playing in *Macbeth*. With Mr. Hatton. But he was not Macbeth. He was the king she plotted to have killed.

The judges from the Court were in the audience. And all the witnesses. The jury, and Mr. Deering and Mr. Mays and the turnkeys, and behind them the prisoners from the gaol. All of them. She held out her hands to them, and they could see the blood. Such a shiver seemed to run through that audience as made a breathing sound of horror.

"Here's the smell of the blood still," she whispered. Looked into her hands and wept. And knew in the dream that she held the audience in those two hands, in the hollows of them like potter's clay, could wrench their hearts. Knew in the dream that here was her future, her reed's song. In that gripping of men's and women's hearts until they were wrung out, and, for a little, purified.

"I will give him up!" she promised. "Give up all last thought of him! Purify myself—" Like a gift—like an offering. "He will not know—I cannot wish him to know—I must not wish it—but I will belong to him forever. No one else. And everything I do shall be his. For him. To weigh for him against—against what? What wrongs could he ever do that would need her sacrifices? "I will pile gifts for him." And the others? All the others? "I will tear out my heart for them. Like the reed." O God, be gentle to me. Do not be too terrible. Only help me to be good. To make amends.

"But I am not strong enough!" she cried out in her dream, and woke crying it aloud. Lay listening. Listening to the morning.

"I am not strong enough," she whispered. Listening to Mr. Solomons's playing. Imagining she heard 'Ang's music answering. The tears growing cold on her face. Lay listening for two swift pairs of feet to climb the steps outside. Or to climb slowly, stumbling with tiredness, with weakness of hunger. Only that they might come. "Let me have that," she prayed. "Let me have that much, that they should be safe, and come back to me." Lay listening, listening. All day long. And in the night.

[330]

Chapter 28

Three years. Four. Bristol. Cardiff. Glasgow. Belfast. The roads. The theatres. Sometimes she half-expected to hear her mother's voice; woke from a few hours' sleep in a strange place and thought for a moment that she was in France still, that she was a child still, and all the interval was no more than a nightmare. And then she would hear Titine, moving about in the room very softly so as not to wake her, or she would feel her asleep beside her, and be fully awake and remember where they were. The road to Holyhead, or to Edinburgh. Or going south again.

It was Titine who had made her well. Coming back to Mr. Mendoza's cellar, leaning on 'Ang's starved shoulder, both of them lame and verminous and thin as gnawed bones. And yet Titine with something like surprise that Kate had been concerned for them. "We was all right," she said. "Wasn't we 'Ang?" And 'Ang had bowed in agreement.

But if the roads and the theatres were like echoes of long ago, their lives were not. Now they travelled in a coach, and had the best rooms in inns. And Kate herself had begun to be spoken of: "Last evening we saw the triumphant entry into the Lists of a new challenger for Mrs. Jordan's crown as Queen of Comedy."

Or "Such a romp of a *Recruiting Officer* we have not seen for a generation."

Or, again, "Here was a Viola as the Bard himself might have imagined her, fresh as an April morning."

Such provincial critics' notices helped a little to reconcile her to Comedy; but somewhat in the way that salt helps to clean a wound, so that it may heal better.

"I am not meant for Comedy!" she had cried to her first manager, Mr. Gosport's cousin in Bristol. Had tried to tell him of how she would play Lady Macbeth if he would only give her the opportunity. Or Desdemona. Or Cordelia.

He was fat and old and asthmatic and made her turn round and round, so that he could inspect her without effort. Judging her like a foal at a horse fair. "The accent ain't so bad as Gosport warned me," he said. "It ain't good, but it ain't bad. But no figure. That's really bad. I couldn't pay a guinea a week with a figure like that, not in conscience I couldn't. Eighteen shillings is the most, and that's only to oblige Mr. Jardine and Gosport. Bristol audiences is very choosy about figures."

"Figures? My figure? But for Lady Macbeth—"

"Lady Macbeth!" Mr. Gosport's cousin had wheezed scornfully. *The Recruiting Officer*, that's what we'll try you out in. A girl dressed up in breeches—if you can't make a go of that, you'll not make a go of anything. Nice tight breeches an' a scarlet coat. Except you needs something under the coat and you haven't got anything. We'll have to do some pads. Yes, yes, that's what we'll give you your start in, and God help Gosport if you makes a mess of it. Eighteen shillings, mind, and not a farthing more, no matter what your Mr. Jardine told you." Voice wheezing like an old bellows, his eyes watering, his clothes so caked with snuff that a small cloud of it rose from him every time he gasped for breath.

Her white breeches needing to be taken in. The coat padded out. A dozen times she had sworn she would not go on, she would not parade herself in this exhibition of a part. And had seen 'Ang waiting for her, or Titine. Thought of meals to be paid for. As though each step she took was downwards, leaving her worse off than before. Eighteen shillings. A padded coat. As though the theatre itself was mocking her.

Rehearsing and rehearsing. That old, fat, asthmatic tyrant of a man tearing her to pieces, waving his stubby fingers in the air as he despaired of her stupidity, her lack of humour, her lack of womanhood, her lack of talent, her lack of any conceivable virtue that might justify eighteen shillings a week. She would cry herself to sleep, and go back to the theatre threatening to kill him, to leave Bristol, to tramp the roads rather than endure another day of him. And would endure another day. And another. Until at last, reluctantly, contemptuously, he said that he had billed her to make her debut on such a day and he had best put her on in case she got still worse instead of better.

It had not been a triumph. But not a fiasco either. And something, something about the small, sad figure in its ridiculous costume, perhaps even that inner conflict between the romping, good-natured jollity of the play and the concealed fury she brought to it, caught the audience's fancy and they decided to take to her, as audiences sometimes do, in a sense of partisanship, of championing an underdog. Perhaps her smallness appealed to them, lost inside her costumes, or looking, in the width of the stage, like a child. A waiflike air about her, about her great haunted eyes, the pallor of her thin face, her very lack of figure. Those self-same qualities, or lack of them, might as easily have made an audience pelt her off the stage. There is no telling about such things. Instead, this Bristol audience decided to be pleased with its new toy. Within a week they had taken her as their own, and within a month or so she could have recited her parts in French and they would still have loved her.

The manager told her she could not act, and never would be able to act—never would be able to say so much as a line in the way that it ought to be said. But he raised her money to a guinea and gave Titine a part in the dancing chorus of the farce, and the entre-acte, at seven shillings.

A year later the one guinea had become five, and Titine could almost have named her own salary. If the theatre's faithfuls loved Kate, they fell at Titine's narrow feet as if they were heathens and she was the golden star of morning. She danced as children dance, not thinking of it. Not thinking of her audience, of what the ridiculous farce might be about—danced like a dragon-fly in summer; like a swan drifting on a lake. Danced for herself, to some inner music that perhaps she shared with 'Ang, but with no one else. Shared only the magic that it gave to her. Letting herself be adored as if it was a privilege she was according to her adorers. Old men offering her diamonds. Young men offering her their broken hearts.

Kate too had her share of offerings. Mr. Jardine came down to Bristol several times. And then followed her to Cardiff. And up to Edinburgh. Once even to Belfast. And Isaac came. Isaac, beginning to grow as adult in body as he had always been in mind. He worked now for a London wholesaler of cotton goods and linens and woollens, and travelled about the country a great deal, both buying and selling in mysterious ways. His black curls sleeker and glossier than ever, his waistcoats and cravats and pantaloons not so much à la mode as a good year and more in advance of it. Once he brought

Mr. Solomons with him, all the way to Cardiff, and Mr. Solomons sat very still and quiet in his box, and then, in Kate's dressing room, broke down and wept, old, old tears.

"You see what they have made of me," Kate said, no longer bitter about it, almost able to laugh at herself. "But do not be sad about it. At least it is more honest than smuggling."

"I am not sad," Mr. Solomons whispered. "I am so happy for you. It is what you were born to do. You are like a little bird that sings, and does not even know that it is singing."

And that too was like a small touch of salt to a wound.

Mr. Jardine did not praise her. Nor make her the kind of offer she had half expected from him. He seemed to have grown wiser again, just as once he had grown so suddenly foolish and young. But he had retained something of that St. Martin's Summer youthfulness that made him very pleasant company, and she was always glad to see him in his box, and afterwards. At supper, with Titine, and 'Ang, and two or three of the company, and Isaac if he was there that evening, and Lord So-and-So and Captain Such-and-Such who were Titine's current, most insistent adorers. When Titine was scarcely fifteen years old, she had already been able to control men effortlessly, not needing to think of it. A look of cool surprise, not even disdain. And provincial Lotharios who had seduced every chamber-maid for miles around took to stammering and making their apologies.

Kate needed to be cruel to achieve the same effect. *And once*, Kate thought, watching Titine, *I imagined that I should be able to teach her how to treat young men.*

Watching Titine growing up with a kind of breathlessness that any creature could become so beautiful. "I am not jealous of her," Kate told herself, many times. Making a swift search of the mirror for comparisons and turning swiftly away for fear of finding them. "Why should I be jealous? They speak equally well of both of us. And as for being beautiful—"

One did not need to be beautiful to act in the kind of parts that she was condemned to. Only impudent. "Such a Viola as Miss Harriott gives us would turn the heart of a Puritan. Boy-girl, girl-boy, she seems to have stolen Circe's wand, and to have the power of changing herself into what she wills." One did not need to be beautiful for that, strutting in breeches and doublet, making one's voice deep and allowing it to crack in order to make the Pit howl with laughter. She had gone almost on her knees to managers to let her play tragedy, and season by season the response grew more pitying, as though they were dealing with an imbecile. A valuable imbecile, who must be cajoled and petted, and bribed to continue with imbecilities. But an imbecile nevertheless.

Perhaps, she thought at times, with the bitterness of a revelation of truth, *they know me better than I know myself. Perhaps I was truly meant for this.*

Until at last she grew almost reconciled to it, as a humpback must grow reconciled to his hump, or go mad of it. She became almost proud of her successes; studied new ways of triumphing, with a fierce, secret contempt for herself and what she was doing that seemed to add a diamond edge to her comedy. Allowed her to stand apart from herself, judge the turn of her head, that pause that gave a word its exact quality of humour, timing her playing as a fencer times his parries and ripostes. And then again would descend into herself with such a ferocity of feeling, such a depth of it as would make of her part something quite new and wonderful. And the audience, without knowing what had happened, almost without consciously interrupting their laughter and pleasure in her playing, would be still for a moment, and see the sadness that lies behind great comedy, see how it links itself to tragedy, leads one into the other and out again. Nothing in the line she had just said. Nothing in the play itself. Only in the way she stood, looked, her eyes great with knowledge, lifting a hand towards some unseen shape of the air.

"How can you laugh?" her attitude, the expression of her body said. "Life is too terrible for laughter." And her hand would fall slowly, slowly to her side, her eyes would turn their hauntedness towards the audience, take light from the candle flames and say sadly, "But of course! Of course! It is the very terror of it that makes you laugh. I know!"

And the audience, without any conscious understanding of what her look meant—and indeed she did not know it herself—would burst into renewed laughter, like relief, as if she had brought them to a cliff's edge, and they were willing to give her their entire hearts in gratitude for not kicking them over it, onto the rocks beneath.

She grew reconciled to it.

And she would sit during those pleasant supper-times, feeling her tiredness like a warm promise of sleep, sipping her wine, and listening to the talk. Thinking of how old she had grown, and how wise. Twenty. Twenty-one. Soon twenty-two. Thinking sometimes of Mr. Jardine. Who had never made the mistake of proposing anything to her, dishonourable or even honourable. Nor the mistake of offering her gifts of any value. Only filling her dressing room with flowers, taking great care about the supper parties that he gave for her, allowing her to sense, in almost indefinable ways, how pleasant it could be to command a banker's fortune. And to need to give so little in return, she also sensed.

His wife was still alive, but failing, he had let her know recently. Grown very wretched in her already wretched state. "No one could wish her to continue as she is, poor woman," Mr. Jardine had said. "Death will be a merciful release for her."

"And Madame?" she had wanted to ask him, gently malicious. But Madame would never now become Mrs. Jardine. She had her villa in Twickenham, and her Negro servant boy, and Mrs. Bunn, and a smart pair of greys to draw her phaeton. And her allowance. She would not have more than that.

How nonsensical a thing to think of! But it was in a way restful to sit there at the head of the supper table, as Kate sat now on this particular, more than particular evening, in this midlands town, with their month's season drawing to an end. And to imagine—oh, imagine a thousand absurd things. That the room was not this rather shabby hotel supper-room, with worn velvet and pewter candlesticks, but a handsome dining-room with menservants behind the chairs, and silver; and outside the tall windows a terrace, and a garden. And trees. Would she truly like such a room, and such a garden? Where she and Titine and 'Ang might walk in the evenings? Truly? Or perhaps not that kind of room, not that kind of house at all. Like the old game of house-imagining she and Titine had used to play. A farmhouse? Very old, with beams and white plaster, and red brick floors, and dark oak furniture. Someone like Mrs. Earnshaw to cook for them—it was a long time since she had remembered Mrs. Earnshaw. And someone like Mr. Biggins perhaps? To see to the horses, and the open carriage? Or a gig? A gig might be more in keeping with a farmhouse, and they could drive it themselves. There would be cows and hens, and an old, deep well, and a fish pond with great lazy carp that would come shadowy up to the bright surface to catch crumbs of bread. And a dovecot. And 'Ang should—

But neither Titine nor 'Ang would wish to come there. They had their own lives complete. They had no need of anything. *Nor of anyone,* she thought, and sat very quiet, looking down the length of the supper table at Mr. Jardine, who was allowing Isaac to amuse him. "And I?" she questioned herself with sudden sternness. "Do I have need of anyone? Have I not learned to do without that kind of necessity, that kind of—possessiveness?"

She put her hand slowly, with seeming carelessness, against her bodice where his letter lay.

"Have I not learned yet? And my promise?" That long-ago promise to give up all thought of him, all wish—But such promises are not truly meant to be kept forever. They are like altar flowers that after a while turn brown and can be honourably thrown away. But there was much more than her promise involved in it. "You did not come to me. Not when I needed you."

"But I did write," his whisper said. "Three times. I would have come to you if—"

"But you did not." She turned her glass in the candlelight, looking at the dark and bright reflections. "Could not you tell how I needed you?"

Three letters. Finding her eventually in Bristol, via Mr. Deering's chambers, and old Mr. Mendoza's house.

The first letter telling her not much more than she had already known. That he had been very ill, and was recovering, at home in Norwich, and that his mother was much beaten down by all that had happened and in need of a deal of care. That indeed Kate had not known. And did not really wish to know, she decided. At least, not at that moment, in his letter. There had followed many right phrases, of how much he had thought of her, and hoped that she had not suffered too much from the experience and—and—and—

Crushing his letter in her two fists, ripping the doubled sheet in fragments. "And I have so prayed for you!" And so prayed for him to come to her. When she lay sick. To hear his voice.

"I cannot stay penitent forever!" she had cried aloud. "I cannot! I know it was my fault. I know, I know! I ruined you, brought you near to death. But I loved you, loved you! And you did not come to me!"

The second letter a fortnight later, reaching her by the same roundabout slow route. And the third a month after that. Lover's letters these both, in every respect, except one. "You still do not be-

[337]

lieve in me," she whispered, holding the second letter against her breast, slowly crushing it. "You say you do, in every line you say it." Along with love, and longing, and all the lover's phrases. But between the lines lay disbelief.

The third letter equally a lover's. Full of reproaches taken back, and made again. All that she had done to him, and she would not so much as write a line of answer. He knew—he had discovered for certainty—that his first letters had reached her. How sorry he was for the delay, still sorrier to learn that she too had been so ill, had taken the gaol fever as he had. "I know what you must have suffered—"

You know? You think that you know one fraction of what suffering is? And the letter that she had held uninjured until then found itself crushed like its predecessors, so that she must smooth it out again to read the remainder of the sheet. Stilted, young man's, young lover's phrases. Wishing her well, success, great good fortune, someone more worthy of her. He must imagine, since she had not replied to him that— And with one part of her mind she saw and almost understood the hurt pride, the feeling that he had been betrayed, fooled, deceived by— *But if he feels that, he does not believe in me. He wishes only to be free of me, to put me out of his mind without any need to feel guilt for it. He cannot really wish me even to reply to him.* And with slow deliberate fingers she tore that letter in half, and half again, and burned it.

"It is finished," she told herself.

She had grown up a great deal since then. Twenty-two. Success, of its own strange kind. Sometimes she remembered Mr. Solomons's conversation about success. "Well, I have paid my price for it, and had something I do not value very much in exchange," And was grown-up enough to begin to accept that that is how life is. And to be half-amused by it, sitting turning her wine-glass, looking at the table, her friends, Mr. Jardine. How safe he was as a friend. How safe he would be as— And tried to feel that she was grown-up enough to consider even that possibility with cool common sense. Safety. Kindness. Wealth. They are not despicable.

She wondered what o'clock it was. A quarter to midnight, the old waiter told her. She had asked him twice already during the past hour, and he looked at her with the beginnings of surprise.

"Your one-time friend Mr. Hatton," Mr. Jardine said, down the length of the table. The name seeming to come at her from nowhere, her mind had been so far away from the table talk. "Did you hear of his book? He has wrote a book of poems."

"Why, yes, I think I did hear something. They are speaking quite well of it in London, I believe." Her voice as careless as she could keep it, not altering the movement of her fingers as they turned her glass. The dark wine now very dark, now bright.

Titine glancing quickly at her, at Mr. Jardine, down at the table. Isaac attempting to change the subject. But Mr. Jardine did not seem aware that the ground he was treading on might be delicate. Or if he was aware, he was determined to tread on it. She had never spoken of Mr. Hatton to him. Nor even of the trial, or of his own share in what had led up to it. And he had seemed to be grateful to leave that part of their lives behind them, and to behave as if their only friendship was through the theatre. This was the first time he had ever spoken like this. And to choose such a public time for it!

It is almost as if—as if he knew something! she thought, and felt her face growing heated a little, and held up her glass like a shield, to consider the colour of the wine more carefully. *He cannot know anything. Indeed, there is nothing to know.*

"His book has made a great stir," Mr. Jardine said. "The radicals are crowning him already as their poet laureate." His eyes watching her.

"Poems!" Isaac said scornfully. "I buy 'em by the yard for Grandpa, for the morocco bindings. Who cares for such stuff as that?"

"Some people do," Mr. Jardine said.

"I have enough to do to learn my sides," Kate said. "I have no time to read poems."

"If I dare," he had written, in that new, fourth letter that now lay warm as lining under her bodice, against her heart—but only by accident against her left side, it might as easily have lain on the right—"If I dared I would send you my poor, wretched volume of verses. But I read such great things of Miss Harriott that—oh, Kate, Kate! Can I still call you that? Do you even remember more about me than my name, and all the unhappiness? And dear God, what could I wish you to remember of me? A solemn, stupid—oh Kate! How long, how long I lay ill and helpless, thinking of you, dreaming—praying that you were well—that I might get well and— You see? I cannot write a connected sentence to you, even after four years. But my pen takes a will of its own, and stammers, and blots the page."

"And did I not lie ill? And think of you?" Kate whispered. "Why are you telling me this again?"

"I thought," his letter answered her, "that in these four years I had grown old, and wise. I have grey hairs in my head, and surely they are a sign of wisdom? And yet I remember you, and my pen makes blots."

"But you did not come to me," she breathed.

"Certainly you grew wise long ago, and put me quite out of your mind. Three letters! And not a line of answer to one of them! There was a time when I never woke in the morning but I thought 'Today. Surely her letter will come today.' And I could not hear the post boy riding up our street but my absurd heart would race and halt and then, as the post rode by, go slowly and greyly on until next morning. I would have gone in search of you, and demanded an answer to face. But first I was so long ill, and then—may I plead my mother's illness as excuse?—could I truly leave her then to spend a fortnight or a month searching the country to find someone who did not seem to wish to hear of me even at a distance? And I told myself, 'I was no more than a pastime for her.' And then thought again, 'No! No! Do not you remember how—'

"It is very hard to grow up of a sudden, when one has stayed too young, too long. But I have grown old enough since then not to ask myself such foolish questions. Only to remember with the deepest of gratitude, the deepest of humility, that once someone very young and beautiful was kind enough to seem my friend. To seem my love. And I look into my candle-flame, and hear the clock strike two of the morning, and listen to the mice run boldly about behind the wainscot. And what I see are two brilliant, beautiful and wicked children, you and your thin golden friend Titine, making malicious fun of a poor simpleton of a librarian. Like one of those tiny pictures in a glass paper-weight. And I hold it in my mind like a treasure.

"I have hesitated a hundred times before writing this foolish letter, and if I delay much longer in sealing it, I shall tear it up, as I have torn up some of its predecessors. 'Tear it up indeed,' Pride says, and is Pride always wrong? But 'Seal it' says—what name shall I put there? Remembrance? I will not put any name except my own. 'Seal it' says your long-forgotten friend, Christopher Hatton, and so I sign myself, thinking that for at least the moments of

[340]

opening these sheets and seeking out the name of the sender to judge if it is worth reading so much cramped stuff—at least for those moments you will hold these pages in your hands, and for a moment or two afterwards will remember me. Although not, my dear, dear Kate, not as I remember you."

Reading and re-reading it. Laying it in a drawer to think of at her leisure. And then going quickly to take it out again in case—Titine would not read a letter not addressed to her—she would not think of it—and yet by mistake—not realising—might— And the idea of Titine's cool amusement, the slight lifting of her eyebrow as she apologised for commencing to read it, gave Kate a sensation she had not felt for a long time, as though not only her cheeks but her throat and forehead were on fire. And she was so angry at that self-betrayal, that unsuspected weakness of mind in herself, that she determined to burn the letter in the first fire she came on. But there was a servant in one room, and someone else in another, and so she put the letter inside her bodice, and kept it there until—

Until she might read it again and decide whether it was even worth the trouble of burning. And rereading it, reading between the lines of it, she thought *He expects an answer!* And was so indignant at the idea that she almost laughed. *After four years! And I am to sit down and answer him! Why, indeed he is right, although he did not mean to be, when he says here that I may not remember more about him than his name. Scarcely that!*

And he seemed to be in the room with her, and there would be a line between his eyebrows, a small crease. As she had seen it that night outside the smoking-parlour. His face grown graver and yet still— *It is not nearly so solemn a letter as I might have—have expected. He was in those days a very solemn young man. Can he have grown more humorous as well as—wiser?* The corner of his letter against her teeth. Almost smiling in remembrance of— But it would be an absurdity to answer him. And thinking of it she grew angry again, and from anger, almost afraid. As if unawares she had stepped near to something unknown and dangerous. What purpose would it serve to answer him?

And lay awake half a night. Thinking. Drafting and re-drafting answers she might make to him. Cold. Disdainful. Angry. Or briefly cool, regretful. Or perhaps—kindly surprised that he should remember her. And she trembled with rage, and then with such a savagery of longing as she had not thought possible. And grew so afraid that she put all thought of answering him out of her mind for days and nights on end. But she did not burn the letter, and it lay in its place against her side, or under her pillow as she slept—for if a servant should find it, and giggle over it in the kitchen? She must be very careful of it for that reason alone.

Until one day, with rehearsals over and nothing to occupy her for an hour, she found a sheet of paper and pens, and ink, and a box of wafers, lying almost deliberately in her way. And sat down at the table in the inn parlour wondering how he would feel if—if the post-boy should at last—at long last bring him the letter he had waited for. It was an amusing idea, and very quickly she wrote his name, their addresses—his, and hers at the inn—on one side of the sheet, and "Dear—" on the other side, where the fold would conceal it. And stayed like that for ten minutes, ruining the quill with her teeth. "Dear Mr. Hatton?" Half smiled at the idea, and heard Titine's voice in the street outside. She would come in, find her here, would ask— But Titine was walking down the hill, towards the centre of the town, her voice receding.

"Dear—"

And realised that it was not possible to write him any truthful answer without humiliating herself. Yet if the answer was not truthful, there was no point in sending it. And she sat staring at the near-empty page as if some answer must grow there of itself. "Why did not you come to me?" seemed to be written there. And "How can you tell how I remember you?" And again, with broad, passionate strokes, "I do not remember you! Not as I once did! Will not! Will not ! Leave me to be quiet!"

The quill broke in her fingers, made a blot on the blank page. And there was no other sheet. She folded it slowly, slowly, so that she might tear it more easily. And saw his direction there, as she had written it, it seemed a year ago. How strange it would be to send him such an answer. She took a wafer, as if she truly meant to seal up the spoiled page, warmed it in the candle flame, fastened it down. It looked very handsome, blue wax, white paper. Christopher Hatton Esq., No. 17 Beacon Street, Norwich. In a fine even hand. And without her being aware of it the old waiter was at her shoulder. He would expect her to give her letter to him for the post. Would think it very strange if she did not.

"I—" she began, and felt herself flushing, and turned away.

"I think as I can just catch the post for you, ma'am. I'll hurry my best."

She had tried to say something, and could not, standing by the window, looking down the hill to where Titine was coming so lightly, so happily back from her shopping, carrying a bonnet box, her feet dancing, as though even in the rain puddles, even on the cobble-stones of the hill she could not walk as any one else would do.

Her slippers will be wet through, Kate thought. As if Titine were a child again. And she herself—

When she turned back into the room the old waiter was gone, and her letter with him, and she wanted to run after him to take it back, and could not think of an excuse. Titine coming up the stairs, into the parlour, showing her the bonnet she had bought.

"Why yes, yes, it is very handsome," she heard herself saying. And the letter would be beyond recovery. "Dear—" and a blank sheet, and a great blot of ink. What would he think of it?

The question had remained with her ever since. For four days. Five. So that sometimes she felt herself burn with shame for it—he would think—he would think that she— *That I sealed up the wrong sheet by mistake*, she tried to tell herself. And then gripped her fists against her heart in rage and humiliation. *How could I have done it? How could I have allowed— It is like a declaration of love! That I do not feel! He will think— I could die of the shame of it!* Covered her face with her hands. Could scarcely sleep and grew hollow-eyed, so that when she appeared on the stage, in these last nights of the season, the audience grew even more tender towards her. Pit and Galleries and Gods and Boxes, as if she were their child, seemed to cradle her with their applauding—their darling, their frail love.

Five days. Two for her letter—for that sheet of paper—to reach Norwich. And three— She had made enquiries of how the coaches ran. He must get himself almost to London before he could turn north again. Three days would be the soonest—but if he did not come immediately, he would not come at all. One does not delay about such things. They are done on the instant or else never. And as the day went on, rehearsals, performance, night, and now this time—one coach, the Flyer, already gone by that might conceivably have brought him—only one more to go by, at half past midnight. She began to grow confident that he would not come and to feel slightly contemptuous, almost offended. And then glad. Heart-felt-ly glad and grateful. How would it have been possible to meet him? To have him announced here?

And Mr. Jardine speaking as if he suspected something. Was testing out the ground.

"There is no ground to test, my dear, dear old friend. I am no longer a stupid child to be—"

The supper was ending, breaking up. Mr. Jardine at her elbow. *He guesses something,* she thought, meeting his eyes for a moment. *Or is it only the book? So that he wonders if because of it I am—remember-ing? And he wishes to—wishes to be certain before—before he—?*

"How good you are to us!" she said. And saw in his eyes that he was afraid. Afraid of losing her. And also afraid of trying to gain more now, before it might be too late, and losing everything by the trial. "You are our dearest friend," she whispered. Laying the light-est of stresses on the "our."

"I wish—" he said, and she put her fingers against his lips.

"Hush," she whispered. "What would we do without you as a friend? I dare not think of it." And saw his eyes grow very sad, and then smile, still sadly.

The old waiter shuffling about, trimming the candlewicks, and wishing them all in their beds so that he might go to his. A saying of "Good nights."

Contriving to be last. To be alone. Sitting in the almost dark, as the waiter cleared the emptied glasses, the wine bottles, looking at her from under his old, worn eyebrows. What did he think of, as he shuffled about this room, and up and down the corridors and stairs?

"I will sit here five minutes longer," she said, "if you do not mind. Leave me here. It is—it is quite restful to be alone."

And sat listening. To his footsteps going away, so old, so slow. Like old John's, in the Hotel in Shoreham, how many centuries ago? Listening to the quietness. A long, long way off she heard the faint echoing of a coach horn. It would be the Challenger, driving hard to keep its time on the long road north to Scotland.

Sat waiting, her hands folded in her lap.

And the sounds of the coach drew nearer, the coach horn loud-er, demanding attention for its greatness, warning the ostlers and the grooms and the waiters of the posting-inn, in the centre of the town, that all must be ready, horses, mails, luggage and passengers;

[344]

hot toddy for the coachman, for the guard. A four-minute change and away, away again, the coach horn high and loud and arrogant, crash of iron wheels on the cobbles, ring of chains and harness. To the North! The North!

Climbing the hill towards her, the sounds shaking the windows of this quiet inn, this room where she sat by candlelight. The coach gone by. Its sounds fading, the last echo of the horn, faint and dying.

How long would it take a passenger, set down at that other inn, to walk the quarter mile up the hill? Three minutes? Four? But he must make enquiries—if there was a passenger—if he wished to find this other inn. Five minutes, say. Or six.

He has not come, she thought. And sat very quietly, holding her hands tight clenched in her lap. *I am very glad that he has not come.*

Heard footsteps, walking fast, the ring of heels on the cobbles. And sat so still she could hear the candle flame, like a soft, soft whispering of shadows. *The footsteps will go by,* she thought. *It is someone hurrying home.*

Heard a great knocking at the street door of the inn, heard his voice. "Open! Open for a traveller!" Heard the old, old footsteps of the waiter, shuffling, grumbling. Going down the stairs. And she lifted her two hands and held them against her heart.